BOSS
hole

ANN GRECH

I0593280

Copyright © 2023 by Ann Grech.
All rights reserved.
The author asserts her moral rights in this work.

This book is a work of fiction. Names, characters, places, organizations, trademarks and incidents are either entirely
fictional or, if they are real, are used in a fictional sense. Any
resemblance to any persons, living or dead, business estab-
lishments, events or locales is entirely coincidental.

This book is protected under the copyright laws of Australia.
No part of this work may be used, reproduced, scanned,
transmitted or distributed by any person or entity in any
form or by any means, electronic or mechanical, including
photocopying, recording and faxing or by any information
storage and retrieval system. For the avoidance of doubt,
no part of this work may be incorporated into or utilized by
any AI databases for the purposes of AI learning or text or
image generation.

This book may not be reproduced in any form without the
express written permission of Ann Grech, except in the case
of a reviewer who wishes to quote brief passages for the
sake of a review, written for inclusions in a magazine, newspaper, journal or online blog – and these cases require written approval from Ann Grech prior to publication. Any
reproduction or other unauthorized use of the material or
artwork herein is prohibited without the express written
permission of the author. Any reproduction, scan, transmis-
sion or distribution consented to must contain the cover as
approved by the author and this copyright page.

Edited by: Hot Tree Editing
Cover Model: Brandon M
Photographer: Wander Aguiar
Cover design: CT Cover Creations

Blurb

He's my boss. I'm his biggest challenge.

I'm a hacker. He's a police detective. Controlling me was never an option—I'm not the good girl he thinks I am. But working for the police has its advantages. It distracts them while I reap the rewards from my skills and live the billionaire lifestyle—yachts, planes, shoes, and men.

Until my bosshole arrests me.

But gathering evidence to exonerate my late mother was worth the risk.

My bosshole has a lot to answer for, especially the kiss that rocked my world.

Now, I can't get them out of my head—my bosshole, my professorhole, and my best friend. I crave them, desperate to be consumed by the fire they ignite in me. I yearn to watch them together.

They're all my fantasies come to life.

It *will* happen too.

If I can prove my innocence.

If I can stop my best friends from being jailed.

I am Queen. I *will* prevail.

Billionaire Boss Girl is a contemporary why choose/polyamorous series. There is no need for the leading lady (or her men) to choose in order to find their HEA.
Bosshole is book TWO of THREE in this slow build, high heat new adult romantic suspense series.

DISCLAIMER

This story refers to the Australian Federal Police throughout. The events in the story involving the AFP do not follow police procedure. This was an intentional decision by the author. All deviations from procedure, ethics, and laws are purely for entertainment purposes only. The author holds the both the AFP and the state police forces in the highest respect, and any artistic decisions should not be taken as a reflection on any of those police agencies.

Content Warning

There are some difficult themes in this book and the overarching series that as author, I wanted to make you aware of. They include, but are not limited to:

Death of a parent and sibling (off page and not lived as a memory);

References to suicide (off page and in the past); and

Drug use (described on page as a memory in chapter 5).

For Dad
We should have had more time with you. But we cherished every moment we had and every memory we made. You'll always be in our hearts.

A CKNOWLEDGEMENTS

They say losing someone and grieving is a process and that it does get easier. As I'm sitting down to write this it's been nine and a half months since we lost Dad. Some days are easier than others.

I hear my friends who have lost people talk about how they see signs that their loved ones are still here, still watching over them. I've struggled with that.

My best friend's father passed away five years ago. She sees those signs. For her, it's rainbows. Peter always paused to point them out and just marvel in their simple beauty. She thinks of him whenever she sees one, and when she's needed her dad the most, a rainbow has always appeared. She knows he's still here. I asked her how she has that faith and she told me she chose to believe. That simple sentence freed me. It let me see past my cynicism, doubts, and my pain to what's been in front of me all along.

I get it now. I see them, Dad. I know it's you.

That's the way Dad would have wanted it too. He liked to let me figure things out for myself and work through my problems in my own way. But he was always there for us, and for everyone else too. We should have had decades longer with him, but the ones he had, he lived to the fullest. He taught us love, kindness, and the unwavering belief that if you can help, you should. Dad left behind a gaping void in our world. But it just proves how important he was to all of us.

I'm so very grateful for the people in my life who make my stories possible. My family—my gorgeous husband and kids, Mum, my cousin (who was also my IT advisor – all embellishments are my own), my beautiful sister-in-law (who was my financial/auditing/insolvency advisor genius on this), my best friend (who I count as a sister), Kariss Stone, and my girlfriends in my MM DreaMMers author group. Thank you for always being there. I'm grateful every day for you being in my life. Words will never be enough.

McKinley Krantz and the team at Hot Tree Editing, thank you for weaving your magic, your encouragement and enthusiasm. I adored working with you and can't wait for the next one!

To Amber, thank you for the work you've done to keep me in line and organized and all the support you give me. I appreciate it, always.

Wander Aguiar and your fabulous team, thank you for the gorgeous photographs of your guys. A massive thank you also goes to Clarise Tan from CT Cover Creations. You worked your magic and both the photographic and discreet covers are stunning. Absolutely gorgeous. Your talent is incredible.

Linda Russell from Foreword PR, my friend, you are amazing. I love working with you. Thank you for all the work you've done and always do behind the scenes for every one of my releases. It's truly appreciated.

To my A-Teamers, I love you guys and girls. You're my safe space to fall and you've been there for me every time I hit rock bottom.

Last and most certainly not least, thank you to you, the readers and bloggers, for your unending love and support. Sharing, reviews, general shout outs and, importantly, reading our words means the world to every author. I never dreamed it would be possible to make a career out of my childhood dream, but you've made it a reality. I'll forever be grateful.

Ann xx

ONE

Zali

"**Zali Rose Stephens, you're under arrest.**" The words echoed in my head like a gunshot. Betrayal sang through my veins. Anger tinted my vision red.

But I didn't know whether it was anger at Ezra or myself.

He'd strode toward me like a man on a mission and gasped my name. His voice cracked as he cupped my face, holding me like I was precious. His hands were shaking. His eyes, the ones that were always filled with warmth and humour, were dull and pinched with worry.

He'd looked me over, searching for something. But I had no clue what.

My skin had pricked with awareness, a sixth sense kicking in. I looked at him, and for the first time ever, I saw him. The man, not the police officer.

I watched him, witnessed that same fear as he frantically searched for Flynn and Ry, his gaze locking onto them when they stepped off the plane stairs. It was as if he'd needed to see them with his own eyes to believe they were still there.

But why?

He'd sagged with relief, a weight appearing to lift off his shoulders. It was a beautiful sight, one I wouldn't forget in a hurry. The breath had rushed into my lungs, the squeeze on my chest no longer restricting my inhale.

Then he'd kissed me.

It was revolutionary. It sent my world spinning off its axis and righted it at the same time. It unlocked a part of me that I'd kept buried. Hidden from everyone, even myself. The part of me that had wanted him, yearned for him, for almost as long as I could remember but had never acknowledged it.

We weren't compatible. He was my police handler, my employer of sorts. He lived life in the light, while I savoured the depths. The shadows. We could never be together.

But for that one moment... fireworks.

I could still taste his kiss. The desperation in it. The need. The way he held me like he never wanted to let me go.

We'd let down our guards and acted on instinct. He was just a man, and I was just a woman. He wanted me, and I wanted him too.

I'd craved his arms around me, his touch. His protection. His passion.

He'd given all of it to me in that one kiss.

But reality had come crashing down on us. Thrust back into our roles, the rigid lines drawn between us had snapped back into place.

So had his cuffs.

That second right there. It changed everything.

Or maybe it was earlier than that—the moment Flynn had turned away from me.

He'd cried out and screamed, "Leave her alone," when the handcuffs closed around my wrists. But that was Flynn to a tee. His big, beautiful heart was in the right place. He was still trying to protect me. But it didn't mean he wanted to be with me anymore.

I never thought it would happen. Never believed for a moment that I could lose my best friend. I didn't want to face a reality where he wasn't in it, but it wasn't my choice to make. And Flynn's message in the plane had been pretty fucking clear.

He'd pulled away from me and slipped his hands into his pockets. He didn't want to touch me. Like I was tainted goods. I'd been good enough for him to stick his dick inside of but not for him to hold my hand. He'd dismissed me, looking out the window instead of at me. He'd told me that he loved me only a few minutes earlier.

What had happened?

Oh, right. The fucking cops.

I'd never fought with Flynn. We'd never had a bestie spat or an argument as kids. We were inseparable from the moment we met.

The sex was... fuck, I didn't even have a word to describe how phenomenal it was. But it had changed things between us. I thought it had opened us up for more, knocking down the wall that had delineated the boundaries between friendship and love. But all it did was risk me losing him for good.

Flynn had been scared that fucking would change us. I'd brushed his concerns aside. I'd been thinking with my cunt, my animal brain needing the release of an orgasm or three. I'd reassured him, telling him I wanted him. I'd promised our friendship would never change.

But it had. I needed him. I needed my best friend. But I also needed the man I was in love with but was only too stupid to realize it.

Had I already lost it all?

What a motherfucking clusterfuck.

Watching Flynn's arrest was like a horror movie.

Officers forced him to the ground. My beautiful, gentle angel had lain face down against the cold, hard concrete. An officer's knee pinned his shoulders in place as he struggled, a gun pointed at his head.

Seeing the cuffs close around his wrists shattered my heart. Like a knife plunging between my ribs, it sliced me open, leaving me to bleed out the broken pieces of my soul.

But not once had he looked at me. Not once had he turned his head to search me out. I wanted to reassure him, to tell him that I was Queen and I would prevail. That we would prevail. But he left me waiting, head hung low even when the officers eased him to his feet.

Ry hadn't looked at me either. He'd fought for me, kicking, shouting, and wrestling the officers trying to restrain him. He'd probably busted one of the coppers' knees and almost punched another. He'd very nearly eaten a bullet for it too.

Point-blank range.

No one could survive a shot that close.

I wanted to vomit, bile creeping up my throat as I thought about how close I came to losing him for good.

He was my shadow, one of the few people who'd had my back through thick and thin. He'd lost as much as I had. He knew what grief was, how un-fucking-fair the world was. How shitty fate could be. I couldn't bear to lose him too.

But I might have already.

I wanted to curl up and cry. To wrap myself in gentle arms and change the direction the last few minutes had taken. Only a day ago, I thought it would have been Flynn's or Professor Reid's arms I'd be seeking shelter in. Even Ryder's. Today it was Ezra's. But tonight? I'd be lucky if I had anyone.

My wrists chafed as I struggled against the cuffs.

I closed my eyes, inhaled slowly, and held the breath.

Exhaled.

Calmed myself.

Stilled my movements.

This was not a time for weakness. I couldn't let it show. I wouldn't. My freedom depended on it, but more importantly, so did Flynn's and Ryder's. They needed me even if they didn't want anything to do with me. I absolutely wouldn't let them down.

I'm fucking Queen.

Shoving every instinct to hide, every weakness, every ounce of doubt and fear away, I slammed an imaginary door closed on them, and locked it up tight.

I could do this. I *would* do this. I had a plan. I needed to stick to it.

The SUV slid smoothly out of the hangar, turning to the squat building sandwiched between the airport proper and the private terminals.

The sun glinted off the corrugated iron roof, blinding me as we drove. Blinking away patches of purple in my vision, I focussed ahead on the open runways in front of us and the tree-covered mountains that formed the hinterland that surrounded it.

The afternoon was quickly turning to evening, the sun setting on a day I'd rather forget. But no matter how shitty things had turned out today, I couldn't lose hope.

I had information now. Data that I could check. It was another step closer to proving my mum's innocence once and for all. I had to trust that Ezra would take care of the USB stick I'd had stuffed in my leather pants. It was the key.

My plan had to work.

I pulled my shoulders back and tilted my chin up.

My time for wallowing was done.

This bitch would succeed.

The wind whipped at the palm trees, picking up significantly from when we were in the air. There would be a storm tonight.

It was an omen, and I was the harbinger.

I smiled, cold satisfaction pumping through my veins. Determination lit me up like the glowing sunset before my eyes. But unlike the blood-orange horizon and the enormous fireball in the sky, I wouldn't fade gently into the night.

Dark rain clouds were gathering, their lining a fiery red. They would sweep in and drench everything, sending people scurrying like ants in a nest. I was the downpour.

Queen.

I twisted my wrists, shifting to ease the bite of the metal against them. No matter how bruised they were, I wouldn't let my pain show.

After all, I liked it rough.

My smile turned into a smirk, reigniting my endorphins from the epic session in my plane. I would never look at that table the same way again.

Ryder had never taken that step before. Unlike me, he'd never once treated our relationship as anything but professional. He was my employee and my late brother's best friend. I was his boss. He kept it that way, except when he treated me like his little sister, scolding me as if I were a child.

Much like the inspector sitting in the front seat of the police car I was sitting in had done.

Less than two hours earlier, Ry had added to his repertoire. Being tied up with my own bra, bent over the table, and spanked until I was writhing under his big hand was exhilarating. Enlightening too.

I'd hated and loved it at the same time. His palm against my arse and cunt set my juices flowing and my blood pumping. His touch was rough, exactly the way I liked it. But he hadn't intended for me to enjoy it—the smacks were a punishment, hard enough to leave me reeling—but it was the disappointment in his gaze that had done me in. The disbelief when I'd gotten the answer to his questions wrong.

It was a mindfuck. But the whole experience only served to heighten the fucking Flynn had given me afterward. It was rapturous, rocketing me into orbit when he impaled me with his pierced monster. He filled me and stretched me. He owned my body, working it until both of us were wrung out.

Sex with Flynn was out of this world. The only thing that topped it was being with Flynn and Professor Reid together.

I bit back a growl.

That man, that piece of shit, was put on this earth to be a pain in my arse. Literally and figuratively. Serious, brilliant, and intense, his laser-like focus was locked on Mum. It still was.

He wanted to prove her guilt. But he'd been dead wrong. She didn't steal her investors' money. His whack job idea that she committed suicide to escape an investigation was fucked in the head. I'd hated him for even suggesting it.

I'd wanted to rearrange that gorgeous face of his. Rip him limb from limb and cut out his insides with a rusted knife.

Instead, I'd gone and fallen for my professorhole and his magic dick. Un-fucking-believable.

He was happy to use both my body and my skills on a computer when it suited him. Ironic, then, that as soon as he got a whiff of how I exercised those skills, he'd gone and pissed off. In some ways I was grateful—if Professor Reid hadn't walked away, he could have been sitting in his own cruiser in our little convoy. But watching him walk away was harder than I cared to admit. The realization that Flynn had cut ties with him as well squeezed the breath out of my chest. Knowing he was hurting made me ache—and there was no doubt in my mind that he was hurting.

Flynn had waited. He'd saved himself for me. He didn't share his body with just anyone, yet within days of meeting Professor Reid, he was sucking his dick. He wouldn't have done it just to please me; Flynn wasn't spineless like that. No, there'd been something between them, something that had encouraged Flynn to drop his guard and open himself up.

Flynn could keep seeing Professor Reid—I would never stop him—but he'd made it clear that he wasn't interested without me. I hated that he even felt like he needed to make that choice, that I'd put him in the position where he was suffering the consequences of my actions.

He was under arrest in the car behind mine, suffering more consequences.

So was Ryder.

I didn't want to hurt either one of them. I would only get one shot at this. I needed to make it right. But my plan had been a little slapdash. It undeniably had the potential to go sideways real quick.

Just as sideways as our escape from the bank had gone. That trigger-happy dickhead security guard firing at us was not part of the plan.

Though I'd known it was a distinct possibility, neither was actually getting arrested.

Queen would prevail. She had to. I had to. Losing everything was not an option.

The police officer stopped the car, and the inspector opened my door after a moment. "Right, missy, come with me."

Pushing my thoughts aside, I channelled Queen. I calmed my mind and focussed. For the moment, I had one thing to do. One job.

I let the inspector wait it out while I imagined myself naked, sinking into the high I got. I exhaled slowly and shifted, opening my legs to climb out of the car. As I was imagining eyes on me, my cunt squeezed, and a pulse ran through me.

Yes, this was it. This was the headspace where I needed to be.

The officers would want me. I'd let them look. Some I'd let touch and some I'd let take me. But I was in control. I was the one writing my narrative.

♟ ♟ ♟

Processing complete, I let the junior officer lead me into an interview room, every ounce of arrogance I owned on display. There was no cowering, no hiding. Chin up, smirk firmly in place, I parked my butt in the plastic chair and stretched out like a cat. I owned the room.

I sighed. "A nap would be lovely. Do you have a pillow?" I asked my jailer.

He sputtered and laughed off my question, mistaking it as a joke. I raised my brows in question, waiting patiently for his answer. If he thought I was being facetious, perhaps I wasn't being clear enough.

"Oh," he huffed. "Um, no."

"Hmm, shame."

I looked around the room, finally taking in my surroundings. It was the epitome of a television cop show interview room. Block walls painted white, cameras mounted to the ceiling to capture every nook and cranny of the room, bright fluorescent lights, and a heavy door painted navy blue. The furniture was plastic, the chairs identical to the ones you find in high schools, and the table was bolted to the floor.

"We'll be back to check on you soon," he muttered before slipping out the door and closing it in his wake. The lock snicked into place.

My breath caught, and my heart rate spiked.

I couldn't let them see me panic. I wouldn't. I exhaled. Relaxed my muscles.

I had this.

As long as they saw what I wanted them to, I'd be fine. We all would be.

Two

Ezra

"**W**hat in the ever-loving fuck was that?" Inspector Puglisi shouted, pointing in the general direction of the hangar. She was right. Kissing Zali had been wildly inappropriate and totally unprofessional, but my give-a-fuck factor was zero.

I'd needed her. I'd also needed to show her what was going on in my head.

The tangled mess that was my thoughts.

I was still trying to wrap my mind around what had happened. A few hours ago, Flynn asked me whether I had access to the Reserve Bank's archives. I didn't, but I'd put in a call, checking to see what I could do for Zali. The head librarian had shut me down. Access to the kind of data Zali wanted was out of the question—privacy laws prevented it. I'd backtracked, claiming that as part of an ongoing investigation, we were analyzing the security protocols in place.

Then, ninety minutes later, the same woman had called, notifying me of an incident. With my heart in my throat, I'd telephoned Zali. Then Flynn, and even Ryder. None of them had answered.

Inspector Puglisi had stormed into my office when I was hanging up the phone. Apparently, the head librarian had made a call to her too. The librarian didn't believe my story, and Puglisi didn't cover for me with the investigation angle either. Not that I expected her to.

"Your behaviour is beyond the pale, detective." Her face turned red, eyes flashing with anger. She was barely five feet tall, but Inspector Puglisi was formidable. She didn't take any shit and was happy to chew you a new one if you screwed up. I was officially on her shit list. "You don't have any control over your assets, you're a loose cannon yourself, and then, after you beg me to handle your asset's arrest, you go and do that? What the hell do you think this is?"

"Inspector—"

"I'm not finished, Fraser." She pointed at me, her fist clenched tight and her index finger coming close to poking me in the chest. I towered over her, but I wasn't an idiot. I knew when to shut up. "You're off the case. She's no longer your asset. She's on her way to jail, and you're on the edge of going with her. A phone call is one thing, but if I find any indication, any hint whatsoever that you knew what she was doing in Sydney, I'm charging you with being an accessory."

"Okay." I nodded.

She narrowed her eyes, her gaze threatening. "Get out," she ordered.

"Not yet." I crossed my arms over my chest and gave her a small smile. The inspector had a few things right—I didn't have any control over Zali, and I was a loose cannon—but if she thought that this case was open-and-shut, she had another thing coming. I'd already thrown Zali to the wolves once. I wasn't going to let it happen again.

"You know as well as I do that if Zali did breach the Reserve Bank's servers, there will be no evidence of it." I paused, waiting for that to sink in. She knew that Zali was the best we had. She knew that the techs and even the other cyber investigators were no match for her. They would only find what she wanted them to. "It's purely circumstantial that she was in Sydney at the time of the break-in." It wasn't quite circumstantial. We had a flight plan, and both the security guard and site foreman had described exactly what Zali, Flynn, and Ryder were wearing. The timing also fit perfectly.

"There's a long way to go before this case is open-and-shut. Confessions from all of them would seal it tight. But there's no way you're going to get them to talk."

The inspector's laugh was one of disbelief. "You think you can do better?"

"I do." I smiled serenely at her and watched as she ground her teeth.

She clenched her jaw tight. "Spit it out."

"I've known Zali for a decade. I've watched her grow up. Same with Ryder and Flynn." A pang hit me hard in the chest. I had watched them grow up. I'd seen Zali become a woman I admired. Adored. She was incredible. Her mind was sharper than that of anyone I'd ever met. She had a body made for sinning and a heart as big as they came. I wanted to protect her, to save her from herself and spare Flynn and Ry too. But first I had work to do, and I could only do that from the inside.

"My personal feelings aside, I know how to work with all of them. Let me interview them, find out why they went to Sydney. I'll get the access code to Zali's laptop and the USB too. It'll save weeks of our techs' time."

Inspector Puglisi regarded me, her scowl lingering as she looked me up and down, considering my suggestion. She sighed and shook her head, rolling her eyes at the same time.

"Fine, you can interview them, but Chisolm sits in the interview room with you, and she's authorized to take over if she deems it necessary."

I nodded. Chisolm being in the interview room was okay with me. She was a straight shooter, by the book, and a damn good cop.

Now, if I could only shake the fear that was settling like an anvil in my gut.

Roe was going to kill me. He would take me apart limb by limb when he found out that I—the man Monroe called his best mate—had been the one to arrest his little girl. I hated myself sometimes. I was dirty, my hands grubby from the way I used Zali and her talents. I'd promised myself just as I'd promised Roe that I'd look out for her. Look where it had gotten us. I had no idea if I could.

The thought killed me. All I wanted was for her to be safe. I'd seen that little girl and her broken dad, and I'd wanted to shield them from the world and all its shittiness. It was why I'd fought so hard to have Zali work for me instead of being charged. My submissions to my superiors had been impassioned, so much so that they'd agreed to let me take her under my wing. It was unheard of. No other rookie had ever had an asset. It had always been senior detectives who'd built up enough experience in the force to cultivate relationships and turn informants. While Zali wasn't so much an informant as an employee, she'd still been a child, another first.

I was still learning the ropes of my own job and juggling how to supervise Zali at the same time. I hadn't expected it to go so well for so long, but I also didn't think it would bomb this spectacularly either. I'd never expected to be arresting her, and certainly not for a crime where the evidence was stacked so high against her.

As a kid, Zali had helped me out with crimes that were safe for her young eyes. She'd honed her talent. She'd learned procedures and where the line was that she couldn't cross. She did good work. She'd also eventually started putting people behind bars who needed to be there.

Why had she gone rogue? Why had she thought that her actions were a good idea? Why had she dragged Flynn and Ryder into it? Although I doubted there had been any dragging. Both men would have insisted on being there, protecting her the same way I wanted to.

I'd always been able to keep at least some of the heat off her. Having Zali on the books meant that the officers focussed on what work she did for me, not what she did in her spare time. But now? I was struggling to figure out a way I could be the armour she needed.

I stood outside the interview room Ryder was sitting in, ready to interview him. Chisolm and another detective were hovering next to me while Inspector Puglisi watched on the video feed.

I pushed through the door, then closed it gently after the other two detectives entered. Exhaling slowly, I crossed the room and then perched my butt on the edge of the table next to where Ryder was sitting. On the surface, his stillness and silence could easily be mistaken for calm. But I could see the restraint he was employing. The way he practically vibrated with anger would make for a tense interview, but I could handle it. Having backups in the room with me was to protect the case, not me.

Ryder's hands were cuffed. At least they were in front of him now rather than behind his back. But that wouldn't do. Not on my watch. They might not trust him, but I did.

"Let me get you out of these," I murmured, gently taking the cuffs off. When I reached for his hand to check his wrist, Ryder snatched it away.

His eyes blazed. His jaw was clenched tight as he launched himself out of the chair. He stood in a fluid motion, graceful like a lion. The plastic seat toppled as if skittering out of the way.

I didn't move.

Tasers were drawn.

The detectives who were with me didn't hesitate.

Fingers on the triggers, they squared their aim.

I raised my arms in a stopping motion.

My heart hammered in my chest.

This man meant as much to me as Zali and Flynn. As Tristan too.

There wouldn't be any stray probes being fired today.

He stood over me, his chest to my face. He breathed hard.

His expression was thunderous. Hatred rippled off him in waves.

Ry clenched his hands into fists.

Unflinchingly, I met his gaze. Silently, I begged him to stay calm.

Electricity arced between us, crackling the air.

He closed his hand around my throat. The pressure he applied was firm—not enough that I couldn't breathe, but enough to exert control.

My eyelids fluttered as my body reacted to his proximity. Heat flashed through me. My mouth went dry, and my hands itched to have him under my palms, skin on skin. My cock thickened, announcing its interest to the world like a goddamn flagpole.

The man was potent.

Chaos had erupted around us, but we were in a bubble of stillness. The squeak of rubber soled boots sounded and repeated shouts of "Drop your hands," from Chisolm and Peterson had rung out.

But Ryder didn't move.

I didn't either.

The officers watching the feed would have already scattered, weapons at the ready as they charged down the corridor. Any moment now, the door would burst open, and he'd be taken down.

I flattened my palms, slowly motioning downward with my hands. "Lower your weapons," I instructed the other detectives, my Adam's apple caressing Ryder's palm as I swallowed.

"You piece of shit," Ryder hissed, gripping my throat tighter. He'd likely leave marks, little bruises where each of his fingers pressed into my sensitive skin. My cock throbbed. I couldn't deny the appeal—wearing his mark would be... I shivered.

"I had no choice," I rasped. He was in my personal space, looking down at me with a mixture of disdain and disgust. Standing, he was only half a head taller than I am, but seated like this, I was at the perfect height to nuzzle his ribs and dip my head lower to his navel. Below that, the delicious V led to a package I'd happily wrap my lips around.

He'd probably take my head off if I tried something so bold.

I wanted to hold him, to touch him. I wanted to wrap my hand around his hip and pull him between my legs. I would show him the truth of my words.

But I didn't.

I pushed my hands down again, motioning for my partners to lower their tasers. "I'm doing my best to get you out of this—"

"I don't give a shit what you're doing. It's not enough." His face was close to mine, his voice a rough growl as he shifted closer, moving between my legs and dominating me. He pressed his hand against my jaw, and I bit back a whimper. The desire flowing through my veins ratcheted up, my cock thickening as he leaned into me.

His harsh breaths, choppy inhales and exhales, washed over my face. The man was a force to be reckoned with.

Potent and intense.

I'd always been captivated by him and the way, even as a teenager, he'd owned the room.

He was a lot like the other man I wanted but couldn't have.

"It'll never be enough," I murmured, dropping my gaze, ashamed of the direction my thoughts were pulling me in. "But I'm trying, Ry. I really am. I just don't know how to get you out of this mess. Talk to me. Tell me something I can use to help."

He stilled, anger draining from his face. Disappointment replaced it until he slammed the walls into place. He dropped his hand, straightening as he stepped back, going deathly calm. "No comment."

"Don't you get it, Ry?" I pleaded with him, motioning to the other detectives in the room. "I can't protect any of you if I don't know what happened."

He rolled his eyes, shaking his head as if I was an idiot. "No comment."

I gripped his shirt, closing my hands around the material and holding tight. "They'll send someone else; they'll throw the book at all of you."

"No comment." He stood stock-still, his chin raised and his eyes on the wall.

"I'm trying to protect you, damn it," I growled, shaking him. Trying to make him understand.

"No. Comment."

I stood, our bodies only a hair's breadth apart.

Unclenched my fists.

Smoothed down his shirt.

The ripples of his abs tensed under my touch, and I breathed his scent in before dipping my head and whispering so only he would hear. "Thank you for protecting her. I'll do my best too."

I turned on my heels and walked out, trusting my colleagues would follow.

Three

Flynn

Everything was falling to pieces, and I hated myself for it. I couldn't do anything to stop my house of cards collapsing. I'd watched in disbelief as Detective Fraser snapped the cuffs around Zee's wrists. It went downhill from there.

None of this was supposed to happen.

Not like this.

We were supposed to pull into the hangar and Zee would have had a few words with the detective. He should have nodded, smiled, and gestured for the others to hop back in their cars. Then after they'd driven off, he would have kissed her, then me, and we would have taken it back to her yacht to explore the promise on those sensuous lips of his.

Ignorance was bliss, and naivety was as hazardous as a toxic waste dump.

I wish I could go back, even just twelve hours. I wish I could forewarn all of us. Give us all a hint of how sideways this day would go. I'd tell Zee to be gentle with Tristan, to not push him away so hard. I'd beg him to stay with us. I wanted his arms around me, around us right now. I wanted him to tell me that we'd be okay, that the tentative relationship we'd been building would survive. I wanted to be back on Zee's yacht, with my girl and my guy safe and happy. But instead, we were like magnets with the same polarity, repelling each other. We were pushing away from our centre further and further apart.

It had only been a few hours, but I missed Tristan. He was probably at work, still catching up on what he missed this morning when I'd asked him to come out to Zee's yacht. I hated that he was hurting, hated the anguish in his eyes when he'd walked away. He'd begged me to go with him, his fear of the unknown, of the potential for any one of us getting wrapped up in Zee's illegal activities, so real it was palpable.

Tristan had been almost desperate to get away from her. He was running. At a guess, it was the memories of his time served.

His attempt to protect me was sweet, if a little misinformed. He had to know that I'd never leave her.

But I would do things differently if I had the chance.

That whole trip to Sydney was one epic disaster. The only saving grace was my conversation with Ry. He wanted Zee—he'd admitted as much. But whether he ever pulled his finger out remained to be seen. I'd nearly combusted watching him take a hand to her butt, but when push came to shove, he'd walked away.

He knew I wasn't going anywhere. He now knew whatever happened between them, Zali would always have other men—me included. Ry needed to accept Zee how she came. There was no trying to fit square pegs in round holes. Being polyamorous didn't mean Zee couldn't be exclusive, but she was wired to love more than one person.

Now all our futures were up in the air.

Even if we somehow pulled out an ace and avoided jail time, there was the whole Ezra-arrested-us issue as well as the Tristan-won't-have-anything-to-do-with-us debacle.

I sniffed, wiping my cheeks and nose with the back of my cuffed hands. My butt was already asleep, the hard plastic on the chair unforgiving. The air-conditioning in the interview room was freezing, making me shiver hard enough to rattle my bones. But even though there were gale-force winds pumping out of the unit above my head, the room still smelled of sweat, mouldy socks, and pee. The harsh light burned my eyes too, which were rubbed raw from crying.

I just wanted out, to blame this on a bad dream. I wanted Zee's bed, Tristan, Zee and me, and laughter. I wanted ice cream too.

But for the moment, I was somewhere I'd never imagined in my worst nightmares. Terrified didn't even come close to describing my state of mind.

I trusted Zee. She always had a plan. At the very least, she said she was organizing a lawyer. But being left in the dark was unsettling. It was like screaming into the void, the echo of my own voice my only company. The silence and the darkness were deafening.

I was back at home, curled up on my bed—the mattress tossed on the floor, piles of clothing and old bedding forming a fort around it. I didn't remember ever sleeping with sheets until I'd stayed the night at Zee's.

All I'd wanted as a kid was to be seen. Zee had done that. So had Monroe, and before she died, Rosa. Now I was being forgotten again. I'd gone back to living in the dark. Zee was doing it so we had plausible deniability. She hadn't told us we were in the Reserve Bank Museum to try to protect us— it was why she'd wanted to drop me off in the first place— but I didn't need protection. I needed to be important enough to someone for them to want to include me.

My wrists were sore, the cuffs tight enough to bite the thin skin there, the nicks drawing blood to the surface. I focussed on the sting of the small cuts, my head down as I mapped the marks.

My breathing was erratic, my heart beating way too fast. I couldn't stop shaking. Shivers skittered over my skin and through my bones.

The memory of Zee calming me down inside the bank floated in my mind's eye. I closed my eyes and mimicked what we'd done, inhaling slowly, holding the deep breath for a moment, then slowly exhaling. With my hands in hers, I'd copied her moves and soaked up her calm.

It wasn't working now.

I quaked, a full body shudder passing through me. My breathing was sharp, coming in fits and bursts. I was on the edge of hyperventilating, my vision spotting and panic churning in my gut.

The door opened, but I couldn't bear to look. Shame crept through me. I shouldn't be a crying mess. I should be strong. I should be demanding to see Zee and make sure she was okay. It's what Ryder would do. Probably what Tristan would do too. But instead of being strong and stoic, I was a blubbering baby.

A bottle of water was placed gently in front of me. I recognized Detective Fraser's hand. My insides wobbled, setting off another shiver.

"I'll get the air-conditioning adjusted in here. It's like a bloody icebox." Detective Fraser sounded frustrated, annoyance colouring his tone. "Lean forward, Flynn."

I did as he asked, still not looking up at him, and his warmth and scent enveloped me. My gaze shot up, locking on his. His eyes were filled with something unreadable. Remorse? Concern? I didn't know what it was, but he'd shown me enough kindness to drape his suit jacket over my shoulders. Why?

There were so many questions spinning around in my head. How did he find out about us being at the museum so quickly? How did they know who to look for? It wasn't as if we were well known in Sydney. We weren't recognizable. It wasn't as if one of the Kardashians or Hemsworth brothers were there. It was just us. Three relative nobodies in a population of a few million.

But I kept quiet, not trusting myself to speak.

"I'm going to spin your chair around, Flynn. You won't fall."

He gripped the chair and dragged it so I was facing him, and I tensed, hating that I couldn't even hold onto anything.

Detective Fraser sank to his knees in front of me and undid the cuffs, dropping them on the table before massaging my wrists. His touch was warm and firm, and I relaxed into it. I couldn't help but admire the difference in our colouring, his skin all golden and tanned against my paler complexion.

"Are you okay?" he asked quietly, his gaze searching. "Are you warmer?"

I nodded, and he shuffled closer, his much bigger body kneeling snugly between my knees.

"Would you like a drink?"

When I nodded, still mute, he uncapped the bottle and waited as I slipped my arms into his jacket and tugged it closed around me. It was big—at least two sizes larger than I'd choose—but it was imbued with Ezra's scent and warmth. My insides whirred, attraction flaring like embers sparking to life with a slow exhale.

My fingers brushed Ezra's as he passed the bottle to me, the warmth like a brand on my cold skin. Condensation dripped off the bottle onto my lap, and my hands shook as I brought it to my lips. The water hit my tongue, and I chugged down half of it, trying to quench the thirst that had unknowingly built up until I was parched.

Breathless, I wiped my mouth with the back of my hand. Ezra's eyes blazed, his lips parting on an unsteady inhale.

Desire slammed into me.

I wanted to sip from those lips. To feel them sliding against my own. I wanted to know if they were as pillowy soft as I imagined them or whether the scrape of his five o'clock shadow would prick my skin. I wanted to watch him with Zee as well. Would he touch us differently? Would he be rough or gentle?

He eased the bottle from my hand and swallowed, his throat bobbing as he did. Our gazes connected and held, his eyes filled with wonder. Ezra touched my face, his thumb leaving tingles in its wake as he brushed it over my bottom lip. My cheek and jawline followed, my breathing as unsteady as his. My stomach swooped and my heart double-timed as want spiralled through me.

I was hard, my cock like a flagpole waving for attention. But getting off wasn't enough. I needed more. I needed to wipe away today. To take us apart and fit all our pieces back together. I wanted to mend the broken bits and smooth the jagged edges, to make us whole again. We were meant to be together—Zee, Tristan, Ezra, and I. Ry too.

But how did I make it happen?

Ezra was so close. All I had to do was lean forward, and I could press our lips together. Would I be able to taste Zee's lips on his? Or would it be all him I was sampling for the first time?

Ezra stood slowly, and my gaze followed him up. Bending forward, he laid a kiss on my forehead, a soft, lingering press of his lips. I breathed him in and stepped off that cliff. My eyes slipped closed, and I reached for him, sliding my hands up his legs and wrapping them around the backs of his thighs. His thick muscles were tense under my palms, the tremble that rippled through him more of a vibration than a shiver.

He drew back, standing to his full height as he threaded his fingers through my hair. I tightened my grip, pulling him closer at the same time that he tugged on me, eliminating the space between us. With my forehead at his hip and his arse nestling in the L-shapes made by my forefingers and thumbs, my breath caught. His scent was heady, engulfing me and taking me higher and higher. I moaned, nuzzling his hip, his hard cock nudging my cheek. I shifted, running my lips over his length, blowing hot air over him before breathing him in. Ezra hissed, his hips flexing and his grip on my hair tightened as I mouthed him.

My mouth watered and cock pulsed. I wanted to taste him, to lick up the drop of pre-cum I knew would be wetting his slit. I wanted him moving inside me like I'd done to Tristan, sinking inside him with every plunge of my hips.

"My boy," he whispered, his eyes fluttering closed.

The door flew open, banging against the cinder block wall. I flinched and Ezra jumped back, separating us. "Detective," a woman snapped. "You were supposed to wait for us before coming in here."

"We won't be questioning Flynn," he choked out, his voice like gravel.

"What now?" she asked, disbelief colouring her tone.

His gaze met mine, our stares locking and holding. My cock was already tenting my pants, but it hardened even further at the lust, the yearning, in his expression. His voice was rough when he added, "Because Flynn would never betray Zali's trust. He's the most loyal man I know. We won't get a single word out of him."

Those words, the way he said them, cracked my chest open. Like taking a cleaver to my heart, he gouged open a gaping wound. Fear burned a trail in my gut. "Please let us go," I begged, balling my fists to stop me from reaching for him again.

He rubbed his chest, the movement pained. "You have no idea how much I want that, Flynn." He reached out as if to brush the backs of his fingers down my cheek, but he let his hand fall away instead. Sighing, his shoulders slumped, he added, "I want you out of here. I want to walk you out that door myself." He shook his head, looking at the floor. His frown was etched by the furrow in his brow and the downturn of his lips. "But I can't. Not until we've gone through the process. This...." He huffed out a breath and looked down at me again, helplessness in his eyes. "What you three did was so incredibly stupid. You've put yourselves at risk. This could be jail time, Flynn, and I can't help you."

I couldn't look at him. I couldn't bear to see the disappointment in his eyes, the absolute certainty that we were completely screwed. Sucking in a shuddery breath, I lowered my hands and tightened the jacket around my shoulders. I pulled away from him, leaning back in the chair and lifting my heels to the seat, curling into a ball. I wanted to disappear. This ride had taken a turn, and I wanted off. It was like a bad trip, nightmarish instead of a mellow high.

"Will you talk to me?" he whispered.

I shook my head, clenching my jaw tight to stop the whimper crawling up my throat.

"Okay." He shoved his hands into his pockets and rocked back on his heels, hesitating as if he wanted to say something more. But instead he spun around and gestured to the other two officers to exit the room. When they were gone, he added, "I'll check in on you again later."

I was alone again a moment later, the door closing with a resounding click. The room was silent except for my shallow breaths and my heart thundering in my ears.

FOUR

___

Ezra

Fuck me.

This was a mistake. I was getting too close. Exposing too much of myself. Flynn had seen how hard I'd been for him. He'd rubbed his face on my fucking dick like a cat and, I'd nearly come on the spot. He could smell how aroused I was. He could see it.

I'd called him my boy. Fuck knows I wanted it. But that was half the problem. If it was only him that I wanted, I could make it work. I would care for him. I would scrub away every doubt and fear from a shitty childhood I'd been powerless to do anything about and shower him with love.

But just like Tristan, he deserved better than my scraps. He deserved all of me.

"I need a minute," I rasped to the other detectives as I turned away from the door.

I didn't hesitate, heading straight for the bathrooms. I needed to get rid of this fucking erection. I couldn't walk around with it, much less head into a meeting with my boss where she'd chew my arse out again.

Closing the door to the stall, I pushed my pants and boxer briefs down to my knees and glared at my angry cock. Why couldn't I make up my mind? How the hell did I get over this? Everything was imploding. My life was in a state of absolute fucking chaos, and my head was whirling around like a tornado. People fell in love with just one person every day. They usually fell out of love with the others before that. Why was I different? And why were they the ones I'd fallen for?

I wrapped my fingers around the base of my dick and squeezed, willing the blood to drain away. My balls were drawn up tight too. With my legs spread, holding up my pants and one hand on my dick, I used the other to pull them away from my body.

A shudder passed through me.

Fuck. Flynn's lips had been divine, his hot breath a whisper of what it would be like to be buried inside that mouth, spreading those perfect lips. How deep would he be able to take me? How quickly would I come?

My cock throbbed, getting harder instead of softening. Gritting my teeth, I ran my fingers over my swollen cock, a hiss erupting from deep within my throat as my nerve endings lit up.

Oh, fuck.

Another shiver. I couldn't do it, couldn't get my cock to stand down. I needed to come. I needed release. Spitting on my hand, I closed it around my length again and tentatively stroked.

Closing my eyes, my mind took over, my imagination running rampant.

Dear god, I could picture it.

Flynn was on his back, those long legs spread. Zali straddled him, her back to his chest. She was picture perfect, her hair a halo around her head as Flynn squeezed her narrow waist and bucked into her, her breasts bouncing with each thrust.

My boy's pretty cock was nestled between Zali's arse cheeks, her hole stretched around him as he pumped into her. I watched, jacking my cock as her juices dripped from her soaked pussy onto Flynn's cock, lubing the way even more.

Ry's grunt caught my attention. He hovered above them, knees spread and thick cock in hand. It swelled, the head reddening as he shuttled his hand over his length, pointing his slit to Zali's mouth first, then Flynn's. His hand was on Zali's perfect tit, twisting and pinching her nipple as Flynn and Zali took turns sucking his dick.

I was perched between their spread legs. I could take either one of them. But the choice was almost impossible. Who did I slide into? Zali or Flynn? A pussy or an arse?

Both.

I wanted both. I'd always wanted both.

Zali's silken folds stretched around my girth as I pressed my cockhead forward. She moaned around a mouthful of dick and my own swelled. Seeing her there, the centre of our attention as we took her to heaven, was every dream come true.

Almost.

I wanted Tristan there with us.

I notched my cock against her pussy and coated myself in her arousal, easing inside her slowly. With nothing between us, she was hot and wet, the pressure of Flynn in her arse squeezing me even tighter. I choked out a moan and surged forward, bottoming out in one smooth stroke.

She screamed, her fingers closing over her clit as Flynn and I established a slow and steady rhythm.

Hands on my arse spread my cheeks and every muscle in my body simultaneously relaxed and primed itself. I whimpered, withdrawing from Zali and canting my hips in invitation. I wanted Tris's tongue on my hole. I wanted him to fuck me the way I was fucking his girlfriend and boyfriend.

Tris kissed my cheek, licking teasingly along the line where my arse met my thigh. I growled, thrusting back inside Zali's warmth only to push back against his mouth as he neared my hole, silently begging him to get closer.

Flynn cried out, and I looked down, watching as Tristan slipped two fingers inside our boy, getting him ready for me.

When Tristan's tongue connected with my star, my legs almost gave out. He alternated quick flicks with slow licks as he prodded me with his tongue tip, pushing inside before he went back to nibbling my rim and licking me again. Heat and sensation washed over me like a tsunami. My cock was buried in the perfect woman, the three other people I was hopelessly gone for right there with me as we slaked our lust on each other. It was overwhelming. A dream come true.

I was burning up from the inside out, rocking my hips forward and back, chasing the high at both ends.

But then he was gone, and I cried out.

Ryder twisted toward me, gripping my face with both hands. "I want inside our woman." He kissed me fiercely, his tongue plunging inside my mouth as he owned the kiss. He pulled back, and I was too dazed to speak, but Tristan was there, controlling my movements. His front was pressed against my back, his strong arms wrapping around my hips and pulling me backward until my cock slipped from Zali. I whimpered at the loss.

Then they were flipping over, Ry on his back as he impaled Zali on his dick and Flynn rushing to plunge back inside her still-open arse. She screamed again as he bottomed out, and both Ry and Flynn groaned. "Oh fuck, that's it, come on my dick," Ry ground out as his hips set a furious pace.

"Get inside our boy," Tristan murmured in my ear, the sound of his deep voice sending a tremor through me. His fingers were nudging my hole, wetting me and getting me ready to take him.

Cross-eyed with lust, I eased my cock past Flynn's pucker and cried out. His hole squeezed my cock so tight. It was like sinking into heaven as I pushed forward. Heat and a vicelike grip surrounded me.

My breath stuttered. My chest seized.

I came.

Hard.

My vision whited out as my balls erupted, shooting pulse after pulse of cum into my boy.

I blinked my eyes open, the sight before me about as far from the one I'd imagined as possible. Sterile white tiles, navy blue dividing walls between the stalls, grey floor tiles. Ropes of cum dripped down the toilet, coating the seat and my hand.

It hadn't even been two minutes. I'd blown a load from my imagination and a spit-soaked hand.

I was in trouble.

The genie wasn't fitting back into the bottle.

Giving in would change everything. My livelihood was already at risk because of where my loyalties lay. I'd be shown the door before long.

But that was only the beginning. Nothing would be the same.

My legs were jelly, and my hands shook as I cleaned up evidence of my arousal.

I had a decision to make.

Or maybe I'd already made it and was now living with the consequences.

I needed my closest friend. But he was the only person I couldn't talk to.

FIVE

Tristan

So, sex noises. Yeah, I'd definitely deserved that one. Barry had hit the nail on the head. How could I have forgotten to mute my microphone? It wasn't bad enough that I'd jacked off in my office to memories of being inside my student and the other inside me. No, I had to outdo myself. Half the department staff had been listening in.

But as the meeting finished and my office was plunged into silence once more, the endorphin high faded fast, and pain more excruciating than anything I'd ever experienced before set in.

I'd only had Ezra for one night, but his walking away had lit a fire in me. It made me want to be a better man. I'd used the rejection as motivation, letting it burn inside me to give me strength.

But this devastation ran too deep. The swooping in my gut when I thought about Zali and Flynn was like being in one of those planes doing crazy acrobatic loops. But now, it was as if I'd been pushed out of it, minus the parachute. The descent was quick and the giant splat at the end was cata-strophic. I'd shattered my insides and imploded my heart, obliterating every cell in my body.

And it was all because I was scared.

I'd destroyed myself. Plunged myself into an abyss where the only thing around me was a vast nothingness. The emptiness was swallowing me whole.

I wish it would.

It hurt to breathe. My chest was too tight, and every in-hale was like razor blades slicing me open from the inside. Closing my eyes conjured up visions of Zali's shy smile and Flynn's warm eyes and fingers threading through my hair. But like mist, they swirled away. The more I reached for them, the quicker they dissipated. The only image that lin-gered was my angel's disappointment and Ryder's scowl. I wanted to smooth it away as much as I'd wanted to make Flynn smile. I wanted him happy. I wanted all of them happy.

Ryder had given me an in with them. He'd helped me show Zali that I was serious about doing this podcast the right way—the fair way—only for me to back out. He was seething when I was on the phone with Ezra, immediately punting Zali from the project. Usually I didn't give a fuck about what people thought of me. But Ryder's opinion had mattered to me. Destroying that hurt almost as much as walking away from Zali and Flynn.

The whole situation was a complete clusterfuck of epic proportions. I'd let my dick do the talking. I'd risked my job to sleep with them—my kitten and my angel. But then my heart had gone and gotten in on the action.

I'd fallen in love with Zali and Flynn.

It was quick—ridiculously so—but so right too. We fit together like puzzle pieces both in and out of the bedroom. Or loungeroom, office, or classroom.

Now I was facing the truth of my reality. Walking away from them was like swimming in lava—impossible. I was coming apart at the seams.

Zali represented everything that I'd tried to shield myself from. I was never going back to jail. I was never serving another day of time in my life. It wasn't an option. I couldn't and wouldn't bend on that. Logically, it was straightforward.

So why the fuck did every instinct scream at me to turn around, march straight back to that yacht, and scoop them up in my arms?

Why was I actually contemplating renting the little cabin in the Sunshine Coast hinterland so I could take them away?

Why did I still want to take them on a date?

I was justified in walking away. The decision was necessary. Saving myself from a world of hurt and trouble was the smart thing. Staying, only to potentially end up back in jail, wasn't an option. It was a no-brainer.

But my heart had other ideas.

It made sticking to my resolve a whole lot harder. It required a level of willpower I wasn't sure I possessed.

The desire to go back to them wasn't a knee-jerk reaction. It wasn't some woe-is-me-I-miss-them-because-I-haven't-seen-them-in-an-hour type craving. It certainly wasn't the need to get off.

No, it was an ache that permeated my very soul. My entire being was tearing in half, shredding me.

The last time I'd lost someone important was a decade ago. I'd been a bad influence, one he was smart to stay away from. He'd pushed me away and kept me at arm's length ever since.

But I'd changed. I'd grown.

I'd fallen deeper for him every day since.

And yet he still didn't want me.

Closing my eyes on a sigh, my thoughts drifted back to the night that had changed the direction of my life.

I exhaled slowly, smoke from the joint curling around my face. I was mellowed out, calm and floating. Ironic considering the speed Andrew was driving at. Stealing the car was his and Murray's idea. He'd wanted to get high. He wanted ice.

They'd waited for the owners to go out.

Andy had gotten into the house easily enough. He'd thrown a brick through the glass sliding door, retrieved the keys, and exited through the garage.

Muz had bragged that Andy was in and out in less than two minutes.

They'd swung by my place on the way to get Muz's stash. I'd piled in, lit up a joint, and enjoyed the buzz as the smoke hit my lungs. I couldn't bring myself to care that I didn't recognize the car, and I cheered Andy on when he sideswiped another car.

Andy chugged a bottle of Jack and revved the engine harder, daring the blokes in the car next to us to race. They'd been down for it, and Andy had taken off like a bat outta hell.

They'd turned off, and Muz leaned out the window, shouting at them. Andy swerved, and Muz squawked, gripping onto the door to stop himself from falling out. I snorted out a laugh, cackling at how much of a dumb-arse he was. Who the hell nearly fell out of a car?

I closed my eyes, inhaling another hit of the pungent smoke. I floated.

The car jolted, mounting the curb.

My eyes sprang open, and I gripped the dash. "Fuck," I screeched.

My breath caught, my heart rate instantly doubling.

Time slowed to a crawl as my pulse pounded in my veins.

A six-foot, double-brick fence was directly in our path. In the beam of the headlights, I could make out the flecks of darker brown and red against the light beige.

The back end fishtailed, wet grass providing no traction.

Andy's laughter bounced around the car.

I couldn't tear my wide-eyed stare from the wall.

The headlight beams narrowed before my eyes. Dad's voice was in my head. "Tristan, you're good for nothing. Useless. You'll end up dead or in jail at this rate."

I was a disappointment. He disapproved of everything I did.

He had a point.

Fear reached out its bony, clawed fingers and wrapped them around my throat. I exhaled on a rush, a whimper of terror escaping me as instinct drove me to bring my arms up and protect my face.

The collision was like a bomb going off. Metal scraped on brick. The squeal from the car grinding against the fence, demolishing it and crashing through the wall of the house, was like fingernails on a chalkboard.

I watched in macabre horror as the front end of the hatchback crumpled like aluminium foil.

The wall folded, teetering for what felt like an eternity, before breaking apart.

Bricks collapsed around us, raining down on the busted-up bonnet.

Glass shattered. Tiny pieces flew at me like miniature missiles.

Bricks landed on me, the impact stealing my breath.

Momentum carried me, the seatbelt catching and branding my chest with a line of fire. I whipped forward, my neck snapping down before being thrown back.

The car stopped.

My head connected with the rest behind me, my neck screaming in protest as I saw stars.

Then stillness.

Everything went quiet, the only noise a hiss coming from the engine.

A soft groan from the front of the car. A whimper from next to me.

I lowered my arms. Turned my head slowly, agony radiating down my spine.

There was a shadow on the bonnet. A dark lump. But the two feet were unmistakeable. One with just a sock on, the other a beaten-up sneaker. Muz.

I blinked. Was I hallucinating? He'd been in the back seat. But he was right there, lying too still.

Another whimper from next to me. I could see Andy from the corner of my eye, crumpled against the steering wheel. His eyes were closed, and blood streamed from his nose. I reached out, grasping his hand.

A bubble formed with his exhale.

His airbag was still partly filled, cocooning him against his busted-up seat back.

Voices in the background slowly filtered in. It was as if I were coming up from underwater.

I needed to move, to get their attention. I needed to help Muz and Andy.

There was a face.

A familiar one.

I hadn't wanted to say goodbye to him, but he'd walked me out. He'd smiled and shaken his head when I'd asked for his number. He'd told me not to swing by his apartment again.

He was fussing over Murray, shifting bricks and touching his head. He was on the phone too, his voice calm. In charge. He was so different to the man who'd pleaded with me to take him deeper and harder when I'd been buried inside him.

"Don't move him," he barked.

I blinked slowly, trying to turn my head more. There was a woman opening Andy's door.

She paused, looking like she was about to argue, but when he added, "Check his pulse and breathing," she nodded.

"He's breathing," I croaked, still woozy from the impact. Or the joint I'd been smoking.

"Tristan? Oh my god!"

I was taken to hospital and checked out. Once I had the all-clear, I'd been bundled in the back of a cop car and driven straight to the station for questioning. I was arrested and charged.

Sitting in the holding cell until my court appearance the next day had been a wake-up call. The disappointment Dad was quick to communicate with me played on repeat in my head. But it wasn't his voice I heard. It was Ezra's. Between rounds, we'd thrown together sandwiches and talked. He was so put together. So grown-up even though he was younger than me. He had a real career, and he was making a difference. I'd joked, telling him I wanted to be like him when I grew up.

He told me to do it. That it was as simple as making a decision. I had to stop making excuses for myself and become who I wanted to be.

He didn't accept my explanation for acting the way I did. They were just excuses, he said, not real reasons.

It had taken an accident, the very real possibility that any of us could have died, or killed someone else, to make me believe him.

Sitting there in that cell was like a come-to-Jesus moment. I'd asked the officer on guard duty for a solicitor. The Legal Aid lawyer had done the rounds early the next morning, and he'd sent her my way. I asked for representation. At my arraignment, I'd pleaded guilty and been remanded for sentencing.

Today was the day. I knew I'd fucked up. I knew I was going to jail. Muz had been in hospital for a week and was still in traction for his broken neck. It was a miracle he could still walk. He'd pleaded not guilty to the drug charges and was awaiting his trial. Andy had pleaded guilty like me, and he was already serving his sentence—two years for a list of offences as long as my arm.

I wasn't part of the break and enter. I didn't steal the car. But I was equally responsible for the damage that we'd caused.

My gut churned as I stood, shifting my weight from side to side as the judge peered down at me. His black robe and white wig set him apart from all the others in the room. He had authority and wasn't afraid to use it. I was flat out intimidated by him. The stern lines around his mouth and eyes were severe.

"Mr Reid, do you understand the damage your stupidity has caused?"

"Yes, your honour," I replied quietly, my head down as shame spiralled through me.

There was a back and forth between my lawyer and the judge, and the police prosecutor interjected a few times. I swallowed, waiting for my fate to be read out.

"Twelve months with time already served with eligibility for parole after six months."

My solicitor nudged me with her elbow, and I nodded. She'd warned me that's what I was facing, but hearing those words was a gut punch.

There was a flurry of activity, and a dude in a uniform came to me with a pair of handcuffs. "Can I have a moment?" a man asked from behind me as a warm hand landed on my shoulder. I'd heard it before, in very different circumstances, but I'd have recognized Ezra anywhere.

Sucking in a breath, I closed my eyes and waited. "Tristan," he started, his voice cracking. I wanted to see him. I wanted to be in his arms again. Turning, I gazed into his chocolate brown eyes swirling with emotion. "I wish that turned out differently. I'm so sorry."

I reached for him, needing to feel his touch one more time. Threading our fingers together, I vowed, "I can change, Ez. I will change. I promise, one day I'll deserve you."

His smile was sad. Bringing our foreheads together, he inhaled slowly, his eyelids fluttering closed. "Take care of yourself, Tris."

"I want to see you when I get out."

"Turn into the man you want to be and then look me up."
He pressed a lingering kiss to my lips and stepped back,
turning and striding away without another word.

I'd done what Ezra asked. I'd tried to carve out a life that I could be proud of. I'd tried to become a better man.

We still had chemistry. It ran hot between us. But Ezra had never caved again. He'd put me in the friend-zone and never wavered.

Seeing him eviscerated me. I'd tried to get him back, but he stomped on my heart over and over. Every time he pushed me away, another piece of me broke.

I couldn't face that again. I couldn't damn myself to another decade of pining. What was the point of being this person and living this life if I couldn't have the three people I wanted?

When did I get to win for a change? When could I have what I wanted?

I'd broken free of my father's stranglehold on my life, only to land myself in jail. When I'd finally seen the outside of those four walls, I'd held the reins of my life so tightly that I might as well have still been ensconced in a cell.

When did I get to live?

When did I get to love?

I wanted to share my life with someone. More than one someone, if I were being honest. I wanted my great love moment. That was it. Surely it wasn't too much to ask.

I hadn't fought for Ezra. Not enough to make him change his mind, anyway. Now I was right back in the same position. Walk away or fight. Be safe or have everything I ever dreamed of.

And that still included Ezra.

It was now or never. It was dive in headfirst or walk away for good.

I had no idea how to do it, how I could convince Ezra, Zali, and Flynn to give me another chance. I was sick of losing.

For once in my life, I was going to fight for what I wanted. I was going to be brave enough to demand more.

I closed my eyes and exhaled slowly. "Fuck it," I muttered, picking up the phone.

But neither Zali nor Flynn answered.

Ezra was my next call. As a start, I needed to apologize.

"Hey," he answered after four long rings. He sounded exhausted, as if he was drowning in stress.

"You okay?" I asked, my own issues forgotten. It had been a long time since I'd heard that kind of defeat in his voice, and the need to shield him from it was overwhelming.

"Not in the slightest," he mumbled, and my heart broke.

What had he come across? What had he seen that left him despairing?

"I'm stuck between a rock and a hard place, Tris, and the whole situation is fucked. I...." He huffed out a breath. "I can't even talk about it. But everything is... *royally* fucked."

My breath caught. *Royally* fucked? Did he mean Zali? Was it a reference to Queen? "Give me a yes or no answer, okay?" I didn't wait for him to respond before I asked, "Are Flynn and Zali in trouble?"

The hitch in his breath said everything. My heart rate doubled, smashing against my chest like cymbals clashing together. But I needed his answer. I needed to hear the words. I waited, silently praying they were okay.

"Yes."

My gut bottomed out, dropping like an anvil. My ears were ringing, and my chest clenched painfully. My fingers itched, desperate for me to do something—anything—to protect them.

"It's been a rollercoaster ride," he added, emphasizing his last word.

The contents of my stomach curdled. I was going to be sick. "Ryder?" I choked out past the lump in my throat, holding onto my belly in a futile attempt to settle it. Fear, real and immediate, swamped me.

"Yeah, that's it," Ezra responded, confirming my fears.

Zali, Flynn, and Ryder were in trouble. By extension, that also included Ezra.

"Tris...," he added, sounding like he'd been winded. He was struggling, forcing down his emotions.

"Are they in physical danger?" Holding my breath, I waited for his answer. Time slowed, each millisecond interminable.

"No."

The breath rushed out of my lungs, relief flooding me. But it was a false sense of security. Like sitting in a blow-up dinghy with a slow leak in shark-infested waters, they were clearly still in some sort of trouble. Whatever it was, whatever they were facing, I needed to help them. I just prayed I could.

"Legal?"

"Very much so."

I exhaled on a rush. It was a relief and terrifying at the same time—I could help, but I also knew the consequences if things didn't work out the way I wanted. I pressed my thumb and index finger against my closed eyelids, rubbing the grit.

Zali was as cool as a cucumber. Her sass and smarts held her rock steady.

Flynn—my angel—was her opposite, but his positivity and that glass-half-full attitude that I loved so much could get him in trouble. He was so willing to help, so fiercely loyal that he would do whatever it took to protect Zali. What would that mean for him?

I'd seen them and spoken to Ezra only hours earlier. Ezra hadn't given me any hint whatsoever that there was something going on. So, whatever had happened since was a new development. If Ezra was involved, they were either under investigation, or they'd already been taken into custody and were facing questions.

But when it came to Ryder, that worried me. He was hotheaded. He reacted on instinct, jumping in feetfirst. If Zali was threatened, he'd breath fire and raze the world. That kind of anger would get him in serious trouble.

The need to protect Ry flared hard and fast in me, the burn intensifying from embers to a forest fire in an instant.

I couldn't explain why, but the instinct to protect him was real. Just as real as the need to wrap my arms around Zali, Flynn, and Ezra. They were in danger. They were hurting. I needed to make it stop.

I needed to step up and be the man they all needed.

Speculation wouldn't get me anywhere. I needed more information, but for the moment, it was enough that Ezra had confirmed they were in legal trouble. I could work with that. I just hoped that my prediction that Zali would get them in trouble wasn't a premonition.

If she had, it was undoubtedly my fault.

Zali had so much on the line, more than any of us, with this podcast looming over her head.

I swallowed back the wariness that came with self-preservation. There was no way I could sit back and do nothing, especially when Ezra was suffering too. I wouldn't squander my chance to help them.

I empathized with Zali's frantic need to protect her mother's legacy. I'd been so pre-occupied with getting the podcast off the ground and hitting it big with my research that I hadn't stopped to count the human cost. Zali and her dad were that cost. They were the ones who would have to live with Rosa's actions being made public. It wasn't their fault, but it was their burden to carry.

I wouldn't make the same mistake twice. I wouldn't discount the impact on them again. I could help, and I would. I had contacts. I knew people in the industry who could assist.

"I'll organize lawyers for them," I promised.

"Okay," he breathed out in a rush. "Please."

"I'll come to you too, okay?" I asked a few more questions and deduced that they were on the Gold Coast. The only offices I knew of there were the ones at the airport. "Is that where you are? The airport?"

"Yes."

"I'm on my way. I'm here for you too."

Ezra's sob was muffled, as if he was biting it back, shoving it down under a layer of professionalism. "Thank you." His voice cracked and he sniffed again. "I've got to go."

The line went dead before I could say anything more, and I didn't hesitate to call the one person I knew would help.

She answered immediately. "Tristan, how are you?"

"Good, Robyn. Listen, I'm sorry to do this, but I need a favour." I paused. "Well, a referral, actually. I need your best criminal lawyer—"

"Are you in trouble?" she asked, concern lacing her voice.

"No, my…. Look, it's complicated, but three people who are important to me need lawyers."

"They likely won't all be able to be represented by one person. But to begin with, we can at least have someone present to make sure they know what their rights are," she advised, audibly tapping on a keyboard in the background.

"Yeah, I don't know about representation," I answered honestly. I had a bad feeling that any lawyer who laid eyes on this case would encourage Flynn and Ryder to turn against Zali to protect themselves, and I couldn't see either one of them doing that.

"I'll speak with Nick, my boss, and see if Jodi can help. She's the best. Can you give me a rundown of what's happened so I can brief her?"

I huffed. I didn't have any information. "My friend is a federal police officer—a detective. He couldn't give me anything other than that they were in trouble. I know they were flying to Sydney today. I happened to ring him, and he's confirmed they're being held at Gold Coast airport."

"Okay, just send me their names, and I'll get someone familiar with federal criminal laws organized for you. I'll see if I can get you the names of a couple of other lawyers in case she can't represent all of them."

We said our goodbyes, and I sent Robyn the information she'd asked for. I had a quick reply—one of their associates was on the case. The need to get there, to show up and be present for all of them was overwhelming.

But so were the nerves and the fear of what might happen to them.

My hands were shaking as I started my car. I wiped my sweaty palms on my black pants and exhaled a calming breath.

This was it.

Six

Zali

"Zali," Detective Fraser greeted with a nod as he strutted in.

I hated myself for the butterflies taking flight in my stomach, swooping at the man before me. He was beautiful, all golden hair and skin with his perfect features and kissable lips.

Another two officers, a woman a few years older than me and a man with a thick beard, followed him in. She closed the door without taking her eyes off me. What was this? Good cop, bad cop? "These are detectives Chisholm and Franklin."

I rolled my eyes and shook my head. How ridiculous. "Detectives," I greeted with as bored a tone as I could muster. I still hadn't decided whether I was pissed at him or myself, so until I did, there was no playing nice.

Ezra slipped into the chair opposite me and interlaced his fingers, leaning on his forearms. "Zali, what's going on?" he asked. His tone was no-nonsense, but it was an act. His eyes pleaded with me, and worry lines creased his brow. His lips were turned down unhappily.

I sat back and crossed my arms, hooking one leg over the other. "Well, you lot"—I gestured around the room, meaning the police in general—"have made a mistake, and I deserve a thank you, not an inquisition. Flynn and Ry do too."

Chisolm barked out a laugh as she pulled out a chair, and the other man huffed almost silently. I smirked knowingly.

"You think I'm wrong." Pushing my glasses up my nose, I pressed my lips together and gestured to her. "Detective Chisolm here thinks she knows what's going on, so you fill me in. What do you allege to have on me?"

Ezra shot her a look that had her closing her mouth and turning her glare on me. I bit back my laugh. She looked constipated, not intimidating.

"Zali," he started, pausing on an exhale. "They have enough on you to prosecute you. You're in deep shit, and you're taking your guys down with you." He scrubbed his hands over his eyes and dragged his fingers down his face before resting his chin on the heel of his hands. He looked tired, weighed down.

He winced. "Is that what you want? You want to see Flynn and Ryder go to jail with you?" He dropped his hands to the table and rested his forearms on the edge. "Give me something so that I can help you. Please." His voice was quiet, the plea clear as day.

"Have you looked at the USB you confiscated from me?" I asked, raising a brow. Without bothering to wait for his answer, I continued. "Well, that assumes you managed to break the password. Try "password," all in caps. When your tech guys have analysed it, come back and see me. Until then, I'm done answering questions." I smiled coldly at him and waved my hand, shooing them away.

"That's it?" he asked. He blinked disbelievingly followed by a small shake of his head.

"There is one more thing, actually," I added. "You can call the lawyer whose contact details are on that USB. She'll be representing Flynn and Ryder."

"Can we have a moment?" he asked the other detectives.

"Don't bother, Detective Fraser. I'm not interested in talking privately with you right now. Just do what I'm asking." It was hard keeping up the act. Everything in me was telling me to drop it, just for a moment. To be real with him. But I couldn't afford any show of weakness. Queen needed to be bad-arse, and to do that, I needed my armour-plated walls locked into place. "I promise you, detective. You won't be disappointed."

"You're making a mistake, Zali. I can't help you if you don't cooperate."

"You remember a few weeks ago you told me that you didn't trust anyone? Same, honey. Same." I narrowed my eyes at him, tilting my head until he read my not-so-subtle message loud and clear.

"That's a low blow."

I sighed and shrugged as nonchalantly as I could. "Yeah, sometimes a person deserves a kick in the nuts." Uncrossing my legs and then recrossing them the other way, I added, "Just look at the USB."

He nodded slowly. "What's your computer password?"

"Morningstar, like the medieval weapon."

He raised his eyes, meeting my stare. Misery surrounded him. He looked at me like I'd kicked his puppy. His normally pristine shirt was creased, and his shoulders were hunched. His hair was always artfully styled and naturally perfect, but it was now a mess. It looked as if he'd run his fingers through it repeatedly and tugged on the ends until it stood up in all directions. The moment of relief I'd seen when he'd spied Ryder and Flynn at the airport was long gone.

Slowly, Ezra rose, bracing himself on the table as he pushed up from the chair. It scraped behind him, the noise grating on my ears. With his arms limp by his sides, he pressed his lips into a ghost of a smile, one that didn't come close to reaching his eyes. He was putting on a brave face. He gestured to the door and spoke to the others, saying, "Let's give tech the passwords."

This time when the door clicked closed and the lock snicked into place, a hollowness enveloped me. They wouldn't find anything incriminating on my hard drive, and I had faith that the USB would get us out of here. It was an easy fix.

I just wished that the rest of this clusterfuck was the same.

I didn't expect the door to swing open only a few minutes later, and I certainly wasn't anticipating the unfamiliar woman who strode in. She was dressed to impress in a navy-blue power suit with white pin stripes, a crisp white shirt and matching navy heels. She was all business. Her dark hair was pulled into a bun, and her small diamond earrings were a match to the pendant hanging on the slim chain around her throat.

"Ms Stephens, my name is Jodi Carter. Professor Reid contacted me on your behalf and urgently asked me to provide counsel for you."

"Professor Reid?" I questioned, creasing my brow, confusion etched in my voice.

"Yes."

She sat down and pulled a notepad and pen out of her satchel. She was old school despite probably only being in her early forties. Resting her forearms on the table, she tapped her pen, waiting for me to ask another question. There was a ruthless efficiency about her that I admired. But I was still stuck on who had sent her.

When she was seemingly satisfied that I wasn't going to ask anything else, she added, "Before we begin, I've had the video cameras and recording devices switched off. We're free to talk, so please be truthful with your answers. I'm here to protect your interests."

I tilted my head before shaking it in disbelief. "Professor Tristan Reid? Why did he hire you?"

She laid down her pen and smiled at me. It was a mix of patient and patronizing, something that would normally get on my nerves, but I had bigger fish to fry in that moment.

"He called one of the associates in my office. She asked me to drop everything and head here. Professor Reid briefed me with the information he knew—"

"What information? Where did he hear it from?"

"Ezra."

The confusion slipped from my face, turning into shock. Ezra? He'd put his job on the line and risked everything to give us a chance. We had a right to ask for representation, but him briefing a friend so that they could help us avoid charges was huge. It was way outside what he would be allowed to do as a cop. He shouldn't have even mentioned us to Tristan, much less given him enough information about the investigation to clue him in on the fact that we might need representation. It had to be a sackable offence, if not a criminal one.

Ezra really was worried. He really was trying to help. I thought he'd been putting on an act, and he had been, but it wasn't me he was trying to fool. He'd been towing the line with his colleagues, framing questions in a way that set my teeth on edge. But it was his eyes that had told me the truth. The pleading in them, the stress he was carrying. The worry and helplessness when I'd brushed him off.

Sitting in that meeting with him, I hadn't decided whether I was pissed with Ezra or myself. But now…. Now there was no doubt in my mind. I couldn't be angry at him;

he was a fucking double agent. He worked for the man, but his loyalties lay with his queen.

Closing my eyes, I thanked the universe for him.

I had my own reasons for breaking into the Reserve Bank of Australia's servers. I doubted anyone in their right mind would think I was justified, but I didn't give a whole lot of fucks.

I wanted what they had, so I took it. They wouldn't miss it. They didn't lose anything. Hell, they weren't even using it. I would. I had a purpose for it, a need.

The locked doors, the passwords, their laws—they couldn't keep me out. They could never contain me. They certainly couldn't stop me.

The police were doing their best, but I had my loyal knights. My men.

First Ryder and Flynn had been there, trying to muscle their way into securing my freedom. Ezra and Tristan had shown a little more flair when they'd jumped to my aid. Ezra had put everything on the line for me.

Tristan had walked away. He'd turned his back. But he hadn't washed his hands of me. He'd reached out, seeking help for us. It may have been self-preservation. It may have been a need to ensure that he wasn't going to be held responsible for my acts, but something in my gut told me that wasn't the case.

No, I had a feeling that my professorhole was still mine.

I pulled my hair out of my ponytail and slumped in my seat. "I… I'm in shock."

"Have they given you any indication of the charges?"

I waved her off. "I'm not worried about that. Do you know who Ezra is?"

"No idea, sorry." She shook her head and pressed her lips together, seemingly biting back a comment in order to move the conversation along.

"It's Detective Fraser. He's my…. Look, don't say anything in front of any of the other police officers. They can't know he called Tristan. He'll lose his job, if not face charges himself. I can't let that happen. He needs to be protected."

"My job is to protect you, not the police."

"He's not the police." I shook my head. On the surface that comment didn't make sense, but I knew where Ezra's loyalties truly lay, and I wouldn't let him be punished for protecting me. "Look, you don't have the whole story, and I don't have time to explain it to you before the detectives come back in—"

"They'll wait for as long as it takes for us to finish our meeting."

"And every minute that we're in here delaying things is a minute longer they can be pressuring Flynn and Ry for information. I understand what you're saying, but I need to answer their questions and get the heat off all of us. It's the only way this will get sorted out—"

She held her hands up in a stopping motion and spoke over me. "I'm all for cooperating with the police when it's appropriate, but you're in federal custody. If they can build a case, the charges you're potentially facing are serious. We're talking significant jail time."

I nodded and waited for her to finish talking, but I was getting impatient.

She laid her hands flat on the table and pressed her lips together before continuing. "At this point, unless you have an alibi or other evidence which will exonerate you, my recommendation is that you force the police to satisfy their onus of proof. Let them build the case. Don't do it for them."

I stood and slipped my hands into my belt loops before walking a lap of the back wall. Turning to face her again, I explained, "I'm a cyber investigator for the federal police. It's literally my job to build the cases you're talking about. I completely understand what you're saying."

She opened her mouth to interrupt again but this time I reciprocated with the same stopping gesture. "I've given a USB to Detective Fraser. He's reviewing the contents as we speak. That's my exonerating evidence. It's the reason why I got on my plane and went to Sydney in the first place. Let me sort this out myself."

"Okay. Look, I need to ask—are you declining representation?"

I couldn't help the smile when I thought about Ezra speaking with Tristan and my grumpy professor pulling out all stops to have someone here to protect me. But I was honestly more concerned for Flynn and Ryder than myself.

"I am. But not for the reason you're thinking. I've already briefed my solicitor on what's happening. I asked her to look after my friends, except she may not be able to represent both of them. It might be better if you represent

Flynn rather than me. At the very least, I know Tristan would want Flynn protected too. My solicitor knows Ryder. She'd probably be more comfortable representing him anyway."

"Okay." She nodded. "I'll let Tristan know and speak with Ryder's solicitor."

"Thank you."

She exited, and I took my glasses off, dropping them on the table. I rubbed my eyes, exhaustion setting in like a rising tide. Biting back a yawn, I would have killed for a comfortable couch to curl up on for that nap.

Closing my eyes and leaning back in the hard plastic chair, I imagined being in my guys' arms. But this time, it wasn't just Flynn and Tristan holding me. Ezra was there too, and Ry was close as well, standing watch at the door.

It seemed like a pipe dream.

When the door opened again what seemed like hours later, I opened my eyes, blinking in the bright light. "Hey," Ezra murmured quietly as he walked in and slipped a paper cup onto the table in front of me. "I got you this. It's not as good as yours or your dad's, but it's hot." The cup was filled with green tea, steam curling from the surface. His shadows—detectives Chisolm and Franklin—stood like sentinels, flanking him.

I yawned, covering my mouth with the back of my hand as he pulled out the seat opposite me and slid onto it.

"Did you look at the USB?"

He pointed at the cameras in the ceiling, and I stopped speaking. I knew the drill.

"We're being recorded—"

"Anything I say can and will be used against me in a court of law, I know." I shot him a teasing smile, and colour rose on his cheeks. Grinning, I nudged him under the table with my foot, and he hooked his leg around mine. That small show of solidarity, invisible to the cameras mounted above us, was as strong as a hug. Warmth spread through my chest.

"You asked if we looked at the USB—we did. Our tech guy is briefing Inspector Puglisi as we speak."

"She's a pleasant one, isn't she?" I deadpanned, swallowing back a laugh when Ezra bit his lip and looked away.

But his playfulness slipped, and he shot me a worried glance. "Wanna tell me what happened? Because, honestly, the screen grabs and package you've put together seems really convenient. I don't know whether the inspector is going to believe a word of it."

I took a sip of the tea and hummed. It wasn't the best, a bit bitter and too hot for green tea, but it would do.

With my hands still wrapped around the paper cup, I nodded. "That's just it—it was a complete accident." I gave Ezra my most innocent smile and shrugged. "I was researching for the podcast. I needed some historical information and looked up what data banks were required to keep and for how long. I discovered that the Reserve Bank held transactional records from during the GFC, not the banks themselves."

"Okay," he encouraged, sitting forward in his chair and resting his forearms on the table.

Tracing the rim of the cup, I continued, "I tried searching the Reserve Bank's online databases, but the information I needed—the raw transaction data—wasn't publicly available. That's why I had Flynn ask if you could access it when he was speaking with you." I gestured to him, and he nodded. That conversation had happened only a few hours earlier, but it felt like a lifetime ago.

"I actually clicked on the wrong thing—I screen grabbed it for you—and it took me into a section of the website that should have been behind a firewall, but it wasn't. It was the Reserve Bank's password registry. Some idiot had created a spreadsheet with the full listing of passwords, then left some of the end points on the API public." I shook my head, bewildered at the potential disaster waiting to happen.

"What's an API?"

"Application programming interface."

He nodded slowly, but I could tell he wasn't really interested in what an API was. He probably already knew. "How did you know the password?"

"A survey in 2022 found that the most popular password was 'password.' It was a lucky guess."

Ezra groaned and dropped his face into his hands, threading his fingers through his hair and tugging on the ends exactly as I'd imagined he'd been doing. I couldn't help my smile. It took everything in me to curb the instinct to reach out and pull his hands away.

He lifted his face, resting his chin on his clenched fists, and I continued.

"As soon as I saw what it was, I didn't even think. I went straight to the sites I monitor for chatter around hacks. I wanted to see if someone was bragging about getting in and leaving it open. But instead, I found what was, for want of a better description, a wanted ad for personal data from Australian banks with a hefty reward for the people who delivered. They were after access to the Reserve Bank."

Ezra's brow furrowed, and he tilted his head, considering what I was saying before giving a small shake of his head. "Why?"

"It's not a bank per se, but the banks share data with it. There's an established upload pipeline between them. The aim would have been to get into the Reserve Bank to find a potential back door entry into the other banks' systems. The complexity of the systems each organization uses, the differing layers of security, and the fact that they need to be constantly updated to keep security at the highest levels would have meant that the Reserve Bank's ISP addresses were simply whitelisted. Once they got in, every bank account in Australia could have been compromised."

"So?" He gestured for me to continue my explanation.

"So, I went back to the Reserve Bank's site. I looked into what else wasn't protected, and it was a hot mess." Shaking my head, I tapped my fingernail on the cup. I continued, "I adapted a patch I've used in the past that's solid. But I couldn't upload it from where I was. I needed to get it onto their servers."

"Why not call them? Why not speak with the head of IT and get them to upload it? Why not call me?"

I huffed out a laugh, but it held no humour. "The password to their password registry was 'password,' all in caps." I raised a brow and pursed my lips.

Ezra tossed me a half smile and nodded, understanding my less than subtle jab at the bank's security protocols.

"I wasn't prepared to trust anyone in that organization, and it was extremely time sensitive. The wanted ad had already generated quite a bit of chatter, and the people taking up the challenge were professionals. They were good enough to get in. As it was, ninety minutes for me to get to Sydney and into the bank's server room was a calculated risk, but I decided that alerting anyone was a greater risk. It would have prompted their IT department to try and fix the issues. They could have opened more holes, or worse, left their entire system unprotected if they got the patch wrong."

He sat back in the chair, gazing at me. The warmth was back in his eyes, but there was still some wariness there, some worry. "You took it on yourself to fly down to Sydney, break into the Reserve Bank, and upload a patch?"

"What's the saying? Something about power and responsibility?"

"Yeah." He huffed out a laugh. "Something like that." His smile slowly slid from his face.

My fingers twitched, wanting to reach out and touch his cheek, to get that smile back.

"Where did Ryder and Flynn fit into your plan?"

I held up my hands, palms in the air. "Ryder is my pilot. You know that. Flynn was with Ryder on my yacht when I found the chatter. I asked Ry to take me to Sydney, and Flynn decided to come with us. Ry was supposed to drop me off, but they followed me inside, thinking they could wait for me at reception until I finished my meeting. I didn't tell them what I was doing. They had no idea where we even were until I entered the server room. Then that damn security guard started shooting at us—"

"Zali—"

"Listen, you know me, detective. You know that when I find something I can help with, I do it. This was important." I shook my head, pressing my lips together as I implored him to believe me. "I couldn't sit back and let millions of people potentially have sensitive information stolen. I couldn't live with myself if I let that happen."

I tucked my hair behind my ear, imploring him to believe me. "Yes, I broke in, if you want to call waltzing straight in the front door breaking in. I used one of the passwords in the registry to get into the server room, and I uploaded the patch. I'm absolutely guilty of all that. But the end justified the means. Prosecute me if you need to, but can you imagine the public backlash?"

Ezra lifted one side of his mouth in a ghost of a smile. "And Flynn and Ryder?"

"Completely innocent bystanders. They didn't do anything. Release them. There's no point charging them with anything."

The door opened, and Inspector Puglisi stepped inside. She looked less than pleased, her lips pursed in a grimace and her eyes still holding a glint of suspicion. "It appears you've done the people of this country a service, Miss Stephens."

I dipped my head in acknowledgement of her reluctant compliment. "I was just trying to help."

"We'll be investigating this further."

"Absolutely." I nodded. "That threat was real. If I can be of any assistance, please call on me."

"Yes. Unlikely," she responded. "You're free to go. But Ms Stephens, don't leave the country."

"I'll be sure to keep that request in mind." I shot her a saccharine smile and held out my hand for her to shake, not bothering to stand. She looked down at my outstretched arm, and politeness and professionalism won out. She shook my hand before stalking away, letting the door slam in her wake.

Smirking at Ezra, I stood, smoothed down my shirt, and added, "Looks like I'll see ya 'round, boss."

"Mmm," he responded, looking me up and down, the hunger in his eyes setting my insides alight.

My cunt clenched and my nipples pebbled. I shivered, want spiralling through me. I licked my lips, chasing the taste of him there. It was undeniable. I wanted him.

"Walk me out, detective."

SEVEN

Ezra

"I'll need my laptop, but you can keep the USB." Zali held out her hand to the tech, who handed back her phone. He slipped her laptop back into its leather sleeve and passed it to her.

We were standing in the front office. Flynn and Ry were waiting for us in reception with their solicitors. I hadn't seen him yet, but Tristan messaged me to say he was with them. A yearning so deep it bordered on painful filled me. I wanted to see them. I needed to. But there were another few hours yet on my shift, and Inspector Puglisi would be after my head. Running away to the Brisbane office was tempting, but two hours in traffic each way was enough to keep my feet planted firm.

"I've mirrored the hard drive. If there's anything on there, I'll find it."

"Knock yourself out." Zali smiled, but it reminded me of a shark rather than the genuinely warm woman she could be.

She turned her gaze to me. I was standing far too close to her, my hand on her lower back as she wavered. Her shoulder pressed against my chest, and she leaned into me.

The tech left, and I murmured low enough that only she could hear, "Where's the yacht moored?"

"Marina Mirage."

"I get off in three hours."

She nodded, her lips parting and her tongue sneaking out to wet her lips. I wanted to bite it, to suck her tongue into my mouth. To feast on her lips.

"Good."

I gestured to the door with a tilt of my head. "Let's get you back to your men."

I knew she wanted to say more, but thankfully she held her tongue. The inspector would be keeping a close eye on our interactions, and I didn't want to give her any more ammunition than she already had.

With a small smile, her gaze lingering on my lips, she nodded. "Yeah."

I walked out into the reception area and watched as Flynn slipped off my jacket and handed it to Tristan before he launched himself at Zali. He embraced her tight, wrapping his arms around her shoulders and pressing their heads together. I couldn't hear the words he was saying to her, but when she wiped her cheeks with the heel of her palm and nodded, my shoulders fell. I'd tried my best to shield them all, and for the moment, it was working, but who knew how badly they could be hurt if the techs discovered anything.

Without letting Flynn go completely, she wrapped her arm around Ry and squeezed him tight. He was rigid, but he kissed her forehead and patted her back awkwardly. I wanted to be right there with them, in the middle just like Zali, even with Ry's discomfort.

But I couldn't.

I looked away, my yearning so palpable, I could have reached out and touched it.

My gaze clashed with Tristan's.

The breath rushed from my lungs, my knees almost buckling.

Dear god, he was potent.

His pale green eyes were smouldering, fire burning in their depths. He possessed an intensity the likes of which I'd only ever seen on one other person—Ryder. Tristan was dangerous to my sanity. To my willpower.

I'd succumbed to him once.

I'd wanted him ever since.

But the timing was never right. After he'd served his sentence and we crossed paths again, I was neck deep in being there while a man grieved for his lost wife and son as well as dealing with a far-too-talented teenager, her side-kick, and their shadow.

I'd wanted more than a one-night stand by then. Tristan wasn't ready to give it. He still came onto me every time we saw each other, but as the years passed, my feelings got more and more confused.

It hit me that Zali, Flynn, and Ry were all grown-up when we celebrated Flynn's nineteenth birthday. Roe and I had taken a six-pack each down to the boat to celebrate. We wound our way through the Maseratis and Aston Martins in the car park, drooling over them and doing the same to the yachts in the marina.

But the picture that greeted me when we got to Zali's yacht was what had stolen my breath. It had solidified a yearning in me, like a picture finally coming into focus. It had also sealed my fate. I was doomed to be single forever.

Zali was lying on the sun deck on the bow, wearing the tiniest bikini I'd ever seen while basking in the late afternoon sun. Ry was aft, barbecuing, and Flynn sat with his legs hanging over the side closest to us, reading a book.

I wanted them, and not just some abstract desire to sleep with them either. The craving to have all of them in my arms and in my bed together was overpowering.

But it would also be the ultimate betrayal.

How could I want them? What was wrong with me that I couldn't decide on just one person? It was ironic that Tristan had become my safest choice.

Instead of accepting Tristan's advances, I'd pushed back against him, blowing him off. I'd told him that he didn't really want something more serious with me, when in truth I was terrified. When he cornered me on Zali's yacht, there was no room for doubt anymore.

Tristan pushed me up against the kitchen cabinets, pressing his big body to mine. He wrapped his arms around my waist before landing on my hips, holding me steady as he kissed a line up my throat, nuzzling the spot behind my ear that made me melt. He'd found it the first night we were together, and when he pressed for me to cave, Tristan played dirty, hitting that button.

"I want you, Ez. I want to strip you of every one of your doubts so you can see exactly what I want," he rumbled against my ear, his breath sending a shiver through me. "I want to love you."

Grinding against me, he pressed his hot, hard length between my cheeks. He slipped his hand lower, palming my dick. My balls drew up tight, pre-cum blooming from my slit, the stickiness against my boxer briefs immediate. My hole clenched. No one had ever taken me like him. No one had ever managed to completely obliterate the world outside my bedroom door like he'd done.

I arched into him, desperate for more of his touch. Needy. Wanting. It had been so long since I'd been with anyone, man or woman, that it wouldn't take much more before my release was inevitable.

But giving in was dangerous.

As time had gone by, Tristan's demands had changed. He promised me everything, the relationship I craved with him rather than just the nights of endless orgasms. But now he wanted more than I could give. I was in love with four people, only one of whom I had any kind of chance with. He deserved better than my scraps.

"Give in," he whispered. "Let me take us to heaven."

I moaned, desperate to let go. To finally hand over the reins to him. To stop thinking and fall into our chemistry headfirst.

Tris gave me a sliver of space, waiting for me to act. Instinct screamed at me to unbuckle my pants and shove them down, but instead I pushed back and spun around. I wanted to have him in my arms, for him to know just how much I wanted him. This whole affair had disaster written all over it, but I was teetering on the edge of reason, unable to think up any more excuses.

Chest to chest and nose to nose, we breathed in each other's air. Our chests came together with every inhale, our hips pressed firm. He was as hard as I was, our cocks nestled together between our thin layers of clothing. Though we were hovering only a hair's breadth apart, I still needed more. Spearing my fingers into Tris's soft-as-silk hair, I gripped his nape and brushed my lips against his.

I think I moaned. It could have been Tris. But it was the final straw, the one that broke the camel's back. Instinctively, we deepened our kiss, our tongues tangling and teeth clashing together.

Then I heard the gasp. A quiet whimper.

Thoughts of Zali, Flynn, and Ryder intruded, and a guilt as heavy as the ocean weighed on me. I couldn't do it.

Stepping back and severing our connection, I held up a hand to stop Tris from chasing me. It took everything in me to force out the one word I knew would hurt both of us, but it was for the best. Disappointing him now was better than doing it later—it would only hurt more if I led him on. "No," I uttered, my tone a mixture of resignation and resolve.

He stepped forward, his eyes blazing. His kiss-swollen lips, still wet from our exploration, were so very tempting.

But I couldn't do it. I had to stay strong. I tried to push him away, but my hands had a mind of their own. It was more of a caress, an excuse to touch him one last time, than a shove. But it was all I could manage.

Walking away from him was one of the hardest things I'd ever done. My feet dragged like I was wading through quicksand. My heart cracked in my chest, every one of my nerve endings already missing his body against mine.

The only thing that kept me going, the only solace I had, was standing in front of me. Zali. It was as if she were the sun and could recharge my batteries. I paused in front of her, cupping her face. I needed her strength, her willpower, to be able to walk away for good. But my hands were trembling, and I couldn't let her see how weak I was either. Kissing her cheek, I gathered my wits and stalked out of the kitchen.

Off the yacht.

I needed space, air, or I'd drown.

"Detective," Inspector Puglisi snapped, jarring me back to the present. "A word."

Tristan slipped around the chairs and handed me my jacket. "You'll get through this. I'm here for you too," he murmured, clasping my waist gently and squeezing. Closing my eyes, I let my head fall forward onto his shoulder and wished for just one moment where I could take what I needed.

But it was impossible.

Holding my jacket in front of my erection, I spun on my heels and followed the inspector into her office without another word. The moment her door was closed, she rounded on me.

"Your girl has gotten away with this bullshit for the last time. There's something more going on here, and I don't like being played."

I sighed, sick of her lecture already. "There's nothing more, inspector. She gave us everything. The contents of the USB backed up every piece of her evidence, and tech have found the threats online that she was referring to."

I shook my head, misery hovering over me like a storm cloud. "The chatter seems real, and you said it yourself that the tone has changed in the last hour. The Bank's firewalls have gotten a whole lot more difficult to crack—that's Zali's patch, and you know it."

"It's too neat," she muttered.

"That's Zali. She does it with every investigation I've worked with her on."

"Get her under control, detective. I'm holding you responsible for her actions." She pointed her finger at me.

I clenched my teeth, resisting the urge to snap it off.

"Next time, this kind of behaviour won't be excused, I don't care what data she allegedly saves. One more wrong move, one more step out of line, and you're both going to jail."

I opened my mouth to speak, but she held up her hand. "I'm not finished. You're skating on thin ice, detective. This is your last warning, too. I'm seeking advice from Ethics about a referral to the Crime and Misconduct Commission. I'm telling you this as a courtesy. Get some advice from your union representative because you might be going to jail re-gardless."

"Am I dismissed?" I ground out.

Inspector Puglisi narrowed her eyes at my insubordina-tion but thankfully didn't call me out on it. Add another strike to my name that the CMC would investigate. "Get out of here. You're done for the night."

Ryder pulled open the security gate to the dock, and the bloke standing next to me handed over the pizza boxes.

"I can help," I offered.

"No need."

I clamped a hand on Ry's shoulder, stopping him from walking away. "I'm sorry."

"Water under the bridge, man. Let's just forget about it." His words were clipped, hollow too. He didn't mean a word he'd said. His scowl deepened, the grooves in his fore-head and thinning of his lips playing off the dim lighting so that he looked like a Roman statue carved in perfect relief.

Ryder was playing nice; he hadn't forgiven me. Not by a long shot.

"They're waiting for you," he tossed over his shoulder as he walked away.

I'd gone home, showered, and changed, swapped my phone to my personal one and caught a rideshare over. Maybe I was being paranoid, but I wouldn't put it past

Puglisi to plant a listening device on me. Sure, anything she got would be inadmissible in court without a warrant, and usually the wheels of the legal system operated glacially slow, but no one liked a cop who was under suspicion. Every judge on the coast would move mountains to help gather evidence to rid the force of a bad apple.

The lights on the Noble Steed were welcoming, and as I walked up the dock, my shoulders unclenched. I didn't have a right to call it home, but it was warmer and more inviting than my lonely apartment.

But before I could cross the gangplank, my phone vibrated. I hesitated, pulling it out of my pocket to check whether I wanted to answer it. Roe.

If he'd heard, he'd call nonstop until I answered. He was probably already at my front door, ready to administer a beat down. And it would be a beat down even though I could defend myself. The idea of using my skills in Krav Maga against one of my closest friends was out of the question.

Especially when he was the father of the woman I was secretly in love with.

EIGHT

Zali

AN HOUR EARLIER

"**S**pill," Ryder demanded the moment I stepped onto the stern. We weren't even on the main deck yet, only just having crossed the gangway.

I was gross and grumpy. Everything hurt, I had a headache, and I was sticky and sweaty. There was no way I was answering his question when he used that kind of tone with me.

"Yeah, I think not," I snarked back. "I need a shower, food, and a drink before I start talking."

"Zee, we deserve some answers," Flynn countered, taking Ry's side once again. "We've waited long enough."

"You can bloody well wait for another five minutes," I snapped, frustration bubbling up. Ry was in a foul mood, slamming doors, driving like a bat outta hell, and growling at me like I was a five-year-old. Even after hugging me, Flynn was still standoffish. It was better, but he still wasn't his normal self. I shouldn't be upset—he'd just spent half the night hours in an interview room because of me—but it hurt too.

"Order delivery so we can eat."

I didn't wait for permission from them, not that I needed it. Fuck that. Instead, I stomped to my stateroom and slammed the door before turning on the water and waiting for it to heat to scalding.

The shower was exactly what I needed, but hiding from them wasn't my style. They wanted answers. I'd give them what they were after. Sighing, I adjusted my shower cap, tucking a stray piece of my hair into it and then scrubbed the lingering scent of interview room and the inspector's unwelcome hands off me.

Within minutes I was dry again and yanking my grey off-the-shoulder knit top from my walk-in closet. It was as soft and snuggly as it was cute, and with the fireworks set to go off tonight, I needed that.

Slipping it on, I let it fall halfway down my legs and slid on a pair of loose socks. I wanted to curl up on my bed and sleep like the dead, but I respected Flynn and Ry too much to blow them off. They were right—they did deserve some answers. My energy waning, I dragged myself back to the deck with heavy feet, and I headed straight for the lounge.

A familiar head of dark hair was waiting for me there. Tristan.

I schooled my surprise and sat opposite him in my usual spot next to Flynn. Tristan's stare bored into me with an intensity that sucked the breath from my lungs. I was suddenly awake. My nipples peaked, and a shiver stole through me as my cunt clenched, instinctively wanting to be filled. Fuck, I loved being the centre of his attention.

Tearing my gaze away from him, I focussed on Ry. Unlike Tristan's intense stare that whispered heat and promised sex, Ry's was angry. He glared at me, his lips pressed in a straight line and his back rigid. I hated that he was being like this, but I shouldn't have expected anything different. Ry had always acted like a big brother, and the resulting clusterfuck from this afternoon's quick trip was bound to grate on his nerves.

I sighed and focussed my attention back on Tristan.

"Why are you here?" I asked him, a note of caution slipping into my voice as I reached for Flynn's hand. He shifted closer, his warm fingers curling around mine as he lent me his comfort.

Could Tristan have changed his mind? He'd shown up at the police station, he'd organized a lawyer for us... so maybe there was hope. But was it just concern for his reputation and what an arrest would mean for the podcast?

It was more than possible he didn't give a fuck about our wellbeing.

Flynn shifted so he sat sideways on the couch. Tugging on my hip, he spread his legs and positioned me until I was sitting with my back to his front. I leaned against him, my head resting on his shoulder as he undid my hair from its messy top knot and ran his fingers through it. He then massaged my scalp, neck, and shoulders, and I groaned as he found all the knots in my muscles, his talented fingers working them out.

Murmuring in my ear, he encouraged, "Listen to what he has to say, Zee."

"I'm sorry," Tristan started before dropping his gaze and staring at his interlaced fingers. His elbows were resting on his spread knees, his back hunched over. "I got scared and I ran. I've shielded myself from anything and everything that could bite me in the arse for a long time—"

"That's no fun," Flynn interjected playfully. "I like biting you."

Tristan's chuckle and reluctant smile warmed my heart. Flynn was good at both diffusing tension and reading Tristan. He knew what the man needed without even having to ask.

But the comment just seemed to incense Ryder. His eyes flashed as he ground his teeth, his jaw bulging as he shifted in his seat. He looked like a lion ready to ambush its prey. And when that prey was caught, there would be no surviving the onslaught.

"Yeah, I like your bites too, angel," Tristan murmured, his voice dropping an octave and taking on a sexy rasp. After clearing his throat, he continued, "When I realized the extent of what you do, Zali, I freaked the fuck out. I mean, I knew—" He gestured to the yacht. "How couldn't I? I'm not a complete idiot, but I let myself be blind to it because there was something I wanted more."

Ry's unimpressed grunt caught Tristan's attention, and he turned to my right-hand man.

Without meeting Ry's gaze, he explained, "I'm not who you think I am, Ryder." He shook his head and huffed. His self-disgust was blatant even to Ry judging by the way his head snapped up to look at Tristan.

"When I was in my twenties, I served six months for being an accessory after the fact to a break and enter and stealing a car, possession—weed—and unlawful use of a motor vehicle. We had an accident that stopped the whole train wreck. But yeah, jail... wasn't fun."

He visibly swallowed, and Ry's scowl softened, a glimmer of concern escaping his stony façade. Ry reached out, squeezing Tristan's shoulder.

He snatched his hand away the second Tristan looked up.

Ry narrowed his eyes, his lips thinning into a feral snarl. Their stares locked.

Tristan inhaled sharply, his body swaying toward Ry.

Desire radiated off Tristan, his parted lips just begging to be kissed.

They were like tinder and a match. Incendiary. Get close enough and they would ignite and as with a wildfire, burn hotter than hell.

But would they fight or fuck?

Ry was the one to break their stare, turning away to study the deck at his feet.

Tristan shifted minutely, subtly adjusting himself. I shivered, and not because of the cool evening breeze washing over the deck.

His sigh snapped the focus back to his story. "It was awful, every day worse than the one before. I was easy prey, but it was mostly taunting. They were trying to scare the shit out of me rather than dishing out beat downs. Still, that kind of mind-fuckery does a number on you."

"Then things changed. Another inmate pissed off my cellmate, and he took it out on me. I was assaulted two weeks shy of being released. It put me in the infirmary for a week before they shifted me back to my cell. The last week I was in there was a waking nightmare. I've never been more terrified in my life. I was just waiting for him to come and finish me off."

Ry looked away, blinking fast, and Flynn's fingers tightened on my shoulders. I couldn't swallow, the lump in my throat like a boulder. Trembling, I brought my knees up to my chest and hugged my legs tight. A sob hitched my breath, and I itched to reach out to Tristan. I wanted to turn back time and save him from the pain. From the fear.

After I'd killed the fucker that hurt him.

All those times I'd pictured ripping Tristan limb from limb and wanting him to hurt burned like acid in my gut. It had actually happened. He'd been injured at the hands of another person. He'd been left bleeding and broken in just the way I'd imagined it. I was going to be sick. Never in my worst nightmares did I ever think it could have happened.

Clutching my stomach, I dashed to the side and dry retched, my stomach heaving as it tried to expel the food I hadn't eaten.

At first I thought it was Flynn gathering my hair into his hands and pulling it back, but when he moved to the side and slowly rubbed my back, I realized it was Ry. "You okay, baby girl?" he asked when I rested my forehead on my crossed arms.

"No, I'm really not," I confessed, shaking my head. I met Ry's gaze, and my heart broke at the deep furrow in his brows. "But it's not about me. I can't believe he went through that."

"Me neither. No wonder he didn't want anything to do with us."

I stood the rest of the way up and looked over my shoulder at Flynn straddling Tristan, his knees on either side of Tristan's hips and their arms wrapped tightly around each other. They were a beautiful sight, one that made my heart ache. I didn't want either Flynn or Tristan to miss out on each other.

"He's strong to have survived that kind of intimidation," I murmured.

His actions—his reactions—were self-preservation. Not to downplay it, but high-school bullying like Flynn and I had endured was one thing. I couldn't imagine how devastating six months of psychological warfare from proven criminals would be to a person's psyche. My chest hurt and my heart broke for Tristan. Tears sprang to my eyes. I tried to wipe them away before they could fall, but Ry saw. He gathered me in his arms and whispered, "You're strong too, Zali. Talk to us, tell us what went down so we can help."

The weight of my criminal actions sat heavy, like an anvil around my neck dragging me under. I had a responsibility to protect Tristan, to protect all these men. No matter what, I could never let my actions come back on any of them. That meant protecting them from me too.

Today was far too close a call for comfort.

"Okay," I agreed. With his arm around my shoulders, we walked back to the couch. Ry hovered as I sat, then he got me a Sprite from the outdoor refrigerator. I knew he was still pissed at me—I'd violated his trust—but his anger was slowly dissipating. He cracked the can open, handed it to me, and gave me a small nod when I'd taken a sip. It was a peace offering that I gratefully took.

Patting the seat next to me, I waited as Flynn climbed off the professor and, hand in hand, they slipped around the table to join me. Flynn and I bracketed him, and Ryder leaned behind us on the back of the couch.

"I'm sorry I put you in that position," I murmured, reaching up to caress his stubbled cheek. His whiskers were soft, his brown eyes slipping closed as I ran my thumb along his bottom lip and over his jaw. He looked tired, the memories of the fear he'd endured taking its toll. My gorgeous, strong man was hurting.

Blinking open his eyes, and with vulnerability radiating off him, he pleaded with a shake of his head, "I can't go back there, Zali. I'm not strong enough to go back."

"Never. I promise you. I'll make sure of it."

He sucked in a shuddery breath, and Ry gripped his shoulder, lending Tristan his strength. Tristan turned, meeting Ry's gaze and holding it for a moment before he diverted his attention to Flynn and then me.

"Walking away from you isn't an option anymore. I've fallen in love with you. I can't...." He groaned and tangled his fingers in his hair.

I blinked, taking in both his words and the tone in which they were spoken. He was conflicted—screwing around with his students was a disaster waiting to happen, and falling for either one of us had career-ending clusterfuck written all over it. But falling for someone like me was downright dangerous. His past, his fears, must have been tying him in knots.

Flynn slid onto the coffee table, his knees between Tristan's. He gripped Tristan's wrists gently, then he eased his hands down and threaded their fingers together.

"You love Zee, like I do?" Flynn asked, awe in his voice and a happy smile lighting up his face as Tristan lifted his eyes to Flynn's.

"Yeah." Tristan nodded. "I do. And you, too, angel." He reached for me, sliding his hand into mine, and I did the same to Flynn. Tristan's move broke the levy on the dam, and my breath hitched.

I pressed a kiss to the corner of his lips and leaned my forehead against his cheek before whispering, "Good. Because I'm stupidly in love with you too."

Tristan's smile was small, but it lit up his eyes. Even if he didn't want to be, he was happy. "I said that I was staying forever, love. I wanted it. So much. But fear pushed me away. I'm still fucking petrified."

I nodded. "I know. I'll do what it takes, Tristan. I'll move mountains to protect you. All of you." I squeezed Flynn's hand and cast my gaze to Ry, needing him to know that my promise included him.

Tristan looked toward the dock, seemingly mesmerized by the way the lights played on the ripples in the water. But if anything, he was staring into space, his gaze unfocussed. The smile slipped off his face. "I kept telling myself that I'd never wanted a relationship before you, but...."

"You've been lying to yourself," Flynn finished for him after his silence stretched out.

Tristan exhaled and his eyes slipped closed. Shoulders hunched and lips turned down, he nodded. "I'm still in love with him." He squeezed my hand tighter and added, "But it doesn't change how I feel about you."

I understood, and I was okay with what he was saying. I looked at Flynn, and he brought our joined hands to his lips. We were connected, each of us holding onto the other.

I hated that Ry was on the outside, especially after the rollercoaster of emotions we'd all gone through today. Hell, less than eight hours ago, he'd given me the spanking of a lifetime, my pants around my ankles and my cunt leaking for him.

But just like only Flynn could do, he smiled at Ry, gesturing to the spot next to him with a tilt of his head.

Ry cleared his throat.

He stalked away.

It hurt more than I was prepared to admit.

"When you fall in love, you love big, don't you?" I asked, my question rhetorical. "Ezra's a lucky man."

Tristan huffed unhappily and squeezed my hand. "That obvious?"

"Yeah," Flynn commiserated. "But after what happened tonight, I'm thinking that he might be open to persuasion. We could work on him as a team. Take all his excuses away."

"I don't want to be scared anymore," Tristan murmured. "I want all of you. Is that terrible?"

"No more terrible than me wanting all of you too," I admitted. Scooting closer to him, I hooked my leg over his knee and snuggled close. He was warm and solid, and as much as I loved getting off with him, I loved these quiet moments just as much.

Flynn brought their joined hands to his lips. He kissed the ends of Tristan's fingers, nipping the pads before letting go and sliding his hand up Tristan's leg. That move, the possessiveness in Flynn's touch and his confidence, was hot as hell. My nipples peaked, a shivery anticipation rocketing through me. I wanted them. I wanted to watch them and touch them as they did the same to each other.

With his hand tucked against Tristan's groin, Flynn leaned in and pressed their lips together. It was slow and sweet, their tongues touching and caressing softly before Tristan smiled against Flynn's lips. When they broke apart, both out of breath, Tristan turned to me.

I wanted to fall into him, get lost and only come up for air when we were all sated and exhausted. I wanted my legs to feel like limp noodles and my skin to be buzzing. But there was something more important. A conversation we needed to have first. I held back like a good little adult and, for once, didn't let my cunt speak on my behalf.

I was growing up. I was so proud of myself.

"I know we still have a lot to talk about," I started, hesitating before I continued. Tristan wanted me to promise no more law-breaking, but I couldn't make that vow. Not yet, and maybe not ever. I couldn't promise him that I would suddenly become some law-abiding citizen. It wasn't me. It just wasn't who I was, and I didn't want to lie to him. Not unless it was necessary to protect him.

"I understand why you're worried, but I promise you that I'll do whatever it takes to protect you. I broke your trust before, and I won't make that mistake again, Tristan."

He nodded, his eyes trained on mine, his kissable lips close enough to taste.

I was only human, and with my broody, beautiful professor sitting so near, I couldn't resist him anymore. I didn't want to either.

My eyes fluttered closed as I eliminated the distance between us, kissing him like I'd been deprived of him for a lifetime rather than a few days. His lips claimed mine, and his tongue possessed me, owning my body. I tunnelled my fingers into his hair and sighed as he clutched me closer, rocking his hard length against my calf. "I want you, kitten," he rasped against my mouth.

"You have me."

A throat cleared in the background, and Flynn's laughter tinkled like crystal.

"Hate to interrupt the love-in, but I deserve to know what the fuck went down before the all-in fuck happens." Ryder stood before us clenching his hands into fists, his eyes narrow slits as he glared at us. Fury boiled in them like a raging inferno.

Tristan stiffened, but when I huffed out a laugh, he relaxed, leaning into Flynn's embrace.

"You're right, you do deserve to know," I conceded. "Sit down, and I'll explain everything."

He moved, sitting across from us, his ankle crossed over his knee. His foot bounced as he waited for me to speak.

I walked them through what I'd found, presenting them with the same story I'd given to Ezra. I detailed everything from the discovery of the information being held at the Reserve Bank, the password-protected spreadsheet, the threat on the bank, the chatter, my decision to act, and how I'd hurriedly adapted the patch I'd used many times before to plug the hole in the bank's systems.

They listened without interruption, until Ry, ever the cynic, asked disbelievingly, "You did all that in the fifteen minutes between Flynn asking whether Ezra had access to the Reserve Bank's archives and telling me we were going to Sydney?"

I winced. "Not exactly. I've been working on it for a few days. When I found out that the Reserve Bank had the data, I started searching to see what I could access, and I stumbled across the spreadsheet."

"How did you get into it?" Tristan asked.

"IT people are lazy. They like easy passwords because they deal with so many of them. The most popular one is '123456.' The second is 'password.' I guessed." I shrugged, playing it off as a simple coincidence. "I got it on my second attempt."

The truth wasn't quite as innocent as that. But the less they knew, the better. By the time Flynn had spoken with Ezra, I'd been at it for nearly thirty-six hours straight, trying to crack the Reserve Bank's firewalls. I finally found a way in, and it was enough to open up the pathway for me as if they'd given me the keys to the vault. But, the information I wanted was only available direct from the server in Sydney if I wanted it anytime soon. The encryption used at the bank was high quality; it would be quicker for me to break into the bank itself rather than going through the servers. So, I'd diverted my attention to that. Was there a way I could get into the server room? Did they do public tours that would get me close enough so I could sneak off? Could I pose as someone with security clearance? Turned out, getting into the building was easier than I'd anticipated.

Except that I needed to be quick, and running a brute force attack to break the password of the door to the server room wouldn't be quick.

That's where the password registry came in. I hadn't ex-pected to find it in a spreadsheet wrapped up in a neat little bow. Of course, I hadn't, quote, "stumbled" across it and promptly guessed the password either. That bit was exaggerated. It had actually taken hours of sustained attacks to force my way past their defences.

But found one I had. It was their accounting software. I discovered a thread which unravelled the more I tugged on it, care of whitelisted ISPs, until there was an opening big enough for me to slip into. I found a list of employees and their ID numbers. It was only a hop, skip, and a jump from there into their wider system.

I'd struck gold.

After that, it was as simple as reprogramming their website to create the link I'd apparently stumbled across.

Setting up the fake profile on the dark web, untraceable back to me, was easy. So was posting in the forums to manufacture the threat. It was a challenge other hackers couldn't refuse—the replies were all legit.

"So did you get what you needed from the server?" Flynn asked.

"I didn't download anything," I lied again. I hating doing it, but it was for the greater good. Tristan had already served time for being an accessory after the fact. If I divulged any hint of illegality, I was putting him in precisely the situation I'd promised him protection from.

My lie was a necessity.

Shaking my head, I explained, "In basic terms, I used my computer to communicate with the server to pinpoint the weakness in their system. Then I uploaded the patch from the USB stick. I could have done it directly, but I wanted to screen record exactly what I was doing. I figured I might run into some challenges, so I wanted Ezra and his team to know where I'd been. That's it."

It wasn't, but again, they were on a need-to-know basis, and they didn't need to know. In truth, I'd downloaded every piece of data I could get my hands on so that I could keep going with my research. The data was safe and sound on my laptop that the police had very kindly returned to me.

They'd been hoping for a jackpot—gigabytes of information that they could confiscate—but there wasn't a single bit. It was for good reason too. I wasn't stupid enough to make a mistake like that.

The login I gave them—Morningstar—activated a honeypot protocol that was a clone of my hard drive with entirely fake information, including a squeaky-clean browser history. Anyone using that password would see only what I wanted them to. The clone would stay active until I disabled the protocol, then my computer would revert to my own. My data was simply compressed and waiting for me to access it.

I'd originally designed the security measures as a hypothetical. It likely wouldn't hold up on detailed analysis of the actual hard drive—eventually the fact that it was a clone would be found—but a simple mirror of the hard drive like the tech had done wouldn't copy across the hidden sectors.

Ry raised his brow, disbelief written all over his face. Silently I begged him not to push, not to press me for any more information. He opened his mouth to respond, but his phone buzzed simultaneously.

"Dinner's here."

NINE

Zali

We all dug into the pizzas when Ry set them atop the coffee table. Carbs and cheesy goodness were exactly what I needed. He knew me well.

"Ezra's here," Ry explained with a mouthful of supreme, hooking a thumb over his shoulder to point at the dock.

Tristan put his slice down, and with a small smile, wiggled out from under Flynn and me, then went straight over to the stairs. He disappeared down them at a jog. I could hear murmured voices and the lap of water against the hull as our conversation ceased, and I craned my neck to try to listen better.

My heart was in my throat. Knowing we needed to have the conversation didn't calm my nerves. I was daring to hope. I'd already had a win—I still couldn't believe that Tristan had come back—but was it too much to ask for?

I also had to hear Ezra's side of what went down first. I needed to know the whole story. Could I trust him? I thought I could, but there were too many loose ends and too many coincidences for me to let my guard down yet. It wasn't even really about me. I was more worried about making sure my guys—Tristan, Flynn, and Ryder—were protected. As much as I wanted to strip Ezra down and sit on his face, I would walk away in a heartbeat if it meant keeping my guys safe from a mole.

Tristan was practically dragging Ezra up the stairs when they finally popped up. My breath caught in my throat. This was what I wanted. All of them. My men.

Ezra had one hand stuffed in the pocket of his ripped jeans, those thick thighs peeking through the frayed sections. I wanted to lick every inch of him.

His footsteps faltered as he spied us waiting for him. Biting down on my lip, I locked eyes with him. Memories of his kiss slammed into me, his hard cock pressing into my belly. My clit throbbed, and wetness coated the tops of my thighs. I shifted, rubbing them together and trying to get some friction against my cunt.

My heart thumped harder. My insides were a tangled mess of desire, hope, and something a lot like nervous anticipation. I couldn't even explain what it was—I'd known Ezra for years, but I was suddenly shy too.

His kiss had rewired my neural networks, mapping a new path to a hidden place I'd only dreamed of entering.

Could I have it all? Could I have all my men? Could they have each other?

I flicked my gaze to Ryder, my heart sinking as his jaw flexed and eyes narrowed. Urgh, he always had to be difficult.

"Hey," Ezra mumbled, then cleared his throat. He scanned the three of us sitting on the couches and swallowed before looking at Tristan. His eyes were pleading, a mix of fear and resignation in them. I hated how uncertain he was, but it was an apt match for what was going on inside my head too.

"Eat up," Tristan ordered the rest of us before turning his attention to Ezra. He stepped close and cupped Ezra's cheeks, pressing their foreheads together. Standing only a hair's breadth apart, breathing each other's air, they were completely in sync.

They looked beautiful too. Dark features against golden, casual versus sharply dressed, a domineering grump and a more go-with-the-flow personality. They were contrasts that only enhanced the way they complemented each other. I couldn't make out what Tristan was murmuring to Ezra, as only his deep rumble was audible over the ebb and flow of the background noise in the marina, but I knew he was speaking.

Ezra buried his face in the crook of Tristan's neck as he reached for our professor. Wrapping his arms around Tristan's waist, he held on tight, connecting them from head to toe. Their bodies perfectly aligned, Tristan engulfed Ezra in an embrace as he kissed his temple.

It took everything in me to stay seated.

"Sit, Flynn."

I tore my eyes away from them at Ry's murmured order. My guy was on his feet, putting his slice of pizza down. But he hesitated, his eyes flicking between Tristan and Ezra and

Ryder. Finally, he sighed and slumped down on the couch again.

"Give them a minute," I suggested. "I think Tristan needs this as much as Ez does."

When they finally separated, Ezra inhaled, squared his shoulders, and gave a sharp nod to Tristan. Flynn shifted to the armchair, and I stood, moving over to Ezra.

"Are you okay?" he asked me, pushing a lock of hair over my shoulder, his hand lingering like he wanted to touch me but wasn't sure whether he was allowed.

Before I could answer, Ryder was in his face, snarling, "Don't. Touch. Her." His hand was raised as if he was reaching to rip Ezra's throat out. But Tristan slapped a hand around Ry's wrist, halting his progress.

I barked out an incredulous laugh and shoved Ry out of the way, stopping Tristan's progress with a hand on his chest.

I asked Ry, "Who the fuck do you think you are?"

"Seriously? After everything? You asked me to play nice and I did, but you're just gonna let him come aboard and what, fuck you?" Ry was seething, fury rolling off him in waves. But he wasn't the only person spoiling for a fight. My legs braced shoulder width apart, I crossed my arms and narrowed my eyes at him.

"Have some fucking respect," Tristan grated out, stepping around me and going toe to toe with Ry.

"You two done?" I snapped, my lips curled in a snarl. "Calm the fuck down."

Tristan stepped back, raising his chin in an obvious challenge to Ryder. It was an I-dare-you-to-test-me look. I didn't know whether Tristan could fight, but Ry was a scrapper, in and out of detention in school and getting suspended more times than I could count because of the fist fights he'd started or finished.

I snapped my fingers, gaining the attention of both. Ry ground his teeth. I spoke, my voice deceptively calm.

"Number one, this is my yacht. I say who comes aboard or not." Counting it off on my fingers to hide the shake in them, I added, "Two, you are *not* playing nice. Pull your head in. Three, I am the one who has control over my body. Not. You." I waved my hand in a circle in an "all-that" motion and spat, "You may think your stunt this afternoon gave you some say over my body, some right to punish or reward me, but you don't. You don't have a claim to me. You don't control me, and you sure as shit don't have a say in who I fuck."

"What did you do to her?" Tristan asked.

Flynn was beside us in a flash, wrapping his arms around Tristan. "It's okay. It was nothing."

"She was fucking gagging for it," Ry gloated.

"And you couldn't deliver, could you?" I shot back, my eyebrow raised. If he wanted to play these games with me, he was going to lose. "Left it up to Flynn to satisfy me."

"I should bend you over my knee again," Ry threatened.

"Try it. I dare you." I stood chest to chest with him, over a foot shorter in bare feet than Ry in his boots. But it didn't matter. I was a powder keg with a very short fuse, begging to be given any more of a reason to explode.

Ry rolled his eyes and looked away.

"That's what I thought. Now sit the fuck down and shut it."

"Whatever, boss." He huffed and spun on his foot, ready to walk in the opposite direction to the couches. "I've got work to do."

"Sit. Down," I snapped. Turning to Ezra, I reached for his hand and took comfort in the way his enveloped mine. I was flushed, rage still boiling in my veins, but I wouldn't take it out on him. I led him to the couch, we sat, and I asked in a calmer voice, "Can you answer a few questions to clear things up for me?"

Ryder, his shoulders tense and back rigid, worked his jaw. His nose flared with each inhale. Tristan eyed him warily, apparently waiting for him to make a move before he did.

Flynn was pale, his eyes wide as they bounced between us. He whispered, "Ry, please."

Ryder exhaled heavily and flicked his gaze to me, glaring. Fury flamed in his eyes as he looked at me, then Tristan. He snarled.

Flynn begged him again, and Ry turned to him, inclining his head in deference. I got the message loud and clear—he was only here because of Flynn.

"I do have a few things I'd like to clear up, Ry. I know you don't trust me anymore, but I'd appreciate it if you listened. I don't expect your forgiveness," Ezra murmured, reaching for Tristan, who'd sat down next to him. Ezra held his hand in an iron grip, Tristan's knuckles turning white as he squeezed.

"Go ahead, Ez," Tristan encouraged, resting his free hand on Ezra's knee.

"I don't even know where to start." He let go of us and scrubbed his hands over his face. He groaned. There were dark circles under his eyes, his shoulders hunched like he was carrying the weight of the world.

"What happened between Flynn's phone call and you picking us up at the airport?" I asked.

He relayed the details, telling us how he'd received a phone call from the Reserve Bank's librarian only a short while after his initial call to her. His boss had gotten involved and set the wolves on us, declaring that it was an open-and-shut case. Ezra had done his best to plant the seeds of doubt, questioning everything, but she'd insisted.

"I was so fucking scared, Zali," he whispered, reaching for me.

I interlaced our fingers and held his trembling hand tight.

"I thought that the three of you would end up in jail. I didn't know what to do. When I saw you, I wanted to tell you to run, to hide out on some tropical island where they couldn't get you, but they would have shot you. They could have killed you." He tore his wrecked gaze from mine and looked at Flynn, then Ryder. "I couldn't risk it."

He closed his eyes and hung his head low. "I shouldn't have kissed you, but I couldn't stop myself. I thought you were dead. But I betrayed your trust. I used you like every-one else did, getting your help when I needed it. I kissed you without your consent. I'm sorry." He shook his head. "I really fucked up."

"How did you betray my trust?" I asked, the pit in my gut growing. "I need you to spell it out."

"I didn't warn you they were going to arrest you—that I was going to," he corrected. His brows were furrowed, and his lips turned down in a frown. "It's my job to protect you, and I failed."

"Did you go to your boss with the information you had on us? With the question Flynn asked you?"

"No." He shook his head, his mouth agape and horror in his eyes. "I'd never do that. It was the librarian. I spoke with her after Flynn asked me what I had access to. She had a go at me for asking for raw data. She told me I should know it was protected by privacy laws. I covered, telling her we were investigating the security of government data and how it was stored. It seemed to placate her—she referred me to the head of their IT department. I wasn't going to call him but got his details as a cover."

He ran his hands through his hair, tugging on the ends in frustration, shaking his head as he did.

"Ninety minutes later she called and reported the break-in and how the security guard unloaded a clip on you. I stuttered out something, I don't even know what now." He choked out a sob. "I thought he'd killed you. I just needed her off the phone. I needed to hear your voices. I tried to call. Over and over again. But none of you answered—"

"We were in the air," Flynn explained, putting the timeline together. Ezra nodded, sniffing and blinking fast to clear the glassiness in his eyes. "I saw a bunch of missed calls from you."

"Me too," Ry admitted quietly.

"The inspector practically broke down my office door while I was leaving another message for you," he explained to Ry. "The head librarian called her. Puglisi didn't cover for me on the investigation angle."

"How did they figure out it was us?" I asked, unsure if I wanted to know the answer.

"The inspector snatched my phone out of my hands and checked my call register." He shook his head, and his shoulders fell. He slumped in the seat, resting his head in his hands. "It was my fault. She saw that I'd called you. She knew exactly who she was looking for. They found the yacht within minutes—apparently, it's Insta-worthy." He lifted his face and rubbed his hands on his jeans, sighing heavily.

"While they had someone come out here to check whether you were onboard, they looked at Brisbane and Gold Coast airports—they figured you would have flown to Sydney if you were the ones to break in. They scanned the car park entry records, looking for one of your vehicles, and found the Range Rover entering at the private hangars. A return flight had already been scheduled, so they ordered virtually everyone in the building to get over there to wait for you to arrive."

"Then you kissed me."

"Yeah." He nodded. Swallowed. Gave me a small smile, but the tension around his eyes remained.

"You were all taken into the interview rooms for questioning, and the techs were trying to break into your laptop. I was with them when Tris called me. I told him what I could. He organized the lawyer and came down. You know the rest."

"You took a big risk, telling me," Tristan stated, reaching for Ezra's nape and squeezing it.

He nodded. "Yeah, I'm being referred to Ethics. Puglisi wants to prosecute me. She told me to get in touch with the union." He clasped his fingers together and rested his elbows on his spread knees. "I did what I had to do; I'd do the same thing again."

"What? Do they think you're dirty?" Flynn asked, confusion lacing his tone.

I swallowed. That was exactly what they thought.

"I'll fix it, Ezra," I assured him. "I'm promising all of you right now that nothing will come back on you. This is my fight, and these are my actions. I *will* protect you."

"I'm not sure you can, Zali," Ezra sighed dejectedly.

"Watch me." I forced a smile, holding my chin high and infusing every ounce of arrogance I possessed into my posture. *I'm fucking Queen.* "They won't know what hit 'em if they try to fuck with the people I love."

Ryder shook his head, stood, and walked away despite Flynn calling for him. He made for the steps to the upper level, taking them two at a time as he stalked away.

"Zali," Ezra murmured just loud enough to get my attention. "I...." He spun to face me and took my hands in his.

But I didn't let him finish.

I knew Ezra. I knew that he would say he wanted me but that we couldn't be together or some shit.

And I was done with all the bullshit.

I wanted this.

I wanted them.

All of them.

Even Ry.

The man drove me fucking crazy, but so help me, I wanted him as much as I wanted Flynn, Tristan, and Ezra.

It was about time I took what I wanted.

I straddled his legs, wrapped his arms around my waist, and dragged his face to mine. My lips connected with his, and I slid them against his mouth. His shock only lasted a split second before he was kissing me back, gliding his tongue against mine. Tangling my fingers in his hair, I angled his face where I wanted it and smiled as Flynn slipped into the spot I vacated, pressing a kiss to the spot under Ezra's ear.

I wasn't sure who whimpered, but it was Tristan who slid his hand between Ezra and me to palm his heavy cock and rub his knuckles along my clit. We rocked together, rolling our hips and devouring each other.

Ezra's hands were everywhere, sliding up my back and to my front, brushing my nipples over the soft material of the jumper I was wearing. I moaned, my cunt clenching as

Tristan palmed my mound and slid his fingers through the wetness coating my thighs.

"Our kitten's soaked," he murmured, his deep voice rumbling over us all. Gooseflesh broke out over my skin, and Flynn hummed, his lithe body straddling Ezra's thigh so my back was pressed to his front.

Tristan slid a finger inside me, and I pulled back, sucking in a breath and arching into his touch. I cried out as he teased my entrance with a second digit.

Flynn eased my jumper up, tugging it slowly up my hips until Ezra could see what Tristan was doing. "Fuck," he ground out as Tristan plunged two fingers inside me. My cunt tightened around him, trying to hold him inside me.

"Greedy aren't you," Tristan teased with a bite to my bare shoulder.

"For you. For all of you."

Flynn grasped the hem of my jumper, ripping it off my body and tossing it aside. I was completely naked in front of three very dressed men, but a rush of empowerment flowed through me. It was like a drug. I was high on it, writhing with desire and desperate for them.

I gasped when Flynn's hands came to my tits, squeezing my nipples and sucking a mark into my shoulder. His hard cock nestled against my arse was a tease—I wanted him inside me again. I wanted all of them inside me.

Tristan pulled free from my depths and reached behind me to cup Flynn's cock. "Ours," he growled, and Flynn choked out a cry, thrusting into his grip.

Ezra trailed his lips down my chest, kissing and licking a path down to my nipple before sucking it into his mouth. He had his hands on my waist, sliding up my ribcage and leaving a trail of fire in their wake. His touch set me alight, sparking every nerve ending in my body.

"You are so beautiful," he murmured, reverence in his tone. "I want to taste you. All of you."

Then I was being moved, laid down and spread out on the coffee table, each of them shifting so their lips were on me, kissing me softly with barely there touches. It was a tease, and I was desperate for a firmer touch.

Throwing my arms above my head, I gripped the edge of the table and thrust my hips, seeking friction. Anything but the cool ocean breeze bathing my body.

My toes curled and my cunt clenched when Ezra smiled at me. I wanted to be his next meal. He looked like he was starving. His eyes full of dark desire, Ezra slipped his hands under my butt, hooking my legs over his elbows and spreading me open as he kissed a line down my body. He ran his nose along my belly, dipping his tongue into my navel before smiling against my flesh as I shivered. He nipped my hipbone, humming as I whimpered, his heated gaze never leaving mine until our line of sight was broken by Flynn and Tristan.

Their lips met in a heated kiss above me, both petting me as I moaned. I loved seeing them together. The way they kissed, the way they touched, was consuming. They were all in. They knew what they wanted and were unafraid to show it. I just hoped that Ezra understood how we were and would be just as okay with it because now that he was with us, I didn't want to let him go.

Flynn and Tristan broke apart, eyes dark and lips wet as their chests heaved. "Strip, angel," Tristan ordered before flicking his eyes to Ezra and adding, "Ez, you too. I want to see what's mine."

As one, Flynn and Ezra stripped their shirts off, Flynn's straight over his head while Ezra tugged roughly at the buttons of his. It sent them pinging onto the deck as he ripped it open, untucking the shirt from his suit pants.

With his hand hovering at the button on his pants, Ezra looked to Tristan for orders. I whined impatiently. I wanted them naked.

Tristan's huff of laughter and Flynn's smirk had me narrowing my eyes at all of them. "Hurry up and get naked. All of you. I want what's mine to fuck me."

After they both stripped out of their clothes in record time, Ezra froze when he saw Flynn.

"Shiiit, I wasn't expecting that." He gestured at Flynn's cock, then reached for him when Flynn pointed his beast at our guy and tugged on his wrist. Ezra groaned in the back of his throat when he closed his hand around Flynn's dick. "I want to feel those piercings on my tongue."

"You can. Anytime," Flynn promised. He tilted his head at me and added, "But first, someone's getting impatient."

Ezra grinned wickedly and dipped his head, flicking his tongue low on my belly, his chin connecting with my clit. The bristles of his stubble tickled me, and I gasped, sensation washing over me.

Tristan and Flynn moved down with uncanny synchronicity, each taking one of my nipples into their mouth and sucking and biting while Ezra lazily dragged his tongue lower, teasing and taunting me. Minutes... hours later, he swiped his tongue over my clit and ever so slowly slid his fingers inside me, crooking them to hit my G-spot dead-on. "So tight," he murmured, his heated breath a caress against my thigh.

Grasping my entire butt cheek in his big hand, Ezra dived in and devoured me, licking me like a lollipop and then spearing his tongue into my cunt alongside his fingers. I writhed, crying out as he nibbled on my clit. "You like that?" he murmured, the vibrations of his voice like a bolt of electricity through me. I shivered and moaned, and he bit down harder until my hoarse shout echoed off the water.

I was sure we had an audience of onlookers watching from the marina. I could feel eyes on me. Intense and burning. But I didn't care. I revelled in it, spreading my legs further in invitation.

My orgasm was like a rising tide, swelling inside me until I was so close to spilling over. Just as I was on the edge and ready to dive headfirst into ecstasy, Ezra shifted, changing the angle of penetration, but held his fingers steady. Unmoving.

He kissed a line down to my inner thigh. I cried out, frustration welling up in me.

So. Close.

Yet so far away.

He sucked a mark on my skin before blowing hot air over my cunt and flicking his tongue over my clit.

My toes curled, my back arching as I pressed my tits into Flynn's and Tristan's faces. I gasped as Ezra gently bit me, thrusting my hips into his grip again, begging him with my moans to make me come.

Ezra curled his fingers once more, connecting with my G-spot and working that bitch until I was writhing. He sucked on my clit, flicking his tongue and lighting up the nerve endings.

The tide rose quickly, and I edged closer.

"Oh, fuck, I'm there," I gasped, my hips rocking as he worked me over. My cunt clenched, and I cried out.

But then he was gone.

Cool air washed over my cunt as Ezra pulled back.

"No," I whined, a sob hitching in my throat.

"Sorry, needed to get comfortable," he explained. "My knees...."

He adjusted his weight, then bent back down, licking me from my clit down to my pucker and back up again, pausing to sample the juices free flowing from my cunt. I was so fucking ready to come, every inch of my body crackling with need. Like a live wire, I existed purely on sensation, chasing every swipe of his tongue and brush of his fingers.

"Please," I gasped. "Fuck me." He slid his fingers into me, stretching me in the best possible way. The walls of my cunt hugged him tight, not wanting to let him go until I'd had my fill. He finger-fucked me, slow and deep, grazing my

G-spot with every pass. His tongue never left my clit, swirling and flicking until I was vibrating.

My walls clamped down.

He pulled his hand away.

It was like a bad dream, my orgasm about to hit me like
a freight train, then suddenly derailed, crashing spectacularly.

"Fuck," I shouted, shaking as adrenaline rushed through
my veins. I palmed Tristan's and Flynn's heads and pushed
them down. "Get me there," I ordered.

Tristan hummed against my belly and cupped Ezra's
nape, dragging him closer. He nuzzled their noses together
before pressing his lips to Ezra's, then swiping his tongue
over Ezra's mouth. Flynn did the same, kissing Ezra with my
legs trapped between the three of them.

Fuck this. If they weren't going to get me there, I would.

TEN

Zali

I slid my hand down and fingered my clit with my thumb while sliding three digits into my channel. I worked myself, shuddering when I began the climb again.

I pinched my nipple, watching avidly as my guys kissed and rocked into each other's grips. Their hands on one another was fucking hot. I loved it, loved watching them and seeing how differently they touched each other from the way they touched me. Tristan was gentle with Ez, worshipping him the way he'd done me when he'd told me he wanted to stay. Flynn was different too. He guided Ezra's hand to his arse, pushing back when he slid his fingers into Flynn's crack. His cock was trapped against my leg, sliding easily with the precum leaking from it as he thrust his hips.

I moaned, shivering as the familiar rush began.

Tristan lowered his hand from Ezra's face to grasp my wrist, tugging my hand free. I fought him, slapping him with my free hand. But it was enough. I fell off the precipice again, the edge of my orgasm subsiding into the mist.

I growled, and Tristan interlaced our fingers. "Love you, kitten," he murmured. My heart melted, and I couldn't help the stupid love-heart eyes I was making at him despite wanting to rip his hand off so I could get back to it.

"Love you too, boo. But if one of you don't make me come right fucking now, I'm gonna kick you off my yacht naked and finish myself off. I have a perfectly good vibrator in my stateroom that'll get me there in no time."

"So impatient." Ezra chuckled, his grin wicked. Bastard was doing it on purpose to edge me.

"You." I pointed at him and narrowed my eyes.

Flynn snorted out a laugh, and I shoved him playfully.

"Sorry." He grinned. "If you're going for intimidating, it's not really working."

"Shut it," I ordered before turning back to Ezra. "You bastard, stop pulling out."

"I thought you liked me releasing you from custody."

"Smart arse."

"Get inside her, Ez. Make her come," Tristan purred, his voice a low rasp as he spat on his hand and curled it around Ezra's length. He pumped him long and slow, twisting his wrist and making Ezra's eyes roll back. "Show our kitten how good it can be when she has patience."

"Wait," Flynn protested.

I grasped his cock hard, squeezing it tight. He moaned, and I gritted my teeth. Fuck he felt good in my hand, but if he stopped Ezra now, I'd bloody well snap his dick off.

"When were you tested?" Flynn asked.

Tristan hummed and shifted slightly. I couldn't see what he was doing, but from Ezra's gasp, he'd done something Ezra liked. "Good question, angel. Ez?"

Ezra groaned, his voice pained. "I can't think straight."

"Put a rubber on, then," Flynn commanded, closing his hand over mine and guiding me over his length, the warm barbells of his piercings bumping over my palm.

"No, wait." Ezra batted Tristan's hand away from his dick before clamping his fingers around the base. But he seemed to be chasing Tristan's hand, pushing back his hips and rocking into him.

"Mmm, so tight. Your arse loves my fingers," Tristan murmured.

Ezra hissed and shuddered.

"Can't wait until you take my cock again."

"Fuck." Ezra breathed hard. "Jesus H Christ." He tugged his balls down, stretching his sac and exhaling heavily. "I got tested six months ago. I haven't been with anyone except for a few bathroom blow jobs. I wore a condom every time, and so did they."

Tristan growled. "No more, Ez. You want that, you come to us. Got it?" He freed Ezra's cock before wrapping his hand around his nape and hauled him in close, their foreheads touching. When Ezra nodded, Tristan kissed him hard, possessing him as their tongues tangled together.

I sobbed in frustration. I wanted to come.

I needed it.

"I have to taste you," Flynn grunted against my lips as I jacked him off. "Want you to ride Ez. Think you can do that, Zee?"

"As long as the fucker doesn't pull out," I huffed.

When Tristan broke away from Ezra, he gestured to me with a tilt of his head, and Ezra moved, immediately scooping me in his arms and lifting me effortlessly. My world tilted again as he spun around and sat back on the table I'd just been spread out on. Tugging me tighter against his body, his arms pinning me to him, Ezra kissed me.

His hard body against mine and his long cock trapped between us scrambled my brain cells. I threaded my hands into his hair, sliding my fingers through silk as I tasted myself on his lips.

Lightheaded and dazed, I pulled back, but Ezra didn't let me go far. "Believe me, Zali, I've waited years for this. I don't think I could pull out once I get inside you."

His eyes fluttered closed, and his kiss was slower, deeper. I rocked my hips, my juices coating his sac.

"That's it, my little jailbird, coat my cock so I can fuck you."

I snorted out a laugh, but it died on a moan when lips—Flynn's—connected with my lower back. Tristan pressed his hand between my shoulder blades while with his other hand, he encouraged Ezra to lie down and me to go with him.

Flynn kissed a line down my spine, spreading my cheeks and running his tongue around my pucker. Like a man starving, he feasted, dipping lower into my cunt. I clenched tight, desperate to be filled.

He brushed his hand over me, but he was touching Ezra, shifting his cock from between us and jacking him. He licked us both, his tongue skittering over my skin before disappearing. Ezra moaned, the tendons in his throat tightening as he tensed.

"Fuck, Flynn, your mouth is magic."

He hummed a response, the sound muffled by the mouthful of cock until there was a pop and he added, "Lift up, Zee."

I did, moaning as Flynn notched Ezra's cock against my opening. With Ezra's hands on my waist, Flynn's at my cunt, and Tristan's twisting my nipples, I arched my back and sank down. He filled me, stretching my cunt around his cock. He was longer than both Flynn and Tristan, and as he hit my G-spot, fireworks exploded behind my closed eyelids.

With my face tilted up to the skies, I ground my hips down, choking out a moan when he bottomed out inside me.

"You're beautiful together," Flynn murmured, wonder in his voice, and Tristan agreed with a hum. Flynn brushed his fingertips over my arse, trailing them down to Ezra, who grunted when he started moving his hips, fucking up into me.

Flynn licked us, his tongue rimming me before shifting down and licking Ezra. He snaked a hand around my hip and pinched my clit between his fingers, working me as he devoured both of us.

My cunt clamped tight, and I rocked my hips harder, bracing myself against his perfectly sculpted pecs as I fucked him. My tits bounced, shocks of sensation going to my nipples with each thrust.

I wanted one of them in my arse and another in my mouth. I wanted dicks everywhere, men touching me, worshipping me. I wanted to be used and filled with cum. I wanted to come until I couldn't stand, until I couldn't even remember my name. I wanted to be an object they fucked, then fucked again, each taking their turn with me until I was wrecked. Stretched and open, leaking cum.

I wanted their mouths, their hands, their cocks.

"Look," Tristan whispered in my ear, his deep voice hypnotic.

Opening my eyes, I spied Ry on the deck above us, his cargo pants pulled down to his thighs, his beautiful cock in his hand. My cunt spasmed, and Ezra cried out.

"You like that, don't you? You're our pretty little slut, aren't you?" Tristan rasped in that sexy growl of his. "Can't get enough of us. You want me in your arse? Hmm?"

"Yes, fuck yes," I gasped.

Tristan licked my throat and I whimpered. "What about Ry? You want him in your arse? Should I get him down here?" Tristan hummed, waiting for me to answer, but before I could, Ezra interjected.

"Or do you want him to tie you up and spank you? Maybe after we've each fucked you? Let him feel our cum running out of you before he sinks into your tight pussy?"

"All of it," I moaned, loving the picture Tristan and Ezra were painting.

"So do I," Tristan admitted, jacking himself slowly. "I want my cock in him too. I want to tame our lone wolf, turn him into a puppy for us. I want to watch him lose his fucking mind when he has three tight little arses to choose between. He'll switch between all three of you because he can't choose. Your holes will be clenching tight, trying to keep him there instead of him pulling out."

My gaze locked with Ry's, and I silently begged him to come downstairs to us. But he didn't. He just narrowed his eyes, his hand speeding up as he neared his orgasm.

I bit down on my lip, wanting to watch him come. Wanting him to paint my skin with it.

"Tris," Ezra moaned. "Need you."

I broke our stares, looking down at Ezra and watching as he reached out to wrap his arm around Tristan's leg and tug him until he was on his knees. Tristan pointed his cock at Ezra's mouth and painted his lips with precum. But Ezra was ravenous, sucking him down until his nose was buried in Tristan's trimmed pubes.

Tristan gasped, running his fingers through Ezra's hair and holding him in place for a moment before pulling back and fucking deep into his throat.

Moans surrounded me, each of us climbing higher.

Flynn shifted back, his mouth disappearing from the point where Ezra's dick was sinking into my cunt. I shuddered, my channel fluttering as Ezra yanked me down, fucking hard into me.

"Zee, you want Tris inside you too?" Flynn asked, kissing a line up my shoulder until he was sucking a mark into the sensitive spot below my ear.

I nodded and moaned, a shiver wracking me.

"Good, 'cause I want Ez and Tris to feel each other again. I want them to share you, and I want my arse." A crack sounded, and Tristan's smooth movements as he was fucking into Ezra's mouth stuttered.

"Your arse wants you," Tristan ground out, his eyes squeezed tightly shut and the pulse point on his throat fluttering fast. He pulled free of Ezra's mouth and leaned down, pressing a soft kiss to his lips. "I want your hole wrapped around my dick too, yeah? Want to be buried balls deep in you. Which one of you is gonna milk my cum out?"

The snick of a cap sounded, and I braced myself for the cold.

"Fuck," Ezra hissed, the tendons in his throat tightening as his body went rigid and his feet scrambled for purchase on the timber flooring of the deck.

Tristan leaned over me, and within moments, Flynn's fingers found my hole. I loved the stretch, the burn as he pumped me full of his fingers. I keened, and Flynn pressed harder, stretched me more, pushing me toward the orgasm I'd been desperate for.

"Come for me, Zee," he encouraged. "Let me feel you strangle me. Imagine it's my dick inside you, fucking you."

That did it. His filthy words—ones that he never spoke outside of when we were together like this—were like striking a match. They lit an inferno in me. My cunt clenched tight, the rhythmic contractions beginning as a wave of ecstasy washed over me. My nipples pebbled, every inch of my body hypersensitive. The cool breeze licked my skin, a thousand tongues and cocks brushing gently against me.

My back arched, and I cried out, presenting my tits to my other men. They took the hint, each latching onto a nipple and biting down. My cry turned into a scream as Flynn stuffed another finger in my needy arse, and I drowned as my orgasm hit me like a tsunami.

My vision went hazy at the edges, my lungs burning as every atom focussed itself on chasing more. More bliss. More cock. More cum.

I sobbed when Flynn pulled his fingers free, the emptiness opening up like a chasm in me. But Tristan was there, pushing into me and fucking deep into my arse in one long thrust. He shouted out, then moaned long and low as his hips danced back and forth.

Flynn's moan was loud, the slap of skin an illicit soundtrack to a show I wanted to watch.

But I couldn't hold myself up anymore, never mind turn to watch them. I fell forward onto Ezra's chest, and his strong arms surrounded me, cradling me as Tristan pulled out to his crown and slammed back into me like a man possessed. Ezra moaned, his deep rumble a symphony in my ears.

God, I loved this. Loved the way they fucked me. Loved the feel of Tristan's thick cock in my arse with Ezra's right there alongside it in my cunt. Widening my legs, I opened myself more, inviting them deeper inside me.

Tristan obliged, gripping my hips and pushing his cock into me as far as he could go before withdrawing all the way. It left me empty and desperate. But he didn't wait before slamming in again. It was fucking delicious, the stretch and burn as my hole was punished exactly what I needed.

I wanted to share Tristan and Flynn with Ezra.

But I was greedy.

I wanted to come first.

Then I wanted Tristan to mark us, to own us.

And I wanted Flynn to fuck him until he collapsed, pinning us all together in a mass of sated limbs and cocks that would eventually find their way back inside me.

I needed Tristan to stake his claim on Ezra, to imprint on him so that he never left, because I was never giving this up. Never giving him up. I wanted to come on his dick and Tristan to paint him with his cum. I wanted Ezra ruined for everyone but us.

This, right here, right now was what I wanted. Every day. Every night. My men with me, inside me.

Tristan slid his fingers between us, pinching my clit as he and Ezra fucked into me, one pushing in as the other withdrew. "Fuck yes," I cried. "More. Harder."

Their movements stuttered, but after a second, they both slammed into me, filling me as one. I screamed, shattering in their arms as my body exploded into a million tiny pieces before being glued back together, changed in ways I didn't know possible.

Cold air hit my empty hole, and I cried out before fingers were stuffed inside me. Ezra.

He stiffened under me, crying out as his legs were lifted in the air and pushed back, trapping my legs against his sides. Tristan's abs hit my arse as he moved inside Ezra, each press deep enough to make Ezra's breath catch. His cock thickened, the walls of my cunt still so sensitive I could feel every vein throb and every twitch as Tristan's thrusts controlled Ezra's movements in me. My cunt fluttered.

Knowing I would soon feel Ezra come inside me was enough to begin the build up toward another orgasm.

"Fuck," Ezra breathed. "Come on my dick again, Zali. Milk my cum out of me." He snaked his free hand between our bodies and pinched my nipple, his fingers pressing deeper into my arse.

"Add another finger. Stretch me more," I begged as I reached for my clit, working the bundle of nerves as Ezra's cock swelled inside me.

"Oh, fuck yes," I shouted. "Fuck," I screamed, my cunt clamping tight on Ezra as his cock stiffened impossibly and he shouted out his own release. Hot spurts of his cum painted the walls of my cunt, extending my orgasm until I was breathless and buzzing from my scalp to the tips of my fingers and toes.

Tristan kept moving, leaning over further and bracing his weight on the table, his hands curled over the edge by Ezra's ribs.

Flynn was breathing hard. His skin and Tristan's slapped together as Flynn pounded into him, taking what he needed. Ezra moaned as Tristan and Flynn cried out, Ezra's softening cock twitching hard as he received a load of

Tristan's cum. They kept moving, kept extending their orgasms with each slowing thrust until they were breathless and hissing with each movement.

The table creaked when Flynn flopped forward. But he didn't stay there for long. He fell back onto the couch, dragging Tristan with him until Tristan was practically on his lap. My arms were like jelly when I tried to push up onto them, but I moved anyway, feeling a lot like a day-old foal with my unsteadiness. Ezra cupped my face, his fingers still buried deep in my arse. He captured my lips in a kiss that curled my toes and sparked another fire deep inside me.

"If you don't let up, I'm gonna need you to make me come again," I murmured against his lips.

"I knew you'd be insatiable," he replied, his lips curling in a smile. "I want every part of you. You're gonna go lie down on your bed and spread your legs as wide as you can. Then you're going to hike your arse up in the air and play with this pretty pussy. But you're not going to come until I say you can. I'll be in there soon so I can fuck your tight little hole. Okay?"

I moaned, nodding. "Can I have Flynn and Tristan too? One in my cunt again and the other in my mouth?"

"You're a greedy little slut, aren't you?" He hummed. "Want us to use you again? Fill you up?"

"Fuck yes."

"Good girl. Get up and go to your room and wait for us. But make sure you don't waste any of my cum. I want to see it still in your pussy when we get there."

I tensed my pelvic floor muscles, and he lifted my arse up with the fingers he had buried inside me, letting his cock slip free before he eased his digits out. He slapped me on the butt, and I shivered. "Go, jailbird. Wait for your jailer to come and take what he wants from you."

"Say it," I dared him.

"Wait for your jailer to come and fuck you in the arse after the other prisoner and your professor fuck you. We'll take you so hard that you won't be able to walk tomorrow. We'll line up and fuck you like the beautiful little slut you are."

I shivered and climbed off him, my legs wobbly under me. I looked up, hoping Ry was watching, hoping he'd seen us together. Hoping he'd fuck me too.

But he wasn't there.

His spot was empty.

Disappointment crashed into me as cum leaked out of my cunt, slicking my thighs. I slipped my fingers into my cunt, plugging it so I could dash to my bed. I followed Ezra's instructions precisely, waiting for each of them to fill me again.

Eleven

Ryder

Moans sounded on the deck below me, the low murmur of voices like a siren's call. It was temptation. Sin and supplication too. I wanted. Fuck me, did I want.

But I wanted too much.

Pacing the deck, I tried to get the picture of the gang bang happening out of my head. I looked out over the water at the yachts bobbing in the calm of the marina and beyond. Barely a ripple, it was perfect for boating. I spun on the balls of my feet and faced the dock, seeing only the lights of the restaurants nearby. We were out of sight from the main part of the marina, another yacht shielding us from the main walkways.

But if I knew Zali, she'd be getting off from knowing that they were in the open and she could be seen. She loved that shit, and it revved my engine right the fuck up, watching her.

Zali.

Once upon a time, she was my best friend's annoying little sister. Then I lost my dad and soon after, Asher. I'd been unmoored, lost at sea. She'd become a safe harbour, shelter in the storm. She'd given me purpose, which let my heart begin the slow process of healing. She and Flynn had saved me. Ezra too. They'd given me something to focus on—a job doing what I loved.

An obsession.

I was jealous. I'd wanted to rip into Ezra when he'd kissed her. But there was a niggle in the back of my mind. A question. Who was I jealous of? I wanted to kiss Zali. There was no doubt about that. But what about Ezra? Did I want to kiss him too? I was beginning to think I did even though I hated his guts for what he'd done after he'd kissed Zali.

It wasn't just that he'd cuffed Zali. It was what he'd done to Flynn too.

I'd seen red, watching Flynn fight the officers. He'd writhed and bucked, trying to push them off him, but they were bigger and stronger. I wanted to raze them from existence. I'd wanted to pound them into the ground, leave them a bleeding pile of flesh for laying a finger on him.

But then sitting in that interview room alone, my thoughts had changed. The other officers had disappeared. My visions had morphed into one of Zali watching from on her throne, naked and sated from so many orgasms that she couldn't even hold her head up. Flynn was on the floor, his smooth alabaster skin sweat slicked and flushed a pretty pink. He was being pinned by Ezra and Tristan, held open for me as he begged for me to give him my cock. His lips were greedy, his tongue eager as he sucked me into his throat. But it was his hole clenching around my fingertip, daring me to sink into him and fill him up that drove me wild.

When I moved, Ezra was there, spreading his legs and jacking himself as he played with his hole. It was a blatant invitation for me to get inside him.

I couldn't decide between them. I hadn't wanted to.

But that wasn't me.

Not the real me, anyway. I'd caught the bug, been tempted by the sexual tension between the three men on the deck below and the woman who'd started it all.

It was just pretend. It wasn't real attraction. That wasn't possible. Not for me, not with them. It was empathy, not desire when I pictured Tristan sinking his dick into me. I didn't want it, but I could imagine that Flynn and Ezra did.

I wasn't turned on by the idea that he'd manhandle me, that he'd pin me down, his hand around my throat like I'd held Ezra, until I did the same things imaginary Flynn and Ezra had done.

My cock wasn't hard.

My curiosity hadn't piqued.

I didn't want to steal into Zali's room and borrow one of those thick dildos I'd seen before on her side table just to try it for myself.

Except that my curiosity *was* piqued. I did want to try it.

And my cock was achingly hard.

Without conscious thought, my feet carried me to the railing overlooking the couches on the deck below. Ezra was laid out flat on his back, his golden skin shining in the glow of the ambient lighting. Zali was straddling him, riding his dick, her breasts bouncing as she moved. Flynn was between Ezra's legs, his face buried where they joined. I shivered, my cock leaking in my boxer briefs.

I'd never tried that before—a tongue at the same time as a pussy—and fuck me, I wanted to experience it.

Ezra was loving life, his expression filled with bliss as the centre of Flynn's and Zali's attention. But Zali was loving it too—impaled on Ezra, being licked by Flynn, and Tristan nuzzling her throat.

My dick was trapped, my cargo pants strangling it. I needed relief. I needed to come. Beyond thought and reason, I was acting purely on instinct. The need to fuck reigned supreme, overruling any common sense telling me to walk away.

They deserved privacy, but I couldn't look away. My body was locked and primed to come, my cock throbbing and balls drawn up tight. The way they were in sync, all working toward each other's ecstasy while feeding their own, was breathtaking.

It was sexier than any porn I'd ever watched, taking me to the edge within moments. If I didn't get my hand around my cock in the next three seconds, I was going to blow in my underwear like a randy fucking teenager.

I shoved my cargos and boxer briefs down to my thighs, biting down on my lip to stifle my shout of relief when I closed my fist around my cock. Precum slicked my way—I was leaking like a tap.

Tristan looked up, his dark eyes blazing as our gazes caught. He gripped his dick, jacking himself and bent down again to murmur something to Zali. Sparks ignited as she turned her glazed eyes up to me. Mouth open, her nipples pink and hard from the guys' attention, she watched me as I touched myself, licking her lips as if she wanted more.

Tristan was saying something to her, his words a low murmur that shot straight to my balls. Jesus fucking Christ, I was going to come.

I squeezed the tip, pinching hard to take the edge off. I was desperate, my skin crawling with desire. I needed to see how this happened. I needed to watch.

"Tris," Ezra moaned, the desperation clear in his voice. "Need you." He wrapped an arm around Tristan's leg and tugged him until he was on his knees and Tristan's cock was teasing his lips. Ezra didn't hesitate, gulping him down to the back of his throat. The effect was immediate. While Tristan tensed, his entire body going rigid as he sucked in a breath and ran his fingers through Ezra's hair, Ezra melted into a puddle. It was almost as if he'd had the weight of the world taken off his shoulders. And maybe he had. Maybe getting fucked into oblivion was what he needed to forget about this shitty night. Or not so shitty where they were concerned.

I was the only one who wasn't part of their clique.

But I couldn't help imagining myself smack dab in the middle. Where would I want to be? Under Zali? Abso-fuck-ing-lutely. But sucking cock? That would be a no, so would licking arse unless it was Zali's. On my knees, my cockhead getting intimate with Zali's tonsils and tight throat muscles? Hell, yeah.

I closed my hand around my achingly hard cock again and slid it down, smearing more precum down my length. Fuck me, I was going to drain my balls before I'd even come, with the way I was leaking.

Flynn shifted, and Zali seemed to brace herself. I wanted to watch Flynn slide his fingers in and out of Zali. But it was Ezra who scrambled for purchase on the deck, crying out as his back arched. My breath rushed out of my lungs, my hole clenching. What would it be like?

No. I couldn't think like that. It was a dangerous path to tread. I wasn't one of those guys.

I worked my dick, shudders passing through me as I placed myself in Flynn's shoes, sinking my fingers into Zali's hole, pressed tight against her. I'd touched her back before—her naked skin was soft and smooth. What would it be like to notch my dick against her arse and press in? Flynn was saying something, his melodious voice barely carrying over the deck to me. I couldn't hear his words, but the sound, the tone, rippled through me.

Zali screamed, her body quaking and locking up tight. She arched her back, and Ezra and Tristan were there, latching onto her breasts. I could see them swiping their tongues over her nipples as they sucked and bit her, extending the ecstatic wave she was riding.

She sobbed when Flynn moved, but Tristan was there, sinking into her, fucking her with shallow thrusts. Flynn shuffled back behind him, wrapping one arm around

Tristan's waist. I couldn't see what he was doing, but Tristan's hiss was a dead giveaway.

"Now, angel," he ordered, pulling his hips back and canting them as if presenting his hole. *Fuck me.* Flynn lined up his dick before pushing inside in one long, slow thrust. Tristan shouted, Flynn moaned, and my eyes widened. I hadn't…. I couldn't…. Flynn was fucking Tristan. My heart crashed against my chest, a sweat breaking out on my flushed skin. I'd never thought for a second that Tristan would be on the receiving end, but I was seeing it with my own eyes.

I sucked in a breath and held it, going lightheaded from the revelation.

Ezra and Tristan were moving inside Zali like men possessed. Flynn didn't take his hands off Tristan's hips, guiding him down onto his dick every time he withdrew from Zali.

"Fuck, yes. More. Harder," Zali begged from her position on Ezra's chest. They picked up the pace and slammed into her, riding her like a rodeo performer does a bronco. Her keening cry made me clamp my fingers around the base of my dick. I wanted to come too. Needed it. But I had to hold out. I didn't know why, but there was something telling me to wait, to keep watching. Maybe it was morbid curiosity. Maybe it was a need to understand them and to satisfy myself that I truly didn't fit in.

Tristan lifted Ezra's legs, forcing them back so that Zali was pinned there. She didn't look like she was fighting to move. Why would she with Ezra's dick still buried inside her. That feeling of fullness, the stretch, the hardness rocking in

144 • ANN GRECH

and out and hitting all the spots to light her up would feel amazing. My arsehole clenched, and I ground my teeth together, hating that kernel of curiosity that had burrowed under my skin. It was like a fucking tick. A parasite that latched on and I couldn't scrape off with my blunt nails.

"Oh, fuck yes. Fuck," Zali screamed. I could only imagine what it would be like to be Ezra or Tristan—impaled by and buried inside another person at the same time.

Zali's orgasm set Ezra off too. Or maybe it was the way Tristan was fucking him with long slow withdrawals of his cock before snapping his hips forward again.

My hand sped up, my balls drawing tight at the image before me. Zali was out of breath, almost unconscious, while Flynn and Tristan took themselves higher as Ezra was still coming. Skin slapped and grunts sounded as they fucked hard and fast.

I bit down on my hand, muffling my cry as my own orgasm hit. But it was no use. Tristan's gaze flicked up to mine, and when our eyes connected, the first jet of cum launched out of my cock. Like it was rocket propelled, it sailed over the edge of the deck, landing almost at their feet. I sucked in a breath, reaching down to frame my cock between my fingers as I continued to work it, my orgasm rushing through me with the force of a freight train. Wetting my lips, I dragged my hand along my cock once more and squeezed my cockhead, more cum dripping from my slit.

Suddenly I wanted to know.

I had to find out.

What did cum taste like?

Bringing my fingers to my mouth, I licked one, moving the salty liquid around my mouth. I shivered, another drip of cum falling from my dick onto the deck. An aftershock tore through me, and I slid my finger into my mouth, sucking on it.

Tristan cried out, and I met his stare again. His heat burned through me, my spent dick making a valiant attempt to rise from the dead and wave hello.

Oh fuck. What had I done?

I spun away from the railing and dashed into the upstairs bathroom. I scrubbed my hands, looked down at my cock, which was still glistening with my own cum, and wanted to slap it off my body. I'd been so fucking horny, so fucking high on watching the gang bang below me unfold that I'd actually gotten off to men fucking. That wasn't me. I wasn't into it. I shouldn't be. What the fuck drugs was I on?

I wet my hand with freezing cold water and hissed as I wrapped it around my soft cock and rinsed it off before grabbing the towel and drying myself. I had to stop this lunacy. I had to stop obsessing over sex and men and what it would be like to have one or more of them inside me or wrapped around me.

I'd kept my desire for Zali in check for years. I hadn't touched her even though I'd wanted to bend her over every surface on the yacht, especially when she paraded around naked whenever she could. I could keep it buried with them too.

I would.

I had to.

♟ ♟ ♟

I slouched further in my seat, the background screen on my laptop—the sexy-as-sin taillights of Zali's Mustang—staring at me. I had a maintenance report to write and flight records to update, but my mind was going a million miles a minute. Every time I tried, I got sidetracked and ended up staring off into space. I couldn't concentrate for shit.

I. Was. Shook.

The night's events had rattled me to my core. After I'd cleaned up, I'd fallen into my chair and hadn't moved. My hands were still shaking, and my stomach was flip-flopping around like I was on a rollercoaster.

I needed time to get my feet under me again, to reset my bearings. It was a good thing that the others had stumbled off to Zali's bedroom and were finally crashed out after hours more moaning and muffled shouts that had tested me to my limits—I'd barely kept the walls I'd built around myself erected, just hearing them. I wasn't sure if I could if I saw them in my current state.

Even though I was wired up, I was utterly exhausted. Weariness had crept into my bones hours earlier. My body was protesting every move I made. But sleep was out of the question. Every time I closed my eyes, I saw them. Tristan and his blazing green eyes, Zali the temptress, the guileless

Flynn, and pretty-boy Ezra were daring me to go down to them.

The four of them would haunt my dreams if I let them.

Hell, they were already in my head every waking moment.

Scrubbing my hands over my face, I groaned. Coffee, whiskey, or both were needed. Sitting here doing nothing except trying not to focus on them wasn't working. I might as well do something. At this point it didn't matter if it was productive as long as I could immerse myself in it.

Like a red-light-district sign—unignorable and in your face but leaving a pit in the bottom of your gut—the USB Zali had given me sat in the back corner of my spotless desk, partly hidden behind my open laptop. I'd been actively ignoring it. I didn't want to go for a waltz down nightmare lane, but it was the only thing that would give me the distraction I needed.

Sighing, I plugged it in and watched as the folder list opened. Anything marine related from the investigation was on that drive—the coroner's report, the marine safety officer's findings on where the yacht was when it went up, where the washed-up wreckage was found, oceanographic maps, her mother's last diary entries, and everything else she'd dug up were sitting in neatly organized folders on the drive.

Zali had delegated it to me, knowing I had enough knowledge to draw my own conclusions about that part of the investigation.

She wasn't giving up. She wasn't letting the threat that Tristan's podcast posed beat her into submission. She just raised the stakes, staring him dead in the eye as she prepared to call his bluff. Zali was looking at every angle, tearing apart the company's investment strategy, and now Rosa's and Ash's deaths too.

Zali wouldn't stop until she could prove her mother was innocent. The allegations Tristan had levelled against Rosa before Zali had started unveiling cracks in his theories were serious—negligent mismanagement at best—and his theory around her death being suicide was equally grave. Zali didn't believe a word of it.

I got it. It was sobering knowing a loved one couldn't face going on despite how adored they were and how big a hole in their loved ones' lives they would leave. It was soul shattering knowing money was the root of what pushed them into that spiral of depression and devastation. Survivor's guilt was as real as it got.

I hated that Zali was in the position at all. Life was a cold-hearted bitch sometimes. I wanted to protect her from anything that could hurt her, but how? If the documents waiting for me to click on them gave me any hint that suicide was possible, rather than the freak accident the coroner had ruled their deaths as, the only option I had was to bury it. But it was like burying a body in a sniffer dog's training yard. Zali would dig up the information without even needing to try.

I couldn't help but think about where a possible suicide left Asher. Had he been collateral damage? Was he an inconvenient liability that needed to be neutralized? My stomach bottomed out, nausea fighting its way up my throat. Had my best friend been killed by his mother in some sick murder suicide? Could Zali have suffered the same fate? Fuck, I hoped not. I prayed to every fucking god around that their lives had been taken in an accident.

But there was only one way to find out. Even then, I might not get an answer. I clicked on the first folder containing the coroner's official findings. I'd heard the details before, but I'd never read the report.

Steeling myself, I began reading.

They set out at 8:00 a.m. on the Saturday. Travelling from the marina where we often moored and straight out the seaway, their yacht would have traversed the very spot where Zali loved to dive—the deep hole.

I shivered, remembering all too well the last time Zali had been in the water there. The bull shark I'd spotted was too close for comfort. But I couldn't get to her—the ear infection giving me grief had meant that I couldn't dive. Even weeks after it had healed, flying had been agony, pushing my eardrums almost to their bursting point.

All I could do was watch the water while Zali was down there, moving the yacht so that the current would bring her straight to us when she surfaced. I shouldn't have been surprised that she brushed off my concerns and strutted around the yacht naked. Zali was an expert at keeping all of us on our toes.

Fuck, that woman tested me.

But I loved her.

That was the day this whole journey had begun—Ezra had talked her into doing Tristan's subject, she'd met the grumpy professor, she and Flynn had fallen head over heels in love with him, and now they'd brought Ezra into their fold.

Happy times.

I kept reading. Rosa had confirmed with the volunteer marine rescue that she and Asher were headed to Cook Island, just off the New South Wales coast to go diving. She'd checked in with the Point Danger coastguard and advised them that she and Asher would be staying for three nights. Then nothing.

But no one remembered the yacht ever being there.

The island was a hotspot for shark sightings. Dive boats frequented the shark nursery there all the time. Surely they would have remembered seeing it. Surely there would have been someone who had a photo with the yacht in the background. Even when social media wasn't as prolific as it is today, people still took photos.

It didn't add up.

Ash had loved sharks. He was utterly obsessed with them. Shark week was a whole event at their house that he never missed. He'd record every documentary, watching them over and over until he could recite shark facts verbatim.

He would have loved diving there.

Did he get to see any of it?

Huffing out a laugh while I blinked away the sting in my eyes, I couldn't help my smile. Asher and Zali were as crazy as each other. Zali wasn't scared of the shark we'd seen—I was sure she'd gotten out of the water just to shut me up—and Ash would have tried to pet the damn thing.

Back when we were kids, our snorkels were practically attached to our faces. Ash had made sure Rosa and Roe knew exactly what he wanted for his tenth birthday. He started his campaign on his ninth birthday and then spent every day for a year after that reminding them that he wanted to do the scuba course. Roe was the first to buckle under his son's pestering power. Instead of a party, we did the scuba course.

I missed Ash like crazy. It was as if a piece of myself had died with him. I missed the way he laughed—his giggle was infectious. He effortlessly pulled everyone into his orbit. In a room full of strangers, he was everyone's best friend. Ash made people feel good about themselves. He made them smile. He lived loud, drawing people into the light with him even if—like me—they preferred sticking to the shadowy corners where they wouldn't be noticed. But as much as I grumbled about his popularity, I would never have given up that precious place as his best friend. He gave me the safe space to be myself.

And I missed the innocent kid I'd once been.

I couldn't say a proper goodbye to him. His body was still out there somewhere in a watery grave, missing its foot. We'd reunited them, scattering the ashes from their otherwise empty coffins at Jumpinpin. But it didn't make it easier.

Inhaling a cleansing breath of the ocean air surrounding me, I rubbed my stinging eyes and forced my vision back to the screen. Focussing on the report, I kept reading, pouring over page after page, taking in the minutia.

Huh.

The wreckage from the yacht had washed up on the north-eastern side of South Stradbroke Island. That was forty or fifty clicks north of Cook Island, well outside the search zone. Even at the most northerly point of their journey, they should have been twenty kilometres south.

It was unknown precisely when they'd gone missing. Had they been at Cook Island for as long as they'd said? Had they come back early because of worsening conditions, only for tragedy to befall them? There had been no further communication with the coast guard. By the time Point Danger had tried to hail them, Roe had reported them missing—he hadn't spoken with Rosa in forty-eight hours and hadn't been able to raise her on the radio or mobile phone either.

Scrolling up a few pages, I double-checked the weather and swell records for the time they were supposed to be away. Set out in black and white, a neat table in the report confirmed exactly how conditions had worsened. The swell got progressively bigger. The calmest day was the one they'd set out on. By the time they were due back, it was over three metres, or twelve feet on the old scale.

Why was the wreckage so far north? They were moored at the city marina—the quickest way to get back from Cook Island was through the seaway. Locals didn't just make the mistake of missing it and choosing Jumpinpin instead. Sure, there were people who would have braved it in those conditions, but I doubted Rosa would have done so in a relatively new yacht with a kid onboard. She was experienced enough to know exactly when to keep away.

The only other explanation was that the winds were strong enough to blow the wreckage north against the southerly flowing Eastern Australian Current.

Maybe it wasn't a mistake. Maybe they'd decided to cruise up to South Straddie instead of going to Cook Island. But 8:00 a.m. was a late start for Rosa. She loved watching sunrises on the yacht. I remembered many mornings when she'd dragged us out of bed and up to the deck, where Asher, Zali, Flynn, and I would lean against each other to stay upright as we were blinded by the sun slowly stretching its rays out over the Pacific.

Zali also told me about her dad's regret that he'd agreed to work rather than start their few days on the yacht. They'd fought that morning, and Rosa had dropped a likely kicking-and-screaming Zali off at her aunt's house.

That's why they were late getting out. That's why only Rosa and Asher were on the yacht. Ash would have been nagging his mum non-stop to head straight to the reef, especially because of the turning tide and, according to the coroner's report, deteriorating diving conditions for the remainder of the day.

Just like I didn't believe for a second that Rosa would have risked crossing the Jumpinpin bar, there was no way she would have made a wrong turn, especially when she would have had the coordinates for the reef plugged into the GPS system.

And why would they have checked in at Point Danger?

The only possible explanation was that something happened on the way back and the wind carried the lone piece of wreckage north of where the yacht actually went down.

I took another look at the table outlining the weather and swell conditions. Typical for that time of year, it had blown from the north, then it shifted to blow from the east. Unless it was blowing from the south, atypical for that time of year but not unheard of, the wreckage wouldn't have ended up where it was found.

Could someone have towed it in? Could they have seen it floating and pulled it up to the beach so that it could be properly disposed of? Anything was possible, but my gut told me something wasn't right.

Something wasn't adding up.

TWELVE

Tristan

I couldn't believe that this day had come. I'd never thought it was possible. I'd all but given up. But here I was, wrapped around Ezra, the big spoon to his little one. We were sharing a pillow on Zali's bed. She was tucked into Ezra's arms. Flynn was wrapped around her, his leg pinning one of hers down. Still fast asleep, only their deep breaths broke the lap of the water against the hull.

Dawn was breaking the horizon, the sky outside turning from the inky black of night to the grey-but-soon-to-be-brilliant-blue of the morning. I was torn between finding Ryder and making sure he was okay and staying put so that I never had to let go of Ez.

It had taken him a long time to fall asleep. He'd lain awake for hours, his hands clasped across his belly as he stared up at the ceiling. I'd kissed his shoulder, drawing his attention, and he'd smiled softly before whispering, "Go to sleep, Tris. I'll still be here in the morning. We can talk then."

We did need to talk, but the longer I put it off, the more time I had with him, the more time I could enjoy touching him in the way I'd dreamed of for a decade. It wasn't even the sex—although that was mind-blowingly good with the addition of Zali and Flynn—it was this. It was him lying in my arms. It was me nuzzling his nape, breathing in the remnants of his shampoo.

I smoothed my hand over his lower belly, spreading my fingers and claiming him. This man was mine. Zali's and Flynn's too. We were his too. Shifting ever so gently, I moulded every inch of myself against him. I didn't want to wake him—he needed sleep after last night—but the instinct to eliminate the space between us was overwhelming.

He was warm and relaxed, but he was starting to stir. He leaned back ever so slightly and slid his hand down my leg, hitching it up so my legs followed the bend in his. I stilled, trying to let him ease back into slumber, but my cock had other ideas. Hot and hard, nestled in the crease between his cheeks, I had to bite back a groan when his breath hitched.

Ezra arched back, letting go of my leg and stretching his arm over our shoulders to tangle in my hair. His morning voice was rough when he murmured, "Good mornin'."

"Mmm, it's very good," I hummed, smiling against his nape as I laid a kiss there. Ezra chuckled softly, gooseflesh rising along his skin as my breath tickled him, and he rocked his hips back, sliding along my length before doing it again.

"You're needy this morning," I mused, teasing a line of kisses on his shoulder, then nibbling along the curve of his muscle.

"It's you." He pushed my hand down lower, curling my fingers around his steely cock. I squeezed, jacking him slowly. His voice was like gravel when he moaned, "You're addictive."

"So are you," I whispered, slicking his precum down his length. "I've been hooked since that first night. Fuck, I've wanted you for a decade." Exhaling, I let go of the fear I'd been holding onto and opened myself up. If I was taking a leap of faith and trusting Zali, I needed to do the same for Ezra.

Especially for Ezra.

"I've loved you for a decade," I admitted.

He stilled, his breath catching. Turning wide brown eyes on me, his brow furrowed and his mouth open, he asked, "You have?" He shook his head in disbelief. "You always made out like you just wanted to fuck."

"In the beginning, I did. I figured one more night with you would get you out of my system. But then I saw you that night of the accident, and I was in awe of you—"

"That was only a few days later—"

I huffed out a laugh. "Like I said, at first. But I was already more than halfway there when you said goodbye the morning after and told me not to call you."

He grinned shamelessly at me before leaning back further into my arms, encouraging me to keep kissing him. It was no hardship, but I needed to see his expression when I confessed what had been in my heart the whole time.

"The night of the accident pushed me over. I fell head over heels in love with you." I ran my hand down his length, slowly working him. But this wasn't about getting him off. I needed him to hear me, to concentrate on every word I said. "You made me want to be a better man, Ez. For you." Laying a lingering kiss on his shoulder, I added, "It's why I started my degree. It's why I cleaned my shit up and got a job, a career. I wanted to show you I could be good for you, that I wasn't some deadbeat who'd drag you down."

Ezra's eyes slipped closed, and he nuzzled his nose against mine. When he finally opened them again, he gave me a small smile and admitted, "I was scared of how much I wanted you." He closed his hand over mine and guided my movements up and down his shaft. We were breathing the same air, both hard and aching, but we weren't trying to get off. Our touch, being so close to each other, created a bubble around us. It was the most intimate moment I'd ever shared with him.

His voice was tortured when he spoke again. "I would have thrown away everything I'd worked for if you asked. I was scared shitless. The only way I wouldn't cave was if I kept my distance."

I shook my head. "I never would have asked you to walk away from what you love."

"I know that now." He pressed his lips against mine in a slow, chaste kiss. "But back then, my feelings were…

complicated." He huffed out another laugh, this one self-deprecating. "They're still complicated."

"You were in love with Zali," I surmised, pressing our lips together for another kiss. Slipping my tongue into his mouth, I tasted him, trying to show him with more than words, with more than sex, how I felt.

"And Flynn. Ryder, too, if I'm being honest."

"Yeah, I get that."

I kissed Ezra again, slipping out from behind him as I did. After shifting him until he was lying on his back, I let the weight of my chest press him down into the mattress. His hands burned a path down my back as he grasped my arse and squeezed. I moaned, and he pulled me tighter against him until I was hooking my leg over his. I deepened the kiss, our tongues tangling as I squeezed his cock and pressed my thigh up high between his legs. His quiet moan vibrated through me as my soul reached out to find another of its perfect matches.

"But it's also why I can't do this," he forced out, and my hand stilled.

I pulled away from him in shock, my brows furrowed and mouth agape.

My voice was a mix of horrified and devastated when I asked, "What? No. Why?"

"Because of Roe. I'm betraying him." Ezra pinched the bridge of his nose, and I almost sobbed at the loss of his hand on me.

He exhaled slowly. "He's one of my oldest friends, Tris. I knew him when his daughter was still a child. How do I explain this to him?" He gestured between us and Zali and Flynn who were curiously still, as if they were both holding their breaths.

If it were any other time, I'd call them out, but I appreciated the privacy they were trying to give us.

"What if he thinks it's been going on since Zali was a teenager? I'd never forgive myself if he believed for one second that I'd groomed her. And when he finds out I arrested Zali last night… I mean, fuck, Flynn was still in cuffs when I walked into the interview room he was in. I was practically shoving my cock down his throat within minutes."

"You aren't giving yourself enough credit," I challenged. "Roe knows the kind of man you are. He knows you wouldn't take advantage of either Zali or Flynn."

Ezra clenched his jaw and shook his head, his lips drawn down in a frown. "He knows about you. He knows it's always been you. How do I explain that it's also been Zali and Flynn and Ry too? How do I make a man who's loved one woman his whole life believe that it's more than getting my dick wet when there are four of you?"

Rising onto my elbow and trying to stem the tide of my rising temper, I hissed, "So you just walk away instead? What about your happiness?" My voice was louder than I intended, but if they weren't already awake, then maybe they should be. "What about Zali's and Flynn's happiness?"

I exhaled, and it knocked the wind out of my sails, my shoulders falling and my heart shattering into a million tiny pieces. My voice broke when I whispered, "What about mine, Ez? I want you. I want to be with you. I want to grow old with you and hold your hand when we have to get our nose hairs plucked because Zali and Flynn still look like a million bucks and we're paunchy and grey."

"You'll be a silver fox." His smile didn't reach his eyes.

"Don't change the subject." My voice cracked, and I swallowed down the emotion, fighting to keep my head above water. "He'll understand. We'll show him how much we love them and each other. Please," I begged.

Ezra blinked, clearing the glassiness in his eyes. Tunnelling his fingers into my hair and bringing my face down to his, he pressed our lips together. "I don't think he will. But help me forget just for the moment. Help me remember what it's like between us."

He didn't add the "one last time." I didn't need him to; the words weighed heavily enough between us without being voiced.

I shifted, aligning our bodies until I was between his legs and our cocks were pressed snug between us, my erection long gone. He ran his hands down my back to my arse, his touch mapping my skin. It was as if he was trying to memorize every inch of me. Maybe he was. It was exactly what I was doing with him.

When Ezra squeezed my cheeks, gripping them until I was sure he'd leave fingerprint-sized bruises, I dipped my head and kissed him long and slow. He wrapped his legs around my hips and held me there.

I rocked slowly against him, our lips never breaking as I touched every part of him that I could reach. His skin burned against mine, a sheen of sweat breaking over us as we moved together. The noises he made—the moans when I ground down, the hitches in his breath when I pinched his nipples, the gasp when I bit his lip—were the sexiest of sounds. My cock woke up once more, and when I slipped my hand between us, gripping our lengths, Ezra's whimper rippled through me like an electric current, lighting up my insides and frying my ability to focus on anything but him.

Desperation clawed at my throat. I needed to get closer, to crawl inside him. I needed us to merge until it was impossible to extricate ourselves. I needed Ezra with me. I just needed him. Burying my face in the crook of his neck, I inhaled, keeping his scent inside me as long as I could. I was dizzy with him, but it still wasn't enough.

Sliding my hand from our joined cocks to cup his cheek, I groaned at the tap on my hand. But before I could pull away from Ezra, a bottle was shoved into my grip. My breathless whisper of thanks earned me a kiss to my shoulder—Zali—and a whimper from Ezra when I flicked the cap open.

I needed a few extra limbs—an extra hand to support myself while I lubed up my man, touching him everywhere I could. Frustrated, I pulled back, shifting my weight slightly so I could rise to my knees. But Ezra's legs tightened around me, stilling my movement. "Ez," I began, his name a devotion on my lips.

"Don't leave," he begged. "Pour it into my hand."

I kissed a line down his throat, sucking on the hollow between his collarbones and tasting the warmth of his skin.

Steady hands found ours, helping me tip the liquid into his waiting hand.

Zali and Flynn were right there, supporting me—us—when I needed it most. She promised me last night that she would protect me. Ironic, considering she and Flynn were young enough to be my kids, that it was one of them helping me ready Ezra. But our ages had never mattered. The connection between us defied logic and explanation. It was fragile and yet rock solid too. I wanted Ezra to be part of that too. I wanted to envelop him into our fold. I wanted him to fight for us like I would fight for him.

Panic welled up inside me. This was it. Unless I could convince him to stay, this would be the last time I got to hold him. The what-ifs bombarded me.

The bars slammed down, fear settling low in my gut as the chill of the concrete block walls seeped into my bones.

Shadows loomed over me.

My body braced for impact.

I knew what was coming.

The beating.

The pain.

A sob tore from my throat. *No, not now. Please, just let me stay here. I want to be with him, with them. I can't go back. Please.*

"Hey," Ez murmured, his fingers nudging my chin.

He applied firm pressure until I lifted my face, but I still didn't dare look at him.

"Tris," he murmured, his voice so full of pleading that I couldn't deny him any longer. "I love you. Be here with me."

Like magnets drawn to one another, the shattered pieces of my heart were pulled back together, held in a tentative bond. It was fragile, but it was enough for the moment. I wiped the tear falling from Ezra's eye before turning to Zali and Flynn. They were curled up together, Zali biting her knuckle, her eyes red rimmed, and Flynn's breaths were ragged. He huffed and blinked away the shine in his eyes before pressing his lips together in a sad smile.

"I love you," I whispered to them before returning my focus to Ezra. "I love all of you. That doesn't change because there's more than one of you. It doesn't make it any less real."

Ezra drew my lips to his and kissed me like a man starving. The memories of this moment—his touch, his taste, his scent—would fade like they did the first time we were together, but this time it would destroy me. The first time we were together was a revolution. The second would be a decimation. But there was no way I would be the one walking away—not when the man of my dreams was in my arms.

Ezra nudged my hip. "Lift up."

I did, and he slicked up my cock with lube warmed by his hand. My eyes rolled back in my head, every nerve ending coming alight with the warm slick I was being coated in.

He didn't bother with stretching himself. Instead, he shifted until my cock was nudging against his hole, and he went lax in my arms. "Go slow."

"I'll never hurt you," I promised and notched my cockhead against him. Sliding my hand down his side to his leg,

I hitched his knee higher and pressed forward, breaching him ever so slightly.

Ezra's breath rushed out of his lungs and his eyes slipped closed.

"No," I scolded, my voice rough. "I need to see you." I needed him to see me too, to see what was written in my soul and on my very being.

I worked inside him slowly, soft pushes and slow withdrawals until my hips were flush with his butt and I was cradled inside his tight warmth. I made love to him, slow rocks and long kisses, tight embraces, and whispered words of praise. His moans spurred me on, his gasps and choked out cries when I pushed inside him like catnip to my ears. We were closer than we'd ever been before. I gave into the sensation and rode the high.

Sweat dripped off my hair and beads dotted his brow as we let ourselves ignite, burning until we went supernova. His hands on me were like a prayer, my lips worshipping him as I kissed him. My body was climbing, nearing the precipice as the tight clasp of his body sent me soaring. I wanted to dive off, to get lost in the bliss that was Ezra, but not without him. I reached for his cock, but Ezra was already moving, gripping my hand and sliding our fingers together. He raised our joined hand above his head and arched his neck. Resting my weight on my elbow, I gripped his other hand and threaded our fingers together, spread my knees, and changed the angle of penetration so my cock dragged along the walls of his channel.

Ezra cried out, "Fuck yes. There."

His arse tightened around me, his cock turning steely between us. Precum leaking from his slit pooled in his bel-lybutton, slicking our stomachs. Dragging my abs against his cock, I snapped my hips forward and leaned down to suck a mark onto his throat. My claim on him would fade after a few days, but the pieces of me I freely gave would last a lifetime.

I wanted him a gasping, shaking mess, coated in our cum and unable to remember his name. I wanted to disassemble him and remake him with pieces of me so intertwined that he would never be the same again. I doubted that I'd get my wish but taking Ez to heaven with me was something I could definitely do. Grinding down, tagging his prostate with every thrust and keeping up the pressure against his cock trapped between us, I rolled my hips and kissed him until he was breathless.

His body locked up underneath mine, and I swallowed his cries as Ez shot pulse after pulse of cum between us. His channel strangled my cock, clutching it like he never wanted me to leave, and his legs clamped around me in a vice grip. I gritted my teeth, begging my body to hold off.

Ezra hadn't been able to come untouched last time we were together, but his prostate orgasm was epic. I wanted to draw another one from him.

He went boneless underneath me and I bit my lip, grin-ning at the blissed out, dazed expression in his eyes. Pump-ing my hips, slowly dragging my cock over his prostate with every push forward, I watched as his eyes widened and his grip on me tightened.

"Jesus Christ," he gasped.

I let go of his hands, then gripped his leg and wrapped my other arm around his shoulders, tightening his clutch on me. I needed him closer as he shattered in my arms a second time. Thrusting and grinding into him, I took us both higher until I was balancing on a single toe on a tightrope above the precipice that I was about to dive into. Gritting my teeth and praying I could hold off until he could come again, I thrust harder.

"Oh fuck," he cried, his body shaking as his channel tightened impossibly around me.

His breathing was ragged, his grip on me bruising as he rode out his orgasm and I crashed headlong into mine. Pumping my orgasm deep into him, I clutched at his shoulders, burying my face in the crook of his neck as I cried out my release.

Eventually our breathing slowed, our sweat cooling and my cock slipping from inside him, but I didn't let go. I couldn't. We watched as Flynn and Zali came together and then lay breathless in the aftermath.

But the sun rose higher, and Ezra spoke those fateful words.

"I need to go."

THIRTEEN

Flynn

"Hi," I greeted Cara, our new friend, as Zee and I slipped into the seats either side of her. She was cute and sweet and so innocent. Zee could eat her for breakfast, but Cara brought out a side in her that was beautiful to see. Cara rambled when she was nervous, but instead of getting impatient, it was as if Zee lost a little of her cynicism and acted her age for once in her life. I loved seeing her with a girlfriend to giggle and have fun with.

"Hi!" Her smile lit up the entire room. "Oh my goodness, you look so stylish," she gushed as Zee gingerly sat on the seat next to her.

Our girl must be sore after last night and again this morning.

Cara wasn't wrong though. Zee looked like a million bucks in her vibrant violet dress that accentuated her curves. The low-cut neckline made me want to bury my face between her ample boobs, and I could just imagine Tristan getting all possessive about how big his hands looked against her cinched-in waist. But my favourite was the flared skirt that was playful and sexy at the same time. It didn't hurt that it barely covered her butt. I'd watched her walk away from me, and that glimpse of the curve of her cheeks had me as hard as stone. I wanted nothing more than to watch Tristan bend her over in his office again.

The door slammed behind us, and I jumped, flinching at the noise. Tristan—Professor Reid—strode in. He was all business in his dark suit, and his scowl upped the intimidation factor a hundredfold.

But instead of being scared, my heart ached. His normally blazing green eyes were dull, and his shoulders were slumped. He was hurting. Anger and powerlessness to stop Ezra from walking away were tearing him apart.

I wanted to go to him, take him into my arms, and help him forget. If it wouldn't prove fatal for his career, I wouldn't hesitate to do it right here and now.

Glancing over at our girl, I saw Zee wince before she turned to me, her eyes filled with concern. Lips pressed in a tight line, her brow furrowed, she flicked her gaze down, silently asking my opinion on our plan to get his mind off things. It was a definite yes.

Zee and I had heard every word of their conversation that morning. Tristan had opened himself up to Ezra, admitting just how much he wanted him. Watching them make love was the most incredible thing I'd ever witnessed. It was a privilege to see them drop all pretences and just let their bodies—their souls—speak. Everything from the way they moved together, the need in their touch, the sounds they made, and the words they said was beautiful.

But then Ezra had reminded all of us that Monroe, his friend, was Zee's dad. Apparently, even though Tristan loved him, Ezra was offering just a one-time-only deal. He'd stomped on Tristan's shattered heart, letting the pieces crunch under his size-eleven boots like broken glass when he walked out without even a backward glance.

Our man was going to get a talking to. No one hurt my Tristan like that.

Zee had tried to stop Ezra, but he'd shaken his head and stepped around her, seemingly without a care. I hadn't bothered with him. If he wanted to leave because things weren't easy, that was on him. Monroe was a good guy; he would understand that Ez had fallen in love with us. Roe knew love. He knew how powerful and all-consuming it was. All Ezra had to do was sit down and explain it. Instead, he was taking the coward's way out.

I'd concentrated on Tristan instead, taking him into my arms. He'd been the one to lift me up, but I hadn't hesitated in winding myself around him like a koala. He'd pulled me tight against him, clutching me for long minutes, his breathing ragged. Without a word, he'd eventually let me down and kissed my forehead before walking away when Ryder interrupted us in the galley.

Tristan was still putting on a brave face, but he wasn't fooling either of us.

"Right, let's get started," he demanded, and the room quickly fell silent. "We have one presentation today, which we'll do in the second half of the class. In the meantime, where are you all up to with your research?" His voice was a deeper rasp than normal, as if he'd screamed his throat raw.

"We've made some progress," a student at the back said. Turning on my chair, I immediately spotted him. He was the same hipster guy—trimmed beard, glasses, and a buttoned-up shirt—who Cara and I had shut down in an earlier class. He was a know-it-all and so arrogant that I wanted to do violent things to him.

"I've worked with the firm who did the liquidation before. They've got offices all over the world. Shortly after the GFC started, they had a massive expansion. I found out that the liquidator who signed off on the report is a partner at the firm, so I called her up—"

"You did what?" Tristan exploded. His voice echoed around the room.

All of us sat in stunned silence. He clenched his fists and glared daggers at hipster guy, his eyes narrowing and his jaw bulging.

Clueless and apparently with a death wish, hipster guy responded nonchalantly, "I called her up to have a chat."

If looks could kill, hipster dude would be dead. Tristan's glare turned even more fierce. He straightened his fingers, then clenched his hands back into fists. A vein at his temple pulsed. Tristan growled, "*No one* has *any* contact with any research target without my explicit permission. Is. That. Understood?"

"Professor," Zee called in a sweet-as-pie voice. She raised her hand and waved to get his attention. "With respect, I'm sure—" She gestured to hipster dude, who hastily said that his name was Jude. "—Jude had a good reason to do what he did."

"Zali, a word. Now," Tristan snapped before stomping out the door. Zee was up and out of her seat in an instant, racing out after Tristan.

Cara turned to me wide-eyed. "What just happened?" she squeaked. "I hope she doesn't get in trouble. Oh man, what if she gets kicked out of class? She's so brave—and crazy for standing up for that idiot—"

"Don't worry, Zee can hold her own," I reassured her. But my heart was pounding, and my stomach was churning. I didn't dare breathe until Zee came back through the door a few moments later and slipped into her seat, her cheeks flushed and biting back a smile.

Tristan followed more slowly, hands in his pockets and gaze pinned to the floor. When he stood back behind the lectern, he scanned the room, focussing on hipster dude. "I apologize. My outburst was unprofessional. I'm bound by my ethics approval to conduct this research in a certain way. As I've explained before, I need to comply with set rules when conducting interviews, so please, no contact with research targets without my involvement so that we don't run the risk of breaching my ethics approval. Nevertheless, Jude, please continue."

"Ah, sure." Jude hesitated. "I did up a bit of a timeline. Can I show it on the big screen?"

Tristan nodded, and they set the display up so that it was mirroring Jude's computer. I was only half listening when Jude began explaining to both Tristan and the class that he had a background in business.

"What did Professor Dreamy Grumpster say?" Cara asked Zee in a conspiratorial whisper.

"I have to see him after class."

"Oh no. He's really mad, isn't he. He's even grumpier than normal today."

"I'm sure it'll be fine," Zee countered at the same time as I added, "I'll come with you."

Cara's sigh was filled with yearning. "I wish I had a sweet boyfriend like you."

I snorted out a laugh. If only she knew what we'd done yesterday. It was anything but sweet. Or maybe it was, just with a little spice added in for good measure.

But then she paled. "Not that I.... I mean... I'm not interested in you, Flynn. Not that you're not good—"

"It's okay, I understood what you meant." I grinned at her, trying not to laugh at how flustered she was.

"He's big... on satisfying my needs. A real keeper," Zee teased, her eyes filled with mischief. I flushed, heat crawling up my throat.

Cara fanned her face and tucked a stray piece of hair behind her ear before she started speaking a mile a minute. "I know we spoke about going out for coffee, but if you're not busy tonight, like an hour ago, I won four free drinks tickets to a pub on the river in Surfers. They have this local guy singing there—Connor. He's pretty amazing, and it's an

LGBTQIA-friendly venue. I don't know if that's important to you, but I like to support businesses that are inclusive."

I thought she'd finished her pitch until she sucked in another breath and added, "But it's okay if you can't. I heard that this boy I like will be there too. He probably won't notice me, but maybe if I was there...." She shrugged and frowned, curling into herself.

"We'd love to come," Zee agreed, hooking her arm around Cara's and smiling like an excited child.

We didn't often go out to bars and pubs—drunken parties weren't really my scene—but this place was on the water and had picnic tables, bean bags, and high tops with stools all the way down the sloping bank. Decent food— nothing like what Ry cooked, but good pub grub—laid-back live music, and a sweet view of the sunset over the mountains in the distance with lights reflecting off the river in the foreground.

We were able to dock the runabout straight up to it too, so we'd been there many times before.

"You would?" Cara asked, wide eyed. "Really?"

I knocked my shoulder gently into hers. "Absolutely. We like inclusive venues too, and I want to meet this boy you like, because even if I have to introduce you myself, he deserves to meet someone as sweet as you."

Cara flushed and looked at me with awe in her eyes. And for what? The truth? This girl was gorgeous. I adored her.

"He's cute, but I don't have a chance with him. He's totally out of my league."

I opened my mouth to refute her, but Tristan com-manded, "All right, settle down everyone."

His voice held more than a hint of annoyance, and as I looked up at him where he was still standing behind the lec-tern, his scowl deepened. But there was a heat in his eyes, fire that turned me right the heck on.

"Jude's ready to give us a rundown." Gesturing to the empty space near the projector screen, he added, "Why don't you come up front?"

"Yeah, so, um." Jude cleared his throat and walked up the aisle to stand on the opposite side of the screen from Tris. "The liquidator wasn't directly involved with the inves-tigation, which isn't normal. Usually, they supervise things while the more junior staff do the legwork. But they had a guy from one of their American offices—an expert in invest-ment firm liquidations—fly over and run the job. The Aus-tralian liquidator largely just signed off on it."

"Did you ask why they called the American in?" Tristan asked, his brow furrowed. His scowl was gone, but the fur-row remained. Now it was concentration and curiosity, ra-ther than anger, marring his features.

"Apparently, she didn't call him. When the firm opened the file for ReimagINC, it was flagged in their system, and the American guy was attached to it. The Australian ac-countants started the data collection, and he took over de-ciding both the scope of the audit and whether it was worth pursuing the sale of any assets."

Jude flipped the slide, and a list of dot points appeared, bouncing onto the screen from different directions. He'd clearly been playing with the animation feature in Power-Point to try to liven up the white-background-with-black-text slide. "They were understaffed, absolutely snowed with cases and they were hiring lots of new, inexperienced graduates. When the American guy said that it appeared to be an open-and-shut case, they closed the company down and moved on."

"What does open-and-shut mean?" another student asked.

"Apparently, given that the director chick disappeared so close to when ReimagINC went under, they were worried it was another case like that director in the '80s or '90s who stole company money and went overseas—"

"Skase," Tristan murmured, nodding thoughtfully.

"But this American guy audited a series of typical investments and found no anomalies. They put it down to a sign of the times."

"So, they didn't do a full audit?" Cara asked. "Is that normal?"

She was resting her elbows on the desk, and I took the chance to cast my eyes over to Zee. She had her arms crossed but seemed okay otherwise. It was good news. It was a relief to hear that the liquidator reiterate that the company collapsed because of bad economic conditions, not Rosa's mismanagement.

"It is when the funds in the company's accounts aren't sufficient to pay the liquidators for a more detailed audit," Tristan explained, his eyes trained on Zee as he spoke.

I loved how he watched her, his stare locked on her like a homing beacon. Anyone else would wilt under his intense focus, but she preened, loving his attention and letting us both know in her unique way that she was okay.

Jude continued, adding, "The liquidators sold off what was left of ReimagINC's investment portfolio, paid their fees, and distributed the small amount that was left. The stock market had crashed, so creditors only got a few cents in the dollar back."

Zali cleared her throat. "What was the liquidator's gut feeling about the director's death?"

"She seemed more worried about ReimagINC than the director." He shook his head and splayed his hands out, palms up. "Normal, I suppose, when your obligation is to the creditors of the business, not the people controlling the company. They did keep their files open until the coroner handed down the report though. I think that if the director's cause of death was ruled as anything other than accidental, they likely would have looked closer at the company's dealings."

"Okay, that's great work, Jude. Let's break for five minutes, and then we'll reconvene for Zoe, Cara, and Mai Linh's presentation on directors' duties."

I signalled to Zee. "Can I speak to you outside for a second?"

Cara hopped up and blushed, gathering all her things in a rush. "It's okay, I'll go. I've got to get ready and show Zoe and Mai Linh the parts they'll be presenting."

Zee cocked her head and glanced at me, one brow raised. I'd caught on to what Cara said too. There was no way Zee or I would let her partner with them again if she'd done all the work.

But that had to wait. Cara shuffled out of the way, and I hauled Zee into my lap. She groaned just as I whispered, "You've got a bony butt."

Zee adjusted her perch, leaning on one butt cheek.

"What did you say to Tris?" I asked, my lips brushing the shell of her ear.

Zee's hum went straight to my balls. "I threatened to drop to my knees and blow him in the corridor right then and there if he didn't perk up."

I snorted out an incredulous laugh as she bit my jaw. My voice was part groan, part breathlessness when I responded, "Bet that went down well."

My eyes met Tristan's. The flare of heat in them was incendiary.

She shivered. "He did that thing with his hand around my throat."

I reached up and mimicked the move I'd seen Tristan do to her a few times before. Her breath hitched, and I murmured in her ear, "Like this? I can feel how much you like it. You're wet, aren't you?"

"Soaked," she gasped when I tightened my grip just a fraction. "He wants to meet us in the library after class so I can do it for real."

"Yeah?" I hummed, my cock as hard as an iron rod against her hip.

"Mm-hmm. Then I told him about my secret." She bit her lip and dropped her gaze to my mouth.

She was all sex, hot and tight, and I wanted inside her with a desperation that bordered on insanity.

"What's your secret?" I asked, my voice strangled. The rasp sounded like I'd swallowed nails.

"You'll have to wait and see."

"I'll go wherever you do."

FOURTEEN

Zali

"This way." I led Flynn by the hand to the spot Tristan had told me. The case stacks in the law library apparently didn't have many visitors these days now that the decisions were digitized. Hopefully there were blind spots in the cameras too because when I showed Tristan and Flynn what my surprise was, there was no way he'd keep his job if we were caught.

I ducked around a corner, following the signs to the tucked-away corner of the library where long, narrow rows of bookcases that rose almost to the ceiling were filled with case law books dating back a century or more. The smells changed—old paper mingled with a stillness, a quietness, that couldn't be taken away by the air-conditioning. These halls were hallowed ground to the law lecturers and students, and I was about to desecrate them. Excitement curled low in my belly, wetness seeping from my core and down the tops of my thighs.

We sidestepped a stool on wheels, one of many placed intermittently along the rows to enable books to be taken off the top shelf, and kept moving, searching for Tristan.

Shadows darkened the end of each row, the lighting dim among the high stacks. It was intimate in a dangerous kind of way, private too, in a sense. But this section was silent, not another soul to be seen. While I loved the thrill of knowing people could watch, that they would get off on seeing my guys take me, I needed it to be just us. I needed to reconnect with them and show Tristan that he was ours and we wouldn't leave.

I pushed down the betrayal and hurt Ezra had caused. I understood why he'd left, but it didn't lessen the blow. I wanted him to choose me, to choose us. But he valued his friendship with Dad more. It was what Dad needed too— they were close, and Dad needed more people in his corner. I think he would always be grateful to Ezra for stepping in and trying to keep me off a self-destructive path. But their bond was more than that. It was respect and a genuine caring for each other. Friendship built initially from gratitude, but then solidified by countless hours of sport, shared meals, and laughter when the world was at its darkest for both of them. They'd both lost someone important to them—Ezra, Tristan and Dad, my mum. But now Tristan came with a side of complication—Flynn and me—and I didn't think Ezra knew how to deal with that.

Still, seeing Tristan's heart break when Ezra walked out, seeing how his hurt had built Tristan's walls back up, forcing the frown and downturned lips back onto his face, gutted me.

One more row, and he was there. Flicking through a heavy hardcover book, seemingly focussed on what he was reading, our professor waited for us. He turned, watching as we drew near.

He was a hunter, and we were his prey, inexplicably drawn to him despite the danger he posed.

But I wanted to be caught.

I wanted to be consumed.

Devoured.

My cunt throbbed, another gush of slickness coating the tops of my thighs as I walked. A shiver wracked my body, desperation clawing at me. I needed to be filled, to be pumped full of their cum. I wanted to be marked by them. I wanted them to stake their claim and own me. I wanted to do the same—to claim them and own them right back.

Ezra had walked away from us. I knew he didn't want to, but it didn't matter. He'd hurt me. He'd hurt Flynn, and he'd absolutely shattered Tristan's heart. The three of us needed to reconnect, to solidify our relationship again. There was no way we could put up a united front and fight for our man without it.

And I wanted a fucking to remember for all the ages.

"Here, now," he ordered, pointing to the floor at his feet after slipping the book back onto the shelf and adjusting the books so they were perfectly lined up.

"Yes, professor," I murmured demurely, looking at him through my lashes.

He held his hand out, but I hesitated, innately knowing it was for Flynn to take. My guy walked over to him and slipped his arm around Tristan's waist, leaning into him. With a brush of his lips against Flynn's temple, Tristan groaned. He rubbed the heel of his hand down his hard cock, his growl deep.

"What do you have to say for yourself, kitten?" he asked me.

"I want to taste you." My response was candid. It was a dare for him to react. But he didn't bite in the way I expected. Instead, his eyes flashed, and his lips parted as he sucked in a sharp breath.

I didn't know whether he wanted me to challenge him or not, but he knew who I was. He knew what he was getting when he played with me.

Flynn's eyes widened in surprise when Tristan stated, "You'll swallow everything I give you." His tone was matter-of-fact, as if my swallowing was a condition of his letting me have his cock.

"No." I shook my head, my boldness growing when Flynn closed his eyes, biting back a smile. "I want you to fuck me, to fill me up."

Tristan raised an eyebrow, and Flynn slid his hand to Tristan's cock, palming it just like I wanted to be doing. My insides swooped, want curling low in my belly at the way Tristan looked down at me, all superior and in complete control. But I knew the truth—Flynn was already looking all sexed up, his lips wet from where he'd licked them and his erection poking Tristan's thigh. But it was the way Tristan held Flynn's shirt in a white-knuckled grip that gave away just how on edge he was.

"Why—" Tristan's voice caught, and he cleared his throat before continuing, "Why should I do that, love? You deserve a spanking for the stunt you pulled in class, not a fuck."

He waited for me to answer, letting the silence linger between us. The tension built, the air crackling between the three of us as Flynn slowly rubbed Tristan's cock through the layers of material, and I dropped my bag to the floor.

Smiling innocently at them, I crossed my legs at my ankles as if I was about to curtsey but instead spun around on the balls of my feet. My legs were spread apart by a hand-span, and I looked over my shoulder. With one side of my lips lifted in a smirk, I mimicked his raised eyebrow before bending, flipping my skirt up, and touching my toes. I probably didn't need to lift my skirt—it was short enough that they could see exactly what I had, and didn't have, on underneath it—but I wanted there to be no doubt about what I'd done.

"Oh, hell," Flynn breathed.

"C'mere," Tristan ordered, his voice rough.

The sense of urgency in his tone lit me on fire. I obeyed without question, taking their hands in mine when they reached for me.

"On your knees, my beautiful little slut. You're going to suck me off and get me nice and wet for you." He leaned in closer as if to whisper a secret, but his words were loud enough that Flynn would have no trouble hearing. "Then

I'm going to slide right into your tight little arse and fuck you until you can't walk straight."

"Yes, please," I eagerly agreed. My heart was beating hard, my clit throbbing. My arse constricted, clenching around the toy held in place there. I was already close to coming apart just from his words. I couldn't wait until he actually pulled out the plug and slid inside me.

I was halfway to my knees when Flynn leaned in and murmured, "And while he's doing that, I'm gonna lick that pretty pussy of yours."

I whimpered, a shudder wracking me as I shot to the edge. I hadn't even been touched yet, and I was already about to fire off like a bottle rocket. But I didn't want that. I wanted fireworks—Sydney Harbour on New Year's Eve or New York on the Fourth of July.

Flynn's smirk was wicked, so unlike his sunshiny person-ality that it had me falling the rest of the way to the floor. The carpet was furry under my knees but didn't provide any cushioning, which only seemed to intensify the sensations racing through me. It was as if I was sinking into an alternate reality, my mind detaching from my body. I was operating only on base desire. The warmth of their hands in mine lit me up, their scents as I breathed them in—their arousal and natural musk mingling—until I was lightheaded.

I wanted to be their good girl, their beautiful little slut.

I wanted to spread my legs and let them take me how-ever they desired. I wanted them to fill me, to fuck me. I wanted every hole stretched around their cocks and their fingers. I wanted their mouths on me, their bodies pressed against mine. I wanted it all.

Opening my mouth, I flattened my tongue, waiting for my professor to feed me his cock. Unzipping slowly, he reached inside and freed his erection, the smear of precum at his slit tempting me to steal a taste rather than waiting for him.

But Flynn beat me to it.

He closed his hand around Tristan's dick and jacked him slowly, swiping up the precum beading at his tip with his thumb. Gathering the glistening liquid on his digit, he brought his finger to Tristan's lips. Smearing it over his bottom one, Flynn leaned in and licked it away.

My pulse fluttered in my veins, my heart thudding in my chest as I watched my guys love on each other.

Carding his fingers through Tristan's hair, Flynn pulled him closer, deepening their kiss. Tristan willingly handed over control to him. It was glorious to watch the trust Tristan placed in Flynn blossom. It was a relief too—I knew, without a doubt, that Flynn would never hurt him.

Letting go of Tristan's hand, I braced myself on his thigh. He cupped my face, then brushed my hair off my shoulder, taking care of me and showing me I was his to love even as he kissed Flynn.

I licked him, tasting his salty precum and humming as I nuzzled his heavy balls with my cheek. Breathing him in, I played with the seam of his sac, teasing him until he was drawn up tight. Moving back to his cock, I took my time, tracing the veins and savouring the teasing drops that had dripped down his straining length.

But I needed Flynn too. I unzipped his white jeans and tugged out his cock. Drawing them together, their cock-heads touching, I licked and kissed them, sucking on both their heads. Next, I jacked them off, rubbing their lengths against each other before sucking on Tristan, then Flynn. I kept going, swapping between them until steady streams of precum were dripping from their slits and their breathing was stilted.

I wrapped my lips around Tristan's crown and slid down his length, savouring his musk until my nose was buried in his short pubes and he was cradled by my throat. I wanted this forever—me on my knees with all the power, and him taking what he needed. I swallowed, and he cried out softly, gasping as I ever so slowly pulled off.

"Up, love," Tristan begged. "I need you."

I scrambled to my feet, then he spun me around to face the shelves and blanketed me with his body. His warmth surrounded me, his strength enveloping me as I sank into his embrace. He was gruff and grumpy, and he'd been on the brink of losing it today in class, and yet there was no-where I felt safer than in his and Flynn's arms.

"Brace yourself, kitten."

Flynn fell to his knees, crawling between my spread legs. He kissed a line up my thigh, stopping to lick my essence that was coating my thighs. His soft lips and smooth face were such a contrast to the wall of muscle and rough stubble behind me. But that was how they worked; they were in perfect counterpoint.

Tristan held me tight like he was too scared to let me go now that I was in his arms.

"I love you," I whispered.

He didn't answer me right away, instead burying his face in the hair at my nape and breathing long and slow. He trembled around me, but I wasn't sure whether it was need or emotion driving him. His hard cock was nestled at the small of my back, but when I reached for him, he grasped my wrist, moving my hand to the shelf in front of me.

"Let me take care of you, love." His voice was low, barely a whisper, but there was an undeniable plea in his tone.

I'd been right. He needed this as much as I did.

He slid his hand up the inside of my hamstring, then followed with his fingers, brushing the plug stretching me. It was ribbed inside, rubbing every nerve ending in just the right way every time I moved. With the barest touch, Tristan lit me up like a Christmas tree, my cunt clenching and a ripple of sensation passing through me. Flynn hummed, the vibration of his voice against my clit ratcheting up my arousal to a whole new level. I breathed hard, biting back a moan as Flynn slid his fingers to my entrance, teasing me with gentle touches as Tristan brushed his fingers over my plug once more.

I was electricity and fire. Sensation. I was already coming apart at the seams. Desperation stole over me, my legs turning to jelly and my cunt clenching hard, begging to be filled.

I cried out, needing more.

"Shh," Tristan murmured in my ear, sliding his big hand up my back until he flicked open the halter holding the top half of my dress up.

My tits tumbled out, the cold wash of the air-conditioning pebbling my nipples. Tristan palmed my boob. He pinched my nipple, and I bit back a moan.

"You need to be quiet, my pretty little slut. Do you want me to get caught? Hmm? Or should I gag you?"

I couldn't help my whimper as Flynn thrust his fingers inside me, stretching me perfectly and tagging my G-spot dead-on. My cunt spasmed, clenching him tight to stop his retreat, and he huffed out a quiet laugh. He bit down on my clit, the pain like starbursts behind my closed eyes. I cried out again, my hips moving of their own volition as I rode Flynn's thick fingers and begged, "Please."

I let out a sob when Tristan pulled his hands away from me, but within seconds he was back, nudging my lips with his rolled-up silk tie. I bit down on it, grateful that it muffled my cries as Flynn took advantage of the snug fit between the plug and his fingers.

"I want your hole, Zali. I want to slide my dick inside you and fuck you like I own you."

I nodded, desperate for him to do it. My body was jittery, my nerve endings firing hard. I was on the edge, ready to come, desperately clawing for it but at the same time resisting as much as I could. I wanted—no, needed—him inside me.

"After I come inside you, I'm going to plug you back up. I want you to carry me inside you, my sexy little cum slut."

I moaned. Fuck, his words. Combined with Flynn's fingers and mouth, and I was powerless to stop my orgasm. "Oh, fuck," I cried out around his tie as my senses were obliterated and the rushing began, my cunt tightening and waves of bliss radiating outward until my legs were barely holding me up. Just as it began to wane, Tristan gripped the base of the plug and tugged it, renewing it with a ferocity that stole my breath.

My head fell back against his shoulder, my back arching.

"Yeah, that's perfect, love," Tristan growled in my ear, yanking the plug free and bending his knees until his dick notched at my stretched hole.

"Please," I begged around the tie, canting my hips so there was no doubt what I wanted.

He didn't hesitate, pressing forward in one long slow thrust that had my eyes crossing and my breath catching. He was bigger than the plug—thicker and longer. The stretch bordered on painful, but it soon turned into ecstasy when he withdrew and snapped his hips forward, fucking me hard and fast. With every withdrawal, Flynn pumped his fingers into me and sucked and bit my clit.

I went onto my tiptoes, white-knuckling the metal shelf as my body climbed higher and higher. Tristan grunted as my channel gripped him tighter. He squeezed my hip. He would no doubt leave bruises, but I loved it. I needed it. Flynn's hum vibrated through me, taking me higher.

He reached up, sliding his hand along my front until he could grasp my tit, twisting my nipple as he bit me. I screamed, rocketing off into outer space as my soul left my body and my world darkened at the edges. My entire being narrowed down to my orgasm blasting through me.

Tristan growled, his bitten-back shout loud in my ear as he bucked into me and shot his load deep into my arse. The heat of his cum scalded me, painting my channel and marking me in the most carnal of ways. I was his and he was mine.

He rested his forehead on my shoulder, our breathing hard and fast. But Flynn's tortured groan had me reaching for him, tugging on his hair to try to get him to stand.

He took the hint and crawled out from between my legs. "Jack me off, Zee. Please."

With shaking hands, I pulled the tie away from my mouth. "Fuck my arse, too. I want you both inside me."

They treated me like a doll, manoeuvring me in exactly the way they wanted. Tristan slid to the floor, lying back, and tugging me forward until I was straddling his face. Clenching my arse, I tried desperately not to let his cum drip from me. I wanted to keep every drop inside my hole with me. His mouth went to my cunt, licking me and sending every nerve ending into overdrive. I was already on edge again, my body needy and primed to explode.

Flynn tilted my hips and notched the head of his dick at my opening. He was panting, his control about to snap, but he held that fucker tight, always reining himself in to make sure he didn't hurt me. But I was already stretched and well used, and I wanted him with the same ferocity that had overcome Tristan.

"Fuck me, Flynn. Slam that cock into my arse and give me your cum. I need it."

Just like that, his control snapped. Gripping my waist, he drove forward, punching his hips until he was buried to the hilt.

His hand landed on the shelf next to mine, and he ground his dick deeper in me, lighting up my nerve endings with his piercings.

"Fuck," I breathed. "Harder."

He obliged, slowly withdrawing before slamming inside me. Again and again I cried out until Tristan had the tie shoved back in my mouth. The only noises in the deathly quiet library after that were the slap of skin, muted cries, and Flynn's grunts.

I shivered, my orgasm racing at me like a freight train. With every movement, Flynn took me higher, and as his cock swelled, stretching me even more, I detonated. My cunt contracted hard, my channel gripping Flynn like a glove as he emptied his balls inside me. Shivers wracked my body, and I moaned. Ecstasy washed over me, taking me higher and higher until I was orbiting the earth.

I never wanted this moment to end, but Flynn was too quick to pull out. I choked out a sob until gentle fingers were at my hole, pushing cum back inside me. The cool silicone plug followed, my arse gripping it in place like a baby does a pacifier, filling me once more.

FIFTEEN

Zali

I was tired and sore after a long day and night. Every one of my muscles ached from dancing and three rounds of epic sex. I'd be an idiot to complain about the non-stop orgasms; my blood was still thrumming, and a delicious tingle danced over my skin whenever the silk of my jumpsuit brushed my nipples or my cunt. That wasn't my problem.

It was the headache. The thump of the music from the DJ's set was still reverberating around my skull, and I was overthinking things. Hard.

It was a combination of everything. All of it was circling around my head in a confusing cyclone of what-ifs and whys.

The night had started innocently enough. Cara asked Flynn and me out for drinks in class. She had free drinks vouchers at a pub on the river. Ry, Flynn, and I had gone, but Flynn had also mentioned it to Tristan on the sly, telling him to accidentally run into us. Tristan had asked Ezra out to talk, and after Flynn and I had danced nonstop for hours, putting on a show for both of them, it made for an uncomfortably hard night. Ezra's self-control had snapped, and he'd caved, taking out his lust-fuelled frustration on my willing body until I could barely stand.

When he'd left this morning, he'd said he couldn't have anything further to do with me, with us. Then he'd followed Tristan to the pub. He'd been standoffish at first, but after our argument, I'd almost walked out. The only reason I hadn't was Cara. Tristan had bought a round, giving me a couple of shots of whiskey and Ezra a few more. It had gone straight to my head, but Ezra was just tipsy enough to lower his guard.

He'd allowed Tristan to touch him while we'd been sitting together listening to Cara and Ry talk. It killed Tristan every time he'd flinched, every time he'd moved away, but the alcohol loosened him up. It relaxed him to the point where he was happy and handsy. Tristan had practically sobbed with relief, holding him like he was the most precious thing he'd ever laid eyes on, while looking at me with an apology in his eyes.

Tristan was dropping Ezra off and I knew he'd come to us the moment he could. It was unfair to force him to choose. So I wouldn't. But it tore me apart to know that we couldn't have everything. Tristan wanted Ezra with a soul-deep yearning. Ezra did too. But as ridiculous as it sounded, Ezra was more stubborn than Tristan. He needed to let go of all the shit going on in his head before he would take what was being freely given.

It was obvious how much they loved each other from the way they'd come together that morning. Then, at the pub when Ezra forgot why he couldn't be with us, the shy smiles he'd shot us and the way he leaned into Tristan's touch was adorable. I still hated him, but maybe I could forgive him if he could make Tristan happy.

I should encourage the two of them to throw caution to the wind. There was no issue with them being together. There were no best friend standing in the way, no career-ending consequences for them if they dated.

Maybe I should step away.

But it wasn't that easy.

It wasn't just my decision to make.

It affected Flynn too.

The way Ezra had all but eye fucked Flynn when we were dancing told me that maybe he didn't just want Tristan. Dragging me into the gardens, stripping me and frantically fucking me until I was screaming wasn't exactly subtle either.

Eventually we'd dropped Cara off at her dorm before heading back to the yacht. My breath caught as we walked up the jetty and I spied Tristan and Ezra waiting for us. Earlier tonight, Ezra had told me we couldn't be together while he was still buried inside me. I'd told him exactly what I thought of him and stormed off in a huff. He'd chased after me, holding my jumpsuit out and begging me to get dressed before I found myself under arrest for indecent exposure. I'd only agreed to avoid a second night in a jail cell. Otherwise I would have told him to fuck right off and strutted my bare arse back into the throng of people.

But there he was, leaning against one of the pylons. He was the big spoon to Tristan's little one as they stared out at the lights shimmering off the rippling water in the distance.

Play it cool, Zali, I coached myself. Ry squeezed my shoulder as he shifted in front of me to get the gangway chain, and Flynn growled as he cottoned on to who was waiting for us.

I stared at Ezra silently, shaking my head. I wanted to give him a piece of my mind, but the self-loathing and shame in his gaze had me biting my tongue. We weren't going to sort through anything without being adults about it. As much as he'd hurt me, and as shitty as his behaviour had been, I needed to be the bigger person. Not for me—if it was just me, I'd tell him to fuck off—but for Tristan and Flynn. I'd do it for them.

I sighed. "Come on up," I invited reluctantly, gesturing to the gangplank. "I could do with a tea and some painkillers. You guys want anything?"

"Tea would be great," Tristan agreed while Ezra reached out to help me onto the yacht.

I hesitated before taking his hand, and Flynn smiled softly at me. At least I knew that he appreciated me making an effort for them.

"Just water for me, thanks," Ezra murmured.

Flynn followed me into the galley and filled a glass of cold water before helping to brew the tea.

"Where do you think this is going?" Flynn asked, his voice soft and unsure. I hated that he was so uncertain. "Did you and Ezra manage to iron anything out while you were off together?"

"There wasn't much talking to be honest," I replied, skipping over our argument. Flynn had gathered enough from my body language to figure out I was pissed. I didn't need to go into detail with him now, not when my head was pounding and I desperately needed sleep. We'd nut it out soon enough.

But for now, I watched his reaction. Nerves bounced around in my belly as he stepped in closer to me. When a sly grin tilted his lips up, the breath whooshed out of my lungs.

He leaned in closer, our bodies only a hair's breadth apart. He ran his nose up my throat, and my nipples hardened, the silk of my jumpsuit brushing the sensitive nubs as a shiver rippled through me.

He brushed his lips over my pulse point. "I can smell the sex on you. It's delicious."

I swayed on my feet, arching into his barely there touch. He grasped my butt and hauled me against him, grinding the erection trapped in his tight jeans against my belly. Massaging my cheeks, he dipped a finger between them and brushed it over my fabric-covered hole.

"Please," I begged, pushing back into his touch. I couldn't resist being stuffed full, but my tender ring protested, a sting arcing through me. I hissed, and Flynn gentled his teasing, sucking a mark into my throat as he rubbed against me. "Second thoughts, my arse is off limits for the rest of the night."

"I can work with that." Flynn hummed, the noise vibrating through his chest into mine lighting up my nerve endings like when his tongue connected with my clit. He added, "Tell me what Ezra did."

I flicked the shoulder strap off, letting it fall to my elbow and exposing my breast. "He stripped me off just like this. I was standing in the gardens completely naked—"

"You loved it."

A shiver passed through my body, my clit throbbing at the memory. "I did. It was like a game of cat and mouse, knowing we could get caught. I was so wet."

"I like these," he rasped, his finger brushing over the twin hickeys Ezra'd left on my tits.

"So do I," I admitted.

"Keep going," he encouraged. "Tell me what he did."

"He slid inside me, and I begged him to fuck me harder."

Flynn reached up and pinched my nipple before sliding his hand down and cupping my cunt. "Did you come?"

"Yes," I gasped as he rubbed my mound, pressing his thumb against my clit. I moaned, widening my stance so he could play. Licks of sensation shot through me, my cunt juices wetting my lips.

"Good girl. I can feel how wet you are again. Is it Ezra's cum in there too?"

I shook my head and ground my hips against his hand. "He felt my arse. Felt how soft I was. I told him you and Tristan had fucked me there. I wanted him to blow inside me too. I wanted to carry around his cum like I'd been carrying yours."

"Did he push inside you? Did he feel how tight you are?"

The rushing started, and my core clenched. "Yes," I breathed, half of me begging him not to stop, the other half revelling in the memory of Ezra spinning me around and impaling me in a single stroke with his iron-hard cock. He'd stuffed me full, stretched me tight around his dick, and gave me another orgasm before he shot his load inside me, his already girthy cock thickening and painting me with hot jets of cum.

Flynn pressed harder.

I hovered on the edge.

That moment of weightlessness stretching out.

Then I fell. I surrendered to the rush.

My body locked up tight as I came on a silent scream. Flynn worked my clit, not stopping until I slumped against him.

"I love that we can breed you. Fill you up until our cum is sliding down your legs. It's hot as heck," Flynn growled against my throat. He licked my pulse point, and a shiver rippled through me, raising gooseflesh on my skin. "I want Ezra to do the same thing to me. I want him to fill me up."

"Can I watch?" I asked as Flynn gripped my tit and dropped his mouth to my nipple, flicking his tongue over the pebbled skin. I threaded my fingers through his silky hair and gripped tight, holding him in place as electric shocks spiralled through me once more.

He sucked me, licking my flesh before releasing me with a pop. I gulped in a breath, my heart thumping against my ribcage as I rubbed myself against him like a cat.

"Hell yeah. But until then, let's get these boys their drinks." Flynn pulled back and slapped my arse playfully before wheeling around and scooping tea leaves into the pot and gesturing to the kettle. "The water's ready."

I blinked, my mouth agape. He'd rendered me speechless.

Without missing a beat, he added, "You might want to pull up your top unless you want Ry wishing he wasn't so stubborn."

Wordlessly, I lifted the strap to my shoulder and took the teapot out to the deck.

Tristan and Ezra were each sitting on an armchair while Ry was on one end of the three-seater couch. There was a tense silence between them, one that continued when I served up their drinks.

I leaned back against the soft cushions and ignored the elephant in the room. My mind drifted as I concentrated on the peacefulness of the marina so late at night. The roads were quiet, the restaurants silent. I yearned to be out on the water again, to see Jumpinpin and go diving. I wanted to feel the rumble of the engines under me and hear nothing but the crashing waves at midnight. I wanted to see stars instead of people and dolphins and dugong rather than cars.

I wanted to ditch my clothes for an entire fucking week.

But being moored at the marina was convenient and, for the moment, necessary.

Resting my feet up on the coffee table, I tangled my legs with Flynn's and leaned against Ry. I closed my eyes and let the lap of the water lull my thoughts into slowing.

We were crossing the seaway, the swell big but not choppy. The yacht rose and fell, riding the swell as we powered out to the ocean.

Asher laughed, his giggle-snort unlike any other person's I'd heard. I loved hearing it. I was bathed in bright sunlight, basking in happiness as I chased Ash. Mum called out, "Zali, stop running, honey."

"Ash is running too," I whined.

Movement caught my eye in the water—a fin, then two more. There was a pod of dolphins swimming alongside the yacht. I squealed. "Dad, look!"

He swung me high, and I shrieked again as he effortlessly planted me on his shoulders. I pressed my fists against my mouth and vibrated with excitement, unable to contain the oohs and aahs every time they surfaced.

But like a cloud covering the sun, a shadow was cast over us.

A wash of unease swept over me.

A sense that something wasn't right.

Colours faded, turning sepia like an old photograph.

I clutched Dad, holding him tight. Fear stole through me.

I needed them safe. My heart stuttered. Where were Mum and Ash?

Frantically looking around, I searched for them. Asher was there, standing on the gunwale, balancing on the edge without hands. He laughed, but the sound was sad.

I reached for him, wanting to pull him back from the edge.

But I was falling.

Water rushed up at me, enveloping me.

The shock of cold froze my breath.

Bubbles erupted before me as the air was punched out of my lungs.

He was sinking, falling deeper. But he wasn't moving. He needed to kick, to save himself.

"Asher," I screamed, but no words came out. Salt water filled my mouth, then my lungs as I inhaled, trying to scream again.

He looked up, his kind eyes filled with pleading. "Keep looking," he whispered.

He sank.

Drifted from me into the darkness.

I followed, kicking my legs as hard as I could.

But with every stroke, with every kick, he slipped further away from me.

I cried out, begging him to come back until all I could see was inky blackness.

He was gone.

Hands were on me, shaking me. "Zee, baby," Flynn cried. "Wake up."

My arms were gripped harder, the shake violent enough to rip me from my nightmare. I gasped, a broken cry shuddering from my lips as I jolted awake. Tristan was on his knees in front of me, his hands on my thighs. Ezra was next to him, his hand on my face, wiping away my tears as Ry grasped my arms and shook.

"Shh, baby girl. We've got you," Ry crooned. I sobbed, curling in on myself.

Ry enveloped me in his arms, pulling me onto his lap. "It's okay, I'm here. We're all here."

My tears soaked his shirt as he rocked me gently, none of my guys letting go. Never letting go.

"I was in the water with him," I cried, my voice a broken whisper. "I couldn't save him."

"It's okay, baby girl. It's not your fault."

"It's not a memory, love," Tristan reminded me, rubbing my back. "You didn't fail him."

"He told me to keep looking." I looked at them through my tears.

"Zee," Flynn whispered, cupping my face and resting his forehead against mine. Ry shifted, wrapping his arm around Flynn. I whimpered, but Flynn hugged me close, snuggling us both into Ry's chest. "You've made him so proud. You've made your mum proud too. You've done everything you can to honour their memories."

But I hadn't. Not really. I had more data, more records to read through and sort out. I had a trail of information that I needed to check. And here I was going out for drinks and fucking everyone in sight.

Wiping my tears with the heel of my hand, I sucked in a breath and pulled on my big girl panties. Fuck crying. It wouldn't do me any good. Action. That's what was needed.

"I need to get back to work." I went to pull away, but Ry tightened his arms around me.

"Not tonight, baby girl. You need rest."

I shifted, tugging out of his arms, and shook my head, clenching my hands into fists so they wouldn't see me shaking. "No. I've missed something. I need to keep looking."

"Come to bed, Zee," Flynn pleaded, tucking a lock of my hair behind my ear.

His touch was gentle, but I pulled away. If I let him—or any of them—near me, I would shatter.

"I'll stay up with you," Tristan volunteered just as Ezra gestured inside and said, "How can I help?"

"You can see if I'm misinterpreting anything in the coroner's report," Ry replied. "I want to reconstruct a timeline and map for their trip."

"I'll take another look at the liquidator's report," Flynn volunteered. "There were a few things Jude said in class that haven't been sitting right with me."

"I agree," Tristan added. "I'll help you."

Tears filled my eyes again, and I blinked them away. These men. My men. "Thank you," I whispered.

"Go and get into something more comfortable, kitten," Tristan instructed. "We've got a lot to get through."

Ry and Ezra got set up around the table with printed maps of the Broadwater and coastline down to Cook Island, folders of information, and a roll of paper taped to the wall.

I led Tristan and Flynn to my office so we could pour over the data we already had—the liquidator's report, the financials for the company, and the investor's details—in conjunction with the data I'd downloaded from the Reserve Bank.

I couldn't believe that barely twenty-four hours had passed since I got it—it felt like a lifetime ago—but now that I had the database records, I was using every bit of data.

"I think we need to look at our assumptions again," I murmured, examining the timeline I'd put up on the wall, filled out with the new notes from our hours-long session. Rubbing my tired eyes, I sighed. I'd tried to push aside the feeling, the lingering black cloud that had hovered since my dream, but it was only getting stronger. Like I was tracking a scent, my nose was firmly planted to the ground. But I didn't know what I was looking for, only that there was something. It was frustrating as fuck.

"What do you mean?" Flynn queried.

"Nothing about the company failing was suspicious. The liquidator concluded that it was simply a sign of the times. It's what I expected; Mum was innocent. So why are we still considering this? Why is the feeling that I've missed something only growing?"

"It's personal," Tristan replied, coming to kneel in front of my chair. He interlaced his fingers with mine, his warm hands comforting me when I needed it most. "You're shaken up from your dream. Maybe you should try to get some sleep and consider things in the morning."

I shook my head and leaned forward, snuggling into his shoulder. I was exhausted, utterly spent. But I had to keep going.

"I'm still not convinced the guy from the US doing the liquidation isn't a red flag," Flynn interjected contemplatively, as he shuffled papers. "Take a look at this notation in the limitations set out in the liquidator's report."

Tristan took the papers and, without moving me, began leafing through them. "You're right, angel. This basically confirms what I was thinking too. Accounting rules aren't standardized across the world. Tax and company laws between the United States and here are entirely different. The report excludes liability for certain errors made by the liquidators. There are always limitation of liability clauses in these kinds of reports, but having this particular clause in there isn't normal. It smacks of a dereliction of duty caused by the American liquidator being given free rein when it should have been run by an Australian expert."

Flynn huffed in disgust. "Hey, the amount of money lost justified a full audit too."

I pulled back and gnawed on my lip, contemplating how to explain to them that I had more data when as far as they knew, I hadn't gotten anything from the Reserve Bank. Stalling, I stood and led Tristan over to the couches they'd been working on.

"I've been able to reconstruct some of the company's transactions. I think we'll get close to doing a full audit of at least parts of the business."

Tristan blinked and swallowed hard. I pinned him with my gaze and silently pleaded with him not to ask the question how. He looked away, and a moment later his shoulders dropped as he exhaled.

"Do I want to know?" he murmured.

Flynn threaded their fingers together in a move that was a plea for Tristan not to leave that also lent him strength.

"Please don't ask me," I begged.

Tristan flexed his jaw, biting hard as if he was trying to get his temper under control. He squeezed Flynn's hand and shook his head in annoyance. I had never promised that I'd give up doing what I did for a living, but I did promise to protect him, and that meant keeping him completely oblivious to anything that even bordered on illegal.

"What parts can we reconstruct?" Flynn asked, moving us along.

I breathed a sigh of relief when Tristan focussed back on him.

"Withdrawals and deposits by customers and most of the investments too, for a limited period at least."

The room was silent for the longest time, the lap of the water against the hull the only sound drifting in from the open window. The dawn's rays were lighting the sky, shafts of sunlight beginning to stream in and warm us.

Tristan cleared his throat. "I've been working on something different while we've been going through all this." He spun around the old laptop of mine that he'd been using. "I've been trying to find some of the senior staff at Reimag-INC so I can interview them. There aren't a lot left. Two died, a few seemed to have simply walked away from the workforce—they don't have profiles on LinkedIn or anything like that—and the others have names that are too common to be able to narrow them down by searching for them on social media. I found a few who could be them, but their presence is either locked down or just don't give me enough information to rule them out."

"How many have you been able to identify?" Flynn asked.

"None." He shook his head, and a pit in my gut opened up.

"Does that make it more or less suspicious?" I asked, dreading the answer. On the surface, the company was operating well until Mum went missing. Things deteriorated rapidly from there, returns on investments plummeting and money disappearing faster than the speed of light. But it wasn't all as it seemed.

"It's not all that surprising, I suppose. The Gold Coast is fairly transient when it comes to its corporate workforce. A lot of people leave for the bigger cities or go overseas after working here."

"Do we know how many people left in the lead up to the company going under?" Flynn questioned. "We should try to find them."

"Realistically, we need to figure out how long the company was having problems previous to going under before we identify which employees to concentrate on finding," Tristan lamented, his elbows on the table and his chin resting in the heel of his hand.

I sighed. I was reconstructing the accounts based on the transaction records I'd managed to pull from the Reserve Bank. "With the benefit of hindsight, months," I answered.

"Their payments back to investors started slowing down in the June of that year. By September it was in crisis."

A knock on the door sounded, and Ry stepped in, effortlessly continuing our conversation. I wondered how long he'd been standing there. "Do you think Rosa would have known?"

"She had to have," Tristan responded, and Flynn and I both nodded our agreement.

"From what we've gathered from her diaries, Mum had her thumb on everything going on. She was the centre of it all."

"So keep digging. I think there's a reason why things aren't adding up." Ezra was leaning on the door jamb, his hands in his pockets and his ankles crossed. He looked like the picture of relaxation, but the dark circles under his eyes and the tight lines around his eyes and mouth were a dead giveaway.

I cocked my head to the side and waited for him to continue.

"You're now seeing the things that the investors were experiencing. Maybe the gut feeling you have isn't unfounded. It's not so open-and-shut." He shrugged, downplaying his words.

"What?" I flicked my gaze to Tristan and Flynn before looking at Ezra again. "Open-and-shut?"

He smiled as if I was finally cluing onto something. "Yeah. Think of it like this—a director starts up this great company, people invest and make a fortune, but the economy changes. The company goes broke, and the director dies in quick succession. The investigations are wrapped up in a neat little bow, but there were shortcuts taken and other things like where the wreckage was found that just don't make sense. Now that you're looking into it, you're finding those loose threads. Keep pulling at them and see what unravels. Keep looking just like Ash told you."

"Mum died before the company went under."

"It appears that way." Ezra nodded. "But I think your parents shielded you from a lot, Zali, and it's possible that you were too young to understand what was happening too. There was a lot of bad press and protests by investors who were demanding their money be refunded before your mum died."

"Dad knew," I rasped, stating the obvious. My gut sank. He'd said that if he was on the yacht, maybe he could have saved them. He'd told me that after Mum went missing, the company imploded. He'd sold everything that had Mum's name on it and asked the solicitors to make it all go away.

"He wasn't oblivious. But Zali, I don't think he appreciated just how serious it was." He paused and looked at Tristan, waiting for something. When Tristan nodded, Ezra added, "We don't think he knew about the threats."

My heart stopped and my lungs seized. "Threats?" I wheezed. What threats? No one had ever mentioned threats being made against Mum. My gut sank, a pit opening up and queasiness washing over me.

If Dad had known about them, if he'd suspected Mum could have been targeted, did he push the police to investigate? Did the police know? How did Ezra find out? If the police had treated it like a murder instead of an accident, would they have found evidence? Would they have kept looking? An accident was the easy choice. It also directed the blame onto Mum. But there were too many coincidences to be disregarded.

"Ry, do you think you'd be able to narrow down where the yacht went down based on where the wreckage was found?"

"Assuming it washed up at that beach, I might be able to, but if it was towed in, there's no chance," Ry responded, shaking his head and looking at me dubiously. "Why?"

"We need to find their remains to know whether they were targeted." I looked between the four men standing and sitting before me.

"Zee," Flynn started, his voice full of sympathy.

But I held my hand up, stopping him. "If there were threats and they got ignored, Mum could have been murdered. Their killer is walking around on the streets while my mum and brother are lying on the bottom of the ocean. I know it's not the focus of what we're doing here, but I need justice."

"If we can get it, we will. This podcast isn't the be all and end all of this investigation, love." Tristan reminded me, his voice allowing no room for dispute. "I agree, if there's a chance it wasn't an accident, we need to try to find where the wreckage might have gone down so we can raise it and get it analyzed." He winced before he added, "I don't know how expensive that is, but I'd need significantly more research funding to make it happen. It'll take a lot to get a grant for that, but I'll find a way," he promised.

I shot him a grateful smile and replied, "Thank you, but it's not necessary. I'll fund it if we ever get to that point. But before we get there, I need to know what Dad knows."

SIXTEEN

Zali

Ezra moved into the room and sat on the coffee table before me, taking my hands into his. "Zali, I'm 100 percent certain that your dad would have pushed for the investigation to continue if he had any inkling of threats being made."

"How do you know about them?" I asked, my voice devoid of any emotion. It was as if I'd been disconnected from my own body and shrouded in numbness.

"Tristan found them. When he—"

"No," Tristan warned.

Ezra huffed. "No, nothing. They need to know."

"We need to know what?" Flynn volleyed back.

"When Tristan received a death threat himself, he started looking into who it might have been. The investors of ReimagINC were ruled out pretty quickly. Why would you threaten someone for uncovering the truth around your lost money? Staff didn't have all that much in entitlements unpaid, so we ruled them out—"

"And you're wanting to interview them? Are you nuts?" I exploded. "You give this to me, and I investigate."

"With what, Zali? It was a piece of paper delivered to my front door."

"In your secure building that has cameras and a fob key entrance. I'll find something." I got up and paced the room. I was vibrating with righteous indignation. How dare someone try to hurt my man. Anger stole through me, and I gritted my teeth, ready to gut anyone who would even think about hurting him. I'd use a rusty knife.

Pointing at Tristan, I ordered, "You're off this project. Until I can find out who issued that threat, you're not looking at another thing to do with my mother or ReimagINC."

Tristan laughed—flat out chuckled—and shook his head, coming to stand before me. He gripped my arms firmly and gazed at me, his eyes full of something unspoken. Something deep and filled with emotion. "You don't need to protect me from that, Zali."

"That's where you're wrong. I know the sort of people who issue death threats, and I promise you, you can't handle them," I growled, shaking out of his grip.

He let me go but stepped closer until I was looking up at him—Tristan was still in shoes while I wore only a pair of loose socks and an oversized jumper. He cupped my face with both hands and leaned down to kiss me reverently, his tongue sweeping into my mouth and short-circuiting every one of my brain cells. "This isn't your responsibility," he breathed against my lips.

"I'm making it my responsibility. I can't risk you, Tristan. I love you too much to see you get hurt."

He slid his hands down my body and up under my jumper to my bare arse, squeezing it tight. "I fucking love it when you get all growly and say you love me," he rumbled.

He lifted me, and I carded my fingers in his hair and wrapped my legs around him, holding him to me as he crashed his lips to mine. This time his tongue owned my mouth, invading every one of my senses until I was panting. "I love you too," he breathed against my throat as he nipped and licked me.

I moaned, wanting him inside me again. I was desperate, needing to banish the fear from my mind while pushing away the memories of how paralyzing the grief was when you lost someone you loved.

Like a mind reader, Tristan slid his fingers along my entrance, spreading the juices leaking from my cunt. "Want to fuck you right here against the wall."

"Do it," I breathed. "I want all of them to watch you. Claim me."

He set me down, and I sobbed out a protest.

"Strip. Let them see how gorgeous you are."

I did, letting the warm sweater fall to the floor before tugging off my socks. I stood before him completely naked. Tristan eyed me like a snack he wanted to devour, and my cunt clenched in anticipation.

He pushed me up against the wall and fell to his knees, hooking my leg over his shoulder. I whimpered when he blew warm air on my lips and sneaked his tongue out to lick me. He hummed as he connected with my clit, tasting me and sending a delicious vibration through my body. I arched my back, threading my fingers into his hair as my empty cunt clenched and begged to be filled.

"Mmm, you want me inside you, don't you, love? I can feel how tight you are."

"Yes," I pleaded, the others' eyes on me ramping up my desire. Standing there naked with a group of them who could all pin me down and fuck me until I was completely boneless—like they'd already been doing for the last day—drove me higher.

My chest expanded, filling with oxygen as I sucked in a breath. I wanted hands and mouths on my tits too. I wanted them to possess me, to use me until I was fucking dripping.

I still had cum inside my arse. Now I wanted it everywhere.

"Pinch your nipples like a good girl. Get them nice and hard. Let your men see how much you love to fuck."

I looked around the room, and every eye was on me. I basked in it, watching as their cocks got harder. For me. They wanted me. Even Ry, who'd walked away every time I got naked, was sporting an obvious erection.

Their desire ramped up my own. My cunt juices leaked from my core, and Tristan eagerly lapped them up, sending licks of sensation through me.

But as much as I wanted to be painted in their cum and for them to fill every hole, I wanted something else too. I wanted Flynn to experience what it was like to sit on Ezra's dick. I wanted to watch his arsehole get stretched like he'd seen happen to mine countless times. I wanted to see him be stuffed full and come as hard as I did. I wanted to share it with him, and I knew Flynn wanted it just as bad.

"Want to watch Ezra fuck Flynn," I breathed, pinching my nipples like Tristan had ordered. My nerve endings were a direct line to my clit, electrifying me every time I pinched myself. I locked my glassy-eyed gaze on Flynn's as a smile stretched his lips and he palmed his cock through his white jeans.

"You want to watch Ezra stretch Flynn? See him sink his cock into our angel?"

"Fuck yes," I groaned, shuddering when Tristan bit my clit as I simultaneously tugged on my nipples. Every inch of me was getting more sensitive the more we played.

Ry stood and blatantly adjusted himself before striding toward the spot where I was standing right next to the door. But I didn't want him to go.

"Ry, please. Stay."

"I'm not part of this orgy," he responded, his voice a mix of resignation and blunt honesty.

"You could be."

"Yeah," he answered, but his flat tone screamed no.

He strode out like a man on a mission, and my heart sank.

But Tristan was good at distractions.

He slid his fingers into my cunt and curled them, hitting my G-spot on the first pump. I gasped, then moaned as I watched Ezra at war with himself. He wanted this, wanted us. His body wavered closer to Flynn, and he reached for our man but dropped his hands before Flynn could step into them. He squeezed his eyes closed and shook his head as if he was trying to persuade himself to walk away.

But Flynn wasn't having it. He stepped forward and cupped his cheek, whispering something to Ezra that I couldn't hear.

Whatever he said melted Ezra's resistance, and he tugged Flynn into his arms. Agonisingly slowly, Ezra popped open each button and peeled him out of his tight shirt. He kissed a line down his throat as he moved his hands to Flynn's jeans. Within seconds, Flynn was naked and Ezra's fingers were brushing his lips.

"Get them good and wet, sweet boy."

The breath whooshed from my lungs, and Tristan rested his forehead against my hip, his shoulders sagging with relief. I hadn't realized that we were both holding our breaths while Ezra made his decision.

"Describe what you're seeing, Zali," Tristan encouraged, his voice a deep rasp that rumbled through me like a thunderstorm.

"Oh fuck," I breathed as Tristan swirled his tongue over my clit, sending shocks of sensation over me. "Ezra's playing with Flynn's hole, softening it up all nicely."

"So hot and tight," Ezra groaned as he pushed a finger inside him to the first knuckle. "God, I can't fucking wait to have you wrapped around my dick."

"Me neither," Flynn moaned, spreading his legs wider and canting his hips.

"Flynn's arse is sucking Ezra in like he's desperate for it." I cried out as Tristan circled my hole.

"Bit like you, my pretty little cum slut."

Flynn groaned, "Want you so much."

Ezra mimicked Tristan's position, falling to his knees and sucking Flynn's pierced monster to the back of his throat. My sweet boyfriend cried out, threading his fingers into Ezra's hair and thrusting in shallow pushes as Ezra added a second finger, pumping deeper than he had before.

Flynn shuddered, and that thread of control slipped as he thrust harder into Ezra's mouth. A garbled response sounded, and Flynn choked out a cry, pumping deeper again.

My breath caught in my throat as Ry reappeared at the doorway, holding a clear bottle. "Flynn, catch," he called and tossed it, stepping back the way he came.

Before he crossed the threshold, I grasped his arm.

If Ry wanted to, he could easily pull away, but he didn't move. He didn't even breathe.

"Be with us," I begged.

He exhaled and let me slip my hand into his. He was connected to us, a part of what we were becoming.

Tristan plunged another finger inside me, and I cried out, pinching my nipple harder with my free hand and rocking my hips as I rode his face. My skin was buzzing, my clit throbbing as Tristan worked me over. I was on the edge, struggling to keep my eyes open, but I wouldn't miss the feast of debauchery before me for the world.

Tristan twisted his fingers inside me, lighting me up, and Ry squeezed my hand. Our gazes clashed, but Ry looked away quickly, his eyes dropping to my tits. He licked his lips, and I watched as he used every ounce of willpower he possessed not to latch onto me. But then he turned to Flynn and Ezra, and he grimaced. His expression said one thing, but he'd gripped his cock tight, his body reacting in a way his mind perhaps wasn't ready to do. The decadent scene before me—Flynn's arse stretched around Ezra's fingers and his cock down my boy scout police officer's throat— sent me hurtling over the edge. I cried out, riding the wave of ecstasy as it crashed into me like a tsunami.

Fireworks lit up behind my closed eyelids until I forced them open, needing to see my men before me, the five of us together, even if Ry wasn't naked and slaking his lust with us.

Ezra swiped up the lube bottle that had fallen to the floor, coating his fingers in slip before stuffing Flynn with a third digit.

Flynn shouted out, his cock an angry red as he alternated pushing his hips back onto Ezra's fingers and pumping forward into his throat.

"Talk to me, Zali," Tristan growled, setting off another shockwave in me, my cunt clenching hard again and trying to keep Tristan's fingers deep inside me.

"Flynn's body was made for fucking. He's taking three fingers now. Ezra's licking his cock like a fucking lollipop and sucking him so deep."

"Want to feel everything," Flynn gasped, his fingers curling around the base of his cock and squeezing as he withdrew from Ezra's mouth.

Ezra's lips were swollen, his hard cock tenting his ripped jeans. Flynn tugged Ezra to his feet and tore his white shirt straight down the front, sending buttons pinging left and right. He yanked at his jeans too, pulling them down to his knees before shoving Ezra backward onto the couch. "Coat yourself. I need you inside me."

Ezra did as he was told but grasped Flynn's hips, stopping him when Flynn went to straddle him. "Turn around. Let them see how much you love me being balls deep in you," Ezra purred.

Flynn hissed, gripping his cock tighter and pulling his balls away from his body.

"You want my cock in your virgin arse, don't you, gorgeous boy?" Ezra purred.

"I do," he admitted, straddling Ezra's legs and bending enough that Ezra would have had the perfect view of his hole. "My hole is yours. You'll be my only." The words were spoken to Ezra, but I didn't miss the way Flynn glanced at Ry as he said them. He wanted Ry just as much as I did.

I tugged Tristan's face away from my cunt. "Watch them," I murmured, and Ezra gripped Flynn's hips and pushed his cheeks open all the way.

He pulled Flynn back before feasting on his hole, spearing his tongue inside and moaning. Flynn cried out, jerking himself off as he dripped pre-cum onto the floor.

Ezra's cock was an angry red, the veins pulsing and pre-cum pooling at the tip before dripping down. I wanted a taste. So did Tristan if the way he moaned and gripped his dick through his pants was any indication.

Ezra pushed Flynn away, sucking in a breath before he guided Flynn down to his dick, reverse cowgirl style. Flynn sank down too quickly, crying out as Ezra's cock stretched him. I loved that part, that moment of being split open, stretched beyond what my arsehole was used to. But I loved the bite of pain too.

Flynn's dick softened a little, and Tristan shifted, crawling over to them and dipping his head. He sucked Flynn's half-hard shaft deep, and my boy cried out, his body battling between pushing into Tristan's mouth and sinking onto Ezra's cock.

Flynn arched back, leaning against Ezra as he rolled his hips, slowly lowering himself with every roll. I gripped Ry tighter and slid my free hand down to my cunt. I was sensitive. I'd lost count of how many orgasms I'd had in a single day, how many times I'd had a different dick inside me.

But I fucking loved it, and I still wanted more.

Variety was the spice of life and all that.

The only thing that could improve the whole scene before me was if I was filled by one of my guys. Tristan and Ry were both wearing too many clothes, and I wanted them naked as well. Though there was something undeniably sexy about having the two most dominant men between us remain dressed while we were all stripped bare.

Tristan released Flynn's dick with a pop and palmed himself. "Fuck me, that's sexy. Watching your tight little hole get stretched around a dick for the first time is in-fuck-ing-credible."

Ry sucked in a breath, and I flicked my eyes toward him, watching as he rubbed his dick through his jeans. "Need some help?" I offered.

"No," he grumbled.

Tristan stood and slowly stripped out of his clothes, his cock a hard rod as he peeled off his underwear. He stalked over to me, and the predatory gleam in his eyes had my cunt clenching hard. I shifted my weight, my essence slicking up my legs as I pinched my clit. My chest heaved, my breasts heavy and nipples straining as he closed the distance between us and lifted my hand away from my core. He sucked on my fingers, humming as he did. His cock was pressed up against my belly, precum slicking me up. It sent the butterflies fluttering, anticipation rocketing through me.

"Climb me, love. Ride my cock like our good boy is doing to Ez."

I dropped Ry's hand and jumped into his arms, knowing he'd catch me. Easily lifting my weight, he shoved Ry up against the wall and pushed me into him, my back pressed against his chest, his hard cock nudging at my arse. I canted my hips, cradling his erection between my cheeks as Tristan impaled me in one sharp thrust.

I screamed, my cunt walls contracting so hard, my vision darkened at the edges. Tristan set a punishing pace, fucking me hard and fast with deep thrusts. Ry's cock pulsed every time I pressed my arse against him. He tentatively reached for my hips, trailing his fingertips over my skin. Gooseflesh pebbled at his touch, and my nipples tightened.

"Ry, my tits," I begged. "God, want you in my arse. Want you to both fuck me."

He was silent, but he reached for my nipples, pinching and twisting them as I fucked his cock through his jeans. Tristan growled and leaned down, licking my nipples over Ry's fingers. The move sent a shockwave through me, reminiscent of a nuclear explosion going off. I choked out a cry and arched up, pressing my arse against Ry's dick and my tits to Tristan's mouth. He thrust harder and deeper, pulling me down onto his dick before pushing me back against Ry's. I watched as his sharp teeth sank into my soft flesh before he closed his lips around my nipple, sucking on Ry's fingers at the same time. Ry moaned, dirty and filled with longing.

I shivered at the sound.

Flynn cursed, and I lifted my gaze to see him erupt handsfree as he fucked himself on Ezra's dick. It was like a geyser coating the table and floor in front of him with perfect arc after perfect arc of cum.

I was fucking jealous of that table.

I wanted it all.

Ezra shouted and bucked up into Flynn, setting off another round of pulses in my man.

Tristan slammed forward once more and grunted, his cock getting impossibly harder inside me. Oh fuck, he was on the edge.

That thought—the knowledge that I was about to be pumped full of cum—set me off. My orgasm slammed into me, rapture coursing through my veins like lava, scorching me. I screamed, writhing on his dick as he let loose, coating me in his release.

Tristan yanked Ry forward by his nape and crashed their lips together, snaking his tongue inside Ry's mouth before he could even react.

Ry groaned, the sound pained as he squeezed my tits to the point of pain. My cunt rippled, gripping Tristan's cock like I never wanted him to pull out. I didn't. Even if they could live inside me and just pump me full of their cum, time after time after time, I'd never be sated.

Heat bloomed against my back, and I cried out again, my empty arse wishing Ry had just shared his load inside me.

Ry pulled back, his eyes hard but his lips still glistening from Tristan's kiss. He snarled, shoving Tristan away. "Fuck you," Ry growled before cocking his fist and punching my man. He couldn't get a proper swing in given the wall, so it wasn't hard, but that glancing blow was enough to have Tristan's cheek immediately blooming red.

He pushed out from behind me, sending me flailing. I hit the wall, Tristan's cock slipping free from my cunt. Tristan gripped me tighter, bracing my weight and stopping me from hitting the deck.

I cursed, hating the emptiness.

Hating that Ry wasn't happy.

He stomped down the corridor as cum dripped down my legs.

♟ ♟ ♟

I pulled up at Dad's townhouse and, for the first time ever, regretted driving my Mustang. Dad could hear me coming from a mile away, so turning around without alerting him to my leaving was an impossibility.

I swallowed.

Ezra's car was parked in my usual spot—he'd left not long after our epic session, making up some excuse about needing to see some people. I hated that he was choosing between us, but I understood it, and I loved that he prioritized his friendship with Dad. I couldn't help but be jealous of Dad though. He got to keep Ezra. He got his friendship and loyalty. So far, we'd only been able to keep him until he'd gotten off. He walked away every time.

I didn't want to be second best. I didn't want Tristan or Flynn to have to watch him walk away again. I wanted all of us to be together, to be happy.

But it wasn't my choice to make. Ezra needed to be all in, and until he came to that decision—if he came to that decision—he'd keep walking away. He'd keep hurting Tristan, and he'd keep Flynn waiting.

I swallowed down the jealousy. Dad didn't have anyone like I did; I was being greedy. I should be happy that Ez was such a loyal friend to him. Even if he was doing the very thing that he was worried would ruin their friendship—me. I understood his reasoning, but only to a degree. If he'd stopped at that first kiss, cut me off cold turkey then, yeah, it would have made sense. But Ezra had caved too many times now for it to be an accident. He kept leaving, using the excuse that he couldn't do it to Dad, but each time he'd come right back to us. At this point, it was feeling a lot more like cowardice than loyalty.

Would Dad understand? He knew love. He knew what it was like to fall arse over tit for someone and have that love last the ages. But I wasn't naïve either. Ez was right. He would never understand Ezra falling for me. Or Flynn. Tristan, yes. But all of us? Never in a million years. If he found out Ezra was fucking me stupid on the regular and then walking away, there would be hell to pay.

I'd never wanted Ez to have to choose, but he already was—Dad would have been the first person Ezra would have confided in and sought advice from—and yet, Ezra wasn't entirely choosing to do the right thing by Dad either.

I sighed. Complicated didn't even begin to describe the clusterfuck we found ourselves in. At least if I hid this thing between us, I could buy us some more time to sort our shit out. I needed to act normal and pretend I'd never seen my hot-as-hell boss naked. Dread settled in my belly, nervous butterflies taking flight. This was easier said than done.

Before I could change my mind and plead that explosive diarrhoea had forced me to turn around, Dad stuck his head out the front door. A smile instantly lit up his face, and he jogged out to me, resting his elbows on my door and leaning into my open window. "You can park, you know."

"I didn't want to interrupt."

"You aren't. We're eating dinner and catching tonight's match."

"Cricket?" I asked, unimpressed.

"No, tennis. Come on in. There's plenty."

I pulled into the closest car park and gave myself a pep talk—*there's no need to freak the fuck out. You can do this. Pull up your big girl panties.*

"Hey," I called as I closed the door behind me.

Ezra stuck his head out from the kitchen, and his wide-eyed look of sheer panic made me snort with laughter.

"Detective, what a pleasure to see you," I deadpanned and continued on over to Dad to give him a hug and steal a cherry tomato. "Whatcha doin', old man?"

"Enough of that, missy," he chastised playfully. "What brings you here?"

"Just wanted to catch up." I smiled, trying to act as innocent as possible, but Dad saw straight through me.

He snorted out a laugh and gestured over his shoulder with a tilt of his chin. "That's exactly what Ez said."

"I'd say great minds and all that, but...," I trailed off and shrugged, tossing a smirk at Ezra.

"Your daughter is so mean," Ezra shot back, eying me up and down like I was a lollipop and he wanted to lick me from head to toe.

Desire flared in me, and I blinked, clearing my throat and looking away from him before I gave myself away.

My phone rang, and I walked out of the kitchen to answer it. "Good evening, Professor Reid. To what do I owe the pleasure?" I asked.

"Is that your professor?" I heard Dad ask Ez.

"Yeah," he answered, moving over to me. His concern was obvious in the furrow of his brow and the way he rested his hand on the small of my back, lending me his support.

Tristan's words registered. "Can you talk?"

"Yeah, I'm at Dad's. What's going on?" I asked, worry prickling my senses. "Are you.... Is everything okay?"

"Yeah, absolutely. Kind of," he mumbled before sighing.

I could practically hear the wheels in his head turning, and the knot of dread that formed with me sitting in the car a few minutes earlier tightened.

"I did a search on our American friend—the liquidator."

"And you found something dodgy," I surmised.

"Yeah. There are too many coincidences."

The breath rushed out of my lungs, and I slumped against the table.

"Some of the search results were on microfiche stored on the other campus. The librarian has just sent it to me." He paused, and I could hear him swallow before he continued. "It's a newspaper article from a few years after ReimagINC went under. The liquidator was charged with a series of white-collar crimes. The company in question was allegedly a front for a crime family."

"Oh," I murmured, his words taking a moment to sink in. I closed my eyes and pressed my fingers to the bridge of my nose. "Do I want to know which family?"

"Martinelli."

The name struck me with the force of two planets colliding. My legs gave out and I slithered onto the dining table chair like a limp noodle. When I'd told Tristan that Reimag-INC had invested in a company that had loose ties with a crime family, I'd hoped that the connection extended only to one of the directors being related through marriage.

But it was so much worse.

Ezra's hands on my shoulders were the only thing anchoring me upright. He played with my hair, soothing strokes that gave me something to focus on other than the blinding fear coursing through my veins.

"Ez, what's going on?" I heard from behind me, but the buzzing in my ears overtook my senses.

If there was smoke, there was fire. The legal system's standards of proof protected innocent people from going to jail. It didn't ensure guilty people were convicted. Prosecutors couldn't always establish that the defendant had, beyond a reasonable doubt, committed the crime. It didn't mean they were innocent, just that they hadn't been found guilty.

But maybe I was wrong.

I prayed to whatever deity was listening that I was blowing this way out of proportion.

Maybe the liquidator was innocent.

Maybe this had nothing to do with the crime family who'd invested in my mother's company. Maybe it was pure coincidence.

I'd been terrified of them for years. I saw the trail of destruction they left behind if you knew where to look—the dead bodies and those who weren't as lucky, the yawning gaps in data where they wholesale deleted anything inconvenient, the influence they exerted to sway govern-ments to their bidding. These people wore perfectly pressed suits and shiny gold watches or evening gowns with sparkling diamonds to hide their rotting, maggot-infested cores. If Mum somehow got involved with them or dared to stand in their way, she wouldn't have stood a chance.

If they knew Tristan was investigating, he'd be next. I whimpered, the sound escaping my throat before I could bite it back. Ezra was there, wrapping his arms around me from behind, shielding me. I sank into his embrace, resting my forehead against his cheek.

"Ezra," I heard in the background.

Tristan added quietly, "There's more."

"Fuck," I hissed, gripping Ezra's hand and interlacing our fingers, holding on for dear life.

"There was a mistrial. Even after extended delibera-tions, the jury couldn't reach a unanimous decision."

"Fuck," I repeated. I knew in my gut what he was about to say, but I hoped I was wrong, nevertheless.

"They suspected jury tampering, but it never went to trial. An arrest warrant was issued for the juror, but the po-lice found them dead by an apparent suicide when they went to execute it."

Bile surged up my throat, my gut churning. The chances that the liquidator was innocent were now Buckley's and none.

Like Tristan had said, there were too many coinci-dences. And too many coincidences piling up meant none at all.

This liquidator worked for the Martinelli family. They were powerful enough to have people on the inside of the global financial powerhouses, one of which acted as liquidators for ReimagINC. I'd bet good money that they'd had a hand in usurping the Australian liquidators in favour of this American "expert." The same expert who happened to have been tried a few years later for white-collar crimes in connection with that very family—the same one connected through marriage to an investor in Mum's company. There was every chance the liquidator got away with his crimes because the family paid off a juror, then killed them to hide the evidence.

"I think I'm gonna be sick," I whispered.

"Ezra, Zali," Dad growled, louder now and from directly in front of me. "What. Is. Going. On?"

"Some information has come to light," Ezra explained. "It's distressing. We'll explain it all in a minute."

Dad glared at Ezra, his lip turned up in a snarl as he gnashed his teeth and clenched his fists. He was getting ready for a fight, and all I could do was whisper, "Tell me he was re-tried."

"No," Tristan sighed. "He wasn't. It was because of a technicality as well—an obscure loophole that hadn't successfully been used to quash proceedings in nearly a hundred years. The state's legislature passed laws preventing it from ever being used again straight after."

"You need to stop, Tristan," I ordered, but my tone was filled with pleading rather than steel. "Stop looking into him, stop searching for him, tell Jude to stop looking into

the liquidators too. Everything. Stop it now. It's too dangerous."

Ezra gathered me closer, his arms tightening their hold
around me as he bodily covered me. His lips were pressed
against my temple, and I was grateful he was there when
the tear slid down my cheek. I couldn't protect him once we
got on their radar—we might have already pushed too far.
I had enough money to disappear. I had enough to take
them all with me to some deserted island where we could
see them coming from miles away. But I suspected my men
would be as reluctant to leave our families and friends as I
was.

"Yeah, I agree," Tristan murmured. There was a pause.
"Where to from here?"

"I don't know yet. I...."

"Hang up the phone," Dad ordered, steel in his voice.
"Now."

"Go," Tristan instructed me. "Be safe. I'm going to get
Ry to go to Flynn's and hang out there. You stay with Ezra. I
think it's better if I distance myself from all of you at least
until we know our next steps."

"No—" The line went dead before I could finish my argument.

"You better start talking," Dad ordered.

"Tristan—Professor Reid—"

"How long?" Dad exploded, rage turning his face red as
he pointed an accusatory finger between Ezra and me.
"What about Flynn? And this professor of yours? You've

supposedly been in love with him for years, and yet you're abusing my daughter? What the fuck?"

I blinked. My laugh bordered on hysterical, but Ezra recoiled like he'd been slapped. "I…. What…? You…."

"You're telling me you haven't touched her? You're awfully familiar with her, throwing your arms around her and kissing her temple like that. How long have you been abusing my daughter? Grooming her?"

"Dad, that's enough," I demanded, standing up and slamming my phone onto the table. "Don't you dare accuse your closest friend of that."

"No? What is it then, Zali? Tell me how it is." He raised an eyebrow expectantly. "How would you phrase a thirty-seven-year-old man touching you. You're barely legal."

"I'm twenty-three, Dad. That's well beyond legal."

"Oh, I'm sorry." He threw his hands in the air dramatically. "Five years, Zali. Five years ago you weren't legal. You were a child." He directed his cold stare to Ezra. "So, I'll repeat my question. How long, Ezra?"

He flicked his gaze to me, narrowed his eyes and daring me to speak. Well, fuck that. I wasn't letting Dad do this.

"Days, Dad. Literally days." It was my turn to narrow my eyes at him when he opened his mouth to interrupt. He needed to hear this, and he needed to really listen to what I had to say. "There was no grooming. There was no abuse. Don't bother looking for evidence because it. Never. Happened." Grasping Ezra's hand, I squeezed tight, but his remained limp, not returning the gesture. But Dad wasn't an idiot either. He needed to know the full story, or he'd never accept my explanation.

"There's no cheating either," I added, and Ezra sucked in a breath.

I waited for his eyes to meet mine so I could let him know that coming out to Dad was as much his choice to make as mine. I gave him enough time to object, to give me any indication that he wanted me to stay quiet. There was never going to be a good time to tell Dad, but I would end the conversation right here and now if Ezra wanted to wait. Finally, after what felt like an eternity, Ezra dipped his gaze and gave me a tiny nod. He squeezed my hand but immediately let go. Was I doing the right thing? Was I going to hurt the people I loved by speaking our truth?

"Explain," Dad demanded, and Ezra sighed.

"Tristan and Flynn both know we're together because we're in a four-way relationship. We're with them too. The four of us. Together."

"Get out." Dad pointed to the door, his voice deathly quiet and eyes trained on Ezra.

"Roe—"

"Don't you dare. Get out of my house. Lose my number and if you know what's good for you, you and your professor had better stay away from my daughter too."

"Dad—" I warned.

"No, Zali. You're young, you're beautiful, you have a lot of money. These men—"

"Don't want me for that," I finished for him, my voice softening. I went to him and slipped my hands into his. "You need to trust me, Dad. You do with everything else. Please, do it with this too."

He shook his head. "Zali, it was my job to protect you, and I failed. They're taking advantage of you. I know you think they love you, but men are bastards. People in general are shitty, not just men. But men in particular think with their...."

"Dicks, Dad. You can say it." I smirked, but he didn't reciprocate, so I leaned in close and whispered conspiratorially, "But, thing is, I have the biggest one of the lot of them."

I pulled him into a hug and squeezed him tight. His arms eventually wound their way around my shoulders, and I snuggled into the chest of the best man I'd ever met—the one who'd been my first love and who would always hold the most special place in my heart.

"I love you, Dad. Don't think for a second that you've failed me because it's not even close to that. You taught me how to look after myself." I pulled back and took his hands again.

"You taught me what to expect from a partner. You showed me how to love big in the way you loved Mum. And we do love each other, Dad. It's unconventional, yes, but they're good men. You know that about Flynn. You know that about Ezra too. Don't let this destroy your friendship with him. I'll never forgive myself."

"It's not right, Zali," he mumbled, but his voice no longer held any conviction.

I looked for Ezra, waiting for him to step up and make this right.

But the room was empty.

Oh, no. He wouldn't.

I whipped my head around to the front door. The screen was slightly ajar.

I groaned and shook my head as the sound of an engine smoothly turning over reached my ears.

"Why would he leave if he knew what you were doing was right?" Dad murmured. "Just saying." He held his hands up in a gesture of surrender when I wheeled on him.

"Men. Fuck me." I threw my hands up and resisted the urge to punch something. I didn't even know what to do. Did I go after him? Did I stay with Dad and keep trying to make him understand?

Dad made the decision for me. He moved around the kitchen, filling a container of delicious-smelling food before handing it to me. "Sleep on it. Think about what I've said."

"What about you?" I asked. "Will you sleep on what I've said? Will you fix things with Ezra?"

"I don't know, Zali. He broke my trust. Shattered it into a million pieces if I'm being honest." He shook his head. "I entrusted you to him, and he took advantage of you—" He held his hand up in a stopping motion when I opened my mouth to interrupt. "It's not just now, Zali. He's been doing it for years—I should never have agreed to let you work with the police despite how much experience you've gained. I know you wouldn't have been able to consult without it, but God knows what evil you've seen."

238 • ANN GRECH

Dad would never know the truth of where my money came from, or I'd have a whole other set of problems on my hands.

"Ezra never let me work on anything dangerous or inappropriate for my age. He shielded me. He still does it now." I shrugged and pointed at the door. "He's just sacrificed himself so I wouldn't have to choose between you or him."

I picked up my keys and phone, pocketing the latter.

Dad sighed and nodded. "Be safe."

"You too." I kissed him on the cheek and lifted the container of colourful salad topped with sliced chicken breast. "And thank you."

The trip back to the yacht was slow going, giving me far too much time to think. Ry was, predictably, gone when I got there, and for the first time in a long time, it was too quiet, and I was too lonely by myself. Taking my dinner, care of Dad, into my office, I locked the door behind me and pulled out the transaction records I'd downloaded from the Reserve Bank. I needed to know once and for all where the money trail went and if Mum had unwittingly become involved with the worst kind of people.

If she had, if she'd found something that made her rethink her investments in their companies, there was no doubt in my mind that her "accident" was anything but.

And if it wasn't an accident, they'd have me to contend with.

SEVENTEEN

Flynn

I was on edge.

We both were.

My heart was beating triple time, and my hands were shaking.

Tristan had telephoned me, told me to expect Ry at my apartment and that Zee and Ezra were together. Then he'd dropped the bombshell of what he'd found, and I was out the door and halfway down the corridor when Ry stepped out of the lift and hoisted me over his shoulder kicking and screaming. He carried me back into the apartment and made Tristan repeat what he'd told me. We didn't know how much of a risk there was to his safety, if any, but Tristan wasn't messing around. He wouldn't let us go to him. He didn't even want us to go to Zee. Wild horses couldn't have stopped me if she was alone, but she was with Ezra and her dad—if they couldn't keep her safe, I'd have no chance at doing it.

But when the clocked ticked past midnight with no word from Zee, I was starting to freak out. Worry was congealing in my belly, making my stomach churn and bile want to crawl up my throat. She rarely stayed that late given her dad's early start time at work.

I called, but she didn't answer.

Neither did Ezra.

Ry had stood silently while I tried again with shaking hands. No answer again. He didn't wait for me to ask.

Instead, he marched straight out the door, beckoning for me to follow as he called Monroe on the way down to the car park. He hung up a moment later with a scowl and explained that they'd left separately hours earlier. Ry's string of expletives would have made a sailor blush. The way he gunned his truck back to the marina had me white-knuckling the grab bars.

He handed me the bat. "If you see anyone that shouldn't be there, don't hesitate. Hit first, ask questions later."

I nodded, swallowing hard.

We slinked onto the yacht, me holding a baseball bat at the ready and Ry carrying a legit bow and arrow. He was as freaking sexy as Jeremy Renner and just as grumpy as the superhero character he played. I, on the other hand, was trying not to pass out from the adrenaline and anxiety.

I'd just as likely vomit on an intruder as break their face.

"Stay behind me, Flynn," he whispered, peering around a corner.

A flicker of movement across the deck caught my eye. I tightened my grip on the bat and crept forward, keeping to the shadows. I planted my feet, muscle memory kicking in and my body priming to crack the softball across the field.

Except this time, I was aiming for a head.

I swung, putting all my years of training into full effect.

Caramel-blond hair registered, and soulful brown eyes turned on me with a startled expression.

"Fuck," he squeaked as he leapt backward, and my bat smashed straight through the window. An arrow whizzed by, catching his collar as he flailed, piercing the interior wall and wedging itself halfway in. "Flynn, what the hell?"

"Why did you leave her?" I demanded, gripping his federal-police-issued vest and shoving him back until he landed on his arse. My voice was far too loud in the quiet of the night, but I was beyond caring.

He was supposed to have been protecting her and Monroe and he just left? Straight after Tristan had spoken to them? Zee was probably shaken up. Heck, I was shaken up, and there was no way this was as personal for me as it was Zee. Why would he do that?

"Woah, woah," Ry warned.

I spun around and saw Zee gripping a kitchen knife like a sword and tiptoeing toward Ry. He stepped out from the shadows, and she froze.

"What the fuck is going on?" she hissed, assessing the mess the three of us had made. "Get inside. You gave me a fucking heart attack."

I pressed the heel of my hand to my chest, willing my heart rate to slow down, and sucked in a slow breath.

"What the hell are you doing?" Ezra growled at Zee, scrambling up from the deck. "You think there's someone breaking in, so you go toward the danger?"

"I came to save your arses, you dumbarse. I pulled up the cameras and recognized you and Flynn, but I could only see part of Ry. I was coming to stop him from killing you."

"You didn't answer my question," I reminded Ezra, pointing my bat at him. If he thought he was off the hook—

"I didn't leave. Not completely anyway." He shook his head and flicked his gaze to Zee, his expression sad. "I moved my car so I could get you guys out easier if I needed to. Then I came back and staked the place out until you left. I made sure Roe locked up and followed you here. I've been guarding you ever since."

"Yet we managed to get onboard," Ry pointed out at the same as Zee added, "You didn't have to leave."

He smiled, but it didn't reach his eyes. "We should do what Zali said and go inside." He gestured for the door she'd come out of.

When we were inside her office with the door locked behind us, he parked his butt on the coffee table, resting his elbows on his knees and intertwining his fingers. He breathed deep, his shoulders curling in on themselves as he mumbled, "I did have to go. Your relationship with your dad is more important than mine is."

Zee went to her knees and cupped Ezra's face, smiling gently at him. She brushed her lips against his, but he turned away, dropping his eyes to the floor. "I can't."

"You can." Her words were firm, but there was no anger behind them. It was as if she was trying to give Ez permission. "Dad will come around. He jumped to the wrong conclusion, yes, but he'll come around."

"I've lost him."

"So to get over losing your friend, you'll walk away from us too? The people who love you?" she challenged, hooking a finger under his chin and lifting his gaze until their eyes met. "You'll hurt the man who's loved you for a decade? You'll push three people away who are waiting for you with open arms?"

When he didn't answer, she shook her head and sighed. "Where were you if you were guarding Dad's and the yacht?"

He shot her a small smile and shrugged a shoulder. "I was in your dad's nextdoor neighbour's garden, and when you got back here, I came aboard. Once you'd locked the door, I set the chain on the gangway and checked all the rooms before I holed up upstairs where I could see the entire dock. I saw movement up the other end of the dock, so I went to the bow and checked it out." He gestured to Ryder and me and added, "As soon as the chain from the gangway rattled, I ran downstairs. I was about to call out and tell Ry that I was onboard when you—" He gestured to me. "—jumped out in front of me and nearly went all freaking Babe Ruth on my head."

I couldn't help my snort of laughter. "Sorry."

"I'm not," Ry grumbled. "I missed."

"Thank you. I appreciate that," Ezra replied dryly.

"Guys," Zee murmured, her gaze bouncing between us, refocussing our attention on her. "I found something."

I looked at her, really looked, and my gut sank. Tension was gathered around her eyes, and she was pale. I thought it had been the shock of our storming the yacht, but something more was going on.

I dropped to my knees in front of her and reached for her hands. She was cold, her fingers white, an unmistakeable tremble in them. "Talk to us," I encouraged.

"There's a pattern in the data." She gestured to the five screens she had set up at her desk, one of which still had the security feed on it. She made to stand, and Ry was there, helping her up and guiding her over to the executive chair rolled halfway across the room.

She pursed her lips before explaining, "The amounts are the same, but the bank account numbers don't match. There's a discrepancy between who the money was paid to in the accounting records and where it was actually sent." She shook her head and exhaled, bringing her feet up onto her chair. She folded herself in half, wrapping one arm around her shins and using her legs as a shield. "No one would have picked it up unless they double-checked every detail."

"Which transactions?" Ez asked. "Are they the ones that the liquidator had connections to?"

Zee nodded and wiggled her mouse, and the darkened screens lit up. "Take a look."

I moved to her side, crouching down as Ry did the same and Ezra moved in behind her.

The screens showed rows upon rows of what looked like spreadsheets, many of the lines highlighted in a different colour.

"The colours don't mean anything. I've used them so that I can easily show where they match up," she explained.

Even just eyeballing it, it was clear there was a pattern.

"Take this transaction, for example." She pointed out one that was a turquoise colour. "It says in the accounting records that this was a deposit into one of the American companies that needed a bailout during the GFC. The funds would have been lost had they been paid into it, so no one was expecting the money back. But instead of being invested, it was paid here instead—different bank account number, different account name but exactly the same amount. Down to the cent."

"So who got that money?" I asked, trying to follow the path she'd mapped across the screens—without success given that I had no idea who the bank account owner was.

She pointed to the next monitor over, one that had more spreadsheet information listed. Names and numbers were highlighted in different colours like on the other screens. "That particular recipient is a shell company based in Seychelles."

Zee then moved her mouse to the fourth one, where she brought up a tab showing a corporate listing. "Each bank account owner where a suspect transaction has been deposited is a trustee, which for an investment firm isn't out of the ordinary. But what's not normal is that they're all based in tax havens. They're also not listed on any exchanges of any type, and they don't appear to have fixed shares that you can buy into or be allocated. So far I also haven't been able to find the documents that regulate the trusts and their shares either, which, again, isn't normal for investment vehicles. But I haven't looked at all of them yet."

"What does all that tell you?" Ry asked.

"Nothing good." She shook her head and sighed. "I have a theory. It's speculation at this stage, but there are too many transactions like this for it to be a simple mistake."

The tight lines around her eyes and her downturned lips had me reaching for her again, resting my hand on her bare thigh.

"Someone was embezzling funds."

"How do we narrow that list down? It could be anyone who had access to the bank account." Ezra asked, his resolve finally breaking as he reached for Zee and ran his fingers through her hair before massaging her shoulders. "What's your theory?"

She groaned blissfully, leaning her head back against his belly. "That feels good."

"I.... That's good." He closed his eyes as if having a battle with himself, but he kept moving his hands.

"So, yeah, theory." She sucked in a breath, and her words tumbled out of her so fast that she spoke in one long sentence. "I think the company somehow got caught up in organized crime. The only explanation for how this was set up, how it all ended, how she went missing—everything— was that Mum found out and was trying to get the company out of it. But that didn't suit someone—whoever it might have been—and they decided that ReimagINC had outlived its usefulness. They tied up the loose ends and got away with murder. Asher was collateral damage."

Zee's voice wobbled, and she fanned her hand in front of her face, blinking back tears. "They killed them," she whispered, her voice breaking.

My chest ached, my throat tightening as I struggled to swallow past the lump in my throat. Unshed tears burned my eyes. I loved Asher like a big brother too, far more than my own siblings who seemed to enjoy forgetting that I was there as much as our parents had. We followed him and Ry around like puppies, trying to be half as cool as them. They were rockstars in our world.

But Asher was so much more than that to Zee. He was her hero. He'd wiped her tears when she was a baby. He'd shared his toys and held her hand when her dad cleaned her scraped knees. He'd crept into her bed and read her stories when Zee couldn't sleep. They whispered their secrets to each other and never ratted each other out. He took his big-brother duties so seriously, being brave enough to pet the neighbourhood dogs first, despite being terrified of them, whenever Zee saw one she wanted to say hello to.

She was shattered when he'd died. Her entire world had been rocked to its core and tilted so far off its axis that Zee didn't know which way was up.

Zee was strong, stronger than anyone I knew apart from her dad and Ry. But days like today when I watched on as she relived every ounce of pain, every grief-stricken moment, ripped my heart out, shredding it to pieces.

Seeing Ry go through the same was just as difficult.

When Ry's dad died, he'd pulled back, retreating into himself. He was sullen and quiet with everyone except

Asher. Ash was the only one who could bring Ry out of his shell and give him a sense of normalcy. They were kids together—they played computer games and took the little tinny out to go fishing or swimming in the Broadwater. They walked to and from school together and did their homework together every night. Ash reminded Ry every day with something far more significant than words—his actions—that he would never be alone. He became Ry's whole world.

Then Asher died.

A piece of Ry went with him.

Ry's world folded in on itself. He erected ten-metre-thick armour-plated walls around an impenetrable vault in which he locked his heart. He hissed like a cut snake at everyone and everything. He lashed out and drove away so many people. His so-called friends abandoned him in droves, leaving him even more alone. He was as rudderless as Zee and Monroe, and as devastated too.

Ry had lost his north star.

Grief reshaped him into someone darker and harder. But inside was a lost little boy.

Just like Ry's mum did to Zee's dad, Zee saved Ry. I wasn't sure whether it was conscious or instinctual, but she gave him something to focus on. She became his purpose until he could navigate his way through the pain that he was drowning in.

At school, he protected her from the cruel kids who wanted to ask the gory details or speculate on how Ash and Rosa had died. He beat any person who opened their mouth until everyone was too scared to even cast a sideways glance at her.

Then when our hormones started racing and they saw just how gorgeous she was, their morbid curiosity changed. They used her as much as she used them.

Ry was there for the good, the bad, and the ugly. He never treated looking after her like a job, but that job was what had saved him. Ry had moulded his duties to be her shadow. He'd protected her from the worst of the men trying to get into her pants.

He'd protected her from herself too—her own destructive spiral was just as vicious as his—but when Zee was involved, Ry put aside his own pain and stepped up for her. I'd done my best to give Zee a soft place to land, to let her know she was safe with me no matter what happened, but it was Ry who'd actually kept her safe. He'd intervened with the dangerous ones, dragged others out by their hair, physically tossing them off the yacht on occasion. He'd made sure she got home every night and that the guys who'd come onto her yacht didn't stay beyond their welcome.

Their bond was iron-clad, and they needed to rely on that to get them through this latest slap to the face that fate was dealing them.

I flicked my gaze to Ry. His eyes were glassy, his lips pressed in a straight line as he struggled to stay composed. He stared unseeing at a point on the wall, his hands fisting and unclenching as he tried to channel his anger and devastation.

Ez shifted, and I met his stare, a silent conversation passing between us. We knew exactly what needed to be done, and we worked in sync like we'd done it a million times before. Ezra spun the chair around, and we reached for Zee's hands, pulling her to her feet. She went to step into Ezra's embrace, but he turned her to face Ry instead. They collapsed into each other, Zee white-knuckling Ry's shirt as he buried his face against her shoulder, his own shaking. I wrapped my arms around both of them and rested my head on her shoulder, needing to be just as close to her as Ry did. Ezra stepped aside, moving around Ry and tangling his fingers in Zee's hair. He pressed a chaste kiss to her temple and sucked in a shuddery breath.

"We need to find these fuckers and make them pay," Ry growled, his voice gravelly. "I'll cut their fucking heads off myself." Rage, deep and dark, vibrated off him, but he held Zee tight like she was his lifeline.

I shifted my hand, moving it up to squeeze his shoulder, only to find Ezra's hand already at his nape.

"I want that too," Zee whispered. "And I want Tristan."

Ry stilled, his muscles locking up tight, and Zee responded by wrapping her arm around his waist, holding him closer. I hadn't seen what happened between Tristan and Ry, but I heard the growled "Fuck you," from Ry, saw the punch, and watched as he stomped away. Tristan hadn't said a word about it, and Zee followed his lead, saying it was not her story to tell.

Ez replied, "I'd rather he was with us too. Do you want to go to him, or should I bring him here?"

"Here," Ry answered without hesitation. It didn't surprise me; Ry was a creature of habit too. He liked his routines and his space. He needed that, and I was proud of him for speaking up.

"Yeah, here," Zee agreed, her voice muffled in Ry's chest.

She looked at Ezra and his gaze softened with adoration. A warm smile tilted up his lips and he kissed her forehead.

"Do you mind?" she asked.

"Not at all. Like I said, I'd prefer he was with us too."

I stared at the wall, shaking my head at the complexity of the graph Zee had created. The map of shareholders and their heirs looked like an upside-down tree with ReimagINC at the top and branches sprouting from it. Apart from the names, there were dollar amounts and bank account numbers listed for every entry. She'd meticulously set out every detail—details that I still had no idea how she managed to get her hands on. Zee had some serious ninja hacking skills to find it all out and be confident enough to rely on it.

It wasn't the first time I'd seen the graph—the earlier version had been pinned to Zee's wall for a few weeks now, but she'd been working on it since then. Some of the boxes at the lowest level were highlighted. It looked like she was progressing through the list in alphabetical order, having done most of the first three letters with a few exceptions.

Two boxes in the As and a lone box in the Bs. The latter stood out among the other branches; it was a level lower than the ones on either side of it. Whoever the investor was, they'd passed away and their heir was listed, or the company had closed and its sole shareholder was listed.

Tristan slipped in behind me, wrapping his arms around my waist. I snuggled back into him. "What are you up to, angel?" he asked, his voice barely above a whisper. I cast a glance at Zee, who was fast asleep on the couch, wrapped up in a blanket. I smiled at the way her nose twitched as a piece of hair fell across her face. Ezra was curled up with her, and Ry was up on deck. I suspected he was avoiding Tristan judging by the frosty reception he'd given the man on his arrival. But now that I'd heard the story, I understood why. It was wishful thinking that Ry would ever be attracted to any of us guys. He was about as straight as they came.

"Looking at this." I gestured to the graph. "I think she's highlighting the ones she's verified, perhaps? I'm not sure what the highlighting is or what the different dollar amounts are."

Tristan dropped a kiss to my throat, trailing his nose up to my ear. "She's incredible. The amount of work she's put into this far exceeds even what I've done."

"It's personal."

"It is." He nodded, his stubbled cheek brushing my own smooth one. I shivered, and Tristan chuckled, tightening his embrace. "I'll keep you warm."

"Wait." I stepped out of his arms, immediately missing his warmth, and frowned. I knew that name. I'd known him as Daz, but Darryl Beckett had been larger than life. His heir, Kristy Beckett, was a tiny woman but a force to be reckoned with. I pointed at the box. "I know them."

"Who is it?" Tristan asked, stepping closer to look.

Brow furrowed, I turned to him. "It's Ry's mum and dad. Daz died, like two months before Rosa did. Ry's mum, Kristy, and Zee's dad are tight."

Tristan's eyes widened, and he inhaled sharply, reaching for me like a lifeline. I held him close, needing the comfort from the gut punch too.

"Fuck," Tristan hissed. He wiped his hand over his face, exhaling on a groan. "You've all been through so much."

I buried my face against his firm chest and closed my eyes, taking comfort in his warmth and the strength of his arms around my shoulders. "Zee and Ry especially."

"How did he die?" Tristan asked hesitantly, his voice a low rumble against my ear.

"I don't know." I shook my head, my heart hurting for Ry. He was so stoic, so guarded, but underneath it all was a soft heart and a fiercely loyal man who'd do whatever it took to keep the people he loved safe. It was his doing that I was in the room with three of them at that moment and why he was up on deck, protecting us against a risk we weren't even sure was real.

"But I do know it was unexpected," I added, letting Tristan reach his own conclusion, likely the same one we'd drawn once we were old enough to understand what could have happened. Seeing this information—his name on the list—was another blow, another terrible hint at what had gone down.

Tristan closed his eyes, and his shoulders slumped forward, his head hanging low. I stepped closer, this time taking him into my arms.

He rested his forehead against mine and sighed. "So fucking unfair."

Eighteen

Zali

"**I** need to go home and get some things," Tristan murmured against my hair.

I was resting my hands on the window ledge in my office, staring unseeing out over the marina. I wanted to be on the water in my happy place where the only thing I could hear was the cry of a circling hawk, the lap of the current against the hull, and waves crashing against the island sheltering us from the ocean.

My gut was telling me Tristan leaving wasn't a good idea, but I couldn't very well keep him a prisoner. Well... he might not appreciate it anyway. I was spooked. Shook. Fear churned in my belly, and I forced myself to uncurl my fingers from the metal of the frame.

"Love, I know you're scared, but I'll be okay. There's nothing connecting the liquidator with the accident other than our speculation. How would he even know that I was doing research on him?"

I whirled around, astounded that he'd said something so naïve. Dressed only in an oversized tee, I was hardly intimidating, but he was being reckless, and I wouldn't stand for it. "The same way that they figured out you were doing research on ReimagINC in the first place." I threw my hands up in the air and paced across the room, my footfalls more of a stomp than a light step. "Wasn't one death threat enough?" I hated the uncertainty in my voice and the frisson of panic skittering through my veins.

But Tristan was also right. I was letting fear cloud my judgement.

I sighed. I understood why he didn't say anything earlier, but I wish he had. "I've set up searches to run in the background and pinpoint IP addresses to track anyone monitoring you. I want you to talk to the IT department at the university about keystroke monitoring and the protections they have in place for you. We can at least be safe than sorry."

"You don't think that someone has been in my office, do you?" Tristan looked taken aback, his eyes blown wide, the colour draining from his face.

I hadn't wanted to scare him, but he needed to understand that if the Martinelli family was any way involved, he had reason to be fearful.

"I'm not ruling it out. These people managed to get into your building to pin a note to your front door. They know enough of what they're doing to be able to access your office too." I swallowed, forcing down the bile that threatened to burn a pathway up my oesophagus. "But they wouldn't even need to." If anything happened to him….

"How about I go with Tristan? Then at least there's two of us going back to his apartment," Ez suggested, his tone soothing like he was speaking to a cornered animal.

In some ways that was exactly what I was. I wanted to lash out, scorch the earth, and inflict pain like those bastards had never experienced before.

No one would hurt my guys.

No one would fuck with what was mine.

"Okay, yeah, but our sticking together like glue is only a temporary solution. I need to figure out who they are. The sooner I can do that, the sooner we can figure out how to eliminate the threat."

"Zali," Ezra warned, but I held up my hand in a stopping motion, silencing him.

I was beyond being reasoned with. My gut was telling me this liquidator was a plant, that my mum and brother had been murdered, and someone had made a shit ton of money from all of it. I was no Robin Hood, but you'd be fucked thinking that I was going to let them keep one fucking cent of their blood money. I'd sooner burn it with their cold dead bodies piled on top than let them enjoy one more breath after they'd stolen all they had from us.

Martinelli family or not.

The door behind me opened and closed with a quiet click. I turned, half expecting it to be Ry, but it was Tristan and Ez. Both had their hair sticking up like they'd run their fingers through it and tugged on the ends. Both were pale, but Ezra had a hard glint in his eye, his mouth set to a grim line, while Tristan looked shaken.

"Is everything okay? Didn't you both have work?" I went to them, guiding them over to the couch Ezra and I had slept on. Ez stuck close to Tristan, never letting more than a sliver of space come between them. Tristan's hands trembled as he clasped them in his lap.

Worry surged through me, chilling me to the core.

"What happened?" I demanded gently as Ry slipped into the room and closed the door behind him. He stood behind me like a sentinel, the warmth from his body seeping into my iced-up veins.

"This." Ezra pulled a clear plastic sleeve from his jacket pocket and passed it to me. It looked innocuous enough, but the breath whooshed from my lungs and my legs threatened to give out from underneath me as I read the note.

Stop hunting. Your prey is far more vicious than you know.

We killed the bitch and her kid.

They begged for it to end.

You will too.

"Fuck," Ry muttered, taking it out of my hands and laying the previously folded-up A4 page on the coffee table that I'd sat on to stop myself from falling.

He parked his butt next to me and grasped my shoulder, squeezing it in solidarity. Shit had gone down between him and Tristan, but I knew without a shadow of a doubt that Ry was loyal to us. He would never waver, no matter what went down.

"Where is Flynn?" Tristan asked, his voice raw and his eyes flicking nervously around the room, looking for our man.

I reached for his hands and squeezed them tight. They were ice cold, the tremble more pronounced when I held onto him.

I tried desperately to keep my voice even and calm when I explained, "He's in my cabin, catching up on some sleep. He's safe, Tristan."

He huffed out a relieved breath and hung his head low. "Ez said that this is out of his jurisdiction. It's a Queensland police matter if we report it. But I only trust the two of you, Zali—"

"I'll find them, and I'll make them pay," I promised him. There was no hesitation, no doubt in my voice. It was a cold hard fact. These fuckers would rue the day they ever crossed my path. "I'll keep you safe, Tristan. We're going to start with security for every one of us. But first we going to make it a little harder for them to sneak up on us."

I turned to Ry, and he nodded without me needing to say anything further.

"Agreed. We're stocked for a couple of days, but it won't be enough with so many of us onboard. I'll put in a grocery order and get it priority delivered. We can leave in a couple of hours. Sooner if they aren't busy."

"That's great. Make it happen, please, Ry." I turned my attention to my guys, my heart warming at the way Ezra knew Tristan needed someone right there with him. "Ezra, take Tristan up to the top deck and get him in the spa. His hands are freezing. He's probably in shock."

Ezra nodded and stood, helping Tristan up. "What are you going to do?"

"Find these fuckers and finish them."

The door clicked closed behind them, and I minimized the screen I'd been staring at. I didn't know how to tell Ry I'd been refunding the amounts investors had given to Mum. I hadn't known his dad had invested money, and the amount had to have been their entire life savings. They weren't rich people—Ry's mum was in childcare, his dad an electrician—a few hundred thousand was likely everything they had. Ry wouldn't want the money. He'd brush me off and tell me that he had enough. But it wasn't going to him. It was his mum's, and I wanted her to be comfortable—I doubted she had any retirement savings, so she was a long way off that. But if I knew Kristy, she wouldn't want it either, especially if what I suspected was true. Daz's sudden death a few months before the company went under was too much of a coincidence. He'd figured out that something was very wrong well before anyone else had.

But as much as I needed to clear the air with Ry, I had to focus on the urgent tasks at hand. I had a job to do, and that meant combing through every one of the company's transactions to follow the money trail.

I poured through every record I could find, meticulously tracing the deposits and transfers out, identifying which ones went into legitimate investments or were paid out to clients and those that didn't match the disclosed destinations. One after another I checked them, highlighting more than I ticked off. Day turned into night, and I kept working, stopping only when Ry and then Flynn brought me food, forcing me to eat it before they left.

The yacht's engines fired to life, and I breathed out a sigh of relief. This was what I needed. No people, no hustle and bustle. Just calm waters lapping against the hull and seagulls floating on the wind currents.

We picked up speed as Ry navigated us out from the marina, but there were more twists and turns than needed to get us up the relatively straight shot to Jumpinpin. He'd taken the scenic, deserted route, winding his way through the quiet waterways, the only witnesses the nocturnal animals who called the estuarine system home.

Ry dropped anchor hours later under the cover of midnight. The blanket of stars in the sky was brighter and the waters silent. No engine noise permeated the air either, and I stopped for a moment, letting the silence travel through me. I wasn't sure where we were, but it was exactly where I needed to be.

Of course, we weren't out of danger. A vessel as big as mine was easily spotted from both the air and the water, and if we were among the narrow channels, we wouldn't even see them coming until they were on top of us.

As tempting as it was to head out onto the deck and watch the stars, I needed to keep going. My eyes were red and sore, dry from staring at the computer screen for hours on end. My limbs were as heavy as my eyelids, but I was close. I'd sifted through months of data, ruling out any theft from the main operational accounts. I'd found countless transactions from the investment funds though. The accounts in which clients' funds were deposited and reinvested in share portfolios, government bonds, direct property, and other long-term assets as well as the shorter, higher risk money earners were like sieves, losing more than was put into them.

The investments had failed, but it had nothing to do with the quality of those chosen. So much money had been siphoned out that I was surprised the investment fund hadn't gone under well before it did. Whoever had stolen the money was good. They hid their tracks well. The transactions in and out precisely matched amounts supposedly being paid into investments or refunded, and they were always consistent—once an account was used for the first transaction, every dollar from that point onwards was paid to the same account. The investments that were supposedly chosen reflected those in Mum's diaries—to anyone looking at the accounts at a surface level, the fund would have had a diverse range of assets that should have set them up for some degree of stability, if not phenomenal returns during what was otherwise a strongly deteriorating market.

Whoever it was also had high-level access—both to the accounting systems and the bank account—to pull off such a sophisticated, ongoing theft. Even if the liquidator hadn't been a plant, I doubted that the deception would have been discovered unless the full audit was completed and each and every bank account checked.

There was no doubt in my mind that Mum had trusted whoever had been responsible. It had to have been someone like her investment manager or head accountant. Regardless, the knowledge that they'd not only breached her trust but caused her death was a bitter pill to swallow.

But they'd get their comeuppance. My face would be the last thing they saw as I slit their throat and watched the life drain from their sorry existence. I'd be there like the fucking grim reaper escorting them to the afterlife for their betrayal, and I'd enjoy every second of it.

I would find them and make them pay.

But first I had a list of bank account owners to find. Their heads would roll next.

It was a task easier said than done though. I could easily check whether the accounts were still valid by attempting to transfer money to them. But masking my account details so I didn't end up with a giant flashing neon sign pointed at my skull would be harder. Finding out who owned the account was a whole step above that level of difficulty.

I needed access to the banks. But hacking their systems wasn't exactly a five-minute job, and I needed answers sooner than would be afforded by me hacking into every financial institution that received a transfer.

How though?

I rubbed my eyes, a yawn tearing free from me. The boys had long since fallen asleep, and I was teetering on the edge of hysteria—staring at the screen, lines of numbers laughing back at me, was sending me nuts. I wanted to sink into sleep, but I had to push through.

Gentle hands shook me, and I surfaced from my dreams with a gasp. They'd been dark and depraved, and not in the good way where I got off. No, these were violent and blood-thirsty, my hands dripping with blood.

"It's okay, Zee. It's just me. Come on, let's get you into bed."

"No, I'm not done yet," I mumbled, sinking back into the fight, launching myself at the faceless person I instinctively wanted to end.

Strong arms lifted me, and I fought the hold until he shushed me. I inhaled, getting ready to scream, but instead of thrashing like I'd been about to, Tristan's woodsy spice filled my senses. I burrowed into his chest like I wanted to crawl inside him.

Pillowy softness surrounded me, the sheets cool under me. I reached out and connected with a warm body, instinctively knowing I was safe with him. I shuffled forward, resting my head on firm muscle, before the bed dipped, and a hard, warm body slipped in behind me. I drifted, cocooned in safety and love.

I startled, my eyes springing open as the dappled sunlight reflected off the surface of the water danced on my ceiling. "That's it!" I tried to pull myself up and out from under the nest of bodies surrounding me.

"Too early, go back to sleep," Ezra mumbled from underneath me. My arm and leg were thrown over him, pinning him to the bed. I hadn't moved in what felt like hours, and our skin had stuck together from the heat of our bodies.

"Have to get up." I struggled, and Tristan pulled back, rolling over and giving me some space. Why hadn't I thought of it earlier? The solution was staring at me the whole time.

It was almost too easy. A few months ago, I'd hacked into a company that acted as an intermediary between businesses in the US and their banks. The system was designed to ping any transaction that dealt with terrorist or other restricted organizations. I'd tinkered with it, adding to their blocked list so that the "charities" which preached hatred and violence against trans kids, fought against women who wanted abortions, and ones that supported underage marriage couldn't receive any funds from their followers.

It wasn't easy, but I'd hacked in through a backdoor entry, piggybacking onto already established data lines so I didn't have to break through all their firewalls. Hopefully, the neat little plug I'd created to seal my entry point was still there. If so, all I had to do was pop the cork.

But before I could move, Ezra lifted my knee, trapping his erection under my leg. "You really want to get up?"

"I'm thinking I could be persuaded to stay," I murmured, my voice still husky with sleep. My tee had ridden up, the hem up around my waist, and Ezra took full advantage, sliding his hand up to cup my arse and tease my folds until they were slick.

My breath shuddered out on a moan, sensation rippling through me as my body awoke to the delicious tease he was dishing out. Tristan shifted behind me, rolling over and sliding his hand up my belly to rest it just below my breast. Playful nips began at my shoulder and worked their way up my throat to that spot behind my ear that made me melt. He was a teasing bugger, that beautiful fat cock thickening and nestling between my cheeks until I was writhing against it.

"Please," I begged, and Tristan hummed.

"Love it when you talk sexy, Zali. Your breathless pleas until I jam my cock into whatever hole I want are intoxicating."

"Want you both."

"What about me?" Flynn asked from behind Ezra, propping himself up until he was lying on top of the man and angling his mouth for my nipple.

Tristan helped him out, holding me steady as I rocked my hips, begging Ezra to finger-fuck me.

Flynn's lips touched my skin, and I cried out, arching into his touch.

"Oh, she likes that," Ez rumbled. "She's soaked."

"Taste her," Tristan ordered, tugging me until I was lying on my back, and Ezra had shifted between my legs.

I loved the way he maneuvered me, flipping and shifting me until I was positioned exactly right. Flynn crawled closer, his arse in the air, and Ezra moaned, licking his lips as he watched him move.

"You love that arse, don't you," I taunted, grinning as Flynn wiggled his hips playfully.

"If you're good—or bad—I might let you have it again too," he teased, pulling Ezra into a filthy kiss, their tongues tangling and lips sliding against each other as they made out.

I watched the way Tristan watched them, his smile warm as the two men he adored kissed. He tore his gaze away and ran his lips along my collarbone as he pinched my nipple until it was stiff and so sensitive that it was sending electric shocks straight to my cunt. Flynn followed his lead, latching onto my other nipple, and licked me until my whole body was throbbing.

Ezra ran his hands up my legs, spreading them wide. I looked like a buffet lying at the ready for them to overindulge on. I was happy to volunteer as tribute.

Working together like a well-oiled machine, they touched and teased me until I cried out with every swipe of their tongues, climbing ever higher to the peak. My body buzzed, my nerve endings crackling with lightning-like energy.

Ezra brushed his fingers along my cunt, teasing from my clit to my core until I was slick with desire and almost mad with lust. Still I climbed, the rushing sensation starting in my cunt as it clenched tight, wanting to be filled.

Then he was there, sliding three fingers into me at once, the delicious stretch and burn rocketing me to the edge of a monster orgasm as he sucked on my clit. I cried out, my back arching and toes curling as my muscles locked up tight.

"Please," I begged again, my voice breathy as I teetered right there, hovering in that weightless moment before my fall into ecstasy.

They didn't let me down. Tristan bit me, marking my skin as he sucked a mark onto my tit.

Flynn swiped his tongue over my nipple, his heated breath washing over me and sending gooseflesh puckering over my whole body. He pressed two fingers against my lips, and I opened immediately, sucking on his digits like they were his dick. I was ravenous for him.

For them.

My cunt clenched again, ready to tip over the edge. One more stroke, one more press against my G-spot was all I— right *there*.

I shuddered, crying out as the rushing in my veins hit me, tossing me around like a buoy in a storm. Over and over, every thrust of his fingers inside me hit the spot. He licked and sucked my clit, the rough scrape of his teeth and the burn of his stubble between my legs branding me and sending me soaring every time the waves began to back off.

"That's it, Zee. Keep coming for us," Flynn ordered, firmly stroking his cock as he watched me come apart.

"Gimme," I pleaded, opening my mouth and flattening my tongue so he could move into place and slide inside my mouth.

Tristan was moving too, both of them shifting so they were kneeling beside my head, their cockheads touching and making for a tempting double lollipop.

They jacked themselves, smearing the pre-cum leaking from their slits on each other while I hungrily lapped them up.

I cried out, sobbing at the loss of fullness between my legs. "Hold tight, love," Tristan murmured. "He hasn't forgotten about you."

Ezra slid his hands under my hips, lifting my arse up and splaying me across his lap. Feeling his thick cock at my entrance, I rocked my hips, trying to get him inside me.

"I've got you, gorgeous," Ezra promised, adjusting the tilt of my hips as he speared me, impaling himself in one smooth stroke.

My moan was garbled around a mouthful of dick. My cunt was filled, and their fingers alternated between gentle strokes and twisting and pinching my nipples. The climb to a second orgasm was swift and all-consuming.

"Oh fuck," Ezra moaned, his hips stuttering as my walls contracted, holding him in place.

His fingers tightened on my arse, and the knowledge I'd have bruises sent me soaring higher. He shouted out, emptying himself in me, the hot splashes of his cum on my inner walls ratcheting up my orgasm.

Ezra fell to the side, breathing hard, and Tristan tapped his hip.

"On your knees, Ez," Tristan encouraged as he shifted between my legs, hooked my knees over his elbows and plunged into my core in one deep thrust.

I shouted out, writhing on his cock as he fucked into me. He didn't give me any respite, his thrusts hard and fast as he rode me like a bucking bronco.

"Oh god," I gasped, another orgasm taunting me from the sidelines as Ezra's dick teased my lips, the final drop of his cum leaking from the slit. I licked our combined essences from his cockhead and choked out a cry as Flynn pinched my clit.

"Come on, love, come for me," Tristan hissed through gritted teeth as he punched his hips forward.

Tingles erupted over my body, an electric current racing through my veins. "Fuuuck," I cried as my body locked up and my cunt milked the cum from Tristan's cock as the rhythmic clenching squeezed him tight.

He shouted out, pressing his hips against mine and unloading inside me. Filling me up.

Tristan shuddered, pulling his hips back a touch before pumping forward again, extending our orgasms with micro movements that fired all our nerve endings.

"Zee, I need you," Flynn groaned, furiously jacking himself.

"Come on me," I gasped. "Give me your load too." I opened my mouth, flattening my tongue and pushing my hair off my chest. I was a blank canvass that he could paint and turn into his masterpiece.

Tristan ran his hand down Flynn's flank, cupping his arse and squeezing while Ezra shifted, poking his head between Flynn's legs and licking his sac.

"Shiiit," he gasped on a shudder and unleashed, pulse after pulse landing on my outstretched tongue, my face, and my tits.

I savoured his salty essence, lapping it up and humming as Tristan leaned down, his tongue tangling with mine as I shared our man's cum. He rubbed it into my chest, his softening cock slipping from inside me.

We groaned, and I wanted nothing more than for him to come inside me again. But I settled for Flynn collapsing next to me, Ezra's head now resting on his outstretched legs while his own legs hung off the bed.

Lazing for a moment and floating in happy hormones, I chuckled. "Sweet distraction, boys."

"Glad we could help," Tristan teased as Flynn poked me in the side.

Ezra added, "Our pleasure." He sighed happily and asked, "Where are we?"

I hummed, making an educated guess. "We're probably just west of Jumpinpin." I lifted my head, trying to see over the pile of bodies to the window to no avail. "There's a cove near the bar, but it's not very sheltered. The channels between the islands are better hidden. There are only a few deep enough for the hull, but Ry can navigate them with his eyes closed."

"He might as well have been with how dark it was last night," Flynn added. "Was there even a moon?"

"Thanks for carrying me in here," I murmured to Tristan. "I don't remember what the dream was about, but it was shitty. Then I smelled you—"

"Do I need a shower?" He lifted his arm and sniffed, his lip curling up in disgust.

"Definitely," Ezra quipped.

"Hush." I shoved him playfully in the head. "It was his aftershave, smart arse. Not B.O."

My stomach rumbled just as Tristan ran his fingers down my body, starting between my breasts and ending at my navel. Quirking his lips up in a half smile, he observed, "Looks like the world outside is calling. We should get some food in you before we're all overwhelmed with work."

Lacing my fingers with his, I responded, "I need to get back to it too. I figured out how to get the information I need." Eyes widening in disbelief, I backed up, trying to keep my guys out of what was going on. I fumbled my clarification though, fooling no one, "Ah, in… in totally legal, non-hackerish ways, of course."

"Of course," Flynn agreed with a perfectly straight face and exaggerated nod.

An hour later my stomach was full from Ry's gourmet breakfast, and I was watching the storm clouds gather on the horizon as my computer did its thing. The humidity had already ratcheted up, intra-cloud lightning flashing across the darkened band in the distance. The wind was whipping the mangroves alongside us, sending the Broadwater into a choppy mess. The sun held a certain bite to it, one that only ever came before a violent storm.

We hadn't had many summer storms this season, but this one would make up for them.

I could hear the guys moving the deck furniture under cover and tying it down. Ry had his process down to a fine art, able to secure every hatch and cover, every door and window within minutes. The others would only slow him down, but I also knew they would want to help.

Another flash lit the air around us, the contrast between the cerulean sky and darkened clouds in the distance was stark. I loved watching it, but I also needed to get some results.

Firewalls and security protocols were beautiful things. But to me, they were just blips. Speedbumps that slowed me down if only for a moment.

None of them held me back for long. I was as inevitable as the rising tide. I trickled in through the smallest of cracks in a levee. No matter how hard they tried to resist my march forward, they always failed.

Breaking security measures down was like watching butter melt in a hot pan. Secured authentication didn't stand a chance, popping and sizzling when I turned up the heat. The company had improved their systems, upgraded their firewalls, and added better encryption since I'd last visited, but I'd learned a thing or two as well.

"Yes!" The last of my algorithms finished processing, and the user interface loaded on my screen. Getting in and out quickly and leaving no trace of my visit was my aim. I only needed to use the system, not corrupt it, so I ran the searches. Records materialized, and I downloaded them, checking only to make sure the information I needed had loaded.

But there were holes.

Some banks weren't connected to the system. There was no information on those accounts available. And the kicker? They were the ones I really needed. At a guess, those three accounts had received transfers of close to eighty million dollars. The value of all the others combined only tallied twenty million. The fact that they weren't traceable using the verification program wasn't lost on me.

I scanned the list, comparing the SWIFT codes, and sighed. The only remaining accounts I had left on the master were the unconnected ones. I wouldn't be able to generate any more results.

The bank that held those three accounts was one of the oldest in the world. It was also one of the most well-known, but only if you were in the right circles. I'd come across their name before, but gaining access as a client was itself a process reserved for a limited few. A personal recommendation by an existing client was necessary. Every potential patron was vetted though an in-person interview conducted by a client relationship manager as well as going through a verification to confirm the deposit amount. Anything under fifty million dollars was unlikely to qualify to open an account unless there were extenuating circumstances—in other words, the person's sponsor was one of the bank's high-ranking clients. The bank had carved a niche market of old money families and corporations and prided itself on being an impenetrable fortress.

Hundreds of the world's best hackers and bank robbers had tried. All had failed.

Monaco's Grande Banque Unie—the Grand United Bank, established in the seventeenth century—was literally the only bank in the world that could boast having never lost a cent of its clients' money through theft of any kind.

"Shit," I muttered. "Why couldn't it be a bank I can actually get into?"

"You okay?" Ry asked, startling me.

My heart hammered in my chest, and I pressed the heel of my hand to my breastbone, breathing hard. "You scared the life out of me."

He smirked. "Sorry not sorry. What's going on?" He deposited a steaming cup of green tea on my desk and leaned back, propping his butt against the timber top.

"I've hit a dead end."

"I find that hard to believe." Ry raised an eyebrow and dared me to disagree.

"The accounts where most of the money was deposited are with the Grande Banque Unie." I rubbed my temples before sipping my tea and sighing happily. "Thank you for this."

"So, hack into it."

I huffed out a laugh, but it held no humour. "It's not that easy. The bank is a literal fortress. The only way into the building is by invitation. Clients are vetted, and you don't just apply for a job there. Accessing their systems is just as difficult."

"Can you get in there via an existing employee?"

"And do what? Kidnap them?" I asked, rolling my eyes.

"No. But you could steal their swipe card." He waved me off, anticipating my next words. "Yes, I know they don't use swipe cards, but you know what I mean. Borrow their identity. Or whatever." Ry shrugged. "It depends how far you're willing to go for this, Zali."

I didn't even hesitate, my cold hard stare locking onto his. He met mine unflinchingly. "All the way, Ry. These fuckers need to pay."

He nodded, his lips remaining in a straight line. "Well, then, we do whatever has to be done."

NINETEEN

Ezra

"Why are you here?" Roe asked me when he pulled open the door to see me, cap literally in hand, standing on his doorstep.

I'd been standing there for five minutes, gathering the nerve to knock. I was sure he'd seen me through the windows, but he'd given me time to pull myself together.

Or maybe it was so he could psych himself up to give me a piece of his mind.

I swallowed, nerves piling on top of my earlier nerves at his less than warm reception. "I was hoping we could talk."

He looked me up and down, crossing his arms over his chest. Roe wasn't a big man—I was taller than him—but he seemingly towered over me in that moment.

"I'm not sure what there is to say. Your actions have shattered any faith I had in you."

"I know. That's why I'm here. Can I come in?" I asked, gesturing to his family room.

Roe stood silently, his stare unflinching until he finally relented and stepped aside.

"Thank you," I mumbled as I walked past him. It had been a long time since I'd felt like a child, but in that moment, I was six years old and getting scolded by my parents for some harebrained scheme I'd thought up.

There had never been any awkwardness between us until now. He was standoffish, and I was anxious and a whole lot scared. My palms were sweaty, and my knees were knocking together. Roe and his friendship meant the world to me, and I'd be a poorer man if I lost him. I'd rehearsed a whole speech, the opening a walk down memory lane of the times we'd been there for each other, the middle arguments why we should still be friends, and my conclusion an olive-branch-call-to-action that I'd hoped would make him realize my sincerity. But standing here in his living room with all those memories smacking me in the face, my practiced words escaped me.

It was a good thing too. Roe would never stand for something so trite. He would expect something more than a prepared speech. He would expect honesty. The truth. Absolute sincerity.

The same things he always gave me.

"You're right to say that I broke your trust in me," I started, twisting my police-issue cap. "You shouldn't have found out like you did, and I should never have taken the leap to begin with."

I paused, mulling over my words. The thoughts that had been jackrabbiting around in my brain were silenced all at once. I was left with the overwhelming knowledge that my words were wrong. I was sorry he'd been blindsided, but how could I regret one moment with Zali, Flynn, and Tristan? How could I say that I was wrong for choosing them, for following my heart after all this time?

"No, that's not right," I corrected myself. "I am sorry I betrayed your trust in me, and I'm sorry that you found out the way you did—that I didn't speak to you first—but I don't regret choosing Zali. I couldn't ever regret that. I'm in love with her, with Flynn and Tristan too. I hate that I've potentially destroyed our friendship and your trust in me and that I've hurt you, but I can't say that I would take my actions back."

I huffed out a laugh that held no humour and scrubbed my hands over my face, groaning at the realizations hitting me like a ton of bricks. "That's not right either. I've been so caught up in trying not to hurt anyone that I've managed to hurt everyone." It had to stop. I had to stop. "That's the part I'd take back."

Roe sighed and gestured to the couch. "Take a load off, Ez."

He sat in his usual armchair, leaving the three-seater for me, and rested his elbows on his knees. He looked like he'd aged a decade in a matter of days, weighed down with worry. "I'm sorry I jumped to the conclusion that you were a paedophile. I know you, and that means I should have known better than to accuse you of that. Zali gave me a dressing-down and pointed out how wrong I was to accuse you. She was right."

"I can understand why you jumped to that conclusion though, especially knowing that I'd been with both Zali and

Flynn as well as Tristan. Two older men in positions of authority with two younger people? It doesn't look good." I dropped my gaze, staring at the floor. I was glad I couldn't see into his mind in that moment, but at the same time, I wanted to. At least that way, I'd see the right hook coming. But that sort of reaction was the absolute antithesis of everything Roe stood for. He was a lover, not a fighter.

As much as he hated me, he'd never try to hurt me like that.

It was why I needed him to understand.

"I promise you, Roe, I never, ever thought about either of them like that until well after they both turned eighteen. Zali and Flynn were both adults when I saw what was in front of me, and like Zali said, nothing happened between us until very recently. She, Flynn, and Tristan have been together for a little while longer."

"Are you and Tristan together now?" he asked, his blue-eyed gaze piercing mine.

"I want to be with him," I admitted. "I've been in love with Tris for a long time—longer than even Zali and Flynn. You know part of his story, but not the whole lot. Suffice it to say that by the time I was ready to reconsider what our relationship could look like, I'd fallen for Zali and Flynn too. He deserved better than a quarter of my heart."

"But Zali doesn't?"

"That's not what I said, and you know it." I exhaled, closing my eyes and forcing myself not to get defensive. He was my friend, and he was looking out for his daughter. I could empathize with how difficult this was for him.

"You know that if you reserve a quarter of your heart for yourself, it'll never work?"

I gnawed on my lip, and he added, "Spill."

"It's for Ryder."

Roe groaned and scrubbed his hand over his face. "Bloody hell, you sure do pick 'em, don't you? Ry doesn't exactly strike me as the type to share—"

"Or be into men?"

"Well, no, but I don't like to assume either. Maybe he hasn't felt comfortable coming out or he hasn't met the right person. Or people, I suppose." Roe flipped his hands over and held them palm-up, giving me a half shrug.

"Yeah, I can't see Ry ever being into me either." I shrugged, trying to play off the disappointment of knowing I had no hope with the man. But no matter what happened between us, it didn't change the way I felt about Zali, Flynn, and Tris. I met Roe's gaze once more and put it all on the line.

"I've been resisting all of them. I want us to be together, but I've been too scared to reach for them. I keep letting go. Then I can't keep away either. The whole cycle keeps repeating itself over and over. I'm hurting all of them every time I do it."

"Maybe that's telling you something," he suggested with a raised eyebrow.

"Yeah, that I'm being a coward. I need to step up."

I'd been hovering on the edge, not committing. Not because I didn't want to. I wanted it more than anything. I always had. But I was holding myself back because I knew it would destroy my friendship with Roe. The cat was out of the bag now, though, and I might lose him anyway. The only thing I'd succeeded doing in keeping the people I loved at arm's length was to risk my relationship with all of them. I didn't want to keep hurting Tris, Zali, and Flynn. Sooner or later, they'd get sick of me walking away and give me an ultimatum—be in it for real or fuck off. I'd pushed Tris away because I'd fallen for Zali and Flynn. But they'd found one another. They were together because they wanted to be, not because I couldn't choose. I wasn't giving them a quarter of my heart. I could give them the whole thing and they'd share it, keep it safe. They deserved that too.

Being with all of them was an impossible dream, but it was staring me in the face.

So what about my friendship with Roe? Where did that leave us?

The realization hit me; it wasn't my choice to make. It was Roe's decision to make, and I had to be okay with whatever the outcome.

"How do I step up, Roe?" I asked, wanting my friend's advice. He'd been there for me for years, always being a friendly ear and a solid confidant. "I want to be as brave as Zali and go for what I want. Flynn too. He's so open and loving. He never lets anything get between him and what's important. I want to take a chance like Tris did. He put his faith in Zali and Flynn and stepped straight off the ledge. It made him vulnerable as hell, but he's happy. They all are."

Roe studied me, his brows furrowed. "Aren't there rules against a professor dating his students?"

"That's what you took out of that?" I huffed out a laugh, but it held no humour. "Yes, there are rules. Tristan can kiss his career goodbye if the university ever found out about him being with either of them, never mind both. The rules protect students from being taken advantage of by a person in a position of authority."

Shaking my head, I smiled fondly. Even just thinking about the three of them had butterflies fluttering in my belly and love hearts appearing around my head like in a cartoon. "The thing is, they're the ones that hold the power. He's so head over heels in love with both Zali and Flynn that he'd do anything for them, including walk away from his job."

Monroe nodded and met my gaze, asking, "Does he feel the same about you?"

I grinned, effervescent bubbles surging through my veins and heat crawling up my throat. "Yeah. He does."

"So, it's all happy times, then? You and Tristan, Zali and Flynn, and Ry whenever you decide to spring that on him. In love and living your happily ever after?"

"I want that, but I also want your acceptance and support. I don't want to lose you, and I absolutely don't want it to affect your relationship with Zali."

"We'll see," he muttered, and my heart sank.

Here I was, hoping that I could pull off the impossible and experience a future together with all of us happy, while Roe was still deciding whether to toss me out of his life like last week's garbage. Talk about putting the cart before the horse.

I looked at him then, and aside from the worry, I saw his resigned acceptance. I saw his reluctant realization that I was genuinely in love with Zali and wasn't going to give up on him either. I wouldn't lose him as a friend because I didn't try—I wouldn't give up fighting for us until he told me that nothing could save our friendship—but I also couldn't let it stand in the way of what I had right in front of me.

"Was Rosa's dad happy when you started dating?" I asked, changing the subject.

He huffed, part annoyed and part sad. "No. He didn't believe that I was good enough for his little girl—I didn't either. I worked every damn day to prove him wrong, to support her in achieving her dreams, but he never changed his mind. He blamed me when she and Ash died, and it destroyed what semblance of a relationship we had. Nowadays they only keep in contact with Zali, but you know what she's like—she's too protective of me."

"She is." I smiled, warmth flowing through me to the tips of my toes. "She's pretty incredible."

He studied me, his eyes never leaving my face as he observed my reaction. "You sound like me gushing over Rosa."

"Yeah?"

He nodded, his gaze going somewhere far off. "I fell for Rosa the moment I saw her. She was standing in the sun and flicked her hair over her shoulder. I'll never forget the way the blond and red in it shimmered in the light. It took me a hot minute to gather up the courage to speak to her." He smiled wistfully and then chuckled. "I took her to opera on the beach for our first date."

I hesitated, looking at the man in front of me and having trouble picturing him in that kind of scene. "That's... romantic."

Roe met my gaze and smirked. "I was trying to impress her, but I'd worked so much overtime that week to afford the tickets, I was struggling to stay awake. She shouldn't have given me the time of day after I drooled all over her, but she asked me for a second date when I dropped her off."

"What did you do?"

"We went fishing."

I snorted out a laugh. That was so much more the Roe I knew.

"I already knew she was the one, but when she pulled up with fishing rods strapped to her roof, I was all in. I gave her all of me without hesitation. I loved her with all my heart." He pursed his lips, still consumed by his heartbreak.

The pain of losing her had been dulled by the passage of well over a decade, but it was still so raw for him. Zali too.

"I want the same for my daughter, Ezra. I want her to experience falling for the great love of her life. Beyond anything she's already achieved, I just want her to be happy."

"I want that too."

"Are you that man?" he asked, peering at me and seemingly staring into my soul.

"I want to be. I might not be the only great love of her life, but I really want to be one of them."

"Is it serious, the four of you?"

"Yes," I confirmed.

I'd gone there seeking Roe's forgiveness but would be walking away with so much more, regardless of whether he ever said the magic words. His words, his protectiveness of Zali and wanting only what was best for her was helping me see my own future. I'd feared losing him, but I didn't need to be scared because whatever happened between us, I knew I'd always have Zali, Flynn, and Tris. If I chose them. If I stopped this wishy-washy bullshit that I'd been pulling. All I had to do was step up and commit. Zali was right—they all deserved better than what I'd given them so far. So did I. I wouldn't hurt them again.

That didn't mean I didn't want Roe's friendship. It would gut me to lose him, but that great love he'd just spoken about—I already had it.

"It's definitely serious, Roe. Zali's not a fling for me. I've loved her for years. I've never taken the leap because of Flynn and Tris. But they're together too. I don't have to feel like I'm not giving enough of myself, because I can give them all of me now. We can be happy. We can give Zali the great love story you want for her."

"How do you see that working?" he asked, shaking his head and holding his hands out in genuine confusion.

"Simple. I'll do whatever it takes to keep all of them safe and happy," I answered without hesitation.

Complete honesty and transparency.

I sucked in a breath and steeled myself. If I truly wanted to repair our friendship, I still needed to fill in some gaps.

"There's more that you need to know," I added, wincing at the dark look Roe sent my way as he waited impatiently for me to carefully choose my words. "No charges will be laid—Zali proved that it was all a misunderstanding—but last week I placed Zali under arrest—" I held up my hand when Roe opened his mouth to speak, imploring him to give me a chance to explain.

He exhaled slowly, his nostrils flaring as he stood and walked away, facing the river.

I continued, my words tumbling out, any semblance of a filter gone. "It wasn't my choice, and I did everything I could to get them out of it, but Puglisi ordered their arrest. I wanted to be the one to do it so I could try to protect Zali."

He whirled around, his eyes flashing and every muscle in his body vibrating. "Protect her, how?" he seethed through gritted teeth.

"I took the lead, interviewing them—"

"Was this before or after you got inside my daughter's pants?"

"Roe—"

He pointed at me, his whole hand shaking as he turned red in the face. "Don't you dare Roe me," he snapped. "Answer the bloody question."

"Before," I said quietly, my gaze dropping to the floor like a scolded child. "After." I huffed, frustration lacing my tone. "I kissed Zali, then I arrested her. Two other detectives arrested Flynn and Ryder."

"Are you kidding me?" he asked, throwing his hands in the air. He shook his head and ground his teeth together. "What the hell were you thinking, Ezra?"

"I don't know," I mumbled. "I couldn't go on. I needed to tell Zali, to finally let her know how I felt. I was going out of my mind, but I shouldn't have kissed her like that, especially not then."

"At least we're in agreement there." Roe slowly turned again and made his way back over to the windows to stare out over the rippling water. He scrubbed his hands over his face and groaned. "Help me understand where Tristan fits into this mess."

"He was in his office. He called me wanting to talk just after I'd taken them into custody." I cleared my throat, trying to swallow past the lump that rose when Roe gave me a death glare worthy of a horror movie.

"I gave Tris all the information I could, and he arranged representation. Zali already had her own counsel teed up, and between the information she gave us and the lawyers she hired for Flynn and Ryder doing their thing, all the charges were dropped."

"Right," he said, drawing out the vowel. "So first it's Tristan breaking the rules, and now you."

I nodded slowly. "I broke every rule there is." Meeting his gaze, I added, "And I'd do it again if it meant keeping them safe."

He cocked his head to the side, zeroing in on my comment. "That's the second time you've said that. Are Zali, Flynn, and Ry in danger?"

He'd just asked the sixty-four-thousand-dollar question. "Not from the police. Not anymore. Zali helped protect a lot of data; she just did it in a way that was... unconventional."

He waved his hand as if dismissing that concern. As angry as he was, he knew I wouldn't lie to him on that. He believed me when I said that the charges were dropped. "From whom, then? I know you hung around after you left that night—I saw you pull away after Zali left. You were tailing her, weren't you?"

"I was guarding her," I confirmed, trying to pick my words carefully. "A couple of threats have been made against Tris that are tied to the podcast. We aren't sure who issued them, but Zali's working on narrowing it down." I paused, trying to sort through my thoughts to word the sledgehammer I was about to deliver with a modicum of tact. "The results of Zali's research for the podcast are suggesting that one of Rosa's staff may have been embezzling funds. They're theorizing that Rosa became aware of it and acted to stop the theft. The threats reflect that Rosa's and Ash's deaths might not have been accidental."

Roe stilled. His body turned to stone, tears instantly springing to his eyes and overflowing, tracking down his cheeks. The heartbreak in his eyes before he slipped them closed stole my breath, ripping out my heart and shredding it to a million pieces.

"You bloody well do your job," he ordered, his voice barely a hoarse whisper, his index finger pointed at me. "Keep my little girl safe, Ez."

"Always," I promised, and Roe nodded, his jaw clenched tight and lips pursed. I made my way to the front door, knowing he would want some privacy. "Yours is the most important friendship I've ever had, Roe. I hope you understand that. I don't want it to be over, but if you decide we're done, you should know that I'll always cherish you. I want your blessing, but I won't wait for it."

"Keep my daughter safe, and I'll give you anything you want." He shook his head and wiped the tears that had tracked down his face.

"I'll do that anyway." I tapped the doorframe with my hand. "I'm sorry, Roe. Not for falling for Zali—I could never be sorry for that—but for not talking to you about it. For disrespecting your position as her dad and my best friend and for dumping this on you. The moment I know something, you'll be the first person I call."

"Protect her, Ez. Please, I'm begging you."

"With my life." I slipped out the door, closing it quietly, and made my way to my car. There was only one place I wanted to be—in their arms.

TWENTY

Tristan

I hung my jacket on the back of my office door and pulled it open again when the quick rap of knuckles sounded. No doubt I looked like a goof when a giddy butterflies-in-your-belly grin split my lips just at the sight of Zali and Flynn.

Zali didn't wait for an invitation before breezing in and grabbing my butt as she walked past. "Is your passport in order?" she asked me the moment I closed the door behind Flynn. But she looked distracted, gazing around my office while a slow, supremely satisfied smile tilted her lips.

She could pull off any outfit, but the one she had on was one of my favourites. She'd paired white sneakers with tailored cornflower blue shorts and an adorable little top that tied up between her breasts. Her hair was in loose braids, the pigtails hanging over her shoulders so damn innocent that I wanted to strip her out of everything and bend her over my desk.

Sucking in a breath, I tore my gaze away from her and immediately zeroed in on Flynn. He was…. How did I get so bloody lucky?

He was our angel. Just as gorgeous as Zali, he was dressed in cream linen pants and a white button-down shirt. The ensemble was the epitome of style in a relaxed summery way, the complete opposite to my dark suits and shirts.

"Tris?" Flynn asked, biting back a laugh as I jumped.

"Sorry, what?"

"He's reminiscing. This office holds fond memories," Zali teased.

"Drooling," I corrected, reaching for them.

Flynn was the first to step into my embrace, and I captured his lips with my own, our tongues slowly exploring together as I tangled my fingers in his hair and moaned into his mouth. God, I'd missed them. We'd been together most of the morning, but having them sit in my class while I delivered a lecture, unable to touch either one of them, was hellacious.

Zali slipped her arm around my waist, and I pulled back, the three of us keeping our heads close. I sucked in a lungful of air, taking their combined scents into me and holding my breath. I wanted them like that forever—under my skin and wrapped around me at the same time.

"Fuck, I missed you," I whispered on a rush, sliding my lips against Zali's.

She deepened our kiss, and the first touch of our tongues was like electricity zapping through my veins, lighting me up and sizzling every neuron inside me.

Flynn cleared his throat, and Zali reluctantly pulled back. "Okay, yeah."

She straightened her spine and lifted her chin, morphing into the woman I'd seen in class that first day. It was like an armour she donned, but this time it wasn't to fight with me. I knew she was pulling herself together, forcing back the desire still swimming in her eyes. If I slipped my hand between her legs, I knew she'd be wet.

Humming, I flicked my gaze down and bit my lip. I wanted a taste. Just a hint. One swipe of my tongue against her core. It would never be enough, but a little persuasion sometimes went a long way.

"No," she chastised me, playfully narrowing her eyes. "No sex. This is important."

I blinked, snapping out of my lascivious thoughts. "Sorry," I apologized, forcing my brain to come back online.

"I've been doing some research," Zali started, and the playful smile that hadn't left my lips since they'd walked in slipped away.

I knew what she did for a living, and I knew she was still doing it. It didn't make it easier to hear. Every one of my fears roared up, blindsiding me. My eyes locked on hers, and the colour drained from my face as fast as my stomach bottomed out. I swallowed, trying to stop myself from being sick, my stomach flip-flopping, and not in the good way.

Flynn's arm around my waist was the only thing holding me up. I leaned against him, absorbing the strength and calm he was lending me.

"Hey," she added gently, taking my hands and squeezing them. "Not that kind of research. The legal kind."

"Okay," I conceded, blowing out a slow breath I hadn't even realized I was holding. I concentrated on them, on their gentle touch and their steady presence. There was no hiding the tremble in my hands or the wooziness that had washed over me with the force of a tsunami.

Zali cupped my face and pressed her lips to my cheek, standing on tiptoe to reach, and I clutched her waist, drawing her close and holding on to her for dear life.

"You okay?" Flynn asked, and I nodded, wrapping an arm around his waist.

"Let's sit," I suggested, gesturing at the bench seat that lined one wall of my office.

Zali slipped onto the bench next to me, and Flynn pulled up a chair. He sat perched on the edge, my knees bracketing his. I held their hands and nodded for Zali to continue.

"I haven't been able to verify the owners of some accounts that RemagINC transferred funds to. Turns out they were all opened at the one bank."

"That can't be a coincidence." My gaze bounced between them.

When Flynn and Zali both shook their heads and agreed, I let out a breath. "So what's the plan? You can't exactly get their names...."

"That's where I need you to trust me." Zali took my hand in hers and squeezed. "I promise you, Tristan, I will keep you safe. Nothing, and I mean, nothing will touch you."

I hung my head and closed my eyes. I believed her. I really did, but fear was a bitch.

"Tris," Flynn murmured, his voice a soothing balm. "I need you to talk to us."

"I'm… okay. It's stupid. Every time I hear about what Zali does, I'm fucking terrified. The walls start closing in, and I can feel the blows raining down on me." I exhaled and rubbed my chest, the broken ribs I'd suffered having long since healed, but the phantom pain was as real as it had been that day.

Zali brushed a piece of my hair behind my ear, but as soon as she lifted her hand, it fell forward. She did it again, her soft touch soothing. "I'm sorry—"

"No, this is on me." I shook my head. "I trust you; I do. It's just a lot for me to get my head around. I've spent so long hiding away from anything that could possibly bite me in the arse that I just…."

"I get it." She gave me a small smile and ran her fingers through my hair again. "I was going to suggest a research trip, but maybe it's better that you stay."

"Is that why I need a passport?"

"It is." She nodded and shrugged. "There's a ball in Monaco in a few days. I thought we could go on that date."

"Monaco?" I stuttered, my eyes going comically wide.

She bit her lip and eyed me like she wanted to eat me. My cock twitched at the intensity of her gaze. "Mmhm. At the Monte Carlo Casino."

Flynn's hand landed on my thigh, and he inched it up until his thumb pressed against my balls. My breath caught, and he chuckled, a soft puff of air against my cheek. I clutched his shirt, drawing him closer, and he shifted, rubbing me through my pants.

"I want to see Flynn peel you out of a tux," Zali murmured, nibbling on my throat.

"Yes," I gasped, my cock rock hard and desperate.

But they stilled as one and pulled back, a silent conversation passing between them.

"The flight leaves tonight," Zali said. "I'd love to see you there, but this is your decision, Tristan. I don't want you to feel forced into anything. No matter what choice you make, I'll still love you."

The sincerity in her eyes drew me in, and I found myself falling for her all over again.

"So will I," Flynn added, bussing a lingering kiss to my temple as he stood. I reached for his hand, squeezing it, trying to hold onto him for a moment longer. "I'll text you the details. If you're not there, we'll text you as soon as we land to let you know we arrived safe."

My cock hated me, but my heart and my mind were on the same page. The weight that had been suffocating me only a few moments ago lifted, and I breathed easy. This was my moment, the one in which I either committed to being all in or the one I used to distance myself from that part of them. I didn't know if I could successfully turn a blind eye. I didn't know whether I could be with them and yet be completely innocent of any wrongdoing, knowing the kind of work Zali did. But the fact that they'd given me the choice meant the world.

"Thank you." Standing up, I gathered Flynn in my arms and kissed him slowly, pulling back only to press our foreheads together before drawing Zali in. When our kiss slowed, I held them tight and whispered, "I don't know if I'll be there. But I'll think about it."

"That's all we can ask." Zali cupped my face and pressed her lips to mine again. "I love you, Professor Reid."

"And I you. Both of you."

I drummed my fingers on the desk, a fast pace that exposed just how twisted up inside I was. Should I, or shouldn't I? The answer escaped me.

I'd downed too many cups of coffee, and I was jittery from the caffeine overload as well as the incessant buzzing in my brain. Wearing a track in the carpet in my office hadn't worked, so I'd walked the quad.

But no answers had come.

The knock on my door startled the fuck out of me. Gripping my desk for support, I growled, "Enter."

I didn't expect Ezra to push through it, but both relief and fear slammed into me when he did. "What happened?" I rasped, my heart lodged in my throat.

No more threats had been delivered to my door, but that didn't mean we were out of the woods. Ry had shadowed Zali and Flynn to the university—he'd waited outside the room while I'd delivered class—and I was under strict instructions to have security walk me to my car. The thought that security would be able to stop something from happening was ridiculous. They were there as a deterrent, not a protective detail. But I'd acquiesced, promising Zali I wouldn't go anywhere by myself.

He closed the door before padding over to me and climbing onto my lap. I grasped his hips and held him close, pressing my face against his throat and just breathing him in for a moment.

"Nothing happened except that I woke up."

Lifting my head, I furrowed my brow and opened my mouth to ask what he was talking about. He pressed his finger to my lips before replacing it with his own and kissing me ever so softly.

"I hurt you, and for that I'm sorry. I was holding back, trying to keep everyone happy, and I realized that instead of helping, I was hurting everyone. You in particular."

I nuzzled his stubbled cheek and let my eyes slip closed, falling into the strength of his arms around my shoulders.

"I'm sorry that you laid your heart on the line and I stomped on it," he whispered.

"What are you saying?" I asked, my heart in my throat. I wasn't sure if this was a final goodbye or something entirely different, but I'd been chasing my tail, spinning around and dizzying myself up until I didn't know which way was up. I needed him to spell it out for me.

"I'm saying I love you." He kissed me, just a brush of his lips against my cheek, but it was one of the most intimate kisses I'd ever experienced. "I'm saying I'm all in. I want this. I want us." Another kiss, another flutter of his eyelashes against my cheek. "I want you." He stared into my eyes and gave me a heart-stopping smile. "Zali and Flynn too. Ry as well, but that's up to him."

I kissed him then, cupping his face and plunging my tongue into his mouth to caress his. Tasting him and teasing him, I drank him in.

"No more walking away," I whispered against his lips.

"Never. I choose you. I love you."

I squeezed him in a bear hug, holding him close. I was home. Finally home. "I love you too."

We sat like that, my chair creaking every time we pressed closer together. It was like we wanted to climb into each other, to meld, our base elements reforming as a compound, bound together at our core.

Our lips met over and over, and even though we were both hard, we never pushed for more. Holding each other was enough.

"Have you spoken with Zali and Flynn?" I murmured when we'd broken apart for air, our lips kiss swollen.

"Not yet. I needed to see you first." He pulled back and reached up to play with the same piece of hair Zali had been fingering. "What's going on?"

"They asked me to go to Monaco with them."

"When?"

"Tonight." I swallowed. "Zali's looking for information. She asked me to trust her. I do, but I'm scared too." I didn't need to tell him why I was terrified. He'd seen the fallout, the aftermath of my stint in jail.

He pursed his lips in a tight smile that was more of a grimace. "Does she know?"

I nodded. "She knows everything."

"Okay." He ran his hand through his hair and exhaled slowly before nodding. "Right, then."

TWENTY-ONE

Zali

The airport buzzed with conversation and the hustle and bustle of people rushing to catch their planes. I was flat, my mood pretty urgh. I meant what I'd said to Tristan and Ezra—I'd respect the hell out of both of them if they didn't come, but damn did I want them to be there and the knowledge that they might not... that they probably wouldn't was like a storm cloud hanging over me. It was official. I was moping.

The disembodied voices on the PA system were almost impossible to understand, but I didn't even try. I played with the handle on my oversized purse and studied the carpeted floor at my feet. I barely suppressed a sigh as another minute ticked by on my watch.

Another announcement came over the loudspeaker, this one from our gate, and my heart sank. This was it. Neither Tristan nor Ezra was coming.

No, don't think like that. At least they had each other while they were here. Hopefully they could sort out whatever was going on between them while we were away.

"This is us." Flynn nudged me and I hoisted my purse over my shoulder as I stood. My sigh was involuntary, and Flynn didn't miss it. He slipped his arm into mine and leaned in close to whisper, "They'll be waiting for us when we get back."

"Yeah, hopefully."

"They will. Have faith and trust them." We joined the queue of first-class passengers shuffling forward as boarding passes were scanned. Each step was like swimming against the tide—harder and harder the stronger the pull was. The pull to Tristan and Ezra was intense.

I didn't want to go without them.

But I had a real shot here at getting justice.

Revenge.

I promised myself that I'd do what it took. Now I needed to follow through with it.

"Wait!" The shout startled me, and I froze, the familiar voice pouring over me like honey. I choked out a sob and Flynn wrapped his arm around my shoulders, holding me tight.

Tristan skidded to a stop at our feet with Ezra right behind him. They were out of breath and flustered, but Tristan took my hands in his and huffed out a relieved laugh. All eyes were on us, the few hundred passengers about to embark the flight to Dubai suddenly focussed on the five of us. But as I gazed into his eyes, everyone else fell away. All the distractions and chatter muted, our group surrounded by a protective bubble.

"We're coming," he said, his voice filled with a promise. "We're here. For all of it."

I blinked back tears. I'd resigned myself to making the trip with the three of us. I was just hoping I didn't get complete radio silence from Tristan and Ezra. I knew Tristan loved us, and I knew Ezra was trying, but I also knew that if they wanted their worlds to stay the same, neither could ever fully accept what I did. Would I walk away for them? Would I put my keyboard down and live life inside a little square box so we could really be together? For the first time in my life, I wanted to fit inside those boundaries that constrained everyone else. I wanted to be a law-abiding citizen, to have a nine-to-five and come home every night to a house full of my men and live the fairy tale.

If it meant having them, remaking myself in that image didn't seem so bad.

"All of it?" I asked, needing to understand exactly what he'd meant.

"Every single thing, good or bad," Ezra murmured, stepping up and running his hand down my bare arm. It sent a shiver through me, and Flynn pressed his hand to the small of my back, snuggling in closer as if to keep me warm. "We're walking into this with eyes wide open, Zali."

"What about your past?" I asked Tristan, squeezing his hand. I was hardly going to go into detail, but we needed to have this conversation, and I didn't want to do it when we were ten kays up in the air in a flying tin can and he couldn't leave.

"It will always be there, but I can't keep letting it stop me from moving forward. You asked me to trust you, and I do. With everything in me."

I let go of his hands and stepped into his arms, his strength and warmth surrounding me. I never wanted to let him go. Burying my face in his chest, I breathed him in. His heartbeat was strong and steady against my cheek, and his words soothed me.

"I love you, kitten, and you, angel." Tristan pulled away from me momentarily, but instead of putting space between us, he tugged Flynn into our hug. They bracketed me as they snuggled closer.

Tristan tilted my chin up and pressed a chaste kiss to my lips, barely a brush of his lips against mine. "I'm coming with you. I'm in this 100 percent. Never in my wildest dreams did I think we could have this." He motioned between us, then gestured to Ezra and glanced at Ry, including him too.

That small action told me just how well he knew me—I needed Ry as much as I needed the three of them. Even if our relationship never turned into something more, he would always have a place next to me. In some ways, he was the most important person in my world, and Tristan's acceptance of that caused a weight to lift off my shoulders.

"I never thought I could be part of something so wonderful, but we have it, and I'll be damned if I walk away." He cupped my face, his green eyes serious. They were filled with a promise that stole my breath. "We do what needs to be done. Together. We finish this. We get justice. And we love each other."

He paused, just for a split second. His wicked grin lit up his face, and I swooned, actually going weak in the knees. Tristan added almost as an afterthought, "And I'm taking you on that damn date."

I laugh-sobbed, and he tightened his hold on me before wiping away my tears with his thumbs and pressing a lingering kiss to my forehead. It was sweet above anything else, but it was worth a million words. It said, *I love you. I trust you. I want you. I accept you exactly the way you are.*

He cupped my nape and held me close. I buried my face in his chest and breathed him in, his spicy scent enveloping me. Tristan lifted his hand to Flynn's face, his fingertips skimming our man's smooth jaw. "Then you're going to peel me out of my tux."

Flynn barked out a laugh, excitement and desire sparking in his sapphire eyes, and he smile-kissed Tristan before doing it again, this time slow and soft.

I reached for Ezra, needing him too. "Everything?" I asked.

"Yes, Queen. Everything." He cupped my face, his rough hands gentle against my cheeks. "I know about you too, Zali. I'm here for it." As if he'd read my mind, he added, "I wouldn't change a single thing about you."

Relief swamped me, but at the same time, my gut flip-flopped, nerves churning through me. I'd managed to keep my online pseudonym hidden from the police for a long time, and here I was in an international airport terminal, about to leave the country in the presence of a federal copper. The man in front of me was freely admitting he knew I was guilty of breaking just about every national and international cyber-security law there was, and he had the power to take me into custody, destroying any chance I had of pulling off this plan.

But all that fear paled in comparison to my biggest worry. Flicking my gaze to Tristan, who'd stepped back, breaking our embrace, I watched as he wrapped an arm around Ezra. I'd never thought of Ezra as a flight risk, and I empathized with why he was struggling, but I couldn't watch him destroy Tristan again. Seeing Tristan's heartbreak was enough for me to ask Ezra to walk away now if he couldn't commit.

I explained, "I don't want you to leave. I don't want you to hurt Tris again."

Ezra shook his head, his eyes shining with honesty. "I'm done doing that."

He turned to Tristan, and the utter adoration in each of their gazes, the love and dedication, stole my breath.

"I'm all in too." He nuzzled Tristan's cheek before turning his attention back to me, a sadness in his eyes that wasn't there a moment ago.

"I was scared of losing your dad, but our relationship has already changed. I was hurting you—all of you—by holding back. I could have lost you. I deserved to, as well. You should have told me to walk away, but you didn't...." He closed his eyes and shook his head before pinning me with his azure gaze, bright and intense. "I'm so grateful for that, Zali. I want a future with you." He looked up and locked eyes with the person standing behind me. Ry. "All of you. Forever."

"I love you," I whispered to him, to all of them.

Ezra tucked a lock of hair behind my ear and ran the backs of his fingertips down my cheek. "I love you, Zali. Every feisty, demanding, intelligent, snark-castic piece of you. Give me the chance to walk with you wherever you go."

I nodded, my head bobbing up and down and my teary smile so broad that it hurt my cheeks. My heart was filled to overflowing. "Yes," I answered in a rush.

The last of the first-class passengers had boarded, but I held back a moment, giving Ezra and Tristan one last chance to pull out. But neither hesitated, handing over their boarding passes to the steward.

Twenty-four hours of travel had landed us in Dubai airport in need of a shower. I was exhausted, yet I also needed to burn off some energy. Sitting sedentary for so long made me antsy.

I'd only been to Dubai once before in the middle of summer on a layover to London for a meeting. The contrast between the two had been spectacular. Heat had shimmered off the surface of the runways, and it was like a slap to the face when I'd left the air-conditioned comfort of the terminal. This time it was like arriving to a Gold Coast winter— perfect jeans and T-shirt weather, except we didn't get to experience it.

Transiting through Dubai was a must for this trip. The designer I'd chosen for my dress was in Lebanon, but he had a boutique in Dubai only a hop, skip, and a jump away from the airport. I'd sent through my measurements, and my gown would be delivered to the first-class lounge for me to try on and have alterations completed. I'd done the same for the suits, tailors gathering en masse to have Tristan's bespoke tuxedo completed and Ezra's and Ryder's off-the-shelf suits perfectly fitted before being delivered direct to Monaco for the ball.

Money spoke, and in Dubai they listened.

They'd come through spectacularly.

Tristan, Ezra, and Ry were standing in front of me, dressed to perfection. I glanced across at Flynn and smirked as he eyed the three of them like they were a buffet of perfectly cooked steaks. As my date for the night, Tristan was gorgeous—dressed head to toe in black, the tuxedo fitted his frame perfectly, hugging his narrow waist and flaring out at his broad shoulders.

Ry and Ezra would be there too but in different guises, and they needed tuxedos to match. I'd managed to get Ezra a security pass to make him look like he was part of the team. His uniform for the night was a burgundy jacket, black pants, vest, and bow tie with a crisp white shirt. The colour only served to highlight how beautiful he was.

Ry was simply smoking hot. Dressed the same as Ezra except for a navy-blue jacket, he was joining the catering crew. His eyes blazed, the hazel in them contrasting so vividly with the dark shades of his tuxedo that I was a whimpering mess.

Flynn wasn't faring any better, pressing the heel of his hand down against his erection when Ry had walked out of the portable change room so the tailor could adjust his suit to get a perfect fit.

The only one of us who wouldn't be getting dressed up was Flynn. He wasn't happy about it, and I hated that he wouldn't get the date that Tristan wanted to take us both on, but at the same time I was relieved to have one fewer person in the potential line of fire. Flynn's role was critical to pulling this whole operation off. All of them were, but it would all come down to Flynn's eye for detail. It was an ambitious plan, and I was under no misapprehension that I could pull it off without them—even with them, it was probably destined to fail spectacularly, but I needed to try. Potentially finding out who murdered Mum and Ash and was now after Tristan would be worth it.

I exhaled heavily, the weight of that responsibility sitting square on my shoulders. But even if I could have done it alone, they would never have let me. Having my guys by my side for this whole trip meant the world to me. Ezra was likely to get fired for walking out of his job without giving any notice, and Tristan's boss didn't even know he was away. If he suspected Tristan wasn't working from home like he'd said, Tristan would be answering some uncomfortable questions. But none of them had hesitated. I'd thought up the plan and set a few balls in motion. Then Flynn and Ry had chipped in and helped with the logistics. The other two had dropped what they were doing and traipsed halfway around the world at a moment's notice. It meant the world to me. *They* meant the world to me.

Truthfully, I hadn't expected Tristan to come, and while I loved having him with us, I would have respected the fuck out of him for sticking to his guns and saying no. I focussed on him, meeting his gaze and relaxing into a smile that was inexplicably shy and a whole lot giddy. Warmth bubbled in my chest and heat crawled up my throat as I looked away, the flush taking me by surprise.

That moment—the one where he'd promised to take us on a date—was burned in my memory as one of my favourites. I couldn't wait to experience it, to be able to walk down the street holding their hands.

Tristan's gaze heated, and he hummed low and sensual, the way he did when he was turned the hell on. It snapped me back to the present. Blinking, I looked around and saw the others waiting expectantly on me.

"Sorry?"

"Are the shoes to your satisfaction, ma'am?" the tailor asked patiently. Clearly it wasn't the first time he'd asked that question.

They were leather, polished to a mirror-like reflection, each pair of Louboutin and Dior shoes slightly different and perfectly suited to my guys' roles. I inclined my head and waited for them to be presented to my guys.

"Very good," he murmured as they completed their outfits.

"Perfect." I smiled and added with a wave of my hand in their direction, "I'll take everything."

He bowed, and our butler murmured in a quiet, unobtrusive voice, "I will have your gown, the tuxedos, and all your shoes boxed and added to your checked luggage, madame. Your driver will take care of it when you land in Nice and safely deliver you to the Villa La Vigie."

"Thank you." I didn't need to dismiss them. They melted into the woodwork, trained to never be seen unless they were needed. I couldn't help but think they were the fairy godmothers of the rich and famous.

Another seven hours and we were in a Lincoln Continental SUV, being whisked to one of the most exclusive villas in Monte Carlo. My head was on a swivel, and excitement bubbled in my veins as the gates to the sprawling estate parted and the driver inched forward along the manicured drive. The stately mansion was perched gracefully atop the peak of the Pointe de la Veille, the grounds lit by strategically placed spotlights highlighting the magnificence of the stone building.

Darkness surrounded us, glimpses of the city lights teasing us every time we rounded a sweeping bend in the drive. I reached for Ezra's hand, squeezing it as I squirmed in my seat and bounced on my toes, trying to peek between the lush forest leading to the crest of the point.

"Wow," Flynn murmured from his spot, cuddled up to Tristan in the middle row.

I shot my gaze right and gasped, the flash of the view such a tease. It was gone as quickly as it had appeared, darkness enveloping us once more.

"It's going to be so beautiful," I breathed.

Our driver pulled up at the base of a stone staircase leading to double glass doors. He got out and came around to open our doors. The sweet scent of roses and night jasmine permeated the air, and I spied the source immediately. A pink climbing rose grew along the trellis, resplendent against the limestone walls.

"This way, please," our driver beckoned, gesturing up the stairs, then waited for us to ascend before he followed. "The view is magnifique."

A patio stretched out before us, lined in terracotta with a stone railing. Lounge furniture was placed in the middle, and although it was tempting to flop down onto them and never move again, the view drew me to the edge of the low railing.

God, I was living in a dream.

The villa overlooked the entire coastline of the Baie de Roquebrune. The water was lit by the moon's silver glow and the lights from the superyachts moored in the bay. The city hugged the coastline. Centuries-old sandstone buildings were lit from below, casting a warm glow over their facades. Modern high rises towered above the stately old buildings, their windows reflecting the light and multiplying it. It was as if we were standing on a carpet of stars glittering in the night sky. It was simply spectacular.

Just like the darkened waters on our left, the shadow of the mountains to our right soared above us. The city was perched on a sliver of land cradled gently between nature's arms.

The view was breathtaking at night. I couldn't wait to see it during the day.

I breathed in the briny air mixed with rose, jasmine, and hints of the pine forest below and reached for my guys. They flanked me, Ezra to my left, Flynn to my right, and Tristan next to him. Joined hands rested at the small of my back, and I leaned my head on Flynn's shoulder, still taking in the sheer magnificence of the view. This moment, the quiet contemplation, would be etched into my memory for a lifetime.

Ry joined us on the patio, resting his elbows on the railing, and my night was perfect. This was how I wanted to remember Monte Carlo—the five of us together, watching the waves lap against the shoreline and the twinkling lights below us.

"Pretty fucking impressive isn't it," Ry murmured, voicing my thoughts to a tee.

"Pardon me, madame," our driver interrupted, his head bowed in apology. "The staff have prepared a light meal for you in case you are hungry. Your luggage has been deposited into the two bedrooms requested, and your vehicle is ready in the garage."

"Thanks, Marco," Ry responded, reaching out to shake his hand. "Appreciate it."

Marco inclined his head and strode away.

"Are we gonna scope out the casino tonight?" Flynn asked, sliding right into his spy role. I snorted out a laugh and he elbowed me playfully. "Hey, you won't let me get dressed up. At least let me pretend to be in on it.

I furrowed my brow, my mouth open and horror in my tone as I grasped his arm. "Is that what you think? That I don't want you involved?" I shook my head, hating that he wouldn't meet my gaze. "It's not that at all. Flynn, I want you in the car because you're the best person to watch the live feed. You have an eye for faces. You'll recognize Moragreiga the moment you see him. You'll be able to tell us exactly who he is if we don't spot him. Sure, Tristan could run the recording, and Ry is the best driver out of all of us. But you'll spot our target from a mile away and direct us straight to him. This whole trip will be for nothing if we don't have the right person."

He raised his gaze to my own, and the gratitude there stole my breath. "Okay." He nodded and gave me a tentative smile. "I can do that."

Tristan rested his hands on Flynn's shoulders and massaged them before dropping a kiss to his hair.

"We should eat, then try to get a few hours' sleep," Ry suggested. "We have a lot of logistics to nut out and a lot to prepare before tomorrow night."

"Do you know what car we have?" Ezra asked him. "I'm glad we won't be relying on a taxi or rideshare to get us out of there, but I'd rather not be trying to squeeze into something tiny either."

Ry grinned. "Oh, she's beautiful. I'm driving her first." He waggled his eyebrows. "My new baby is in the garage."

If I'd thought the night before was gorgeous, the morning had stepped it up to a whole other level. The sun had risen over the Mediterranean, and although I'd seen a hundred sunrises before, it was something special knowing we were on the opposite side of the world. I'd drunk my tea in silence—speechlessness, actually. I'd looked around at the city below us, and I was lost for words.

But the ballroom had me awestruck. It was elegance personified. Marble columns supported the towering lime-washed arched ceilings. Intricate crystal chandeliers hung from the beams, scattering warm light over the expansive room. Every column, beam, and ornately carved medallion was inlaid with gold leaf. A sense of luxury permeated every corner of the ballroom.

Between the soaring arches of the ceiling, Renaissance frescos adorned the walls. They were a hundred and fifty years old, and each one was a masterpiece. The brushstrokes and the colours were incredible. There was no AI to tweak the images, no digital enhancements to clean up the edges. These murals were hand drawn and took years to complete. I could imagine the artists standing on top of scaffolding, perfecting each tiny stroke, correcting and recorrecting each piece until they were finished. The artists would have been up there for years, dealing with the complexities of heat and cold, light and dark, and the only technology they had to aid their work were brushes, scaffolds, and candles. It was inspiring.

"They're remarkable," Flynn murmured in my earpiece that was hidden by the curls tucked over my shoulder. "I wish I could see them for real."

I wished Flynn was in here with us too, but like I'd told him last night, I needed him watching our video feeds and running facial recognition software in case we missed spotting the face of the Grande Banque Unie. Tristan's and my only aim for the night was to engage Felipe Moragreiga in conversation. To distract him for just a moment.

"It's indescribable," I murmured, half to Tristan and half to Flynn.

My mic was disguised by the diamond choker I wore, and my camera was fitted into the diamante clip in my hair. My intricate Swarovski crystal mask was a perfect match to my jewellery and my red Elie Saab gown. My whole getup—including the technology that we were about to deploy—was more *Mission Impossible* or *007* than real life, but apparently that was my life now.

"Sorry to rain on your parade, but we've got a limited timeframe to do this," Ezra whispered apologetically.

He was right. I needed to get my head in the game, but ever since coming down those stairs in the villa to four men gazing up at me watching my every step, I'd been floating on air.

"We'll try to come back," Tristan promised. He was fitted with an earpiece too, his camera hidden in the top pocket of his tuxedo, and his throat mic was tucked safely under his shirt. Tristan's mask was almost bronze, the delicate patterns a contrast to the masculinity he was oozing. "Let's get a drink and mingle."

With a hand resting on the small of my back, he guided us through the upper-class echelons of Europe. I'd already seen a movie star or two as well as a few sports stars—a Formula One driver and a soccer player and their entourages. It was no wonder the casino had taken on extra security for the night; it was the perfect way for Ezra to sneak in under the radar.

Crystal glasses clinked together, the sound of money talking. The hum of voices was reserved, the boredom of old money only showing a glimmer of excitement when they came across a famous face. The spark of excitement it caused in the volume of conversation sent a frisson of electricity through the crowd and set my heart to thrumming. It was beating hard, rising in cadence with the string quartet tucked onto the stage as they reached the crescendo of the piece they were playing.

I looked in their direction, spotting Ezra instantly. Even in a suit designed to blend into the furniture, he stood out like a beacon. The beauty of Baie de Roquebrune at his back and the glittering lights of the city surrounding it were no match for him.

The Villa La Vigie was across the bay, and as ridiculous as it sounded, I wanted to be back there. The opulence, the money—none of it was me. None of it was *us*. I wanted to get back to the villa and watch the sun come up after I'd stripped my guys naked and rode them until we were hot and sweaty.

All of them.

Tristan closed his hand over mine, slipping in closer to me. I leaned in, grateful for his warmth at my side. My gown was incredible, but there wasn't much of it. Even with the heaters in the ballroom set to toasty, my skin was prickling with the cold. Coming from a sub-tropical summer, the European winter, no matter how mild it was, still required a fuck tonne of adjusting. The layer of silk that barely covered me wasn't doing much to help.

Ry circled the room, holding a tray of champagne flutes aloft as he moved.

"Any sign?" Ezra asked, his disembodied voice a deep whisper in our earpieces.

"Not yet," Flynn responded. "But we've still got time. He's not due to make the speech for another hour yet."

Minutes ticked by as Tristan and I made our way around the room, exchanging pleasantries with Europe's socialites.

A beautiful woman eyed me up and down, smiling politely as we neared. "Your dress is stunning," she gushed, holding her delicate hand out. "Benedikte, pleased to meet you."

I shook her hand, her grasp surprisingly firm compared to the some of the people who'd shaken my hand that night. "Zali, and the pleasure is all mine. This is my partner, Tristan."

They shook, and she exclaimed, "You're Australian! My boyfriend, Nikolai, and I are moving there soon to study."

"We are. Where are you moving to?" Tristan asked just as Flynn's voice came through my earpiece.

"Nikolai is Count Nikolai of Denmark. He's literal royalty. Benedikte is his girlfriend."

"Sydney. We have been accepted into the University of Technology."

"UTS is one of Australia's best universities," Tristan responded with a smile, adding, "And Sydney is one of our most beautiful cities."

We spoke for a few minutes longer before Benedikte excused herself, and Ry swept past us, gesturing to his right at the couple standing nearby. He offered us glasses of champagne as he whispered, "Train your camera on the white tux for me. I think that's him, but I need Flynn to get another look."

I couldn't see more than the man's shoulder, but the woman he was with was the picture of elegance. In a glittering emerald evening gown with long chiffon sleeves and a plunging neckline, she was beautiful. She could easily be mistaken for his daughter, but Moragreiga's type was early twenties and gorgeous—he was the Leo di Caprio of banking, never dating anyone over twenty-five.

The man he was talking to shifted, and I got my first glimpse at him. Filipe Moragreiga was in his late fifties, dressed in a traditional tux complete with a white jacket with tails. His steel-grey hair and black leather mask provided a stark contrast to the white of his shirt and jacket. But I wasn't interested in any of that. It was his glasses that held my attention. They were perched on his nose, resting over his mask. Moragreiga flicked through a series of palm cards, seemingly scanning the details on each of them.

As chief operations officer for the Grande Banque Unie, Moragreiga was a regular on Europe's social calendar, and his dates were always a favourite topic. I didn't much care who he had with him. I was more concerned with what he was wearing. Moragreiga attended all the important parties, races, and business transactions on behalf of the bank, and every time he was shown with glasses, he was wearing the same pair. Boxy, heavy black frames that were indistinguishable from the pair Ezra was currently holding.

"That's Moragreiga in the white tux," Flynn confirmed in our earpieces. "Glasses are a match too. Do your thing."

We converged on the couple, Tristan and I coming in from behind while Ezra strolled around from the opposite direction.

When we were only a few feet away, I set our plan in motion. "Baby, we should dance."

Moragreiga took off his glasses, holding them by the frames as he looked over at us, the volume of my voice catching his attention.

I put on a pout when Tristan shook his head and said, "Not yet, my love. I need a few more drinks before that."

I twirled around and danced backward, shimmying my hips and tugging Tristan toward Moragreiga and his date. "Then let's get some more champagne."

"What—careful, kitten," he warned just before I slammed into Moragreiga, almost sending both of us tumbling to the floor.

"Steady." He grasped my arms and righted me before reaching out to our target. "I'm terribly sorry, sir. My date is... enthusiastic."

Tristan distracted Moragreiga's date, murmuring softly to her, while I stepped in.

"Oh my. I'm so sorry," I gushed. Just like I knew the man always had Europe's most beautiful young women hanging off his arm, I also knew that he spoke five languages and would understand me when I spoke.

Taking Moragreiga's hands in mine, I gathered them close, pressing his hands against my boobs. "Monsieur, I apologize. I wanted to dance."

His gaze barely flicked over my face before travelling down and stalling, glued to my tits. I'd chosen this gown over the others I'd tried on because of just how much it revealed—the perfect carrot for our resident playboy banker. The shoestring straps looked like the slightest tug would tear them, and the bodice was secured only by the smallest amount of Hollywood tape. If I moved the wrong way, my entire tit would break free. The dress was backless too, cut so low that I knew it would be the perfect tease for him.

"It's not a problem, mademoiselle," he answered with a posh Spanish accent. "You love to dance?"

"I do. But my date doesn't want to." I pouted, pressing my boobs harder against his hands.

"I would be glad to accompany you." He lifted my knuckles to his lips and stared as goosebumps broke out over my skin.

My nipples pebbled and I inhaled on a gasp. Moragreiga's eyes darkened, and his tongue darted out to lick a trail along his lips, but it wasn't him or his touch I was reacting to. My visceral response was to Tristan. Standing to my side, blocking Moragreiga's date's view, he'd run those gentle fingertips teasingly down my spine, stopping just at the top of my cleft, only inches from the holes I couldn't wait to be filled.

Moragreiga tugged me closer, and I let him pull me off balance, falling against his chest. He slid his finger inside the front of my dress, brushing my nipple before slipping his card into my hand. "My personal cell is on that card. Use it."

I fluttered my eyelashes and sank my teeth into my bottom lip, staring into his eyes. "I'd like that very much."

"Monsieur, mademoiselle, is everything all right?" Ezra asked. He stared at Moragreiga, his eyes hard.

But the other man didn't flinch, letting me go and taking his spilled palm cards from Ezra.

"Yes, yes." Moragreiga waved off Ezra's concern, pocketing the cards and slipping the glasses Ezra had passed to him into his jacket pocket.

"I will see you on the dance floor, monsieur." I dipped my head in deference to him. Before I stepped back, I leaned in and added, "And perhaps afterward for something a little… sexier."

I flashed him a smirk, the whole time biting back the urge to slap him silly. He'd just come onto me in front of his date. I wanted to scrub my skin clean of the feel of his greasy mitts on me. I fantasized about getting naked in front of people, of being fucked in a crowded room where men would line up and use me, getting me off until I couldn't stand anymore, but he would definitely not be on the invite list.

I'd seen Ry glaring at Moragreiga when we were talking. He'd been hovering nearby, just like Ezra. I met his gaze, and he swept in, lowering the tray for me to take a champagne flute.

"Thank you," I murmured, our gazes locking and sending heat whispering through my body.

"Did he hurt you?" he ground out. The possessiveness in his gaze, the flicker of anger and desire that were simmering below his seemingly calm façade, were visceral.

And I really wanted him to unleash.

My cunt clenched, my juices coating my lips as he set me alight with the want in his eyes.

"No. He just copped a feel."

Ry's gaze turned thunderous, his jaw cracking. He'd ground it together hard enough to shatter a molar, but Flynn's disembodied voice snapped him out of his murderous thoughts.

"Well done, team. Ez, you especially. Nice swap," Flynn congratulated, breaking the spell Ry and I were under.

Tristan hummed and gathered me closer, his erection pressing into my arse, then shifted his hands to my arms. His thumbs brushed the outside of my tits, slipping underneath the edge of my dress.

Ry's gaze darkened. My nipples pebbled again, and I ground my arse against Tristan.

He whispered, "Feel that?"

Ry's head snapped up to my man's, and I shivered as they stared off, their intensity palpable.

"It's for you."

"Thanks," Ezra responded, dragging us back on track once more. "Let's hope we get what we're after."

"Let's fuck," I demanded, taking a step toward the door.

Between Tristan at my arse and Ry in front of me, burning up my retinas with his heated stare, I wanted to get naked and become the buffet dinner. But knowing Moragreiga was in the same room was a hell of a motivator to behave.

"I promised you a dance," Tristan rumbled in my ear, his hot breath against my skin sending another ripple of desire through me.

Ry's nostrils flared, but he stayed calm enough until a man took a glass off the tray. He shot him a murderous glare, and the guest scampered away.

Tristan's silent chuckle vibrated against my back.

He led me in the direction of the empty dance floor, stopping only when we'd reached the centre. He took my hand and clasped it right above his heart, bringing me in close and sliding his other down to my arse, shamelessly slipping it below the plunging backline of my dress. He leaned in close and whispered, "That pig had his hands on you, kitten. He's lucky he still has them attached to his body."

"Distracted him though, didn't it?" I challenged, loving the possessive glint in his gaze.

"Mmm, it did. But that's not the point," Tristan pushed.

I couldn't see Ry, but I heard the growl of agreement he let loose. It was predatory, so very Ry.

Just the way I loved him.

Tristan spun me around and pulled me tight against his body. His hardness nestled in the curve at the small of my back again, his fingers digging into my hips. Ezra had returned to his post near the stage, directly in front of us. His gaze was locked on us, the rigid outline of his cock tenting his pants.

He ran his fingers town my arm, then lifted it, encouraging me to clasp his nape. Tangling my fingers in Tristan's hair, I held on as he swivelled his hips. He moved me with him, and we swayed to our own beat. I could get lost doing this. Close my eyes and drift away, but I also loved the attention of the people openly staring at us. My cunt clenched. I wanted to be filled right there and then. I didn't give a fuck who was looking.

I whimpered, and Tristan hummed. "You like that, my pretty little slut? Are you wet for us?"

I nodded, and Tristan splayed his hand over my belly before kissing my throat.

He spun around, turning me so I could watch Ry's reaction. He shamelessly squeezed his cock, his eyes glued on us, the empty tray down by his side.

"Good, because only we're allowed to touch you." Another kiss. "To kiss you." He bit down on my lobe and tugged gently. "To spread those sexy legs of yours and fuck your pretty holes."

I moaned, the tops of my thighs slippery with my juices.

"That worthless motherfucker wanted you. What are you going to do about it?"

"Nothing. I'm yours. Only yours," I breathed, my clit throbbing as I rested my head on Tristan's shoulder. "All of yours."

"Mmm, what are you going to let us do to you?"

"Anything. Everything," I gasped as he slid his hand lower, brushing the top of my cunt.

"You going to let us slip these tiny little straps off your shoulders? Push this scrap of material fall to the floor? Hmm?"

"Yes."

"We're all going to watch you, aren't we? We'll see your beautiful tits, all perky and tight, ready for us to suck on." I whimpered, and he continued, "What about your tight little snatch? Are you going to spread your legs and let us all have a taste?"

"Oh god," I breathed. "Yes."

"You going to let us slide our cocks into all your holes? Fill you up with our cum? Use you until you can't walk?"

The rushing in my blood took me by surprise, but my body had taken over, priming itself to come. Without any hope of stopping my instinctual reactions, my hips pressed back and ground against Tristan's cock, wishing that we were naked. Wishing that he was filling me like the fantasy scenario he'd tantalized me with.

"You going to come for me, kitten? The thought of us all fucking you going to send you over? Hmm?"

I turned my face, my body primed and ready to detonate. Tristan's words, Ry's steely gaze and the molten lava underneath it, and Ezra's open desire had set me on fire.

"Come for us, Zee," Flynn demanded urgently, and I fell, a wash of ecstasy flooding me as I let go.

Tristan turned my face, spearing his tongue into my mouth as he kissed me and I shattered. Quaking in his firm hold, Tristan held me as I rode it out, his kiss gentling as I panted.

"Hurry the fuck up with this speech," Ezra mumbled.

As if on cue, the song finished, and the emcee spoke a few words in French. People clapped, and I recognized Moragreiga's name. I may not have understood her words, but it was clearly his introduction. People gathered closer, and Moragreiga slipped his glasses on, took to the microphone, and greeted guests, first in French and what I thought was German, then in English.

"We're getting readings," Flynn said, excitement lacing his tone. Moragreiga adjusted his glasses, pushing them up his nose so they sat tight against his mask and looked out over the guests, continuing to talk.

Flynn squeaked. "Oh my God, we've got a full scan. It's enough. I've got enough."

Moragreiga wrapped up his introduction after another minute, inviting us in three languages to enjoy the remainder of the night before thanking the quartet and striding off the stage.

That was our cue.

TWENTY-TWO

Ryder

Zali had pulled it off. She'd done it. She'd managed to find the right frames with the right prescription and inbuilt retinal scanners. Not only that, but she'd done it in a matter of days.

Other than her talent for finding out the exact information she needed, I knew she'd thrown stupid amounts of money at the manufacturers to make and ship the glasses to us in record time. They'd only just made it too.

Now we had the scans. We had a way in. And tonight, we were done.

We were going back to the villa, and they were gonna get their freak on. And I was... not.

At least I could get out of this penguin suit.

I looked around, searching for the other waiters. Not seeing any close by, I discreetly slid the tray of empty champagne glasses onto a high-top table. It was on the edge of the ballroom, out of the way in a dim corner. A few people mingled nearby, chatting privately, but didn't take any notice of me.

Pulling my shoulders back, I tried to look like I was actually supposed to be here—ironic considering how I so wasn't—and slinked backward, avoiding attention.

I moved quietly toward the door, spinning on my feet as I ducked around the stage, ready to waltz straight out of the ballroom.

Instead, I slammed straight into him. The man I'd been avoiding all night—the grand head honcho of the waitstaff. His arms cartwheeled backward, and he looked like he was about to land on his arse.

Fuck. Of all the days luck wasn't on my side.

My reaction was instant. But by grabbing on to him to steady him, I sealed my fate. It wasn't bad enough that he'd seen me. No, I had to go and walk right into the fucker, nearly knocking him off his feet.

He'd been barking orders and carrying on when I'd slipped in a few minutes before the doors opened. His final instruction before guests were welcomed was that any time we weren't serving food, we needed to be carrying a tray. I wasn't working here, but I didn't want to blow my cover either.

"Watch where you're walking," he hissed, his face turning scarlet. A sneer curled his upper lip, and he flicked his cold gaze to my hands before looking around the room. "Why is your tray over there? Pick it up. Carry it at all times. We do not leave trays with empty glasses lying around in the Casino de Monte-Carlo."

If I did as I was instructed, I'd have another full tray of glasses in hand before I could back out of the room. But my first priority now had to be getting the hell out of Dodge.

If Moragreiga realized he wasn't wearing his own glasses, we ran the risk of being found out. If he looked closely enough at them, he'd realize they were slightly heavier than his too. Knowing that his bank access came from a combination of his username and retinal scan, he would lock down his access, and any hope of getting into the bank would be crushed. That meant us sneaking out and Zali hacking in and getting the information she needed before Moragreiga's night was over.

We didn't want any attention drawn to any of us. Our Aussie accents stood out like a sore thumb among the people here, and Zali and Tristan had already been doing the rounds. How likely was it that there was a security guard and a waiter who also hailed from somewhere as far off as Aus?

Fuck. Fuck, fuck, fuck.

Ezra crossed my line of sight, gesturing to the doors with his chin. I rolled my eyes. How stupid did he think I was? Flynn's confirmation that we had the scan was our cue to get out. But I couldn't just walk away.

Could I?

What was the worst that could happen? The manager didn't want to draw attention to any of us. He wouldn't exactly shout across the room to stop me.

"Act drunk," Ezra demanded urgently in my earpiece. "I'll get you out."

I gave a small shake of my head, breathing out a "Nah-uh," against my throat mic, hoping that it was sensitive enough to pick up my whispered words. Instead, I stepped away, walking in the opposite direction to the tray. Chin up, I strode past the manager, ignoring his demand.

But as I passed, he shot his arm out, connecting with my chest.

I hesitated, irritation thrumming through my veins. I didn't want to get pissed off at him, but he was making it hard.

"Now," he hissed.

Fuck. "Duuude," I drawled, putting on the worst American accent I could manage. I wrapped my arm around his head until his face was pressed into my pit and added, "Chill, man. Relax." I staggered, making him stumble, and dragged him toward the dance floor. Unless he stopped me, we'd both literally be in the spotlight real quick. "Let's dance."

"Stop it," he growled, a hint of panic in his voice.

I couldn't help my smirk. Time to turn it up a notch.

We had the attention of a couple in their sixties who were looking at me with pursed lips as I took a step. "Hey, hot mama." I moved my hand like a cat's claw and added, "Rawr. Can I be your meal tonight, cougar?"

That was enough for the manager to stop pussyfooting around. He broke free of my grip and glared daggers at me before turning his attention on the couple. "Monsieur, madame, I apologize for this man's behaviour. We will be escorting him out immediately."

"Duuude, no need to hate. I was just lookin' for some lovin'."

"Get in the break room," my pretend boss ordered through gritted teeth. He gripped my elbow, squeezing hard, and tried to yank me back behind the stage.

I pitched my balance sideways, spinning as he pulled me. This was either going to get me kicked out or arrested. I hoped it was the former—I didn't feel like spending another night in an interview room, or worse, the lockup.

"Weee," I cried out, faking a delighted laugh. I spotted a glass of champagne with a lone sip left in it sitting on the stage. I lunged for it, toasting the woman. "See you in my bed tonight, hot mama."

"Sir, you'll need to come with me," Ezra insisted, his tone brooking no argument. He grasped my arms, holding me in place as he met my gaze and gave me the barest dip of his head. But I understood. *I've got you. Trust me. Let me lead.* His stare was piercing, waiting for my acknowledgement and agreement. I couldn't look away.

My heart slammed against my chest, beating rapidly and I sucked in a breath. It had to be the adrenaline coursing through my veins, but my cock twitched, thickening as it hardened. Shaking off the manager's hand, I stepped closer to Ezra, putting my trust in him.

He licked his lips, and I followed the path his tongue took. My cock hardened to the point of pain, and a shiver ran through me. What would it be like to press my dick between those lips—*fuck!*

Stop. Jesus fucking Christ. Why?

I exhaled slowly, lifting my gaze back up to meet his. Desire, hot and thick like lava, flared in his eyes, his lips opening on a sharp inhale as he saw something in me that I definitely wasn't ready to admit. I tried to get both my mind and body back under control, but it wasn't working. Ezra filled my senses, short-circuiting my brain and overruling my natural fight-or-flight instinct with his sexed-up looks.

Ezra adjusted his grip, his thumbs beginning a slow massage inside my elbows. It was as if he had a direct line to my cock. It shouldn't happen like that. I shouldn't get harder. I shouldn't imagine him naked and on his knees for me or my shaft sliding into his tight little hole.

I didn't want it.

I didn't want a man.

If I told myself that enough, I might actually believe it too.

"Get him away from the guests," the manager hissed at Ezra. "You're a disgrace. You'll never work in Monte Carlo again."

My laugh was loud and surprised boss man. He turned an angry shade of red as he glared at me through narrowed eyes. He was a bully and a shit boss. I didn't think, I just reacted, tossing the contents of the glass at him before dropping it on the carpeted floor.

Ezra stepped between us and directed, "That's enough for you tonight, sir. I'll see you safely to your ride."

I instantly missed the feel of his hands, the strength in his hold. Wavering on my feet, I wasn't sure if it was an act or if I really was unsteady without his touch.

The flash of approval in his gaze told me the whys didn't matter as much as the appearance. He wrapped his arm around my waist and hoisted my arm over his shoulder, readying himself to guide me bodily out of the room. I sank into him, secretly enjoying the weight of his body against mine.

No. I stiffened, mentally slapping myself stupid.

I faked tripping over my own feet, staggering as he led me out. Moving slowly, I didn't fight him, but I did try to wander off, moving toward the dance floor until he pulled me tighter against him. I kept telling myself that it was all part of the act, but when another security guard tried to grab my other arm, I shoved him away none too gently.

"I've got this one," Ezra explained, tugging me out of the security guard's reach. "Keep your eyes out for the waiter that has champagne all down the front of his shirt. He was hitting on a woman near the stage. Her husband didn't look impressed."

We picked up speed, my stumble more of an arm-in-arm race to get to the doors of the ballroom.

"Fuck me," Ezra breathed as we pushed through them. "You were amazing."

"Let's get the fuck outta here," I muttered. "Tristan, Zali, where are you?"

"Right on your tail," Tristan answered, coming up alongside us. We speedwalked down the corridor and into the main hall like our arses were on fire. I didn't want to wait around to find out if someone was chasing us.

My heart was beating triple time, banging around inside my chest. I was riding an adrenaline high, my feet barely touching the ground as we pushed through the wide doorway and into the cold night.

I tore my jacket off without hesitating and draped it over Zali's shoulders. Tristan shot me a half glare, half grateful smile at my action. Biting back a laugh, I pressed my lips together in a smirk and scanned the forecourt for the Maserati. Where was my baby waiting at?

My steps skidded to a halt as Ezra shot his arm out, stopping me from walking straight into Flynn's path. He eased the masterpiece around the corner, bunny hopping it and revving the engine too hard. I had no idea how he managed it. It was an auto, for fuck's sake.

"Out," I ordered, opening the driver's door when he pulled to a stop.

Flynn didn't hesitate, sliding over into the passenger seat without another word as the others piled into the back.

Revving the engine, I listened to her purr. The rumble was like a caress. I tilted my lips up in a lovestruck smile and sighed happily. Yeah, this girl was my happy place.

TWENTY-THREE

Zali

Ry ordered, "Buckle up," and dropped the Maserati into gear, the tyres chirping as he fishtailed it out of the forecourt to the casino. I was sure there'd be people giving him the what for as we pulled out, but frankly I didn't give a shit.

I. Was. Pissed.

"What the fuck was that?" I hissed through clenched teeth, startling all my guys.

"What, love?" Tristan asked, his tone a mixture of curiosity and confusion.

"Ryder. Coming onto some old lady? Hot mama? What the fuck?" My voice rose, my indignation getting the better of me. He'd been holding me at arm's length forever. It was one step forward and three steps back with us every damn day. And now I find out that he's into some old woman?

Tristan opened his mouth to reply, but I held my hand up, silencing him. "No. I want an explanation. Was a plan developed in the three seconds it took for me to adjust my earpiece after it fell out? Or is that the reason why—" I stopped mid-sentence, halting the flow of words from my mouth. I was giving too much away.

But maybe it was time to lay my cards on the table.

"The plan was for Ry to act drunk," Ezra explained. "He decided on a bad, horny Kelly Slater impersonation."

Unimpressed, I huffed and crossed my arms over my chest. "Fine." It was hard to avoid Ry's gaze in the rearview mirror, so I didn't. I narrowed my eyes at him and glared, but it was hard to keep a straight face when he grinned shamelessly, clearly getting off on my discomfort.

I'd give him discomfort.

Licking my lips, I flicked the shoulder strap of my dress down, tugging at the Hollywood tape until it slipped down and revealed my boob.

Tristan hummed and cupped my tit, brushing my nipple with his thumb. "Ez, I think our girl is telling us something."

Flynn spun around in the seat, his ocean-blue eyes darkening as he watched Ezra slide the strap down my arm and peel off the tape until both my boobs were hanging out. With Flynn's gaze locked on my chest and their hands on me, I arched back, loving being the centre of their attention. The flicks of their thumbs over my nipples were like lightning rods sending charges straight to my cunt. Ezra pressed a kiss to my shoulder, then one lower to my cleavage, his heated breath a promise of what I hoped was to come. I rubbed my legs together, needing some friction, but Tristan wasn't having it.

"No, my pretty little slut, that's our pussy. We look after you." He ran his hand down my leg to the bottom of my slinky skirt and tugged it up, Ezra following a heartbeat later. "Lift up. Show us your pussy. Show us how much you want us."

I did as they asked, but Tristan didn't stop pulling it until he'd whipped it off entirely. I was naked save for my high heels, sitting in a car with three of my lovers and the fourth man who I wanted with a ferocity to rival the others. "Make me come," I ordered, meeting Ry's stare in the rearview mirror.

Ezra hooked my leg over his knee and trailed his fingertips up the inside of my thigh. "If I remember correctly, you've already come tonight. Hmm? Thinking about how we'd fill you up. You all wet again, gorgeous girl?"

"Touch me and find out." I hooked my other leg over Tristan's thigh, opening myself up to them and sliding down the seat a little to give them better access to my cunt.

Flynn licked his lips, and Tristan pressed his hard cock against my thigh. "You want a taste of our kitten, angel?"

"Yes, please," he breathed.

Tristan didn't hesitate, spearing me with two fingers. I cried out, my cunt gripping him tight as he stretched my core around his thick digits. But as quickly as they were there, they were gone again, and Flynn was licking them like a lollipop. "Mmm, my favourite."

"Get that sexy dick out, angel. I want your cum on the windshield by the time we get back to the villa."

Flynn groaned and unzipped his pants, then shoved them down off his hips until his cock sprang free and slapped his belly. Ezra whimpered, and I shifted, reaching down for my cunt. If they wouldn't help me along the way, I'd bloody well do it myself.

Like the grumpy arsehole he was, Tristan tsked me and took my hands into his, stopping my movement. "Did you forget that this is our pussy? Hands on our shoulders, and don't move them unless we tell you to."

I grumbled but did as he said and threaded my fingers into their silky hair, trying to push their heads down.

Flynn's slow glide over his cock was hot as hell. He squeezed on the upstroke, and a drop of pre-cum pooled at his slit. I wanted to lick it away. I wanted my arse up with Tristan and Ezra inside me and Flynn and Ry's cocks stuffing my mouth.

I shivered, my nipples peaking and a rush of gooseflesh rising over my body.

"Our girl's desperate tonight," Ezra mused, his fingers still trailing a slow path up the inside of my leg. My cunt clenched again, desperate to be filled, and he groaned. "Oh, I like that."

Tristan was there too, the two of them only a hair's breadth away from my core. They teased and taunted me, delicate swipes of their fingers against my lips the only thing they were prepared to give me.

"She's leaking everywhere," Tristan mused. "What about you, angel? You dripping for us too?"

Flynn grunted, his hand speeding up, his eyes locked on me. I watched Ry, his head turning subtly every time he pulled his gaze away from the road and locked it on Flynn before flicking back to mine in the mirror.

My guys finally stopped their teasing and joined their hands together, thrusting a finger each inside me. I cried out, my hips flexing as my core muscles squeezed them tight. I huffed out a sob when they retreated, but they were done teasing. Finger-fucking me in long, slow strokes, they dipped their heads and each latched onto a nipple, alternating between sucking and biting me.

My moan was long and loud, my eyes instinctively drifting closed. But the visual before me was too tempting to shut out. Flynn jacking off, his body turned into Ry's so he could watch and Ry struggling to concentrate on the road, his gaze bouncing between the mirror, road and sideways to Flynn.

I gripped Tristan's and Ezra's hair tighter and gasped, "More," as my legs started to tremble and the tingling at the base of my spine began.

With his thumb on my clit, Tristan slipped a second finger into me, and I hissed, "Yes, more." I wanted the stretch. I wanted the burn.

Ezra was there for me, adding another digit, and I detonated, crying out as wave after wave of ecstasy crashed into me, carrying me on the tide until I was floating dreamily under a star-strewn sky.

Tristan slipped his fingers free of me and straight into Flynn's mouth. His muffled moan ricocheted around the car, and he stiffened, pointing his dick toward the dash. Cum shot from his slit, painting the glove box and windscreen with every stroke of his hand. A ripple of jealousy pulsed through me that the car got his spunk and not me.

Ry moved his hand as if he was pressing his hand down on his dick and clenched his jaw, before hitting the remote on the visor to open the estate's gates. Maybe with a little luck, this taste would have been enough to persuade him to drop those final barriers and join us.

No words were spoken, but the air was ripe with sex and anticipation as we sped through the wooded front entrance and up the point to the garage.

Flynn opened the door first, the chill in the air immediately pebbling my naked skin. He stumbled out, his linen pants still undone and his boxer briefs tucked under his sac. But he stopped to open the door for Tristan while holding his pants up by the belt loops. We slipped out, and while they worried over the leather in the Maserati, I strutted up the marble stairs to the entry foyer. I'd had nowhere near enough, and before I did anything else, I wanted their attention on me.

The round table was the first thing I saw in the foyer. There was a vase filled with white tulips in its centre, but it was the perfect height. Before the boys could come up the stairs, I shifted the vase and rested my arse on it.

Jesus fucking Christ.

The marble was like a block of ice. Gooseflesh broke out over every inch of my body, and I shivered, the cold passing through me like a shock wave.

I hissed.

I panted and tried to summon up the courage to lie back. But pressing more of my flesh against the centre of a glacier was going to take a little more persuasion.

Voices in the stairwell had me taking the proverbial plunge, falling back in the way you do when ripping off a Band-Aid—all at once.

Draping myself artfully over the table was easier said than done. I shook my hands and wiggled my toes, clenching my jaw tight and shivering. Waiting for the marble to warm under me took an age. Why the fuck wasn't the entry table made out of carved timber? Hell, at this point, even literal ice would have been warmer.

At least it was the perfect size—long enough that my butt was hanging off it when I rested my head on it, but shimmying up a little, I managed a comfortable spot. I lifted my arm and bent my knee, giving them an enticing peek at the goods. The marble did wonders for my tits, my nipples peaking hard.

Ezra rounded the corner and stopped at the doorway, watching me with a smirk. Tristan was there a moment later, resting his elbow on Ezra's shoulder and holding Flynn's hand.

"Not done yet?" Ezra asked.

"Not even close." I beckoned them closer with a curl of my finger. "Get your sexy arses over here and fuck me." I slipped my fingers down my belly and rubbed my clit, widening my thighs to show them just how wet I was.

Ezra peeled off his jacket and dropped it on the floor, and the others followed suit. Clothes were shed everywhere, and it was like a buffet. I didn't know where to look or where to touch. Good thing I didn't have to choose. I could have them all.

And I would.

Each patch of naked skin revealed somewhere I wanted to lick, to bite, or to kiss. I rubbed my legs together, needing friction, my own fingers not thick enough to quell the unquenched fire smouldering inside me.

Licking my lips, I focused on the one closest to me—Flynn. His innocent looks were deceiving. Golden curls and smooth chest with a wide smile made him look like a golden retriever. But his hardening cock revealed the secret deviant underneath. Those piercings were made for Tristan and me—to rub us both in all the right places. He stroked himself, his hand so sure and confident, and I bit back a moan. It was easy to forget his inexperience. He'd only ever been with us. He'd waited, saved himself for me. I wanted to give him everything. My whole heart. And he had it. All my men did.

Ezra stalked closer, coming around my other side. His gaze was fixed on my tits, and I flicked my thumb over my nipple, my cunt spasming as sensation shot straight down to my clit.

He kicked his pants, underwear, and socks off, leaving himself naked for my viewing pleasure. With all that golden skin on display, I wanted to lick him. I reached for both Flynn and Ezra, my hand closing around both their cocks. I moaned, their hardness such a turn-on. I pumped them, gliding my fist down their lengths, and revelled in the power I held over them. There I was, lying naked and exposed while they were hovering over me, and yet I was the one to cause the catch in their breaths. I was the one who could offer them my body, to take and use as they wanted, to fuck whatever hole they wanted in whatever way they chose.

I knew I'd get orgasms out of it. They were experts at that, but it wasn't my real reward. No, it was their cum. The way they lost their control and pumped me full of it until I was overflowing. I loved how it dripped down my legs and lubed my arse so that they could fuck me again and again. I was wet and aching. I needed to be filled.

Spreading my legs wide, I offered myself to Tristan standing at the foot of the table and groaned when he licked his lips and stroked himself, his eyes fixed on my cunt and arsehole.

Ezra ran his finger between my tits, instantly making me shiver. "I wanna fuck these gorgeous boobs tonight. Give you a sexy-as-fuck pearl necklace."

Tristan hummed and stepped closer, squeezing my arse hard enough to leave a bruise. He brushed his fingertip over my hole, and I cried out, "Yes, please."

"Mmm, your mouth or your sweet pussy?" Flynn debated. "Which to choose?"

"My cunt," I begged. "I need you stretching me."

"You'll have a free hole," Flynn murmured, leaning down to kiss me on the corner of my mouth.

It was a tease, not even a taste, but I was so worked up that it was like a lifeline. A breath of fresh air to a person drowning.

"Get Ry to help. Need you to fill me up," I begged.

"We need lube," Tristan mused, and Flynn smirked, dropping to his knees. Tristan groaned and gripped Flynn's hair as he pumped his hips into Flynn's willing mouth.

I widened my legs and lifted my head, needing to see more.

What a sight.

Fuck, I loved seeing them together. Tristan's face was tense, his whole body quaking as Flynn took him deep while working him with his fist.

Ezra hummed and bent down to swipe his tongue over my nipple. I arched into his touch, and he closed his teeth over me, biting down. I yelped, and he smacked the inside of my leg so close to my cunt that I jumped. The sting from his handprint radiated through my nerves, and a gush of juices leaked from my cunt.

"Hug your legs, gorgeous girl. I'm hungry."

Gripping behind my knees, I lifted my legs and spread them wide until I was bent in half for him. He kissed a hot line along the red handprint on my inner thigh and swirled his tongue over my pucker. I cried out, the zing of desire overwhelming. I loved arse play. Loved the stretch and burn, the bite of pain and the overwhelming sensation of being filled.

He tongue-fucked me, stretching my hole. My nerve endings were alight, rocketing me to the edge of an orgasm. Fingering myself as well, I turned into a trembling mess on the table. My cunt was leaking, my juices lubing the way to my hole too.

"Oh fuck," I gasped, so close to coming apart.

But he pulled back, pressing my hand against my belly so I couldn't even reach myself. The sob wrenched from my throat was one of sheer frustration.

"Oh yeah, gorgeous girl. I like that."

I shifted on the table, trying to get more friction, but his hand didn't let up.

"Your pretty little hole wants to squeeze tight again, but you're stretched open. You want Tris in your arse? You want him to fuck you?"

"Yes," I moaned, "I need it."

Tristan groaned and pulled back from Flynn like it was the greatest of efforts. He squeezed the base of his dick and breathed through his nose, visibly pulling himself back. "Angel, you have the mouth of a devil," Tristan murmured.

Flynn's cheeks pinked but his smile was pure smugness. And it looked bloody good on him.

Flynn and Tristan converged on me like predators, stopping only to wait for Ezra to jump up on the table. He straddled my chest, his knees at my armpits and his sac resting on my sternum. He thrust his hips, dragging the soft skin against my own, and my eyes rolled back in my head. *Oh yeah.*

Ezra spat in his hand and stroked himself, his eyes locked on mine. Heat burned in them, and his sharp inhale when I licked at his cockhead had me repeating the action. But my mouth was reserved for another. Our fifth. The man I'd wanted for a decade but who'd never crossed the line.

Tonight was the night.

My cunt leaked as I watched Ezra lube up his cock until it was glistening wet. I loved how he was going to take me, to fuck my tits and use me until he came all over me. I pinched my nipples, my cunt clenching as the ripple of electric current ran through me, my nerve endings already on fire from the visual of Ezra hovering over me. Dominating me.

I wasn't sure who, but Tristan or Flynn twisted my hips, turning me as best they could to access my holes. Ezra shifted, lifting his foot and trapping my thigh with it. With my other leg hitched over Flynn's shoulder, I was open to them. I waited, my hips rocking impatiently as my guys tortured me, rubbing their cockheads over where I wanted them most.

"Fuck me, already," I grumbled. "Give it to me."

"Hold your tits together, Zali," Ezra instructed, rolling his hips forward again.

His movements were like water, flowing perfectly over me. I scrambled to obey him, shuddering as his hot flesh pushed through the resistance I created. I squeezed tighter, my nipples between my fingers as I plucked at them, and Ezra began a steady rhythm.

Tristan pressed forward, breaching my tight ring. He didn't stop though, burying himself in one deep thrust.

I screamed, the pain/pleasure ripping through me, pushing me straight back to the edge of an orgasm. Flynn was there too, pinching my clit with one hand as he guided his cock into me.

They fucked into me hard and fast, one pushing forward as the other withdrew. But then Tristan pulled all the way out and was gone. I sobbed, desperate to be stuffed full again. He spat on his cock, rubbing it against my hole before plunging in again as Flynn pulled out. My choked cry was one of pure bliss, the stretch and burn quickly morphing into flames licking at the wildfire of the orgasm that was about to consume me.

They tag-teamed me perfectly, overwhelming me with their rough touches. They didn't hold back, didn't shield me or try to go gentle, and it was exactly what I needed. To be taken. To be pinned down and fucked within an inch of my life. I wanted to be owned. To be used. To be stretched and filled. To be so full of their cum, I leaked it everywhere. I wanted to be dirtied up. I was their horny slut who couldn't get enough of their dicks.

"We own these holes, Zee," Flynn growled. "They're ours to fuck anytime we want. You're gonna stay naked for the rest of the time we're here. We'll spread you open and fuck you whenever we want."

He pulled his cock out and waited, twisting my clit between his fingers.

I screamed, "Yes, fuck yes. Yours."

He slapped my cunt.

Hard.

My orgasm crashed into me, my core tightening impossibly. But Flynn was there, forcing it to stretch, to accommodate his thick cock as he pounded into me. My orgasm didn't have a chance to wane before I was coming again even harder than before. Breathless, I sobbed, still needing more.

"Stay," Tristan commanded, and I opened my eyes. "She wants you, Ry. Stay here and fuck her mouth. She saved it for you."

Ry shook his head, backing away before Flynn pulled free of me again, and I cried out, reaching for him. But all it did was loosen the tight clasp I had around Ezra's cock. He froze, his eyes hardening. He shook his head, and I rushed to comply with his unspoken demand.

Flynn stood before him and held out his hand, waiting for Ry to take it.

"Flynn," Ry growled in warning.

"I'm asking you to stay too. Please." He gestured to us, all of us looking in their direction. "You don't have to touch us, and we won't touch you. But stay for Zee. Let her suck you off."

Ry stood rigidly, the erection tenting his pants the only indication that he wanted in. Flynn came back to us and propped my ankle back on his shoulder. He pursed his lips and exhaled slowly, the disappointment that Ry hadn't immediately accepted radiating from him.

"Hey," I croaked, nudging his ear with my toe. "I love you."

Flynn smiled, the joy lighting up his face with a radiance that made my breath catch. He nuzzled my ankle and guided his cock into me, slower than before.

I moaned, and my eyes slipped closed as my guys took me to heaven, their movements slowing down after the frantic pace they'd initially set.

"Zali," Ezra whispered, and I opened my eyes, gazing at him.

He flicked his eyes to the side, and I turned my head in that direction. Ry stood there, watching us. His eyes were locked on my body, flicking between Ezra at my chest and Flynn and Tristan between my legs. His hand was wrapped around his dick. My mouth watered at the sight, the veins in both his hand and his dick like ambrosia. He jacked himself, a bead of pre-cum forming at his slit. He'd only unzipped his pants, tucking his underwear under his sac. His vest was still buttoned, but he'd pulled the bowtie and top button of his shirt open. It was a fucking good look on him.

I moaned, and Ry met my stare. Air punched out of his lungs, and a larger drop of pre-cum leaked from his slit, dripping onto the floor.

"No," I cried. "Mine. I need it."

Ry moaned, and like a domino, it set the others off too, the deep masculine sounds ratcheting my desire up.

My guys were giving me everything. All of themselves. But I still wanted more. I wanted Ryder.

Was I a greedy bitch? Without a doubt.

Did I care? Not in the fucking slightest.

I wanted him to eliminate the distance between us, to feed me his cock. But I wouldn't push him into it. He needed to want me. He also needed to be okay with sharing me with these men.

I wasn't sure, though, of any of it. Was he forcing himself to be here? Did he really want to watch the live-action porno in front of him? His shoulders were tense, his body vibrating. But his cock was as hard as stone, his cockhead leaking like a tap.

He was close, ready to come apart in front of us.

If only he took one more step so I could get a taste.

I moaned, desperate for him, and opened my mouth in invitation. Ezra's movements stuttered. He grunted and flooded my neck with the pre-cum steadily dripping from his cock.

My cunt tightened. I loved watching them take their pleasure from me. Ezra's tight body filled my view, his abs flexing and biceps bulging as he held his weight and fucked my tits.

Flynn gasped, then rolled my clit between his fingers, pushing deeper into me. His thrusts lost their rhythm too. We were all hovering on the edge, teetering on the precipice. I wanted us to fall over together and float on a cloud of happy hormones for as long as it could carry us.

Tristan shifted to spit on his dick again, and then he thrust in at the same time as Flynn. It was like they had the instruction manual to my orgasms, knowing exactly what buttons to push, exactly what part of me to tune in to to make me fall apart in their arms.

My body buzzed, my clit pulsing and waves of ecstasy radiating outward to envelop me. I shivered, despite the warmth surrounding me now.

"That's it, kitten. Come for us again."

Hearing the words, the rasp in his voice, the desperation there, his restraint was all it took. I keened and rode the waves of my orgasm, my cunt clenching hard around Flynn and Tristan. Flynn moaned, his forehead pressed to my shin. The hot splashes of his cum inside me were like a brand. An ownership mark only we knew about.

Ezra was right there too, his cock swelling and hardening impossibly before he unloaded on me, his cum mixing with the diamonds in my necklace.

"Ry," Tristan barked. "Let go. Give it to her."

Ryder stepped forward, and my heart stopped, anticipation thrumming through my veins. This was it, the moment that would change everything. I'd wanted everything he'd give me for so long, and I was finally getting it. On the inside, I was squealing and doing a happy dance. Relief and wonder warred for prime spot.

I couldn't tear my eyes away from him, from the way he held himself, the intensity in his eyes. It was as if he was a storm and I was a lightning rod, reaching up to him, beckoning his spark to connect with me.

He moved his fist fast, sliding it over his thick cock. Watching him get closer again, almost within touching distance was a tease. A temptation. *He* was a temptation. Effervescent zings danced under my skin like champagne bubbles popping inside me.

Ryder groaned, his body going rigid as he pointed his cock toward my mouth. Pulse after pulse of his cum landed on my tongue, and I greedily lapped it up, swallowing all his salty essence. God, just seeing him come was enough to ramp me up again, to send me soaring toward the edge of another orgasm that would claim me.

Flynn thrust again, just enough that Tristan would feel every one of his piercings caressing his cock through the thin walls between my cunt and arse. I choked out a cry and shuddered, my entire body oversensitive and buzzing.

Tristan roared, pressing deep inside me and emptying himself into my body.

Ry fed me his cock, pressing his softening dick inside my mouth. "Clean me, baby girl," he ordered.

My eyes rolled back in my head as I laved my tongue over him, sucking him clean. Ezra fell forward, dropping his weight on his elbows, his hand brushing Ry's sac as he moved. Another spurt of cum landed on my tongue, and I greedily lapped it up, but he was gone before I could take him all in.

Spinning on his heel, he strode out of the room like his arse was on fire, the soles of his shoes clicking on the timber floors.

TWENTY-FOUR

Zali

I was wrapped up in the down quilt from one of the spare rooms, my laptop on my knees and a cup of steaming tea in my hands. It was still early, not even 11:00 pm, but it was quiet at the villa. My guys were all inside doing their thing, but I'd needed a moment to decompress. Things were intense between us and I loved it, but I also needed to keep my head in the game. I could easily crash and sleep for a week—the ball and orgasms had worked me into an exhausted stupor—but if I did that, I'd risk the entire mission. As it was, guilt ate at me. My number one priority should have been to get into the Bank's site, not get laid. But the progress I'd made with Ry was worth it.

Now, though, I needed to act. I had a limited window of opportunity when I knew Moragreiga wouldn't be trying to log in to the bank's systems and I needed to jump on it. I couldn't just log in either. I had to get my computer to "talk" to their system as if it were a legitimate piece of hardware. Having an image of Moragreiga's retinal scan was irrelevant if I couldn't trick the security protocols in the software the bank used into thinking that my computer was a retinal scanner. Not only that, but if Moragreiga tried to log in at the same time as I was in the bank's system, it would lock both of us out and I'd have no hope of getting the information I needed.

My laptop pinged. Looking down, I grinned, nervous energy fluttering in my belly like a kaleidoscope of butterflies. I'd gotten through the first layer of security. I thought I'd have to credential stuff the page, but it wasn't necessary. Moragreiga's username wasn't his employee ID or another randomly generated number. It was his email address—the very same one listed on his card. When would people learn? Most of the weaknesses with IT security were because of human error or laziness.

Now I had to link in so that I could upload the retinal scan. I opened a terminal—a command prompt—to upload the first bot that I'd programmed. It was to help me get into their system and upload the saved scan. Taking the picture from the glasses was a calculated risk. People tended to open their eyes wider when performing scans, so if the image was only a partial and didn't have enough matching points, no amount of programming would get me in. Short of kidnapping Moragreiga, this was my best shot.

Tying him to a chair and doing a live scan of his retina was plan B. But that meant I'd probably need to get naked with him, a suggestion that my guys would not be on board with and one I wasn't at all psyched about either.

The second bot was a trailing program. It followed close behind me, jumping in front of the site's audit system and scrubbing the logs so that any trace of my visit was wiped and my tracks were covered.

The third was "a just in case" measure, but it wasn't a stretch to imagine the incorporation of anomaly detectors running on the network to beef up security. If they were tripped, the site would clone itself, hiding the real data and sending the hacker to a honeypot filled with fake records. Most hackers wouldn't even know that it had happened.

Good thing I wasn't *most hackers*.

I was intimately familiar with honeypots. I'd designed a few of my own, including my Morningstar protocol, but it was much better hidden than the average honeypot.

I knew what to look for: the triggering of the anomaly system, the activation of the cloning, and the redirection to it. My bot disabled the anomaly system, temporarily tricking it into thinking that all was well so that the clone wouldn't even be generated.

I was hoping with everything in me that my bots would work. There were so many things that could go wrong.

With shaking fingers, I entered the code to upload the scan. Nervousness danced in my veins. I held my breath as I waited to see if it would work. The command prompt flashed, running the comparison. My knee bounced, nervous energy escaping the only way it could. I held my breath.

The wait was interminable.

Could I get in? Or was my plan doomed to fail?

The screen flashed.

The terminal disappeared, going blank.

My stomach dropped. A pit of dread yawned open before me. *Fuck.*

I'd blown my chance.

I'd failed.

The screen lit again. The user interface loaded in an instant.

I whooped, equally filled with joy and shocked amazement. My heart pounded in my chest, my pulse fluttering like a hummingbird's.

"Fuck yes!"

I'd never seen a more welcome sight—the Grande Banque Unie logo. Tears welled in my eyes. I couldn't believe it. Shock held me immobile while I tried to comprehend the gravity of what I'd pulled off.

I blinked.

Sucked in a harsh breath.

Then I squealed, excitement pulsing through me like I was a Swifty at a Tay Tay concert.

My tea sloshed all over my hand as I dumped it on the table.

The French doors behind me bounced off the stonework as bare feet slapped across the terracotta tiles.

"What's wrong? What's happened?" Tristan breathed, panic in his tone.

"Get inside," Ezra hissed.

I turned to him, my brows furrowed as he shifted Tristan behind him.

What was going on?

But then I saw the knife.

"What the fuck?" I squeaked, hugging my laptop to my chest to protect it. I ducked down, making myself as small a target as possible. "Who's after me?"

"You hear Zali scream, and you run toward her un-armed?" he berated Tristan after he'd scanned the area, looking for danger and found nothing obvious. "Especially after you've received death threats?"

Naked as the day he was born, Ezra still made an impos-ing figure. But Tristan didn't flinch at his harsh words. In-stead, he cupped his face and kissed him, sliding his tongue into Ezra's mouth.

Flynn stumbled out behind the others. "Zee?" he asked, rubbing his eyes. His hair was sticking up everywhere, once side of his face with crease marks on it from his pillow.

"What's happening?"

A throat cleared from above us. I looked up, and my heart lodged in my throat. Ry was there, dressed head to toe in black, tossing up and catching a throwing knife. He looked like he'd been there a while, a blanket draped over his lap. Without a word, I knew he'd been there like a silent sentinel, protecting me from risks I didn't even know ex-isted.

"Ry?" I called, my voice cracking.

He nodded, his lips turning up in the briefest of smiles. "Stand down, Detective Fraser. Zali has something. There's no threat." He gestured to my computer, and my sleep-deprived brain finally connected the dots.

Incredulous faces stared back at me.

"Sorry?" I shrugged. "I didn't mean to scare you."

"What's going on?" Ezra asked, sliding into the seat next to me. I reached for him, clasping his shaking hand in mine.

"You're going to catch your death out here, angel," Tristan muttered, rubbing his hands up and down Flynn's bare arms.

They spoke quietly, but I tuned them out, turning my attention back to my screen.

Excitement surged inside me once more. A little pride too. Monaco's Grande Banque Unie was no longer unhackable. Queen had succeeded where every other hacker the world around had failed.

"I'm in," I exclaimed, the surprise in my voice obvious. I turned my laptop to face them.

They looked at the screen.

"Oh shit," Tristan exclaimed, his eyes lighting up with excitement and awe. "You did it. Do you have the account details to search, or do you need me to get them?"

I nodded and blew out a breath. "I have them." I flicked my gaze up to Ry, who was still tossing up and catching the knife. Where the hell did he get it from? *Why* did he have it? "Ry, would you come down? Please?" I asked.

He stood, pocketed the knife, and went inside before appearing at the door on our level a moment later as Flynn came back out, dressed in a hotel robe with a couple spares for Ezra and Tristan.

"Thank you," I said softly to Ry as he peered at the screen. "I don't know how long you were there, but I appreciate you watching over me."

"I've been here the whole time." When I tilted my head, silently asking him to explain, he added, "I heard you go outside after your shower. The guys were already asleep, so I checked on you. When I saw that you were wrapped up, I got dressed and sat on the balcony so I didn't disturb you."

"It doesn't matter what I'm doing, Ry. You're always welcome to sit next to me." I patted the seat and shuffled closer to Ezra so the three of us could fit on the two-seater. It was snug, but I didn't mind, and when Flynn and Tristan leaned over the back of the wicker chair, looking over my shoulder, I wanted to sink into the moment and enjoy its simplicity.

But it was anything but simple.

This was it. This could be the most pivotal moment of this investigation.

Of my life.

I might find a lead identifying who was responsible for Mum's and Asher's deaths. The person who stole from the company. The person who ordered their murders. The person who might have watched them die.

The person who'd threatened to do the same to Tristan if he didn't back off.

Or I might find nothing at all.

I wasn't sure which possibility was worse.

I looked out at the horizon, taking in the early morning vista trying to imprint this moment in my mind. The sun had risen. The sky was a pale blue, unmarred by even a single cloud. Aquamarine water stretched as far as the eye could see, small ripples radiating on its surface from the gentle breeze.

To either side of us, steep slopes stretched above the city. It was so different during the day compared to night. The city was just waking up, stretching its arms in the dawn's rays. Trucks navigated the narrow roads, and street sweepers were out cleaning up. Restaurants were preparing for their breakfast serving, the early morning cafes opening their awnings and shifting chairs and tables onto the footpaths. Joggers ran along the foreshore, and a few dedicated people swam in the bay.

It was all so decidedly normal. The people below us were settling into their daily routines, and I was facing the possibility of my entire world being turned upside down. I tried to push the thought away for just a second longer, giving myself one more minute of peace.

As I peered down through the gaps in the stone balustrade, the sun's morning rays lit up the dew on the verdant lawns like scattered diamonds. They were trimmed to perfection all the way to their edges where they were intersected by formal gardens and the sweeping drive.

The temptation to say, "Fuck it," and go out somewhere—anywhere—and experience everything this city had to offer, to just experience life, was huge. I wanted that. I wanted to lie on a tropical beach somewhere and drink out of a coconut with an umbrella in it. I wanted beach bonfires and dancing. I wanted sand between my toes and warmth on my face. I wanted to go diving again too.

Maybe that's what had me so unbalanced. We'd spent most of the summer moored rather than in my favourite spots diving and fishing. The sex had been incredible, but I wasn't myself. I needed things to change.

Except that I had a responsibility.

I owed it to Mum and Ash.

I owed it to Dad.

And to me.

Flynn squeezed my shoulder, Tristan kissed my temple, and Ezra leaned closer, all giving me the support I needed.

But it was Ry who gave me the courage to start my search when he said, "Whatever happens, baby girl, we're together until the end."

I smiled at him and rested my head on his shoulder, absorbing his strength. "Let's do this," I stated, my tone a hell of a lot more assured than I felt.

I copied over the first of the three account numbers and held my breath. It was closed. After downloading all the data I could find on both the client and their transaction history, I moved onto the next one and repeated the process. It was dormant. No transactions had been processed on it for years, the balance just sitting there, accruing interest.

Until I checked the third and final account on my list.

I opened the file and my heart stopped.

My blood ran cold. A cold sweat broke out over my skin.

My breath caught. I choked out a sob.

My hands shook.

I turned at the sharp inhale from Ry. But I couldn't see him. Tears blurred my vision.

No.

I had nothing. Worse than nothing. They'd ended her life. Then they'd stolen her identity.

Seeing her name in black and white—Rosa Weatherall— shattered something inside me.

I shook my head, clenching my jaw tight. They would pay for this. They would bleed for trying to tarnish my mum's name.

These bastards were living on borrowed time, and they didn't even know it. Once I found them, I'd shank the fuckers.

They would fucking beg me for mercy.

Instead, I'd watch them bleed out on the cold concrete. I would be the last thing they'd see as the life faded from their eyes.

Just like they watched my mother and brother die, I'd force them to go full circle. The daughter and sister of their murder victims would get justice.

No. She'd exact revenge.

They thought they could get away with it.

They thought wrong.

It was time for Queen to become their worst fucking nightmare, to terrorize their very existence. A cold smile split my lips.

She was no benevolent ruler. No, she would be their misery. Their torment.

Queen would be their executioner.

♟ ♟ ♟

Haven't had enough of Zali and her men?
Download the bonus chapter:
https://bookhip.com/CCGPXDV

The series will be completed with Alphahole. Pre-order now: https://books2read.com/Queensalphahole

Someone stole her identity. Now, I'll destroy their life.

Proving my mother's innocence has never been more important. I'm so close to catching the person responsible for her death. I can almost taste my vengeance.

Ryder, my brother's best friend, is on my side. He's my ride or die. He's with me to the end, just as determined to seek retribution.

Together we will raze the earth to find out who killed my mother and brother.

But I want more. I want *him*.

I want *us*. All of us.

I'm not the only one either. My guys want Ryder as much as I do. My professorhole, my bosshole, and my cinnamon bun are all secretly in love with him too.

But convincing Ryder that a relationship with me—with my guys—is exactly what he needs is easier said than done. He's a lone wolf, the alpha, and his walls are iron clad.

But I am Queen, and I want him as my king.

I won't let anything stand in my way.

Billionaire Boss Girl is a contemporary why choose/polyamorous series. There is no need for the leading lady (or her men) to choose in order to find their HEA.

Alphahole is the FINAL book in this slow-build, high-heat new adult romantic suspense series and should be read after Professorhole and Bosshole.

Pre-order Alphahole now:
https://books2read.com/Queensalphahole

I appreciate your help in spreading the word, including telling a friend. Reviews help readers find books! Please leave a review on your fave review site.

About Ann Grech

By day Ann Grech used to live in the corporate world and could be found sitting behind a desk typing away at reports and papers or lecturing to a room full of students. She graduated with a PhD in 2016 and is now an over-qualified nerd. But the grind got old, and the voices got louder. She still has the librarian look nailed, but she's a little freer to be herself now.

She's never entirely fit in and loves escaping into a book—whether it's reading or writing one. But she's found her tribe and loves her book world family. She dislikes cooking, but loves eating, can't figure out technology, but is addicted to it, and her guilty pleasure is Byron Bay Cookies. Oh and shoes. And lingerie. And maybe handbags too. Well, if we're being honest, we'd probably have to add her library too given the state of her credit card every month (what can she say, she's a bookworm at heart)!

In 2019 she was an Award-Winning Finalist in the Fiction: LGBTQ category of the 2019 Best Book Awards sponsored by American Book Fest for her story In Safe Arms.

She also publishes her raunchier short stories under her pen name, Olive Hiscock.

Ann loves chatting to people online, so if you'd like to keep up with what she's got going on:

Join her newsletter (you'll get two free books!):
https://landing.mailerlite.com/webforms/landing/d8m4r2

Follow her on Instagram:
@anngrechauthor

Follow her on TikTok:
@authoranngrech

Like her on Facebook:
https://www.facebook.com/pages/Ann-
Grech/458420227655212

Join her reader group:
https://www.facebook.com/groups/1871698189780535/

Follow her on Goodreads:
https://www.goodreads.com/author/show/7536397.Ann_
Grech

Follow her on BookBub:
https://www.bookbub.com/authors/ann-grech

Follow her on Amazon:
https://www.amazon.com/~/e/B00IJPO3EM

Visit her website for her current booklist:
http://www.anngrech.com/

She'd love to hear from you directly, too. Please feel
free to e-mail her at ann@anngrech.com or check out
her website for updates.

ANN GRECH'S BOOKS

BILLIONAIRE BOSS GIRL

Professorhole (why choose/Polyamorous – MMMMF)
Bosshole (why choose/Polyamorous – MMMMF)
Alphahole (why choose/Polyamorous – MMMMF)

RULE OF THREE

Three Hearts (MMF) (Also available in audio)
Yes, Captain (MM)
Triple Beat (MMF)
Threepeat (MMF)
Third Time's A Charm (MMF)
Triple Threat (MMF)

PEARCE STATION DUET

Outback Treasure I (MM)
Outback Treasure II (MM)

SPINOFF FROM PEARCE STATION

Three of Us (MMF)

UNEXPECTED

Whiteout (MM)

White Noise (MM)
Whitewash (MM)

MY TRUTH

All He Needs (MMM)
In Safe Arms (MM)

STANDALONES

Home For Christmas (MM)
The Gift (FMMM - free for newsletter subscribers)
Take Two (MM – free for newsletter subscribers)

M/F TITLES

One night in Daytona
Ink'd

GERMAN TRANSLATIONS

Outback Treasure I
Outback Treasure II

www.ingramcontent.com/pod-product-compliance
Lightning Source LLC
Chambersburg PA
CBHW030510120726
47904CB00005B/1409